Very BAD People

Also by Kit Frick

See All the Stars
All Eyes on Us
I Killed Zoe Spanos

Very BAD People

A NOVEL BY

KIT FRICK

Margaret K. McElderry Books

New York   London   Toronto   Sydney   New Delhi

MARGARET K. McELDERRY BOOKS
An imprint of Simon & Schuster Children's Publishing Division
1230 Avenue of the Americas, New York, New York 10020

Text © 2022 by Kristin S. Frick
Jacket illustration © 2022 by Gee Hale
Jacket design by Debra Sfetsios-Conover © 2022 by Simon & Schuster, Inc.
Map and ghost illustrations by Mike Hall

MARGARET K. McELDERRY BOOKS is a trademark of Simon & Schuster, Inc.
For information about special discounts for bulk purchases, please contact Simon & Schuster Special Sales at 1-866-506-1949 or business@simonandschuster.com.
The Simon & Schuster Speakers Bureau can bring authors to your live event. For more information or to book an event, contact the Simon & Schuster Speakers Bureau at 1-866-248-3049 or visit our website at www.simonspeakers.com.
Interior design by Irene Metaxatos
The text for this book was set in Garamond 3 LT Std.
Manufactured in the United States of America
First Edition 10 9 8 7 6 5 4 3 2 1
Library of Congress Cataloging-in-Publication Data
Names: Frick, Kit, author. Title: Very bad people / Kit Frick. Description: First edition. | New York : Margaret K. McElderry Books, [2022] | Audience: Ages 14 and up. | Audience: Grades 10–12. | Summary: Sixteen-year-old Calliope Bolan joins a powerful secret society at her new boarding school, hoping to find answers about her mother's death, but she becomes involved in a dangerous campaign for revenge that threatens her new friendships. Identifiers: LCCN 2021024092 (print) | LCCN 2021024093 (ebook) | ISBN 9781534449732 (hardcover) | ISBN 9781534449756 (ebook) | Subjects: CYAC: Secret societies—Fiction. | Secrets—Fiction. | Justice—Fiction. | Death—Fiction. | Boarding schools—Fiction. | Schools—Fiction. | LCGFT: Novels. Classification: LCC PZ7.1.F75478 Ve 2022 (print) | LCC PZ7.1.F75478 (ebook) | DDC [Fic]—dc23 | LC record available at https://lccn.loc.gov/2021024092 | LC ebook record available at https://lccn.loc.gov/2021024093

Sadie Lou, this one is for you,
not about you. Mostly.

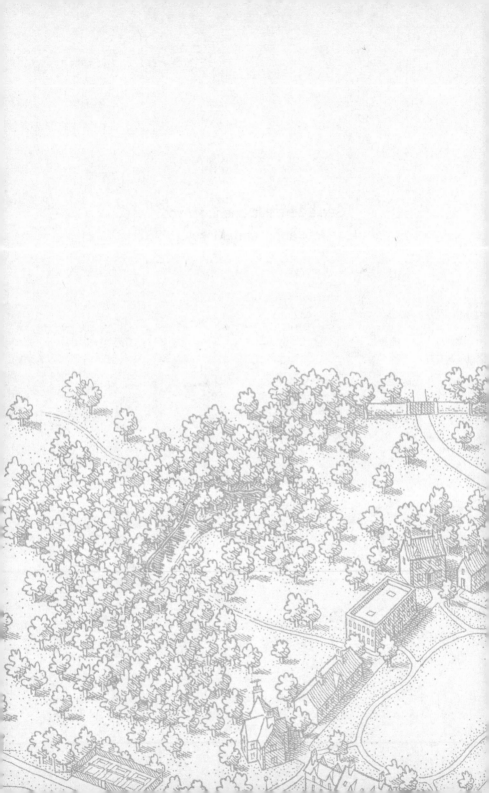

Glossary of Terms:

Tiptonian: Student at the George M. Tipton Academy

Bunker: Boarding student

Aly (pron. *alley*): Day student

Prefect: Student dorm monitor

Upriver: Fall trimester

High Bluff: Winter trimester

Long Trek: Spring trimester

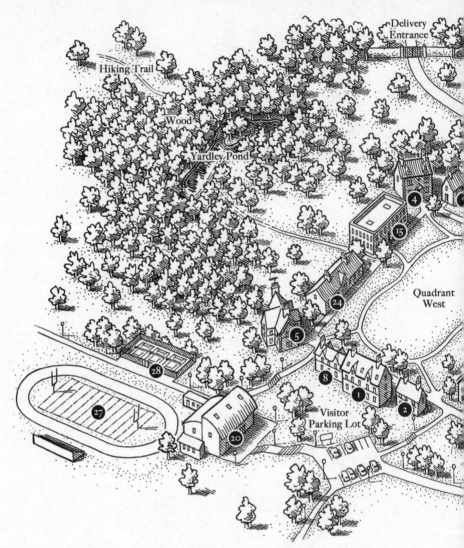

Delivery Entrance

Hiking Trail

Wood

Yardley Pond

Quadrant West

Visitor Parking Lot

Student Dormitories

1 Anders
2 Carrington
3 Chandler
4 Hadley
5 Kiley
6 Lynd
7 Stratton
8 Wright/Calhoun

Academic Buildings

9 Ashbourne Theater
10 Booth Design Lab & Maker Space
11 Fortin Hall
12 Henry Hudson Library
  a Back door to the Den
  b Brown Rock
13 Hunt Studio Arts Building
14 Perry Cottage/The CW
15 Preston Music Building
16 Sloane Humanities & Social Sciences Building
17 Tobin Science & Mathematics Building

Other Buildings

18 Academic Advising Center & Peer Tutoring Center
19 Brisbane
20 Fleet Sports Center
21 Gray Space
22 Mail Room
23 Manny's Joint
24 Rhine Dining Hall
25 Security Hut
26 Student Health & Wellness Center
27 Teal Athletics Field
28 Tennis Courts

Faculty & Staff
Parking Lots

Quadrant
East

Sugar Maple

Main
Entrance

To the town of
Alyson-on-Hudson

I
ORIENTATION

1

We are the Bolan sisters. Calliope, Lorelei, and Serafina.

If our names sound like they were plucked from a fairy tale, it's because they were. Momma wanted, above all things, to live in a fairy tale.

We have pale, freckly skin and dark auburn hair, which we refuse to cut. It falls in long jumbles down our backs—thick and wavy for Lorelei and me; wispy curls for Serafina. We are tall for our ages, respectively. We are clumsy. We have mammoth feet and delicate wrists. We see the world with perfect vision. Lorelei and I have green eyes. Serafina's eyes are brown. When we are together, we collect stares we'd rather return. *See? It's the Bolan girls. The ones who survived.*

We don't live in a fairy tale, but people regard us, sometimes, as if we are more story than girl. More myth than flesh that hurts and bleeds and grieves.

Serafina is seven, the baby. Lorelei and I are so close in age, so close in appearance, *so close* that we are often mistaken for twins. I am the oldest, sixteen. My sister is fifteen, a year and change behind me.

Our mother loved all magical stories and consulted a variety of sources when naming her daughters. My name, Calliope, was drawn from ancient Greek myth. Lorelei owes hers to German folklore. Serafina is from seraphim, angels of the highest order in Abrahamic religious lore. Put us together, and we are part survival story, part fable, part cautionary tale.

We live with our father in a small village in the Adirondack Mountains. Our house is large and drafty and far from other houses. There is a nearby lake, from which our village takes its name. There is a grocery store and a general store and a movie theater with one screen. In the summer, the vacationers and second-homers move in, and the village hums with life. In the winter, we hunker down, shrinking to a quarter of our size. About eight hundred families live in Plover Lake year round; at school, we average 11.7 students per grade. In harshest winter, you could pack us all into a snow globe and shake.

The Bolans have always lived here, before the accident and after.

When I was little, I loved our house, our school, our postcard town. In my fantasies, I would always live here with my mother, my father, my sisters, and our dog. I could not fathom growing up and moving away. What could possibly tear me from the place that held all my memories, my family, my firsts?

Now, the village is crushing me. It is so small. It has eyes and claws and teeth.

There is a fairy tale like that.

Tomorrow, I am leaving. I might never come back.

Thruway Tragedy: New York Woman Drives Minivan Into Lake

BY SAMIRA FARZAN
September 26, 2016

An investigation has been opened by local NY authorities.

GREENE COUNTY—On Friday, an upstate New York woman, who was with her three daughters, drove a Honda Odyssey off the road and into a lake bordering the New York State Thruway. The woman, who has been identified as Kathleen Marie Bolan, 38, was found dead. Ms. Bolan's oldest daughter, 10, led the rescue, getting herself and her two sisters, 9 and 14 months, to safety. From the side of the road, the girls were able to flag down a driver who called 911. Police, assisted by a dive team, found the vehicle submerged in the lake. The body of Ms. Bolan was inside.

Local authorities are investigating possible causes to what the police chief calls "a tragic event."

Peter Bolan, the girls' father and husband to Ms. Bolan, says his wife pulled his two oldest daughters out of school early that day without notifying him. "I have no idea where she was headed or why. There was no history of mental illness. Kathy would never drink and drive. You hear stories like this. I never thought it would be my wife, my daughters. Me asking the question—why?"

Why this happened is the question on everyone's minds. The medics responding to the scene said it is "a miracle" all three daughters survived with only minor injuries. The girls, who are all in stable condition, did not describe any strange behavior from their mother leading up to the crash, and police report no immediate evidence of alcohol or substance use.

"Possibilities include a mechanical failure or distracted driving," says Chief Mason Sumner of the Greene County Regional Department of Public Safety, who is investigating the crash. "A suicide and triple homicide attempt has not been ruled out as a possible cause. We haven't ruled anything out at this point. The autopsy may turn up more. I hope we'll be able to get answers for the family."

Chief Sumner says he does not believe any other vehicles were involved. Police are trying to determine what happened just before the crash and are seeking the public's help. If you have any information about the collision, which took place Friday around 4:00 p.m. on 1-87, near the Athens exit, please call the Greene County Regional Department of Public Safety at 518–958–2461.

2

If Momma had gotten the air-conditioning in the minivan fixed, we wouldn't have been driving with all the windows down that day six years ago. A curse when the water rushed in fast, so fast. Then a blessing, an escape. But our mother hated to spend money on practical matters, as if the air-conditioning might fix itself, or the leaky bathroom faucet, or the clogged gutters. Or as if those things didn't matter.

It wasn't because we didn't have the money. Dad had a steady job and Momma was always "saving her pennies for a rainy day," which was a bit of an exaggeration because those pennies came from a generous trust set up by the wealthy grandparents we rarely saw, and rainy days could be any day, filled with fun things like ice cream and adventures with her girls.

Dad was the voice of reason. Dad did the shopping, the upkeep, made sure we were clothed and fed and had the right number of subject notebooks and a full pack of pencils on the first day of school. Momma made sure we had treats stashed in our bags and scavenger hunts on our birthdays.

If Dad had known about the broken air-conditioning, he would have seen that it got taken care of, but only Momma ever drove the minivan. And so that Friday in September, as we sped away from the elementary school—Lorelei and I in the middle row, Serafina, the baby, in her car seat in the back—and toward one of our mother's secret adventures, destination unknown, we had the windows open, and a warm breeze was rushing through.

Momma was in a good mood that day—the best mood. Her gold chandelier earrings danced back and forth across the tops of her shoulder blades as she drove and belted out Fleetwood Mac and Tori Amos and Florence + the Machine and all the music she only put on when she was feeling a little nostalgic and a lot giddy about some surprise she had in store. Her voice was throaty and lilting. She smelled like the lilac perfume she wore for special occasions. She threw us kisses in the rearview.

At some point, we stopped for gas and car snacks. When we got back on the road, the afternoon sun was warm on our faces. My sisters and I dozed off.

When the van swerved off the highway, smashed through the guardrail, and sailed into the narrow strip of water along the side of I-87, my sisters and I were still sleeping. Dad was at work. Sebastian, our blue-eyed Aussie puppy, was at home. Momma was driving.

Lorelei always says I sleep like the dead. When we hit the water, I didn't wake up right away. I was dreaming about Six Flags. We were on The Comet, and everyone was screaming. The roller coaster trembled just slightly on its rails; the wooden beams were white slashes below us, beside us. The clouds were so close I could touch them with my fingertips. I left trails in the sky. The leaves were orange and yellow flames streaking through blue. As we whipped through the park, the spray from the water rides splashed against our faces. We screamed and screamed.

I woke to cold water—rushing in, filling the van, dragging us under. Screams and screams. Only our mother was silent in the front, slumped over the steering wheel. *Momma!* Dark streaks, dancing in front of my eyes. Lorelei's bare foot, tangled in something. The seat belt. I clawed at mine, got it off, and the water kept rushing in, greedy, greedy. I got Serafina out of her car seat. I'd helped our mother fasten and unfasten her plenty of times; plenty of times she was wailing, screeching, inconsolable, but this was harder, scarier than anything I'd ever done. *Get Momma,* I screamed to Lorelei, but my sister was frozen, staring.

Then we couldn't scream anymore because the water was everywhere, snatching our voices, sucking up all the air. I clutched Serafina to my chest and groped for Lorelei's hand, pulled hard. I half climbed, half swam, dragging Lorelei at first, until something finally clicked, and she started moving behind me, toward the front of the van, the open passenger's side window.

The dashboard, lit up like Christmas. Lorelei's pink jelly shoe, rising on the water, rushing past me into the back. Momma, still slumped over the steering wheel, hair floating in a dark cloud around her, the gold sparkle of her earrings tangled in the strands. No air. Water, everywhere. *Momma!* I needed to stop, to get her out, but my lungs burned and my baby sister squirmed against me. There was no time.

I pulled myself out through the passenger's side window, into the lake, and Lorelei followed. The stretch of water was deep but narrow. We swam to shore.

My sisters and I survived, but our mother never woke up. Kathleen Marie Bolan, forever thirty-eight, forever preserved in sticky amber—Momma. Never aging for us, never graduating to Mom or Ma. Something terrible happened while your three princesses were sleeping. Maybe something scared you, caused the wheel to jerk. A witch, a wolf, an evil queen.

People say a lot of things. That you were irresponsible, distracted. That you wanted to die. That you tried to take us with you. I stuff cotton in my ears, push those voices out. Some fairy tales are dark, hideous, pulsing with blood and sorrow. But I know you. That wasn't your kind of fairy story. You wanted the dazzling ending, fireworks in the sky, the happily ever after.

Dad says that sometimes, bad things happen to good people. Six years later, the cause of the accident is officially "inconclusive." Dad says that it was a terrible tragedy, and maybe that's all we'll ever get to know. This is enough for him, or at least he says it is. But I don't think it will ever be enough for me.

3

Orientation day one, Tipton Academy. Lunch was a picnic on "Quadrant West," which normal people might call "the west quad," but we would never adopt such a pedestrian moniker here at Tipton. Dinner is the first unorganized activity for first-years and transfers (eight sophomores, the three other juniors, and me), which is not to say it is disorganized, but rather that we have not been broken into groups or sorted by dorm or assigned a buddy. At six, I find myself standing at the front of Rhine dining hall, clutching my tray, and feeling very much alone.

"Calliope, over here!" My head swivels, I hope not too desperately, in search of the voice currently butchering my name. Callie-ope, like Callie-nope.

An arm, a wave. It's Nico Hale. Year: junior. Dorm: Chandler. Learning styles: auditory and kinesthetic. Super-power: graphic design. (Our afternoon "Getting to Know the Secret You" breakout sessions were led by the orientation leaders and our prefects, a schmancy boarding school name for the senior dorm monitors. Nico, our group's orientation leader, encouraged each of us to "disclose" a superpower to our breakout group, a not-so-cleverly-masked way of asking, "What's your favorite hobby?" I panicked and went with knitting, which isn't really true. This summer, I knit three scarves: one for Dad and one for each of my sisters. I wanted to say *I'm sorry I'm leaving*, and *I love you*, and *this isn't about you*. I'm not sure my scarves said any of that.)

I make my way to Nico's table in the center of Rhine. Many tables are unoccupied, and I'm grateful to not be haunting one of those empty seats. Two more days of orientation stretch ahead of us, then the weekend will bring the rest of the returning students before classes start on Monday.

"Thanks," I say, scooting into an open seat at Nico's table. I recognize two other orientation leaders and another junior transfer, Marjorie. The others must be prefects or fall athletes. "But I have to tell you, it's Ca-*lie*-uh-pea. Not Callie-ope."

Nico laughs, and his grin splits his face wide. His hair is a light shade of brown, and it spills into his eyes. "I know. I was just trying to get your attention. Didn't want you to wind up with the lacrosse team."

"Clever." I pierce a piece of summer squash from my quinoa and pulled chicken bowl. Nico is cute and artsy, which is maybe my type? I try to decide. I've never dated anyone before, and I'm fairly certain I know each of the 10.7 other juniors at my school back home too well to consider any of them as a potential romantic partner. Who even says romantic partner? This is how little I know about dating.

"So what brings you to Tipton?" The question comes from Prisha, another junior. She's been leading one of the first-year orientation groups. I know from the morning's welcome session that Prisha grew up in New Jersey, she visits her grandparents in Odisha every other summer, and she is a setter on the Tipton volleyball team. I do not know her superpower.

How to answer Prisha's question. The same way I've been answering it all day, or the truth?

I settle for the easy route. "My high school back home is very small. I wanted the opportunities afforded to all the . . . Do people actually say Tiptonians?"

"We do," Nico solemnly affirms. His eyes twinkle.

"Right, then. But also, my mom and her sister both went to Tipton in the nineties, and my aunt still lives here, in Alyson-on-Hudson. My father would never have considered allowing me to leave home before the age of eighteen without family nearby. Hence Tipton."

There are several things I don't say to these people I barely know:

- My father and Aunt Mave are not close. They have never gotten along, and I have never really understood why. Aunt Mave and her wife, Teya, used to come to visit a lot while Momma was still alive. Dad would spend all his time talking to Teya and ignoring Aunt Mave.
- Even so, Dad must fundamentally trust her because in the end, Aunt Mave was a deciding factor in his ruling about Tipton. I am sworn to have dinner with her every Sunday night, come hell or high water, without fail.

- I have been here for less than a day, and already I miss my sisters so badly that the space behind my eyes burns, and I have been clenching my teeth so hard they threaten to spill out of my mouth and scatter across the dining hall floor.
- After Momma's accident, a village of eyes has followed me for six years, pitying, hawk-like, marveling, probing. I don't tell them about that.

Prisha has now turned the question to Marjorie, the other junior transfer at our table. Marjorie was in my afternoon breakout group with Nico. Her superpower is baking.

Marjorie says something about wanting to go to Yale, and I spear another piece of summer squash, then a piece of chicken. Momma went to Yale, and Grandmommy and Granddaddy hated that she "never did anything" with her fancy degrees. I wonder what my mother would think if she could see me now, at Tipton. I hope it would make her happy, but I don't really know.

The whole truth is this: I am here because Tipton is my escape route from Plover Lake. But there is another reason too. I am here to get to know my mother in some fundamental way. Walk the paths she walked when she was my age. Sit in the classrooms where she sat. Take Creative Writing, her favorite class. Tipton is a gateway to my mother's past, the princess and her kingdom. Maybe if I can get to know the person she used to be, I can start to figure out who I want to become.

Nico, Marjorie, and Prisha keep talking, but my thoughts

stay with my family. At home, Lorelei and Serafina are sitting down to dinner with Dad around the big oak table in our dining room. My seat is empty. This morning, we left home super early to drive here. They got me settled in at Anders, my dorm, then I waved goodbye so they could get back on the road. It's been just over nine hours, but it feels longer. I am happy to be here, away from Plover Lake. But I am not used to being apart from my family.

We have a video call scheduled for later tonight. I set an alarm on my phone.

4

What I have learned today about being a student at Tipton:

- Call the school Tipton, not Tipton Academy, and never its full name, the George M. Tipton Academy. Anything aside from Tipton is pretentious.
- The *M* stands for Mansfield, also pretentious.
- The website and brochures project *we are elite*, but also, *we care.* An oft-lauded financial aid initiative provides full funding to all admitted students with family incomes below some salary marker. *(See? We are not that pretentious.)*
- 80 percent of Tipton students are boarders. We are called *Bunkers*, which is meant to conjure images of summer camp or sound somehow less steeped in privilege.
- Day students are called *Alys*, which is pronounced "alleys," as in "never walk alone down dark alleys" and is derived from Alyson-on-Hudson, the quaint valley town nestled at the bottom of the hill where

Tipton towers, all redbrick and white trim.

- Collectively, we are Tiptonians.
- We number 933.
- Our school colors are white and teal.
- Our school mascot is a winged stallion named Manny.
- The year is divided into three trimesters, each bearing perplexing names: Upriver (fall), High Bluff (winter), and Long Trek (spring).
- Tipton has been co-ed for all seventy-five years of its history. We approach academics with rigor, with a collaborative spirit, with intellectual curiosity.
- We do not wear uniforms.
- We do not tolerate prejudice, alcohol, bullying, or hazing.
- We welcome everyone's voice, even if we do not agree.
- We welcome new students with warmth and good cheer.

Or so I am told.

5

We "Bunkers" do not sleep in bunk beds. I sit on the foot of my extra-long twin in Anders 2C, which is now outfitted with brand new, yellow polka dot, extra-long twin sheets, and my roommate Clarice sits on the bed opposite me. Her bed is made up in oranges and reds, and I think it looks like a sunburst in here. Or a fire.

"I'm not here on scholarship," she tells me. She says it like it's a challenge. "Just to clear that up."

I assume she is telling me this because I am white. Because she assumes that I, a white girl, will assume her Black roommate is here on one of Tipton's generous financial aid packages. I don't blame her for this assumption. I haven't given funding much thought today, but if I had, I might have assumed she was here on aid because I assume that I am here on aid. The truth is we never discussed the money when I was accepted here, but Dad's bartending salary definitely wouldn't cover the tuition.

I do this sometimes—project. I need to be more aware of making projections, applying myself to the outside world. Who do I think I am?

"I think I'm getting funding," I say. "But I don't really know."

"If you don't know, you're probably not here on scholarship," she says.

I think about that.

Clarice has dark brown skin and skinny dreads that reach past her shoulders but not as far down her back as my wavy jumble of hair. She wears plastic cat-eye glasses, but the frames are clear, which I've never seen before. I think she looks cool but also studious. I'm not sure how I look to her. Probably nervous but also eager but also sheltered. A deer caught in the headlights that are Tipton.

"Where are you from?" I ask. When I arrived this morning, Clarice was not in our room, but all of her stuff was unpacked. I didn't think you could move in before eight, but maybe she got here last night.

"Manhattan, born and raised. Do you know the city?"

"A little." I shrug. "My mom grew up in Westchester, so she went to the city all the time when she was a kid. She used to take us when I was younger. She liked Central Park and the Metropolitan Museum of Art."

"Everyone calls it the Met." Her voice is not unkind.

I blush. I didn't know that.

"I live in Tribeca," she says. "That's downtown, south of the Met and Central Park."

"We went to Chinatown a couple times," I say. "I love all the markets."

"Tribeca is near Chinatown. But it's also a different world. You're from Vermont?"

I shake my head, no. "Upstate. Well, further upstate. Adirondacks."

Clarice stands abruptly. Have I offended her in some way? Would she want to hang out with me if I was from Vermont?

"I have to go. Cross-country hang. My teammates are waiting." She sounds apologetic. It's not about me. *(Not everything is about you, Calliope.)*

"Right, okay." Then she's gone, and I am alone on my bed with yellow polka dot sheets. I think about hanging a poster on the big blank wall above my bed, or maybe the watercolor Lorelei painted of our house. I can't decide if it will make me too homesick.

What would Momma have hung on her walls? I stare at the white paint and wait for it to tell me something. It doesn't.

Eventually, I settle for tacking my dog calendar to the corkboard above my desk. Then I place a framed photo of my sisters and me beside my computer, and for now, I am done.

6

They are huddled together on the living room couch: Dad, Lorelei, Serafina. Dad has the tripod set up so no one has to hold the phone out awkwardly. I just saw them this morning, but that was a thousand years ago. The long Renaissance.

"I'm thinking about going by Cal here," I tell them. "What do you think?"

"No. Full stop." Lorelei twists her face, which is so like my face yet so distinctly Lorelei, into an ugly scowl.

"Definitely not." Serafina shakes her head back and forth, back and forth. Her fine curls whip against Dad's neck.

"Dad?" I implore. I don't need their blessing. But I need their blessing.

"Why do you want to change your name?" he asks.

"It wouldn't be changing my name. It's a nickname."

"I see." Dad's voice is thoughtful. He adjusts his glasses against the bridge of his nose, which he does when he is considering something. "I think it's not up to us, pumpkin."

"You wouldn't fit anymore," Serafina whines.

"She's right," Lorelei agrees. "Serafina, Lorelei, and *Cal*?"

I think about that. If the nickname would sever me from my sisters, I'm not sure I want it anymore.

"Do I have to tell everyone here about the accident?" I ask.

"Of course not," Lorelei says. "I've told you this. Is that why you want to change your name?"

"No. Maybe. I just don't want to have to tell it over and over."

"You don't have to, pumpkin. You can share whatever you're comfortable with, whenever you're ready."

At Tipton, Momma was Kathy Callihan, her maiden name. Current Tiptonians probably don't have any reason to know about an alum dying six years ago, before they were even at Tipton. Besides, my sisters and I weren't named in the news articles about the crash. It feels strange after six years in the spotlight, but Dad is right. Here, I get to choose.

"Thanks. I think I'm going to stick with Calliope. People are already calling me that anyway."

"Good," Lorelei says.

"Good," Serafina agrees.

"What did you do today?" I ask.

School won't start for my sisters for another week and a half. Lorelei will be a sophomore and Serafina will be in second grade with Ms. Florence. I liked second grade with Ms. Florence. She smells like lavender and plays guitar.

"Same same," Lorelei says. She twists a strand of long auburn hair between her fingers. "Dad took a nap when we got home, and I took Serafina out in the kayak. Then Dad went to work and we went to the library."

"It was story hour," Serafina adds. "Lorelei read about bees."

Lorelei does this. Of the two of us, she is the more social Bolan by far, but she can retreat into a book for hours and hours. She will drop Serafina off at some children's activity at the library, then scour nonfiction until she finds a book about salt or freegans or Szechuan food and she won't stop until she's read everything on the topic—and shared her newfound knowledge with the three of us and all her friends. She will now be an insufferable font of bee facts for weeks.

She clears her throat. "Did you know there are no bees on Antarctica? Here in North America—"

"Don't start," I implore. "Have mercy."

"Fine." Lorelei frowns. "What did you do today? Let us live vicariously through you."

"I thought you didn't want to leave," I say. Dad didn't want to see any of us go, but when I'd made my boarding school intentions clear, he'd been diplomatic. The offer had been extended to Lorelei as well. She wasn't interested.

"I don't," she says. "Why go through all that upheaval when I can stay put and you'll tell me everything anyway?"

"Mmm." She's right. I will always tell my sister everything. "I was oriented. We had a welcome meeting and ice breakers and a picnic lunch and breakout sessions. There was a tour. I unpacked. I met a boy."

Serafina makes a face. Dad pretends to stuff earplugs in his ears.

"Nothing happened. Nothing will probably ever happen. But I think he likes me. He mispronounced my name."

"So that's why you want to change it," Lorelei says at the

same time that Serafina asks, "How does that mean that he likes you?"

I ignore Lorelei. I don't know what made me want the nickname. That impulse has passed. "He was trying to get me to talk to him," I say to my baby sister. "Boys do silly things like that sometimes, if they like someone. At least I think they do. I'll feel it out and report back."

Dad pantomimes removing the earplugs. "Is it safe now?" he asks.

"God, Dad. You're so embarrassing."

"I know." He grins, a flash of white teeth against the gray-and-brown scruff that covers his cheeks and chin. "This is my job."

"I thought being the best bartender in Plover Lake was your job." And solo parenting three daughters, a job I know he'd never imagined. All in all, he does a pretty good job. After the accident, he ushered us through four years of family therapy. He keeps all our schedules straight and makes sure homework gets done. He'll never be bursting with imagination and creativity like Momma, but that's not his fault. One thing we talked about again and again in therapy is how it's not fair to expect any of us to fill Momma's shoes now that she's gone. We all have to be who we are and do our very best.

"That too," Dad says, pulling me out of my thoughts. "But I'm not on at the bar again until dinner tomorrow, so I can hang around and be embarrassing all night."

"No need," I assure him. "I'm embarrassing myself plenty here all on my own."

I don't want to get off the call with them. But I don't

want to be the girl who spends her whole first night at Tipton on the phone with her family either. I should go out to
the Anders common area, find someone to talk to. Maybe try
my hand at Ping-Pong, which requires less talking but more
hand-eye coordination than I can probably muster. But I
should try. I'm here. I need to try.

7

We are on an excursion, orientation day two. Today we are grouped by dorm, so I am walking through town with all the Anders first-years and Marjorie (superpower: baking). Two of the first-years are Alys and could give this tour themselves, but they are here to bond. I learn that each day student is assigned to a dorm, and Alys participate in dorm-sponsored social activities with us Bunkers. I wish Nico was with us, or Prisha, but they are with the groups from Chandler and Lynd, respectively. Three full-time Tipton staff members, our chaperones, trail behind.

The Anders student leaders are Brit Bowen, our prefect, a tall senior with very good posture and a long blond ponytail, and Lee Fenton, a small girl with pale skin like mine but even more freckles. Her electric blue tank top is overshadowed by an explosion of red curls. It is difficult to focus on anything else about her; Lee's narrow shoulders and skinny arms are swallowed in a blaze of red. I wonder what she would look like without her hair, and I can't picture it. She tells us that she is a senior, and the primary reason she volunteered to be an orientation leader was to get back to campus early. I wonder if she is escaping something at home or running toward something at Tipton. I wonder if someday I will know her well enough to ask.

It is strange to not know anyone here. For no one to know me.

I pull out my phone and check the group chat I have going with Erica and Beatrix. Aside from my sisters, they are my two best friends in Plover Lake, the only two friends I stayed close with after the accident turned me into a local celebrity. There's nothing new from them today, probably because they are hanging out with each other. Their lives continuing, of course, without me. *I miss you*, I type. Then I am afraid of sounding desperate, so I snap a selfie, my face haloed in sunshine, caption it: *Boarding school babe lol*.

Later, I will tell them the real story, how I am excited and relieved to be here but lonely and homesick too. How I wish I could have taken them and my family with me and left the rest of Plover Lake behind.

Phone back in my bag, I return my focus to Brit and Lee. We are becoming acquainted with the highlights of Alyson-on-Hudson. Some places are familiar from visiting Aunt Mave and Teya, but a lot has changed, or I don't remember, or I never knew where the post office was located or how to get a public library card. Momma used to take us to visit her sister several times a year, but after she died, we've come less often. I try to remember the last time I was here. I think it was two years ago; Dad dropped us off for a long weekend the summer before I started ninth grade. Aunt Mave and Teya have come to visit us in the mountains twice since then, on days when Dad was working double shifts, and we went kayaking or hiking or swimming. They never stay over. They always bring us home, then drive back to Alyson-on-Hudson.

I will see them on Sunday, the first of many scheduled dinners. For now, Lee and Brit are leading the Anders group down Chicory Lane, which is like a main street but not called Main Street. The sun is hot on our backs, and I weave my hair into a loose braid as we walk. Lee keeps hers down and I think she must be hot, but also if I had hair like that, I would never tie it back, ever. We are appraised of the Thai restaurant favored by Tiptonians, the bookstore that will carry our course texts, the yoga studio that offers a student discount, and the smoothie place where three sophomores got food poisoning last spring.

Toward the end of the Chicory Lane commercial strip is a small coffee shop called Frances Bean. Brit says the owners moved here from Seattle and that they're stuck in the nineties. Everyone laughs. I smile and pretend to know what she means. I shouldn't do that so much—pretend I understand something when I don't. Admitting you don't know something is uncomfortable. It's so much easier to smile and nod and look it up later. But it's not very honest.

Brit opens the door and ushers us inside. As I pass by her, it strikes me that she is very pretty in a carefully composed way. The skirt and top she's wearing look expensive; they're definitely not from Old Navy. Her makeup is understated and flawless, and her blond hair is pulled into a high ponytail not with a hair tie, but with a slender gold clasp lined with tiny pearls. I return her placid smile with my toothy one and try not to feel too scrubby in my cutoffs and favorite black-and-white striped tank.

Inside, Lee hands us each a neon-green slip of paper and tells us the orientation committee has prepaid for one large drink for everyone. All we have to do is present our drink ticket to the barista at the counter when we order. If we want any snacks, that's on us, and some Tiptonians may be spoiled rich kids who don't tip, but we are better than that. I check the small leather satchel with brown leather fringe that Lorelei calls my hippie bag and am relieved to find my wallet inside.

When it's my turn, I order a large passion fruit iced tea with lots of sugar. The barista points me toward a small counter near the window with sugar, honey, and three kinds of milk. I thank her. I don't forget to tip.

"No caffeine?" Lee is also at the counter, fitting a lid on her coffee cup. I tear open three sugar packets.

"Coffee makes me jumpy," I admit. "I like herbal tea, but it's bitter."

"Hence triple sugar." Lee smiles. Her teeth are small and straight. Everything about her is small except for her hair. She is one of the most interesting-looking people I have ever met.

"Exactly."

I stir sugar into my iced tea and look out the window. On the sidewalk across the street, a man my father's age is walking with his hands shoved into his pockets. His hair is a dark shade of blond, and he walks with his shoulders thrown back. He pauses to examine the flyers posted on an old-fashioned bulletin board hanging on the side of a squat brick building.

Then he turns, and for a moment, he is staring straight at me through the coffee shop window. His cheeks are sunburned, and his eyebrows are very thick. His eyes lock with mine through the glass.

I drop the straw I've been using as a stirrer. Then he breaks my gaze, turns, and keeps walking.

"Calliope? Hello?" Lee is still talking to me. She's not at the counter anymore. I didn't notice her sit down at one of the little café tables.

I turn to face her. "What?"

"Is everything okay?" she asks. "Other people might want sugar."

I spin around. A small line has formed behind me. I am hogging the counter.

"I'm sorry," I mumble, stepping aside. I leave my iced tea sitting on the countertop. "I have to go."

I push through the door, onto the sidewalk. The sun is in my eyes. The man is nowhere. I cross the street and start jogging in the direction he disappeared.

"Calliope!" Lee's voice. I haven't made it far. I freeze three storefronts down from the building with the bulletin board, let her catch up to me. He could have turned down any side street or stepped into a store. He was just here, his eyes locked with mine, and now I've lost him.

"You can't run off like that. Jesus."

"I'm sorry. I thought I saw . . ."

She narrows her thin red eyebrows. "What?"

The sun is hot. It needles into my scalp. My throat is

scratchy and dry. "Someone I recognized. The blond man reading those flyers." I point at the now vacant patch of sidewalk in front of the bulletin board. "Did you see him?"

Lee frowns. "Come back in. Your ice is melting."

I let her touch my elbow, guide me back inside.

8

A Wolf at the Door

A brand new memory—
There was a man that day, six years ago.
Dark blond hair, thick eyebrows, sunburned
    skin.
Inside the van, riding in the passenger's seat.

A handsome prince or a hideous beast?

I am drowning in questions—
Did he steer us into the lake?
How did he escape before I woke?
How did I forget him?

The Pied Piper, piping his beguiling tune.

He was with us that day because
he knew our mother, or—

he was a hitchhiker, or—
he forced Momma to
let
him
in.

A wolf at the door. A wolf inside.

Six years later, he lives here, or—
he followed me. Did he come to finish
what he started? Does he remember me?
Am I in danger?

9

Later, when Clarice goes to dinner and I'm alone in our room, I call Lorelei.

"A man?" she asks, cutting me off. I am speaking too fast. I am rambling.

"In town," I say. "Today. But also on the day of the accident. He was in the van."

My sister frowns into her phone screen. She is in her room, back pressed against the giant blue pillow on her bed, chin propped on her hand, the way she likes to sit.

"No," she says, emphatic. "There was no man in the minivan, Calliope. I think I'd remember."

"We went through a trauma," I say. "And we were just kids. Momma died. We almost died."

"I was there," Lorelei says. "I know."

"I'm just saying, I think it's perfectly possible that we got things mixed up, after it happened. If you'd've seen him today, you would remember him too. He was this perfect stranger outside the coffee shop, but I *knew* him. The moment

I saw his face, I could see him clearly that day, sitting in the passenger's seat."

Lorelei presses her lips together. "You know I love you. But you're out of your mind."

"I need you to think, that's all. I need you to try to remember."

Lorelei lets out a frustrated huff. *Pfff.* "How am I supposed to remember someone I've never seen?"

She has me there. Point Lorelei.

"Maybe if you just think about that day," I implore. "Maybe if you try—"

"What is this really about? Is it about Momma?"

It is about the man with dark blond hair. I saw him. I *remember*.

When I don't respond, Lorelei says, "I know you don't want it to have been her fault. None of us want that. I believe you saw someone today, probably someone you've seen in Alyson-on-Hudson before. Maybe someone Aunt Mave knows. But I think this is just your brain trying to connect dots that aren't there. Searching for a reason to let Momma off the hook."

What my sister is saying, it makes sense. It's perfectly reasonable. But she's wrong. I know what I saw—today, six years ago. A man. A wolf.

10

Lee Fenton's walls are plastered with eight-by-ten portraits: extreme close-ups; self-portraits; Tiptonians standing on a boulder somewhere near campus, made tiny against its craggy gray mass. I hover in the doorway, unsure if yesterday's invitation to stop by had been serious or just one of those things people say but don't really mean. She'd been kind, back in Frances Bean. She rescued my iced tea from the counter and sat with me while I drank it. She told me to come find her in Anders 3F anytime.

The door is open, but Lee doesn't see me. She is sitting at her desk, which faces a window looking out on Quadrant West and Brisbane, the main administrative building where Dr. Naylor, our head of school, and the various deans have their offices. I rap my knuckles against her open door.

Lee turns in a blaze of red curls. Her face lights up. "Calliope. You came by."

I take one step through the threshold. It's Saturday morning, and we new Tiptonians are fully oriented. Returning students have already begun flooding across the quads, pouring into dorms, clogging up the waffle line at brunch. It's a lot. I knew, of course, that everyone would be coming back today, but I wasn't prepared for the noise of it. The bodies, everywhere. Cars squatting in front of dorms, doors flung wide, all of Tipton in motion.

"I needed a break," I say. "It's nice to see a familiar face."

"Move in can be overwhelming. Come hide out in here with me." Lee gestures to her bed, which is spread up in a pale gray duvet. Like all seniors and some juniors, Lee has a single. Aside from the photographs, which cover almost every inch of wall space, the room is unfussy. Gray duvet, gray rug, small mirror on the back of the closet door. I take a seat on the corner of her bed.

"Thanks. And I'm sorry about yesterday. Again."

Lee waves my apology away. "You want to talk about it?"

I do want to talk about it, but I don't want to scare Lee off. "Tell me about your photographs," I say instead.

"These are old. I'm dying to get back in the lab and print the series I did this summer."

My eyes land on a cluster of prints to the right of Lee's desk. They are of a girl who looks like Lee, but turned at an angle. Longer features, fewer freckles, same wild halo of red hair. "Your sister?" I ask.

She nods. "That's Lacy. I took those three years ago, when she was a senior here."

"She's beautiful."

"She hated having her picture taken." Lee frowns. "She put up such a fight about doing that shoot. It was one of my first projects, when I was a first-year. The photos aren't great, but they're still some of my favorites. Now that she's not here anymore."

"I know what you mean," I tell her. "I've never been away from my sisters. I didn't think it would be so hard."

"Anyway," Lee says abruptly, standing up and stretching. "Tell me about your passions, Calliope. What are you into?"

"Oh." This question keeps coming up, but I still don't have a good answer. Everyone here seems to be "into" something, to already know where they want to go to college, what they want to be when they grow up. Or they're just better at faking it than I am. "I guess I'm still figuring it out. That's part of why I came to Tipton."

Lee smiles, waiting for me to say more. What are my passions? Not knitting.

"My mom liked to write when she was a teenager," I say finally. "I'm taking a creative writing elective. Maybe that will be my thing."

Lee's eyebrows narrow. "Who with?"

"I'm not sure." I pull out my phone and log into Tipton Teal so I can look up my class schedule. "Ellis?"

Lee sits up straight, and I realize she'd been hunched over, waiting for my answer. "You should switch sections," she says, "before the trimester starts."

Before I can ask why, there's a figure darkening Lee's doorway. He has light brown skin and thick black hair that skims his shoulders. Lee squeals and rushes toward him, wrapping him in a four-limbed hug. He stumbles out into the hall, laughing.

"This is Lucas Morales," she says, extracting herself. "Lucas, meet Calliope Bolan."

He walks back into the room and perches on Lee's desk. "Sick name."

I shrug. "Thanks."

"How was your trip?" Lee asks. She flops down on her bed.

"Epic. Ninety minutes to Santiago, then two hours in the airport, then ten and a half hours to JFK. I stayed with Quinn in Brooklyn last night and we drove up together this morning."

I stand and run my hands down the front of my shorts. I feel like I'm intruding.

"Lucas is from Chile," Lee explains. "And Quinn is awesome. Where is Quinn?"

"They're with Tina, I think. At Gray Space."

I take a step toward the door. "I should let you catch up."

Lee doesn't argue. Lucas, who is maybe her boyfriend or maybe a friend, twists around to look out the window. "Look who's walking into Brisbane with Ms. Correa."

Lee casts a glance outside. "Later," she says, thin-lipped. Then she turns to me. "Switch out of that class. You'll thank me later."

I say I'll look into it, then I step out into the hall. "Nice to meet you, Lucas."

"Come say hi at dinner," Lee says. Which is a nice offer, but not quite as nice as suggesting we go together.

11

I eat dinner with Clarice and her cross-country friends. It's better than sitting alone, but not by much. Clarice's friends are nice enough, and occasionally they try to include me, but mostly they forget I'm at the table. Right now, they're talking about ghosts and when they're going to make their first appearance of the trimester. If this campus is haunted, I'd like to know which buildings to avoid after dark, but the conversation is moving too fast for me. Before I can ask for a little context, the topic has shifted to their coach's new haircut and whether or not the man they saw her talking to in the faculty lot this afternoon is her boyfriend.

Being new at Tipton is like picking up a book and starting to read somewhere in the middle. For everyone around me, the story already has a beginning and rising action and well-rounded characters. I'm just lost.

Lee is nowhere. I scan the dining hall for her one more time before I excuse myself and walk out onto the path. Maybe she came to dinner as soon as Rhine opened, or maybe she and Lucas decided to go somewhere off campus. I trudge up the path, past the music building, then two buildings that I think are dorms, then Brisbane, the main administrative building. I'm meeting people every day, but those people have people already. Where do I fit?

My hand travels to my bag, to the outline of my phone against the leather. I could call Lorelei again, but Lorelei only wants to talk about bees. Instead I pause on the path and tap open my group chat. Erica and Beatrix have sent me a bunch of photos from the annual back-to-school shopping pilgrimage to the outlet mall. It's an hour and a half from Plover Lake, and usually the three of us go together. This year, Dad took me a few weeks ago since my school year was starting earlier, and now I can't decide if flipping through pictures of Beatrix modeling a pair of red pleather pants she'll never buy and Erica licking a giant soft pretzel with the grossest topping—sour cream and onion, her favorite—is making me feel included or even more homesick.

"Hey, stranger."

Nico's voice draws my eyes away from my phone. He gives me a wave from his perch on the low stone wall in front of his dorm, Chandler. I haven't seen him since our excursion into town yesterday, and even that barely counts. His orientation group split off in a different direction early in the day.

Nico is alone, but he doesn't look lonely. A pair of white earbuds stick out from between messy strands of light brown hair, and he's using some kind of stylus pen to draw on a big, fancy-looking tablet. He removes the earbuds and tucks them into his pocket.

"Hey," I say back. I'm not sure what to do with my hands,

so I flip my phone over and over. Nico is wearing a green graphic tee with a cartoon rat triumphantly lifting a slice of pizza above its head. He gives me a wide smile, and my eyes focus in on a small chip in his left front tooth.

I'm staring. I avert my gaze upward, to the dorm behind him.

"Evening stroll?" he asks.

"Something like that." I keep my eyes trained on the front of the dorm. Like most of the buildings at Tipton, Chandler is redbrick with white trim and a slate black roof. The buildings here look timeless, like there's knowledge and tradition mixed in with the brick and mortar. When it seems like I've safely not-stared for long enough, my eyes drop back down to Nico's face. Why does everything I do feel so awkward?

"What were you listening to?" I ask out loud.

"It's the audiobook for *The Poet X*. We're reading it for Contemporary American Lit, and I'm getting a head start." He pats the wall next to him, and I pull myself up, grateful for something to do.

"I never think to listen to audiobooks."

"I retain information better that way. And you should definitely listen to this on audio. It's amazing."

"Thanks." I'm not taking Contemporary American Lit, but I make a mental note to check it out. My gaze falls on the large tablet resting on his lap. "Is that Lee?"

"Yeah." Nico grins. There's that chip again. It might technically be an imperfection, but now that I've noticed it, I can't stop thinking about his mouth. Oh god. I look back down at the screen.

"That's amazing. Did you draw that using . . . ?" I motion toward the stylus.

He nods. "Takes some getting used to, but I like drawing digitally this way. I got the tablet over the summer, and it's opening up some really cool new possibilities. I'm excited to get back into the design lab." He slips the stylus into a slot on the side of the tablet and rubs his hand against the back of his neck. "I probably sound like a giant dork."

"No, that's awesome."

Everyone here really does have a talent or something they're passionate about. I was on honor roll back home, and I did some clubs and activities—student government, Amnesty International, I even organized a library book club last year—but I'm not sure any of that defines me in some key way like Lee's photography and Marjorie's baking and Nico's graphic design.

"Knitting's not really my 'superpower,'" I confess. "This fall, I am going to find my thing." My voice brims with more confidence than I feel. Connect with Momma. Find my passion. Adjust to a new school two hours away from home. I'm setting myself up for a lot, but why else did I come here?

"Tipton can be a lot," Nico says. The boy is reading my mind. "Just keep your eyes open. You'll find your place here."

I give him a smile. He makes it sound so easy. "Thanks."

"Where were you headed?" he asks.

"Back to Anders, eventually. I was kind of taking the long way home."

Nico is quiet for a moment. His eyes travel down to the

drawing of Lee. "I heard you saw something yesterday, outside Frances Bean."

I wrap my arms around my waist. "News travels fast here."

"Don't get mad at Lee. All the orientation leaders had to give a report at our closing meeting last night. She just said she was a little concerned, that's all. It's okay if you don't want to talk about it."

I do want to talk about it, though. With someone who is really going to listen, unlike Lorelei. At home, I never have to talk about the accident because every single person in our village already knows. But it's there, always, hanging over me like a rain cloud or a halo, depending on who's doing the looking. I didn't think I'd want to talk about it here, but seeing the man with dark blond hair—this stranger who is somehow not a stranger—changed that. There's so much I need to figure out.

I study Nico's face. His eyes are brown and wide and there's no judgment there. He already knows I made a fool of myself running out onto the sidewalk, and yet he's still sitting here, talking to me. I draw in a deep breath.

"When I was ten, I was in a bad car crash. My sisters and I got out, but our mom died. We've never understood what happened to make the car swerve off the road, and the police investigation was inconclusive. My mom was driving, so by default, people assume she was to blame. Best case scenario, she was distracted behind the wheel, or worst case, she had some kind of mental break and drove us into a lake on purpose. None of the theories ever seemed right. I've always thought there must be some other explanation for what happened that day."

Nico is a good listener. All his attention is on me, but he doesn't interrupt with questions or condolences or awkward shoulder pats. He lets me tell it at my own pace.

"Then yesterday, I saw this man walking down Chicory Lane, outside the coffee shop. He was a stranger, but he wasn't. Seeing him triggered this very clear memory about that day. He was with us in the van, riding in the passenger's seat. I think he might have caused the accident—done something to my mom or grabbed the wheel."

Nico waits for a beat, to make sure I'm finished speaking. Then he says, "I'm so sorry about your mom, Calliope. And . . . wow. Do you think you had amnesia?"

"I think it's more like I didn't realize the man was important at the time, so he didn't stick in my memory. When I woke up after the crash, he wasn't in the van anymore. The lake we drove into was this narrow strip of water. If he pulled himself out of the window as soon as we crashed, he could have gotten to shore pretty quickly. My mom dying, my sisters and me almost drowning, that took up all of the space in my brain. I don't remember much about what happened that day before the accident, or the EMTs coming, or going back home. Everything else got crowded out."

"And your sisters?" Nico asks. "Do they remember him at all?"

"Serafina was only fourteen months, so she's too young to remember any of it. But Lorelei is a year younger than me. She thinks there was never a man in the car with us, that I'm losing my mind, but I'm not. That memory was real."

"I believe you."

Nico's hand is resting on his leg. Before I can think about it too hard, I place my hand on top of his. He shifts, and I think he's going to pull away, but he turns it over so our palms are touching. He laces his fingers with mine.

My heart stops.

The sun dips below the tree line.

The air is exactly still.

I am holding Nico Hale's hand.

"I'd like to help," he says. "Maybe we can find him, or figure out who he is. Why he might have done something to your mom."

I smile. "I'd like that."

Then we sit there for a long time, on the wall outside Chandler, holding hands and not saying anything else.

12

Classes begin tomorrow. On Sunday afternoon, I walk to the bookstore in town to buy my course texts. I'm not used to buying books for school. At home, books were assigned and recycled year after year. Here, textbooks will be passed out in class, but for English and Creative Writing, we buy our books and keep them.

Dad has set up an account for me at the bookstore, and I buy everything I will need for English 11 and my elective, which is still with Mr. Ellis. I did take Lee's advice and check if I could switch, but the sections with Ms. Correa are all full, and I really want this class. If he's a hard teacher, fine. I'm up for the challenge. Maybe writing will be my thing like it was for Momma.

I walk back to campus slowly, keeping my chin up, eyes open. The man I saw is nowhere, but I don't stop looking. As I start up the hill to campus, I see Marjorie and wave. She is walking into town with a sophomore transfer and two girls I don't recognize. I wonder if they are already friends, if everyone is having an easier time finding their place here than I am. Then I think about Nico, his fingers laced with my fingers on the wall outside Chandler last night. I have one friend who is maybe more than a friend. Maybe I am doing okay.

Tipton's main entrance is an arch at the base of the hill, GEORGE M. TIPTON ACADEMY spelled out in black wrought iron between two redbrick pillars. The mail room is the first building you pass on the path, trudging up the hill. Unlike most buildings at Tipton, the mail room is small and constructed from pale gray stone. We are to check our mail daily, because although it is the twenty-first century, we are told that some Tipton teachers do not like to communicate by email or through Tipton Teal, the online campus portal. Delivering notes to a mail room staff member to distribute to student boxes seems highly inefficient, but there is a permissiveness for the outmoded here, a reverence for tradition.

Inside, the mail room walls are lined with small wooden doors. For privacy, each student's box is accessed by a three-digit combination. I turn the small bronze dial—3-22-14—and open the door. I have a package slip that will have to wait until the mail room staff returns on Monday and a postcard with Plover Lake on the front and a sweet note on the back in Serafina's careful, round letters. The third item in my mailbox is a thick card envelope with my name written across the front in a sloping black scrawl. I flip it over. The cream envelope is secured with a red wax seal; below the seal is a note: *Open in private. To be read by the addressee only.*

I sit on one of the narrow wooden benches that stretch across the center of the room. Two other students are sifting through mail, tossing coupon sheets and L.L. Bean catalogues into the trash. While I wait, I pretend to read a discarded flyer advertising a show tonight at Gray Space, the student-run performance venue at the far end of Quadrant East. When the mail room is finally empty, I flip the envelope over and lift the seal. The wax is imprinted with the outline of something that looks like a ghost baring its teeth.

> *Dear Calliope,*
>
> *Welcome. You don't know us yet, but we know you. You are cordially invited to join us in the early hours of Monday morning, one o'clock sharp, under the sugar maple on Quadrant East. We hope you will choose to attend.*
>
> *You must trust us, as we have decided to trust you. This invitation is for your eyes only and will be rescinded immediately if you violate our privacy. No photos, no posts, no sharing of any kind.*
>
> *One o'clock. Bring this card. Don't get caught.*
>
> *Your Fellow Ghosts*

I read the note three times, then return it to its envelope. Something one of Clarice's friends said at dinner last night sticks in my mind. Something about when the ghosts were going to make an appearance. Maybe this is what she was talking about.

The door to the mail room opens, and I drop the invitation into my bag along with the package slip and Serafina's postcard. Dorm check-in is ten o'clock on school nights. I continue my walk up the hill toward Anders and try to decide if I'm brave enough to sneak out tonight. If I want to find out who the ghosts are. If I want to be one of them.

13

I have no car and no driver's license, so Aunt Mave will be picking me up for our weekly Sunday dinner dates. At six thirty, while the rest of the Bunkers head to Rhine or an off-campus destination with friends for the last dinner before classes begin, I lean against the Tipton arch at the base of the hill and wait for Aunt Mave to arrive. The invitation from my "fellow ghosts" is still nestled in my bag. The instructions were pretty clear—don't tell anyone. Does Aunt Mave count? Probably.

At six thirty-one, she pulls up in a small orange car. I get into the passenger's seat and buckle up. Aunt Mave has looked exactly the same for as long as I can remember—petite frame and dainty features accented by a pixie cut, which she dyes white blond. She barely looks related to Momma, who was tall like me and wore her auburn hair long like her daughters. Her smile is the same though—broad and warm.

Today, however, there is one change. Aunt Mave is wearing a pair of green-rimmed glasses. I don't ever remember her wearing glasses before, and I try to remember how old she is.

Momma was three years older than her sister, so that would make my aunt forty-one now.

"I like your glasses," I say. If I ever have to get glasses, I think I'll get a pair with green frames too. They bring out the green in my aunt's eyes, which is something else she has in common with her sister, and with me.

"Oh god," Aunt Mave groans. "They say when you turn forty your vision goes to hell, and it's true." She backs out onto the main road and steers the car toward her house, which is a ten-minute drive from campus, give or take. "I have to wear them for driving now."

"Well, they're cute," I tell her. "They suit you."

"Thanks, hon."

Fifteen minutes later, we're sitting in Aunt Mave's kitchen with Teya, her wife. Sebastian, our blue-eyed Aussie puppy who is now a full-grown Aussie dog, is flopped at my feet. Dad has never been much of an animal person. After Momma died and Dad was suddenly a single parent to three young girls, Sebastian went to live with Aunt Mave and Teya. I protested, declared I'd take on full responsibility for him, but the puppy on top of everything else was too much. I reach down and let Sebastian lick my hand under the table.

It's been six months since I saw them, maybe a little more, but it doesn't feel that long. Teya is younger than my aunt by a couple years; she's in her late thirties, I think. She is Black and Filipina and wears her hair in two long braids that she coils on top of her head. When she lets them down, they hang almost to her belly.

"Tell us everything about Tipton." Teya props her elbows

on the table and leans forward while Aunt Mave ladles gazpacho into bowls and arranges thick slices of sourdough bread and a runny white cheese on a pretty wooden cutting board. Teya grew up in Chicago and teaches history at Roosevelt, the public high school in Alyson-on-Hudson. She is not Tipton's greatest fan, but her interest seems sincere.

"It's very pretty," I say. "And the food is better than I thought it would be."

Aunt Mave laughs. She sets our bowls down on the table. "Glad something has changed for the better since I was there."

"There are two all-gender dorms now too," I tell her. "Hadley and Carrington."

"That is truly something. Tipton evolving."

"Did you like it there? The real answer." When I've asked Aunt Mave about Tipton before, she always says something vague, then changes the subject.

"The real answer, huh?" She dips a piece of sourdough into her bowl. "I did and I didn't. I had a lot of fun, being away from home. Probably too much fun. But Tipton in the nineties was a difficult place to realize you might be queer. I didn't come out as bisexual until my midtwenties, even to myself. I think if I'd been in another environment, things might have been different. And I wasn't much of a student. Your mother thrived there. Kathy was at the top of her class, but I was perpetually struggling. I have always suspected that your grandparents bought my way in."

"Could they do that?" I have never considered this. Grandmommy and Granddaddy are very wealthy, but they retired from Westchester to Florida a long time ago and never come to visit. We grew up with Nana and Pop-Pop, Dad's parents, who live five minutes away from us in the Adirondacks. I sometimes forget that I have another set of grandparents.

Aunt Mave shrugs. "Why not? Tipton loves a major donor."

"Is that how I got in?" At my feet, Sebastian rolls onto his back, and I reach down to rub his belly.

"Definitely not," Teya interjects. "You got in on your own merit."

"But they're paying," I press. My thoughts travel back to my first night here, to Clarice's words. *If you don't know, you're probably not here on scholarship.*

Aunt Mave shrugs. "You'll have to ask your dad, but I'd guess your tuition is coming out of your mother's trust. So indirectly, yes. But you got in because you're bright and curious about the world. Have some faith in yourself, Calliope."

"Someone should listen to her own advice," Teya interjects. "Your aunt's grades were not as bad as she's making out. She could have gone to college if she'd wanted to, but that wasn't her path."

Aunt Mave's path involved staying in Alyson-on-Hudson after graduation, much to my grandparents' dismay. This I already know. They wanted both of their daughters to go to Ivy League colleges, "marry well," and become doctors or lawyers or business moguls. Essentially, to have it all, but that was *their* dream. Momma went to Yale, then disappointed them by marrying a bartender from a rural village and getting a part-time job in a flower shop. She was always more interested in being a mother than a career woman, a concept my grandparents could not get behind. Their younger daughter disappointed them too, by skipping college altogether and marrying a woman. Aunt Mave is a cheesemonger and owns a specialty cheese shop in town, which I think is very impressive, but her parents expected her to be running Microsoft by now.

"What was Momma like at Tipton?" I ask.

"Kathy was three years ahead of me, so we only overlapped for one year. Most of the time she was there, I was still at home in Scarsdale, suffering through middle school." Scarsdale is the wealthy suburb of New York City where Momma and Aunt Mave grew up. "But I was a first-year at Tipton when Kathy was a senior. She worked hard, really excelled academically. And she was social too—she had a ton of friends, and they never invited me to do anything with them." She laughs. "I think part of her resented her baby sister being on her turf."

This is hard to imagine. "But you were always so close," I protest.

For a moment, Aunt Mave is quiet. She spreads some cheese across a slice of bread, and I do the same. "Most of the time, yes, we were very close," she says finally. "But all siblings fight. I'm sure I don't have to tell you that. Things got better when she left for Yale, then they got bad again four years later. There was a time we weren't close at all. But then Kathy met your dad, and by the time she had you, we were thick as thieves again."

"What did you fight about?" I think about Lorelei the other night, insisting I was out of my mind. Are *we* fighting?

"Being too close, then too far apart. Boys." She laughs and slides her hand into Teya's. "It was a long time ago."

Teya asks me about my classes, and I pull up my schedule on Tipton Teal to show her. We finish dinner, then move to the living room. Teya pours us all mugs of tea. I sit on the floor with Sebastian and let mine get cold. Teya has to teach in the morning, so when it's time to go, she stays home to prepare while Aunt Mave drives me back to campus.

When she pulls up to the main entrance, I don't unfasten my seat belt right away. "Can I ask you something?"

"Sure, hon."

I trace the outline of the card in my bag, but my gut tells me not to ask about that.

"Do you know a man, about your age, with dark blond hair and thick eyebrows and ruddy cheeks, like they're sunburned?"

Aunt Mave frowns. She adjusts her glasses on her nose. "Here in Alyson-on-Hudson?"

I nod.

"That could describe a lot of people," she says. "Lots of people hike and fish and bird-watch around here. At this time of year, a little sunburn isn't uncommon."

"So no one in particular comes to mind?"

"I guess not. Why?"

I shake my head. I am not ready just yet to open up to Aunt Mave about the memory, my suspicions. But maybe I can rule out Lorelei's explanation—that he's someone I've met here through my aunt, and my brain is mixing things up.

"No real reason," I say. "I saw someone the other day. I

thought maybe he was a friend of yours. Or I recognized him from your shop."

"Maybe," Aunt Mave concedes. "But I can't think who that would be."

"Forget about it," I say, fixing a bright smile across my face. I unfasten my belt so I can lean over and give her a kiss. "I'll see you next Sunday."

I walk up the hill to campus, mentally composing what I'll say the next time I talk to Lorelei. *You were wrong. He's not a friend of Aunt Mave's. I'm not losing my mind. He was* there.

II
INITIATION

14

Back at Anders, I walk the perimeter and locate all the exits. Anders is a midsized dorm, forty girls living on three floors. Our resident faculty member, Ms. Joy, lives in an apartment with her family at the far end of floor three. Brit Bowen lives on floor one. Clarice and I are on floor two. I think I will be able to do this, but anxiety ties knots in my stomach and won't let go.

When I've finished scouting things out, I pack my bag and wait.

Here's how things work at Tipton: At ten o'clock on school nights and eleven on weekends, Bunkers congregate in dorm lobbies all over campus to check in with their prefects. I'm sure there's an app that would be much more efficient, but this is the way things have always been done at Tipton. In Anders, Brit holds a clipboard and crosses names off a list. She stands tall, shoulders thrown back and long blond hair pulled up on top of her head with a rose-gold clasp. After check-in, Bunkers return to their rooms and security goes around and locks up for the night. Then we have quiet time, followed by lights out.

Back in our room, I tell Clarice about dinner with Aunt Mave and Teya and show her pictures of Sebastian on my phone. Clarice shows me pictures of her boyfriend, Will, who lives in New York City. She says she will be gone a couple weekends a month, so I'll get the room to myself. I wonder if she'll want Will to sleep in our room when he comes to visit, but Clarice doesn't seem like the rule-breaking type.

I don't think I will be able to sleep, but just in case, I set an alarm on my phone, then connect my earbuds so only I will hear. At 12:50, it is shrill in my ears. I look over to Clarice's bed, but she is breathing deeply. I trade my pajama shorts for a pair of leggings and lace up my sneakers in the dark. Then I grab my bag from the foot of the bed and slip out into the hallway, silently closing the door behind me.

Sneaking out doesn't seem too hard. It's getting back in that I'm worried about.

Right across from our room is a stairwell down to the first floor. There is a back exit I can use so I won't have to pass by Brit's door. I hold my breath and keep my feet quiet on the stairs. I close doors softly behind me. At the back exit, I hesitate. You can walk right out, no problem—locking us in would be a major fire hazard—but student ID cards aren't coded to unlock dorm entrances once campus has been locked up for the night.

Outside, I wedge the cardboard tube from an empty toilet paper roll between the base of the door and the frame. It's propped open just enough to keep it unlatched, but not so wide that you'd notice if you were just walking by. If anyone else comes through this door, my plan will unravel, but that's a chance I'll have to take. It's 12:56. I have four minutes to get to Quadrant East.

Campus is silent. I avoid the lamp-lit paths and walk in the shadows of buildings. The moon is a fat, round orb in the sky, and there's just enough light to keep me on my feet instead of my face as I walk.

Tipton looks changed in the middle of the night. There's a different quality to the darkness now that everyone is sleeping. It's the same sky overhead, the same redbrick buildings all around me, but everything is completely still. The air itself seems frozen, like it's holding its breath. Only the shadows reach out, catch at my feet. A cold tendril zips up the back of my neck, nerves or something darker.

When I round the corner of Lynd, the large dorm where Prisha lives, the lamplight snares a student on the path to my right. I freeze. He is walking fast, head down, hands in pockets. The path leads directly between Tobin and Sloane, the two large academic buildings that divide Quadrant West from Quadrant East. I wait until he's almost out of sight, then continue my route through the shadows, doubling my pace. It is one minute to one o'clock.

As soon as I step out of the shadows of Tobin and Sloane and onto the grassy lawn, I can see why "the ghosts" picked this spot. Quadrant East is tree-lined on all four sides, and it's one of the farthest points on campus from Brisbane, the main administrative building. The security hut at the main entrance is likewise far out of sight, down the slope of the hill, although the night guards must do rounds at some point. It's very dark away from the path, and I squint, searching for a sugar maple. What I see is one body moving in the darkness, then another. I follow.

15

I arrive at the sugar maple at 1:01, on the heels of two other Tiptonians, but no one chides us for being a minute late. No one speaks at all. I scan the faces around me, counting, looking for anyone I know. Lee. My face lights up. Lucas, Lee's friend from Chile. And Brit—my prefect. My breath catches. I'm about to stammer out an excuse, something, but she flashes me a small smile, then raises her finger to her lips. There are eleven students in all, a few more faces I recognize, but no one else I know by name.

"You're late." Lee frowns. Her gaze is focused behind me, and I turn. Two more students are jogging across the quad toward us.

"Sorry," the first student gasps. He brushes a curtain of long blond hair out of his eyes. "There's another sugar maple. At least I think it's a sugar maple."

"I followed Josh," the other student says. She has light brown skin and brown hair that frames her face in tight, springy curls. I think she's a junior, like me.

"Blame Lucas," Brit sneers. She folds her arms across her

chest. "There is, indeed, another sugar maple."

"It's obscured behind a fir." Lucas holds up his hands defensively. "This is *the* sugar ma—"

"Enough." Lee cuts them off. "We're all here now. Juniors, please present your invitations. And place your phones in the bag—no exceptions."

Everyone except Lee, Lucas, and Brit digs in bags and pockets, producing their phones and ten identical creamy white envelopes. While Brit collects them, I steal glances at the faces around me. Of the ten juniors gathered here, I am the only transfer student. Everyone looks a little nervous, but no one is asking questions. I wonder if I am the only student here who has no idea what a ghost is. Who has no idea why they received an invitation in their box.

"The others are waiting," Lucas says. "Walk quickly. No talking."

The others?

I fall in line behind a girl with feathery blond hair. Lee, Lucas, and Brit lead the way across Quadrant East, back in the direction we came from. We stay off the path, away from the lamplight. Halfway across, we take a hard right. Lucas leads us through a break in the tall trees that line all four sides of the lawn. It's just a row of trees, but the act of passing through in the darkest part of night, leaves and low branches clutching at my hair, feels significant in a way that pricks at my skin. *Pay attention.* I have the hazy, intoxicating sensation of moving from the ordinary world into some hidden reality. It's the kind of feeling you'd brush aside quickly in daylight, dismiss as childish or silly. But right now it feels true, thrilling, impossible to ignore.

We emerge in the shadows of a large brick building. I try to place it from the campus tour, but it's unfamiliar from the back, shrouded in dark. Lucas leads us along the side to a gray-painted door. He stands aside to allow Brit to step up. She has a key.

"Watch your step," she stage whispers, shoulders thrown back. Her blue eyes flash sharp and cold in the moonlight. "We're going down."

Brit runs her hand along the wall inside the doorway, and a thin yellow light illuminates a set of stairs. Whatever building this is, we're headed to the basement. A small voice at the back of my head says this might be a bad idea, but a louder voice says to keep walking. My fingertips find the railing, and I follow feathery blond hair down into the stairwell.

We're in the Henry Hudson Library. More specifically, we're in the stacks in the library basement. Brit leads us through a narrow aisle lined on both sides with floor-to-ceiling steel shelving. Books upon books upon books. At the end of the aisle is a windowless door with a wooden sign: READING ROOM CLOSED. Brit pulls out a key.

"Wait here," she tells us.

We hover outside while Lee, Lucas, and Brit enter. Before she closes the door, I catch a glimpse of several more students sprawled on couches and sitting cross-legged on a large braided rug.

"I have been waiting two years for this," the girl with light brown skin and curly brown hair says reverently. There are murmurs of agreement all around me. I shift my weight to my right foot, then my left. Waiting for what?

When the door swings back open, the mood has shifted entirely. No one is lounging across couches or parked on the rug. The windowless room is dimly lit by several table lamps. It has the distinctive air of a well-worn clubhouse. Furniture foraged from yard sales and dorms. Tapestries hung on the walls. A hodgepodge of bookcases. Only the wall opposite the door is free from clutter. The others are regular white-painted plaster, but this wall is exposed brick. On it is painted a larger-than-life version of the symbol I recognize from the envelope seal—the angry ghost. Its looming presence casts a grim pallor across the room, which might otherwise look cozy. Lee, Lucas, Brit, and seven other seniors stand in a row against the wall, the ghost at their backs. They wear floor-length robes in a crimson so deep it is almost black. I shiver.

Lee motions for us to enter. We file in, and Lucas instructs us to line up so that we each face one of the robed students. Ten juniors facing ten robed seniors. Lucas shuts the door, and I wince as it locks behind us. No one else seems to notice. I take my place in front of Lee, focus my attention on her spray of freckles and cascade of red curls.

"Congratulations, initiates," she says. "You have been tapped to join the Haunt and Rail Society, the only currently active secret society at Tipton. If you successfully pass your initiation period, you will sign your name in the book and officially become a ghost."

16

A senior who introduces herself as Akari holds up an ancient-looking leather-bound volume, and someone lets out a small gasp. It is slim but larger than a regular book, like an old encyclopedia. Branded on the front is the angry ghost.

"Welcome to Haunt and Rail," Akari says. She wears her glossy black hair in a sharply angled bob, and her bangs are dyed purply-pink. Chunky black boots peek out from beneath her ceremonial robe. "Our society takes its name from two pieces of Hudson Valley history. 'Haunt' is a nod to *The Legend of Sleepy Hollow*, and 'rail' to the Mohawk and Hudson line, the first railroad to run through New York State. Hence the ghost with railroad tracks for teeth, our symbol. But our name also speaks to our mission."

She opens the book to its first page and reads. "The society's purpose will be to *haunt* and *rail*, that is to clandestinely observe injustices, inequities, and bad actors at Tipton Academy, and to rail against these wrongs." She looks up from the page. "Haunt and Rail was convened at Tipton in 1956, nine years after the school first opened. Six Tipton seniors founded the Haunt and Rail Society in an effort to pressure the administration to admit more students of color after several members of the board tried to halt the school's civil rights–era integration efforts.

"In its sixty-six-year history, Haunt and Rail's campaigns have been responsible, in full or in part, for many important changes on campus, including an increase in student and faculty diversity; the passing of the financial aid act of 2002; daily vegan options in Rhine dining hall; the termination of library fines; and the change from a one-day Columbus Day holiday to a two-day Fall Break."

"Don't forget the overhaul of Gray Space's policies on exhibiting student work," Lucas adds.

"Right," Akari agrees. "Haunt and Rail's campaigns have addressed large-scale social justice concerns and smaller campus life matters. As long as it has a broad impact on Tiptonians, we'll consider it."

"Our campaigns are carried out in the form of one or more larks," Lee says. "You'll hear people call them pranks, but we don't use that term because nothing we do is a joke. The addition of a campaign to Haunt and Rail's agenda requires the unanimous vote of all twenty members. You will gain voting privileges after you are officially inducted into the society."

"Haunt and Rail is not an anarchist organization," Lucas says. "Ghosts believe that there is a place for action through official channels. Some of our members belong to Tipton student government, which is crucial to Haunt and Rail's work. These ghosts serve as our eyes and ears on the inside, and our campaigns often dovetail with initiatives being discussed by student leaders. But throughout the years, Haunt and Rail's work has demonstrated that it often takes a radical, visible action to make faculty, administrators, and other students sit up and take notice."

"Which brings us to our motto," Akari says. She reads again from the large leather-bound book. "*Actiones secundum fidei*. Latin for *action follows belief*; in other words, ghosts act in accordance with our beliefs. Having ideals is one thing. Taking action to back them up is another. That's what we're about."

"We mentioned an initiation period," Lee says, "but the Haunt and Rail Society does not participate in hazing. In fact, think of this as an antihazing week. As initiates, you must keep your noses clean—no infractions, no calling attention to yourselves, no trouble. Acting alone, each of you will complete one initiation rite by this Friday morning: Sneak into a classroom after hours and draw the Haunt and Rail symbol on a whiteboard. Send us a picture, and leave it up for the class to find in the morning—and don't get caught."

"Isn't that hazing?" one of the juniors asks. He has strawberry-blond hair and a dusting of fine stubble across his jawline.

"It is not," Brit says. She stands stick-straight, and her voice is dead serious. "Hazing activities expressly humiliate or endanger participants. Our initiation rite tests your skills, but it does not subject you to any abuse or put you at risk of anything worse than a possible detention. In which case you will say you were simply copying what you've seen other students do around campus this week, and you've never had any contact with the Haunt and Rail Society. If you're not up for ghosting a classroom, you won't be up for Haunt and Rail's larks. We are rarely wrong about an initiate, but if we are wrong about you, you can simply walk away."

"No way," the junior says. "I'm in."

"Me too." I don't know why they've picked me. I don't know if I'm cut out for this. But I want it. What had Nico said the other night? *Just keep your eyes open. You'll find your place here.* Maybe this is what I've been looking for—my thing. Ten seniors, ten juniors, twenty beating hearts in a windowless basement room surrounded by sagging furniture, old books, and decades of Tipton history. I am scared and nervous but also buzzing with energy. Over the years, the ghosts have been a part of so many meaningful changes at Tipton. I want to be a part of that.

There is a chorus of *"me too*s" and *"I'm in*s" all down the line. They want it too. My fellow ghosts.

"Um, one question?"

Nineteen eyes turn to look at me.

"Aren't there cameras? I mean, won't we be caught on security tape?"

Brit laughs and flashes me a pitying look. "This isn't *public school*, Calliope. This place has its issues, but the elite realm of Tipton Academy is far from a surveillance state."

"There's one camera at the main entrance," Lucas says. "Records traffic coming and going from campus, when it's switched on, which is occasional at best. The main thing you have to watch out for are the guards. Security does rounds on the half hour, so start paying attention to the patrol schedule and the routes they take. You'll catch on quick."

I nod. I can do that.

"If that's settled," Lee says, "you will each need to swear to uphold the secrecy of the Haunt and Rail Society." She gestures toward a table on which ten large manila envelopes have been laid out, each bearing the name of an initiate.

"Go on," Brit says. "Open them."

The other juniors and I cluster around the table, locating our envelopes. Before I can tear mine open, the boy next to me groans. Then there's a gasp from a girl at the far end of the table. My heart starts to race.

Inside my envelope is an agreement between my tenth-grade chemistry teacher, Mr. Ewing, and me, laying out the terms of my discipline for cheating on my final exam. I'm suddenly freezing. I jam the paper back inside the envelope.

"How did you get this?" I choke. My eyes dart from Brit to Lee to Brit again.

Brit ignores me and addresses the group. "Consider your envelope's contents to be collateral. Do you know what that means?"

The initiate with reddish-blond hair speaks up. His envelope reads *Wesley*. "I'm guessing you have something embarrassing on each of us."

"Or something that could get us kicked out of Tipton," says the girl with feathery blond hair. *Kadence*.

Akari steps forward. "Precisely. Everyone has something they'd rather hide, and the ghosts have been paying attention. Your secret is collateral to ensure you will keep ours. Don't breathe a word about Haunt and Rail to anyone, and your secret will be safe with us. Forever."

"The first rule of Fight Club . . ." Wesley murmurs beneath his breath. A few nervous titters rise up around me, but this is no joke. My palms break out in a cold sweat. When I cheated on my chemistry final last spring, I had already been admitted to Tipton. I was floundering in class, and I panicked—I thought Tipton might change their mind about admitting an honor roll student who was suddenly no longer on the honor roll.

Of course I got caught. Mr. Ewing took pity on me, maybe because he's known me forever and I'd never cheated before, on anything. He let me retake the test, and in return for a ten-page paper on honesty and an endless string of volunteer hours after school, he kept the record of my cheating between the two of us. Or so I thought—but somehow here it is, in my hands.

Tipton has a zero-tolerance policy when it comes to academic dishonesty. If they find out about this, I'm screwed.

I try to breathe normally, ease my heartbeat from a gallop to a canter. I am not a rat. Like Akari said, as long as I keep Haunt and Rail a secret, I don't have anything to worry about.

Lucas clears his throat. "We take Haunt and Rail seriously, and we expect you will too. We're not here to threaten you. You were selected to join the society because we know you have real value to add. We *want* you here. But if even one member slips up, your bad judgment threatens the existence of the entire group. Your collateral is a reminder of the crucial role you play in keeping Haunt and Rail alive at Tipton."

All around me, initiates are nodding, murmuring promises of silence. But I'm still stuck on how they got their hands on this. Mr. Ewing promised he wouldn't turn it over to the school administration, and presumably he didn't, because Tipton didn't rescind my offer of admission. Which means the ghosts got this from *me*. After we'd signed an agreement, Mr. Ewing kept the original, and I used the school photocopier to email a copy to myself. Someone hacked into my email.

My eyes scan the faces of the seniors, but they don't give anything away. It hits me that the person who hacked me might not even be in this room. Ten senior ghosts would have graduated last spring; it wouldn't surprise me if Haunt and Rail has been keeping tabs on me since I got admitted. My chest feels tight, and I make myself draw in a deep breath. I can either dwell on how violated I feel, or I can focus on everything Akari said earlier, all the positive changes Haunt and Rail has brought about at Tipton. The ghosts are powerful. And of course they need to take precautions to protect themselves.

I decide not to dwell. I want this. And besides, what Lucas said sounds reasonable. Haunt and Rail has been around for six decades, and its cover hasn't been blown yet. Which means everyone's collateral has stayed safe. I'm not about to buck that trend.

"Okay," Lee says. "Let's make those good intentions official, shall we? Before we disperse for the night, each initiate will swear to an oath of secrecy. Calliope, you're first."

17

What I have learned tonight about Haunt and Rail:

- There are always twenty members. The society taps ten juniors to join the ten existing seniors each year. No exceptions.
- At least one senior ghost serves as a prefect because prefects have ID cards with twenty-four-hour dorm access and other special privileges that Haunt and Rail uses to their—our—advantage.

    This year, there are two: Brit and Quinn, who uses "they/them" pronouns and is the prefect at Hadley, one of the all-gender dorms. (My cardboard tube proves unnecessary, as Brit and Quinn slip silently around campus, letting us all back in when the meeting adjourns.)

- Juniors are tapped for a variety of reasons including academic and athletic merit, involvement in student government, potential to secure a prefect position for senior year, activism, artistic talent,

technological savvy, family history with Haunt
and Rail, and any number of special circumstances
or qualities deemed desirable to the society. Each
initiate has received a unanimous yes vote from the
existing members, but the reasons for our selection
will not be revealed to us.

Do not ask. Seriously.

- I suspect I have been tapped because I was the
  student council historian at my old school. As one of
  the five junior class representative spots on Tipton
  student government is reserved for a transfer student
  each year, I have an excellent shot at earning that seat.
- Under no circumstances are we to reveal the identity
  of any current member of Haunt and Rail.
- From this point forward, communication will be
  conducted via password-protected texts.
- The basement room where we met tonight is called
  the Den. It has been our clubhouse for two decades
  now, ever since Ms. Bright (fellow ghost, Tipton class
  of 1992) returned to join the library staff in 1999.
- Following the end of the initiation period, we will be
  issued a key to the Den. We will enter through the
  back and meet there weekly, Monday nights at 1 a.m.
- If we wish to access the Den at other times, we must
  ask Ms. Bright for a pass to visit the stacks. She will
  only grant us a pass if there are no other students or
  teachers in the stacks at that time.
- Like Tipton itself, Haunt and Rail has always been
  co-ed. It has become increasingly diverse over the

years and values diversity in its selection process.
- There are over six hundred ghosts living all over the world.
- Haunt and Rail is the only currently active Tipton secret society, although there have been others over the years.
- Secret societies are expressly forbidden by the administration. Tipton is very aware of the ghosts' presence on campus, but so far, Haunt and Rail has not been caught.

It is our job to keep it that way.

18

When my alarm goes off at seven, I'm not tired. I'm exhilarated.

I am a ghost.

7:45: Breakfast. I pick up oatmeal and a tea at Manny's Joint, the grab-and-go eatery on the northeast corner of Quadrant West. It sits opposite Tobin, the large science and mathematics building, and bears the likeness of Tipton's white and teal winged stallion above its entry.

I sit on the lawn and eat slowly, watching the stream of faces go by. I can picture Momma sitting right here, long, dark hair fluttering around her shoulders like mine is right now, sun lapping at her back and face. Watching, collecting ideas for her stories.

8:30: Classes begin. Physics with Ms. Stone is first. I slip a bright green book cover over my new course text.

9:30: Assembly. All Tiptonians gather in Fortin Hall for announcements from faculty and student groups. We file into wooden auditorium seats by dorm, Bunkers and Alys together. My eyes stray to Brit again and again. When assembly ends, she wraps one arm around the waist of another senior prefect named Jeremiah, who I learn is her longtime boyfriend. She does not acknowledge me. We are a secret.

10:30: English 11 with Mrs. Stiver, who wears rings on each finger and has her long gray hair swirled up in a complicated-looking bun. Mrs. Stiver believes in jumpstarts, not soft launches, so we will begin the year by reading *Othello*. After class, she pulls me aside, tells me she had Momma when she was in eleventh grade. She says she is glad to have me in class, and I feel warm all over.

11:30: Creative Writing (elective). Mr. Ellis asks us to write about our favorite place in the whole world, which he says is a way of introducing ourselves. He is young and energetic and friendly, and I wonder if Lee might be wrong about him.

Momma wrote fantastical stories, filled with magic and mystery. She kept them all; I've read them hundreds of times. I write about a different kind of magic—the sun-drenched dock on Plover Lake where my sisters and I have spent countless summer afternoons. How the wooden slats soak up the rays, even on cold days. How time moves more slowly there, and a single afternoon can hold three lifetimes.

My sisters don't start school for another week. I wonder if they are headed to the lake now, and I press my eyes shut when I've finished writing, picture myself there with them.

12:30: Lunch. On the way to Rhine, a text from Nico: *Sit with me?* I find him at a table with a few other juniors. The girl from last night with light brown skin and tight brown curls is there. Aymée Rivas. She is Cuban by way of Miami.

I've been to Florida once, to visit my grandparents. But I was still little, and anyway, they are in Fort Lauderdale.

Nico has saved a seat for me. I introduce myself to Aymée as if we haven't met, as if we didn't walk back to our dorms together at three in the morning, whispering beneath our breath. Aymée plays along, and our performance makes me feel guilty. I don't want to lie to Nico, but Nico is not a ghost. I steer the conversation toward the afternoon—what happens after classes. Nico has soccer practice, but then there is a break before dinner. He says he can meet me in the library to help with my family history project.

I smile. We also have a secret.

1:45: History: Europe Since 1945 with Mr. Wheeler, who has tiny glasses and a hipster mustache and says, "I love it, I love it," any time a student displays the slightest degree of enthusiasm in class.

3:15: I will have to join a sport or take PE in another trimester, but that is a trial for Future Calliope. For now, I am signed up for theater tech during the afternoon activity period. Once rehearsal for the fall play gets underway, we will build set pieces and paint backdrops, but today's meeting is mostly introductions and a tour of the backstage. Lorelei does theater tech back at our old school. Every year, she paints the most detailed parts of the backdrops. I am not that talented. I think I signed up because I miss her.

Mr. Cruz lets us go early, and I slip back to my room in Anders to lie on my back and stare at the ceiling until it's time to meet Nico in the library. Last night's lack of sleep is starting to catch up to me. I doze off.

5:08: I am eight minutes late to meet Nico, who is sitting at a table with his laptop open in front of him, waiting for me.

"I'm sorry I'm late. I fell asleep," I admit.

Nico smiles, warm and wide, and my eyes zero in on that tiny chip in his left front tooth. I force myself to look away from his mouth.

"First day of classes can be exhausting," he says. "How'd it go?"

I sit down at the table across from him. The library is quiet; no one has much homework yet, and everyone is out enjoying the sunshine.

"Okay I think? I didn't get lost."

"That's a start."

"Barely." I grin. "It's a lot to take in. I'm used to small classes, but not the seminar tables. There's nowhere to hide."

Most Tipton classes are conducted around a circular table, the teacher sitting with the students. At my old school, we sat in rows. There's no back of the room here, no ducking out of the discussion.

"My middle school was huge," Nico says. "Tipton was an adjustment for me too."

I fiddle with the fringe on my bag. "So what's the plan?" I whisper, even though there's no one within earshot.

"I thought we'd start with the online directory," Nico says. "Just in case the man you saw works at Tipton. It's a big employer in Alyson-on-Hudson, so worth a shot." He motions for me to come around and sit next to him, and I do. Nico scoots his laptop over so it rests right between us. "Almost everyone has a photo posted, so if he's faculty or admin, it shouldn't be too hard to find him." He angles the keyboard toward me.

My fingers skate across Nico's track pad. A lot of people work at Tipton, more than I'd realized. There are a few white men with blond hair, but no one who looks even remotely like the man I saw.

I shake my head. "Not here."

"Okay," Nico says. "Let's try Roosevelt High too. They're another big employer."

He pulls up the site, which is clunky to navigate, but I click slowly through the faculty and staff directory. I point out Teya's picture when I get there, but the man with dark blond hair isn't a Roosevelt teacher either.

"One more idea," Nico says. "Some Tipton alum live here in Alyson-on-Hudson, and even more land in New York City after college, so it's pretty common to see alum around town. How old did you say he was?"

"I don't know exactly. Midforties? Around my dad's age, I guess."

Nico shuts his laptop and gestures for me to follow him. We take the stairs to the second floor, Nico, then me, and my eyes jump from his light brown hair to his slender neck to the worn blue cotton of his graphic tee. It looks soft. I picture my cheek pressed against the fabric, then wipe the image away.

"Yearbook archives," Nico explains as we arrive at our destination. "Every class dating back to the beginning."

"Let's look at the nineties," I suggest. "My mom went here; did I tell you that already? She graduated in ninety-five."

"Oh yeah?" Nico says. "We'll look around that year."

We grab a few yearbooks and spread them out on the floor around us. I start with 1995 and flip to the senior class photos. First-years through juniors are printed in black and white, but seniors get color, which makes the process of elimination a little easier.

It takes the full hour we have to go through all the pictures. I pause on the C's, 1995—my mother's face peers up at me. *Kathleen Callihan*, her maiden name. I've seen this photo before. In it, Momma looks very serious, facing the camera head-on, barely smiling. It's not my favorite picture of her. She looks like she's trying to appear grown up, but Momma was most herself when she was goofing off, having fun. Dreaming. I show Nico, then quickly turn the page.

By the time we have to pack up for dinner, I have three names jotted down—seniors from 1994, 1996, and 1998 who might, possibly, be adolescent versions of the man I saw. It's a starting point. I snap pictures of their photos, then we slide the yearbooks back onto the shelf.

19

"Honey bees have five eyes. And they love the color blue." Lorelei's voice is reverent. She wants me to be as excited as she is. "Bees mate high in the sky. Can you imagine how amazing that would be? A queen can lay up to two thousand eggs in a single day. But after they mate, the male bee dies— *blam.* Just like that. You have one life purpose, Mr. Bee. Then your work is done." She laughs.

"Bees are cool," I tell her. "As long as they don't sting me."

Lorelei groans. "Bees pollinate over a hundred crops in the US. Don't you understand how important they are?"

I do understand. I just don't want to talk about bees.

"Do any of these names sound familiar to you?" I ask. "Jesse MacDonald. Samuel Pateman. Kurt Devin Wood."

Part of me feels bad for forcing a subject change, but we both know Lorelei has already shared her top bee facts of the day with Dad, Serafina, and probably half of Plover Lake. After the accident, I found the most comfort in my family. Lorelei went the other way. She is constantly out with her friends, testing Dad's boundaries when it comes to parties and curfews.

"Is this about the man in town again?" she asks. "Are you still on that?"

"Just answer the question," I insist. "Did Momma ever mention any of those names?"

"I don't think so. They don't ring any bells."

There is a muffled sound on the other end, then Lorelei groans.

"What's going on?"

"Sorry," she says. "Reagan won't stop texting me. I should go."

There is usually some minor social drama going on in my sister's life. When I was home, I got sick of hearing about what Reagan said or what Emma did. Now, I feel disconnected, cut off. I make a mental note to check in with Beatrix and Erica later. I've fallen behind on our chat.

"Put Dad on first," I say. "I want to ask him."

Lorelei sighs. "Are you going to tell him about what you think you saw, in the passenger's seat?"

"No. I don't want Dad to think I'm 'losing my mind,' as you put it. He'll show up here to check on me."

"So you admit that you sound crazy," Lorelei says. She sounds pleased with herself. She thinks she's caught me in a trap.

"I do not. But you seem to think so. Just put Dad on."

"Fine."

"Hi, pumpkin."

I tell him I miss him. I do not tell him about the man in the passenger's seat. Instead, I tell him I was looking through old yearbook photos. The years Momma was at Tipton. Did she ever talk about her classmates? I repeat the names. *Jesse MacDonald. Samuel Pateman. Kurt Devin Wood.*

"Sorry, pumpkin. I don't recognize any of those names."

"What about a boy with dark blond hair, thick eyebrows, and sunburned cheeks? Did Momma have a classmate like that?"

"That's very specific," Dad says. "Why do you ask?"

I think about the best way to respond. I do not want Dad to show up here, to worry about me, to suggest maybe I should come home.

"In town the other day, I saw someone who looked like that," I say finally. "Maybe he was familiar from Momma's school photos."

"Maybe, pumpkin. Your mother might have had a class-mate who looked like that."

"Not too tall," I add.

For a while, Dad is quiet. Then he reminds me that he did not go to Tipton, did not meet Momma until after she had finished college.

I get off the phone. I don't know where to go from here.

20

Tuesday morning, three classrooms have been ghosted.
All over campus, there are whispers. *It's happening again.* And
I heard they make initiates drink blood. And *it's just a stupid hoax.*
The teachers talk too. *I bet I know who is responsible.* And *at
least they're not defacing school property.* And *there are proper chan-
nels here at Tipton.*

Three students have completed their initiation rite.
Which leaves seven of us. The others have a leg up; they are all
beginning their third year here, know the arteries of this campus, its beating heart. I have been here for less than a week,
have not yet split Tipton open, seen its anatomy at work.

I have until Thursday night to complete my mission. Part
of me wants to get it over with as soon as possible. My stomach clenches at the idea of leaving this to the last night, elimi-
nating any possibility of a second chance, but I force myself
to slow down. Pay attention. For two days, I observe building
locations, cleaning schedules, club meeting spots. More rooms
have been ghosted when we file into class on Wednesday
morning, then Thursday. I collect the whispers, count seven,

eight, nine. I am the last initiate left, but no one said this was a race. By Thursday, my plan is in place.

Perry Cottage is a small academic building off Quadrant East, adjacent to the library. The first floor houses a seminar room, where my Creative Writing class meets, a student lounge, and two faculty offices. Upstairs is an apartment, occupied by Mr. Ellis. Like the library, the back of Perry faces a thick row of trees, shielding the south-facing windows from sunlight—and roving eyes. With a faculty residence on the second floor, it's a risk, but Mr. Ellis lives alone and his car has not returned to its parking spot on the north side of the building until 9 p.m. for the past two nights.

Trash is collected from seminar rooms daily. On Tuesday and Wednesday, a peek through the windows reveals that cans have been emptied and rooms locked for the night by the time I'm back from dinner. You can't ghost a classroom before the janitorial staff comes through unless you want to risk them seeing your work and erasing the whiteboard. But they lock up the rooms, so you either need to hide out in the classroom or find another way in. I opt for option B.

On Thursday, when everyone is at lunch, I slip back into Perry Cottage and open the locks on the back south-facing window in 100, the seminar room. Then I remove the screen and tuck it into the storage closet in the back of the room and slide the window open, just an inch from the bottom.

I am as ready as I will be. The Linguistics Club meets in the Perry student lounge on Tuesdays and Thursdays at seven thirty, then there is a half hour window between the end of their meeting and the time Mr. Ellis has been getting home.

I sit on Quadrant East with a book and a book light, back pressed against a tree, and listen. Most of the lawn is lit up by lamps, but it's dark under my tree. At eight thirty-five, I hear voices and the sound of a heavy wood door swinging shut. The Linguistics Club has adjourned.

Eyes still trained on the book in front of me, I wait for three more minutes. Then I switch off my book light and make my move. I wiggle my fingers between the windowsill and the base of the frame and nudge the window up, then up some more. Check to the right; check to the left—all clear. Then I hoist myself up until I'm balanced on my belly and gracelessly worm my way through the window and onto the thin blue carpet. I'm inside.

It's dark in the classroom, but I don't want to risk turning on a light. I slide a dry erase marker, pilfered this afternoon from another class, out of my bag. It only takes a matter of seconds to draw the ghost, its angry railroad track teeth. I snap a picture, return the marker to my bag, and freeze. Outside Perry, a car door slams shut, followed by the *beep-beep* of the lock.

Mr. Ellis is home early.

I drop to my knees and begin crawling back to the window. The building's front door opens, then bangs closed. Mr. Ellis needs to pass by the classroom on his way to the stairs, but as long as he doesn't stop to look through the door's square window, I'm safe. If he does, though, the whiteboard is plainly visible from the doorway, even in the dark. And faculty carry keys.

So far, I have stayed on Mr. Ellis's good side, but Lee's

warning is still a low hum. I picked Perry Cottage because I'm here every day, and the classroom is on the ground floor. But maybe I wasn't being smart. If Mr. Ellis catches me, I'm risking not only my initiation into the ghosts but also my reputation with one of my teachers.

I flatten myself against the floor below the window and stop moving. The blue carpet is scratchy against my cheek, and I try not to breathe in the dust. Footsteps outside, coming closer, closer, then stopping. My heartbeat booms in my ears, drowning out all other sounds. Is he at the door? Does he see me?

Then footsteps again, heading up the stairs. Heading away. I let out a long breath, then shove myself to my feet. Tumble back through the window, and I'm gone. A ghost.

21

"Calliope!"

I am not a ghost. I am solid, flesh and bone.

I am *seen*.

Not by Mr. Ellis—by Nico Hale.

"Nico, hey." I lean against the back wall of the library, just a couple yards from Perry Cottage, in a way I hope looks casual but am sure looks staged.

He turns the corner and joins me. A flashlight beam bounces at his feet. Did he see me sliding out of the Perry Cottage window a minute ago? Did I just blow this?

"What are you doing back here?" He looks genuinely curious. He doesn't look like he knows what I've been up to.

"I cut through Quadrant East," I fib. "I thought the library had a back entrance."

"Nah, this door's always locked." Nico leans against the wall next to me and scrapes his hair out of his eyes.

"Right." I stare at the door Brit led us through on Sunday night. The door that leads down to the Den. "I'm still learning my way around this place. It's not even that big."

"No, I get it," Nico says. "There's a lot to take in. There are layers to Tipton. Like that building."

He points to Perry Cottage, and my heart leaps into my throat. "What do you mean?"

"Its official name is Perry Cottage, but no one calls it that."

"Really?" This is news to me.

"Well, faculty do sometimes. But mostly people just call it the CW."

I scrunch up my nose. "Like the network?"

"Because it's the creative writing house. But yeah, also because of the network. Someone started calling it that years ago and it stuck."

"Oh." I feel silly. "I should have known that. I have my elective in there."

Nico shrugs. "This is my third year here, and I'm still learning things. There's Tipton, and historical Tipton, and Tipton culture and lore."

"Layers," I repeat. I wonder how much Nico knows about the Haunt and Rail Society. If it's as secretive as it claims to be, probably not much beyond whatever "larks" they've done on campus over the last two years. It feels strange that there might be a piece of Tipton I know better than Nico, although with Haunt and Rail, I have the distinct feeling that I've barely scratched the surface.

"I should let you go," Nico says, shoving off the library wall. I stare at him blankly. "You were going inside?"

"Right." Heat rushes to my cheeks. "I was just dropping off a book. I can do it later."

Nico smiles. I can't catch the chip in his tooth in the dark, but I know it's there. "Walk with me then?"

We slip through the break in the trees and out onto Quadrant East. It's much brighter out here, the lawn lit up by tall lampposts.

"Any luck with those three guys?" he asks. "From the yearbooks?"

"Not really. I asked my family about them, and they were no help." I don't tell Nico that I got the strange sense Lorelei and Dad were keeping something from me. "But then I did some searches online, and I found current photos for the Samuel Pateman and Kurt Devin Wood who graduated from Tipton. The man I saw in town wasn't either of them. So that leaves Jesse MacDonald, class of 1996. His name is too common; he's been harder to track down. But honestly, I'm not holding out a lot of hope that it was him."

"Huh." Nico frowns. We're across Quadrant East now, headed back toward our dorms. "I'm sure my Google skills are no more refined than yours are, but let me know what I can do to help."

"Thanks." My hand brushes against his in the dark, and he doesn't pull away. "I'll let you know if I think of anything."

22

Friday morning, I get an email from Campus Housing. My request for a single has been approved. I may move downstairs into Anders 1D this afternoon.

I reread the note; it is definitely intended for me. But I made no such request. And I like living with Clarice. She's not around a lot, but when she is, she always invites me to eat with her friends, and it's nice having someone else's stuff around. It reminds me of having sisters.

My eyes stray to her side of the room. She's been gone for over an hour; she's always up early for cross-country. What am I supposed to tell her?

My fingers hover over the keyboard. Maybe I should just write back and say there's been a mistake. Before I can do anything, my phone buzzes. A new text from a number I don't recognize. When I click to open the message, a box pops up on the screen:

Enter your password.

Oh. My heart picks up speed. Akari's words from Sunday night come rushing back. *Once you complete your initiation rite,*

Haunt and Rail communications will be conducted via password-protected texts.

No one responded last night when I sent the photo of my angry ghost to the number I'd been given. But someone must have received my message. I'm in.

I turn back to my computer and open the Tipton daily email, which is sent from Dr. Naylor, our head of school, at eight every morning to all students, faculty, and staff. *The password changes daily at 8 a.m. It is the eighth word in the Tipton Daily Update, or the ninth if word eight is shorter than four letters, or the tenth if word nine is also short, etc.* I scan the opening sentence, then return to my phone.

As the first week of a new **Upriver** term draws to a close, I am reminded of the intelligence, talent, and compassion present in each member of the Tipton community.

The message opens.

Enjoy your new single, Calliope!
Two first-years will be available
to help you move following the
afternoon activity period. Be
ready. Tonight, meet in the Den
at 1am. The back door will be
open. DELETE THIS MSG
—YFG

YFG. Your Fellow Ghosts.

I delete.

Later in the afternoon, I receive a second message, instructing me to tell Clarice that I have SAD—seasonal affective disorder. They are moving me to a room on the other side of the building so I'll get enough sunlight. Making up a disorder is definitely wrong, and I feel guilty lying to her, but it's better than letting her think I'm moving *because* of her. Which would also be a lie. And the truth—that Haunt and Rail pulled strings to move me to a first-floor single so I can easily sneak out at night—is out of the question.

I lie.

At twelve thirty, I am lying awake in my new room. As promised, Brit showed up with two Anders first-years as soon as I got back to my dorm from theater tech, and we packed and moved all my stuff in under an hour. I imagine having prefects in the society is handy in myriad ways. And Clarice seemed to buy my excuse about more sunshine. I don't know. I still feel bad about that.

But at a quarter to one, I am grateful. All the precautions I took on Sunday are unnecessary tonight. I get dressed with the light on and lace up my shoes. When I slip out into the hallway, I walk right past Brit's door and exit out the back, letting the door click softly shut behind me. This time, I know Brit will be there to let me back in.

Once I'm outside, I stick to the shadows like I did on Sunday, but I move swiftly, bolstered by the confidence of knowing exactly where I'm going. As promised, the door at the back of the library has been left unlocked, and I hurry down the stairs with Aymée and Quinn, who arrive at the same time. Quinn gives me a small smile, and I return it. Their glasses catch the yellow stairwell light, and their short brown hair, which is usually gelled back, is sticking up in spikes tonight.

The Den is lit up by candlelight. It looks like a scene out of *The Phantom of the Opera* in here. Three huge candelabras are positioned on the long table, which has been pushed against the brick wall, illuminating the angry ghost in flickers of shadow and light. More candles burn in jars around the rest of the room. The seniors wear their crimson robes from the other night, and on the table in front of the candelabras, ten new robes are laid out. On top of each robe is a silver door key. Looks like we all passed our initiation.

In the center of the table sits the large leather-bound book.

"Ghosts," Lee says when all twenty of us are assembled, "tonight we welcome ten new Tiptonians to Haunt and Rail. After tonight, you will no longer be initiates. The senior ghosts are here to provide counsel, but we are an egalitarian organization without a top-down leadership structure. We conduct business by group consensus. After tonight, you will be one of us."

I stifle a laugh at Lee's choice of words. *One of us.* The candles, the robes, the turn of phrase. If someone stumbled in on this scene, they'd think we were joining a cult.

"Initiates will all take a place in front of the table," says Spencer, a short, toned senior ghost with dark brown skin and thick black hair that melts into a neat fade on both sides. We file over. "Keep your key somewhere secure. *Do not lose it.* It opens both the back door to the library and the door to the Den. Beneath your key is a robe. We only wear our robes on ceremonial occasions, and they are stored here in the Den. You may put yours on."

We pocket our keys and do as instructed.

"I hope our three juniors who were not already in single rooms are enjoying their new accommodations," Akari says. My eyes skim her purply-pink bangs, which look freshly touched up. "A single will be vital to maintaining your secrecy. For everyone, if you have any concerns about the exit path from your dorm room, talk to Quinn or Brit after the meeting."

Then Lucas speaks up. Tonight, his shoulder-length black hair is tied back in a neat, low ponytail. "Stay in line, but step away from the table. Josh"—he nods toward the junior ghost who went to the wrong sugar maple last Sunday night—"please head over to the corner with the green armchair. Everyone, follow Josh, then turn back around to face the table. Aymée"—he nods toward the foot of the table, where Aymée occupies the last position in our row—"you will be first in line to sign your name in the book and be sworn in."

We do as we're told, ten junior ghosts in crimson robes shuffling toward the far corner of the room. Lucas steps up to the center of the table and stands beside the leather-bound book and a tall fountain pen resting on a marble stand. We spin around to face the table in a single-file line, and the remaining senior ghosts form a semicircle around us. Lucas opens the book and moves aside a red ribbon, which had been marking the page.

"No blood offering?" Wesley asks. He's grinning, but he looks nervous.

Kadence, a petite junior with feathery blond hair and bangs so long they tangle in her eyelashes, elbows him in the ribs. "Don't give them any ideas," she hisses.

Brit laughs, but it's a hollow sound. Her face is smooth and cool, like polished marble in the candlelight. "Hardly. No presence on the dark web or ties to the Illuminati either. Whatever you've heard about Haunt and Rail, it's probably a lie."

My eyebrows arch up. I must be the only junior ghost who arrived tonight with zero expectations.

"Aymée Rivas," Lucas says, and she steps forward. "Welcome to the Haunt and Rail Society. You may sign your name in the book."

Aymée lifts the fountain pen from its stand and signs. When she bends over the table, her chin-length brown curls fall forward, casting a shadow across the book.

"*Actiones secundum fidei,*" Lucas says. *Action follows belief.* "For all time, a ghost."

Aymée straightens up. "*Actiones secundum fidei,*" she repeats. "For all time, a ghost."

I am fourth in line. When Lucas says my name, I approach the table and reach for the pen. He steps in front of the marble stand and holds up his hand—*wait*—a gesture meant only for me.

Something is wrong. Did I mess up after all? I fidget beneath my robe.

Lucas bends over the book and flips back and back and back. Then he straightens and allows me to look.

My eyes scan the rows of names. Beside each signature is the printed name of the initiate and the date. I'm looking at a page from 1993. Halfway down is my mother: *Kathleen Marie Callihan, September 6, 1993.*

I lift my head, and Lucas meets my gaze. He smiles, then turns the pages until the book falls open again to the current date. I lift the pen.

"Calliope Bolan, welcome to the Haunt and Rail Society. You may sign your name in the book."

III
A Lark

23

Enter your password.

The first September weekend has arrived in the **Hudson** Valley, and it's shaping up to be a glorious fall on campus!

The message reads:

Hi Calliope. On this verdant Saturday morning, swing by Student Activities and self-nominate for junior class transfer student rep. You will be running unopposed. DELETE THIS MSG
—YFG

There are only three other junior transfers, Marjorie (superpower: baking) and Art and Ava, twins from Wisconsin who keep mostly to themselves. So the odds of running unopposed are surely in my favor, but how do the ghosts know for sure?

I shove the thought aside and sit up in bed. My first morning in my new room. There *is* more sun in here; the too-short shade is probably to blame for the fact that I'm awake before 9 a.m. I take a shower and get dressed quickly, then walk to Brisbane to complete my first mission as a ghost. It feels a little strange to be joining student government because a group of seniors told me to, but I'm sure I'll enjoy it. I liked serving as historian at my old school. And Clarice is a class rep too, so at least I'll know someone. Besides, it'll probably be good to have an activity outside theater tech; it's not like the Haunt and Rail Society is something I can put on college applications.

Inside Brisbane, the main administrative building across Quadrant West, the sign-up sheets are hanging in the hall next to the Student Activities director's office. Elections for nearly all the positions took place last spring; only the class representative spots for first-years and transfers are open. The other sheets have a variety of names scrawled across them, but as predicted, all the spaces on the junior class self-nomination sheet are empty.

I write my name in slot one and wonder if it's a coincidence that no one else wants to run, or if somehow, the ghosts made sure it would happen this way. If it's the second thing, am I okay with that?

On my way out of Brisbane, Lucas falls in step next to me on the path.

"Morning, Calliope."

I adjust the strap of my bag against my shoulder. I'm not sure how much we're allowed to talk about Haunt and Rail outside of meetings and texts, but there's only one way to find out.

"Can I ask you something hypothetical?"

Lucas gives me a glance out of the corner of his eye as we walk toward Rhine, where brunch is in full swing and Nico is saving me a seat. "Hypothetical is fine."

"Say you had a really good reason for doing something, but you knew the way you were doing it wasn't very, I don't know, ethical. How would you resolve those two things?"

Lucas grins and wraps one arm around my shoulders. I'm used to boys topping out around my height, but Lucas is tall and his muscles are wiry but strong. It's a friendly gesture, but his arm feels heavy across my back.

"Here's the thing," he says. "Contemporary society places a premium on ethics, right? But we conflate moral authority with political authority. When systems are corrupt, we have a moral obligation to push back. Sometimes that means doing things that may seem 'unethical,' but really what we mean is 'unlawful.' Laws are created by humans, not gods, and they're not always right or good."

"So . . . okay, that makes sense. Following the rules isn't necessarily the same as doing the right thing."

"Exactly. And I have a hunch that in your hypothetical scenario, the moral right bests the legal right. Or 'the rules.'"

I think about that as we arrive at Rhine, and there are suddenly far too many other Tiptonians swarming around for us to continue the conversation. I hear what Lucas is saying, but Tipton isn't exactly a corrupt government regime. Or maybe I'm not thinking critically enough. Akari said Haunt and Rail was created by students who wanted to push Tipton to admit more students of color. The civil rights movement seems like a long time ago, but that's a privileged way of thinking. Those injustices weren't solved in the fifties and sixties—I know that. I'm not quite sure how all this applies to locking in my seat on student government, but Lucas is on to something. Haunt and Rail is going to force me to question a lot of my assumptions. I think that is a good thing.

Lucas drops his hand from my shoulders and holds open the door. We step inside the dining hall, and he waves to a group of mostly international students sitting at a booth near the salad bar. Before he goes to join them, he tilts his head down so his mouth rests beside my ear. "History forgets the rule followers, Calliope. Remember that."

Midway through brunch, there's some commotion at the table nearest the buffet. I spot Brit and Quinn and a few other seniors I recognize as prefects gathering around; the poor first-years seated at the table are picking up their trays and relocating to an empty table near the back.

"What's going on?" I ask Nico.

He smiles. "Watch and see."

In a minute, two senior prefects are standing on top of the cleared table at the front of Rhine. Brit, her boyfriend Jeremiah, and several others cluster around. Martha, a curvy prefect with wide-set eyes and perfect teeth, strikes a pot with a wooden spoon while Quinn calls us all to attention.

"Good morning, Tiptonians!" they call out. Quinn is wearing a loosely fitted purple blazer over a black ribbed tank top and dark-wash jeans. Their glasses and the gel in their hair glisten under the yellow dining hall lights. "Who knows what today is?"

"Saturday!" one student calls out.

"Fajita night!" another student shouts.

Everyone laughs. I scan the faces around me. The first-years look as confused as I do, but everyone else is at ease. This is a dance, choreographed. Everyone knows the answer to Quinn's question.

"Today, my friends, is the Saturday following the first week of Upriver classes." Upriver—the peculiar Tipton name for the fall trimester. To be followed by High Bluff in the winter and Long Trek in the spring. "Which means today is the day for . . ." They stop midsentence, cueing a chorus all around me.

"Hoards of Gourds!"

Martha bangs on the pot again in a not entirely successful attempt to regain Rhine's focus. "Festivities begin in Quadrant East at noon!" she shouts. "Prefects, please remind your Alys! Adjourned!"

"Hoards of *Gourds?*" I ask Nico.

"Indeed." He grins. "I could explain it, but you should probably just see for yourself."

24

At noon, all 933 Tiptonians—or nearly—gather in Quadrant East. A pickup truck filled with pumpkins, gourds, dried corn, and wreathes woven from twigs and brambles has pulled up to the far end of the quad, by the sugar maple, and prefects are assembled around the truck bed, handing out instructions to groups of students.

Quadrant West, Rhine, Wright, Tobin and Sloane, Hadley, the CW, the mail room, Anders, Brisbane. First-years and sophomores get decorating assignments and a tote bag to fill from the truck. I sit on the lawn in front of the Ashbourne Theater with Nico and Aymée, eyeing the hot cider cart setting up on the path.

"I feel like I should be doing something."

"Nah," Nico says. "The underclassmen have it covered. Your only job is to kick back and enjoy the autumnization of Tipton."

"And a cider donut," Aymée adds, "courtesy of Chef Andrea. She bakes them every year."

"And the musical stylings of Alyson Effect, Tipton's boys

and enby a cappella group." He points behind us, where a group of twelve Tiptonians in white skinny jeans and bright teal blazers are assembling on the theater steps. Among the singers, I recognize Jeremiah, who is tall and model handsome and looks exactly like a boy I'd imagine Brit would date, and Colin, a junior ghost I haven't really gotten to know yet.

"Wow. Who does all this?"

"The prefects set it up," Nico says. "Comes out of the student activities fund, I guess. It's not really a surprise, but they always pretend it might not happen until the day-of."

"It's the Tipton way," Aymée says, brushing a rogue curl out of her eyes. "Traditions we like to pretend are spontaneous. And students are always trying to create new campus culture, leave their mark."

"The latter usually fails," Nico says. "But it's fun to watch people try."

"Oh my god, remember the frog floats at the end of Long Trek first year?" Both Aymée and Nico burst out laughing.

"Explain," I demand, nudging Aymée in the shoulder. Am I on the outside or the inside? Sometimes it is hard to tell.

"Sorry, sorry," she says. "The last day of classes our first year here, Cameron Hunt and Harry Pearce, two of the biggest trust fund douches in the senior class, built these giant frog floats that they 'set sail' in Yardley Pond." She snickers.

"Yardley Pond?" Behind us, Alyson Effect begins to hum, then they break into the opening notes of a OneRepublic song that is constantly playing in the grocery store at home.

"Have you been?" Nico asks. "It's out beyond Rhine,

toward the woods. It's just a big pond, not much to see. Sometimes there are ducks."

I shake my head. Was that an invitation? Does Nico want to go out to the pond with me? My mind instantly conjures up the image of the two of us walking across the field, together, my hand brushing Nico's again. In my fantasy, he weaves his fingers into mine. "I guess I didn't know there was anything out beyond Rhine," I say out loud. It's possible I am putting far too much thought into this.

"Anyway," Aymée says, "they made a big giant deal out of issuing written invitations to every student mailbox and promising this spectacular site at Yardley Pond at sunset. Tons of people showed up."

"And then the floats just sank." Nico makes a diving motion with his hand. *"Blub blub blub."*

Aymée bursts out laughing again, and Nico is saying something about the look on Cameron Hunt's face, but I am frozen. Behind me, Alyson Effect is burning money and counting stars. In front of my eyes, cold water—rushing in, soaking the floor of the car, rising up to the seats. Sinking. *Blub blub blub.*

"Hey, you okay?" Nico's hand on my elbow. Nico's eyebrows drawn together. Alyson Effect's cheerful harmonies. *Sink in the river, the lessons I've learned . . .*

"Sorry." I shake my head, shake myself out of it. The memory doesn't come often, but when it does, it is consuming. It wants to drag me back down. "I'm fine." I don't want them walking on eggshells around me. I need to get it together.

"Oh shit," Nico says. "That was insensitive of me. I wasn't thinking."

"No, really," I say. Aymée looks confused. I know I don't owe her an explanation, don't owe anyone anything when it comes to my trauma, but I like Aymée. I want us to be friends. At home, everyone knew my business. Here, no one does, which is both a relief and a responsibility. I have to decide who to tell and when. And I don't want the accident to become an unspoken weirdness between us.

I turn to her. "I'm going to tell you something, and then we're all going to get up and try those cider donuts. Deal?"

She nods.

"Six years ago, I was in a bad car accident. My sisters and I got out okay, but my mom drowned." Momma, whose life ended at thirty-eight. Momma, who, when she was my age, was a brand new member of Haunt and Rail. Maybe later, when we're alone, I'll tell Aymée that part too.

"Oh my god. I had no idea."

"Of course not. And the frog floats, that's hilarious. Sometimes my brain is a total traitor." I smile. "Now let's get those donuts."

The line at the cider cart is ridiculous, so Nico motions us to follow him away from Quadrant East with the promise we'll come back for refreshments in a bit. "There's another Hoards of Gourds tradition you need to take part in," he says.

On the lawn in front of the library, a group of students is gathered around the seven-foot boulder Tiptonians call Brown Rock.

"Brown is really anyone's guess," Aymée says. "Brown Rock

gets painted at the start of each trimester, so who knows what color the rock is beneath all those layers of paint. It's always an autumnal theme for Upriver, cool colors for High Bluff, and pastels for Long Trek. Grab a paintbrush."

I find an unoccupied corner of Brown Rock and dip my brush in a can of red paint. Someone has already given the boulder a base coat of pale orange, and all around me, students are painting pumpkins, ghosts, and leaves. I picture Momma crouching down here when she was my age, painting the rock like I am now. Momma loved anything creative; she would definitely have taken part in this Tipton tradition. The brush feels warm between my fingertips. I touch the bristles to an open patch of stone, draw the first stroke of a small red leaf. It's a small thing, but I can feel my mother's energy coursing through the brush. It is like magic. Next to me, Aymée paints the face of a black cat with bright yellow eyes and whiskers that look like curls of smoke.

"This looks fantastic. Nice work with the eyes there, Aymée."

I look up, and Mr. Ellis is standing behind us, hands tucked in his pockets. Aymée isn't taking Creative Writing, but she has Mr. Ellis for English 11. He's handsome in a teacher way—a dusting of scruff on his cheeks, thick brown hair, bright smile punctuated on each side with a boyish dimple. He looks like he's barely out of college, but I know he's taught here for a while, so he's probably in his late twenties. It's the weekend, but he's wearing a corduroy jacket with his jeans, as if it might make him look a bit older.

"Thanks, Mr. Ellis." Aymée pushes herself to her feet and

takes a step back so he can get a better view.

"You girls probably know I live right over there," he says, motioning toward the CW with his chin. A big, guilty grin spreads across my face. But Mr. Ellis has no way of knowing that I'm the student who snuck in the other night, ghosted the seminar room.

"So as you can imagine," he continues, oblivious to my discomfort, "I'm always very invested in what you students do with Brown Rock. It's the view from my kitchen window."

"We're just getting started," Aymée says. Her eyes are on Lee, red curls bouncing off her shoulders as she approaches with two fresh buckets of paint.

"Oh." I step back, letting Lee in. Two ghosts may socialize in public, but if a third arrives, one ghost must leave. The rule makes sense; if we all hung out together on campus, it would be much easier to identify the rest of us if one ghost was caught.

I give Aymée what I hope is a meaningful look. "You keep painting. I'm going to go take a peek at the donut line."

"See you on Monday, Calliope." Mr. Ellis flashes a dimpled smile in my direction. "We've got some fun stuff ahead in the flash fiction unit."

"I'm excited," I tell him. I'm not as creative as Momma was, but Mr. Ellis's class is still shaping up to be one of my favorites.

Nico says he'll come with me, and we turn back toward Quadrant East. Lee doesn't acknowledge me or Mr. Ellis. She settles into the spot I left behind and dips her brush into a can of mossy green paint.

25

By late Monday night, the Den has been restored to its original appearance. Gone are the candelabras, robes, and serious faces. At a few minutes after one, all twenty ghosts are assembled on couches, easy chairs, desk chairs, and beanbags for our first regular meeting of the trimester. An eccentric collection of lamps burns all around the room, and Lucas passes out bags of chips. Take us out of a hidden room and set the clock back a few hours, and this could be the meeting of any student club on campus.

Almost.

For the first time with the ghosts, I feel something resembling relaxed. I'm not hungry, but I do accept a can of Diet Coke from a mini fridge humming near the closet door. I may regret the caffeine jolt when I'm slipping back into bed in an hour or two, but I'm not used to being up in the middle of the night, and I will not be the girl caught yawning through the first meeting. Aymée plucks a Red Vine from a large plastic container on the table where, two nights ago, we were sworn in, then settles on the wide arm of the easy chair where I'm slowly sinking into the upholstery. I've never been great with naps, but I am beginning to see the benefits.

"Okay, newbies," Lucas says, "listen up. Haunt and Rail meetings are partly social, since they're the only times we get to hang as a group, but they're mostly about society business. Before we get into some serious planning, any questions, comments, or concerns from your first week as a ghost?"

"I have one," Josh says, shifting uncomfortably in his beanbag. Josh is in my physics class, and he's quiet, but when Ms. Stone encourages him to speak up, he always has something smart to say. I don't think I've exchanged two words with him directly, though, and I barely know him any better now than I did that first night when he arrived late after going to the wrong sugar maple.

"Yeah?" Spencer leans forward in his desk chair to listen. He has a notepad open in front of him. He must be Haunt and Rail's secretary or historian.

"I live in Wright, and there's a kid two doors down from me who always sleeps with his door open. I have to pass by his room to get to either exit."

"Your prefect's Connor?" Quinn asks. "I'll talk to him."

"What if this kid's scared of the dark, though? I don't want to upset him or anything."

"Don't worry," Quinn says. "It's taken care of."

Kadence asks about a sticky key, and Spencer takes notes on the pad in front of him. My eyes skate over to Josh, who is leaning back in his beanbag and chewing on a cuticle. I'm not the only one wondering what Quinn meant by *it's taken care of*.

"Okay," Lucas says, "let's get down to business. To bring the new ghosts up to speed, at the end of last year, student government was attempting to work with the administration on a wage increase for our food service staff. Fill us in, Akari?"

"Right." Akari jumps up on the long table to make her presentation. She is wearing a fitted black top with a black, knee-length skirt. Her purply-pink bangs and bright blue tights pop against her all-black palette. Lucas pulls himself up beside her. He looks more casual in jeans and a faded concert tee.

"For the unacquainted," Akari says, "Tipton employs about twenty staff members between Rhine, Manny's Joint, and campus catering. They work for Fresh INC, a food service company that has a contract with Tipton. Anyway, we found out last year that the old food service company Tipton worked with in the early two-thousands was unionized, but Tipton brought on Fresh INC in 2014, and Chef Andrea and the rest of the staff haven't had a raise in over four years. Their contract is up for renewal at the end of the month, and the administration refuses to commit to the food service staff's request for a three dollar an hour wage increase."

"Basically," Lucas says, "since the staff aren't directly employed by Tipton, since they aren't unionized, and since twenty employees are small beans to Fresh INC, the Tipton administration can get away with screwing them on this new contract."

"We've been trying to make sure that doesn't happen through student gov." Akari brushes a flyaway from her bob out of her face. "This topic was on the agenda all last semester, but Dean Sadler kept tabling the discussion since the contract wasn't up for renewal until this year."

"This is precisely why Haunt and Rail is essential," Lucas says. "If we rely on the administration to do the right thing, we get burned. Nothing gets done." He looks directly at me, and I hold his gaze. Our conversation from the weekend is still fresh in my mind.

"We *do* get shit done in student gov," Akari counters. "Sometimes. But even if Dean Sadler gets on board in our first meeting, there's no way he'll be able to get new terms through the administration before time's up. If the ghosts don't intervene, our food service workers could be locked in for another four years at the same rate."

"We propose that the Haunt and Rail Society take up their case as our first fall campaign," Lucas says. "Everyone loves Chef Andrea, but most Tiptonians don't have any idea what she or her staff make or how their contracts work. We need a campus-wide action that will bring this issue into the popular consciousness and make it impossible for the administration to get away with lowballing them."

"Thank you, Akari and Lucas." Brit stands, high ponytail swishing behind her. "Your proposal is heard and acknowledged by the society. Do you wish to hold a vote?"

"We do," Lucas and Akari say in unison.

Brit moves to the head of the table to address the group. "The society votes by show of hands. In order for a proposal to pass, the yay votes must be unanimous. If a proposal receives three or more nay votes, it is permanently off the table. If two or one nay votes are received, the presenting members may revise their proposal and present again at the next meeting. The results of a second vote are final. Any questions from the new members?"

"I have one?" The statement comes out more like a question, and I flinch at the echo in my ears. I need to work on that, stop apologizing for simply having a voice.

Brit nods at me, a formal gesture. "Calliope?"

"If we vote to accept Lucas and Akari's proposal, what happens next? I mean, how exactly will we stop the administration from writing a bad contract?"

"The nature of a campaign is agreed upon after a proposal passes," Brit clarifies. "Right now, we're only focusing on the philosophical question at hand. Is this an issue worthy of Haunt and Rail's intervention? If we agree to take it up, then we will craft a corresponding lark or larks. Any further questions?"

Philosophically, as Brit put it, I'm all in. But how are we going to take a stand while maintaining our secrecy? We can't hold a march or stage a sit-in in Brisbane without revealing our identities. So what exactly is a yay vote agreeing to?

I press my lips between my teeth. Haunt and Rail has been operating for over six decades, and they've influenced an impressive number of important decisions at Tipton. The seniors have been a part of this for a whole year. I keep my mouth shut and trust they know what they're doing.

"If there are no other questions," Brit is saying, "I move that we vote."

"Seconded," Lucas says.

"All in favor of adopting Akari and Lucas's proposal for action in the Fresh INC case, vote in the affirmative by raising your hand."

As my hand floats into the air, I look around. There's no secrecy now; a nay vote would stand out like a beacon. I wonder if an anonymous voting process would be fairer, but questioning Haunt and Rail traditions probably isn't a good look for my first week as a ghost.

"All the votes are in," Brit says. "The proposal passes unanimously. Congratulations, Lucas and Akari."

Spencer makes a note of the vote's outcome, and there is a polite round of applause. I join in. It's all very serious and professional. *Adult.*

"All right, all right!" Lucas jumps down from the table, his celebratory tone breaking the reverent mood. "Now it's time for the good stuff."

"Help me down, you jerk." Akari is leaning forward, reaching for Lucas's hands.

"Sorry, dear." He spins back around and takes Akari's hands in his.

She hops to the floor and gives the room a little curtsy. "New year, still got it."

Quinn leans over toward Aymée and me. "As our eyes and ears on student government, Akari is one of our most frequent presenters. I hear you'll be joining her, Calliope."

I swallow. Am I going to be expected to stand on that table and make proposals to the whole society? When I filled out that self-nomination form, I wasn't really thinking about what all it would entail.

"Don't worry!" Quinn gives me a little nudge with their elbow. "You've got this, okay?"

"Yeah," I mumble. "I can do that."

"Okay, ghosts." Lucas claps his hands together. "Let's plan a lark."

26

By the time the second week of Upriver classes is nearing its end, Tipton's glaring newness has begun to soften around the edges. A few things are becoming familiar, routine: Grabbing breakfast at Manny's Joint on the way to physics. Lunch with Nico or Aymée. I've even hung a few pictures on the walls of my single, and when a vendor fair sprawled across Quadrant West on Tuesday, I bought an oversized poster to hang above my desk—trees flaming red and orange, the Hudson River snaking through. Autumn is coming. I live here now.

Student government meets in the evening club period, two Thursdays a month. There isn't much time for campaigning for the few available seats, and fortunately running unopposed gets me off the hook entirely. Akari is the treasurer and tells me that the regular spring election for the major positions is a much bigger deal. I am glad to be quietly ushered in, no fanfare. Students cast their votes in a ballot box at the front of Rhine earlier this week, and by Thursday, the new class representatives—five first-years, plus the transfers—are chosen.

On Thursday evening, we meet in the student lounge on the second floor of Fortin Hall, above the large auditorium where Tiptonians gather for morning assembly. There are more students involved, and the setting is nicer—in my old school, we met in the cafeteria—but otherwise, the trappings of student government are comfortingly familiar. We are joined by a few adults—at Tipton, it's Ms. Shannon, the student activities director, and Dean Sadler, the dean of students—who sit with the rest of us in a loose circle of cushioned chairs. Clarice is also a junior class rep. I find her clear-framed cat-eye glasses among the sea of faces and slide into the empty seat to her right.

"Hey, stranger." She flashes me a smile. "I feel like I never see you anymore."

She's not wrong. Clarice and I don't share any classes, so without our room to draw us together, we've been released to different Tipton orbits over the past week. Her world of cross-country and honors classes doesn't intersect much with mine.

"I'm glad you're on student gov," I tell her. "I've missed you." And I mean it. Clarice and I aren't close exactly, but she was a fixture of my first week at Tipton. I feel a little like I'm being reunited with an old friend.

A senior with close-set eyes and limp brown hair named Madison Blythe is the Tipton student body president. She calls us to order from her seat in the circle, and I can't help comparing the relaxed atmosphere in here to the fervor of Monday night, Akari and Lucas leaping onto the table to make their presentation. My gaze lands on Akari, her bright bangs and a different stylish black outfit, but she doesn't make eye contact.

Madison is telling us that tonight's meeting will be short. "Housekeeping," she calls it. The new reps stand to introduce ourselves one by one. When it's my turn, I tell them I'm Calliope Bolan from a small village in the Adirondacks they've probably never heard of. My favorite thing about Tipton so far is the opportunity to challenge myself every day.

Inwardly, I groan. Who even is that girl? I always clam up when I'm asked to speak in front of a group. Lorelei would excel at this. She is great with new people, outgoing and inquisitive and engaged. But of course, Lorelei isn't here, and I need to do this on my own.

No one seems to register how cheesy I just sounded, or maybe it was the right thing to say. We finish up introductions, then Madison reviews the process for submitting items for the agenda and asks for volunteers to help out at the upcoming clubs and activities fair. Akari gives us a brief overview of the budget and thanks Dean Sadler and Ms. Shannon for approving this year's funds. And then we are released.

As we collect our stuff and grab cookies from a tray by the door, it hits me how right Akari and Lucas were on Monday. The first full student government meeting won't be for another two weeks. We could get the Fresh INC contract on the agenda, and we could move to file a petition to the administration, but the outcome is ultimately outside student government's control. It would be hard to make real progress here, and definitely not by the end of the month.

I make plans to meet Clarice for a catch-up lunch tomorrow, then step outside into the lamp-lit semidarkness of Quadrant East. Something brushes my wrist, and I look up. Akari gives me a slow smile, then disappears up the path.

27

Back in my room, I video call Serafina.

"How was your first week of second grade?"

"It's not over yet," she reminds me. "Tomorrow is Friday."

"I know, silly. But how has it been so far?"

Serafina draws her lips together in concentration. "Ms. Florence is nice. She plays 'Here Comes the Sun' every morning while we walk in."

In my head, Ms. Florence is nine years older but still wearing the same denim dress and cranberry lipstick. She is perched on her desk in her classroom with all the succulents in the windows, strumming her guitar and singing softly.

"Where are Dad and Lorelei?" I ask.

"Lorelei's out with Emma and Reagan and Marcus and Ray. And maybe Jodi, but Jodi and Reagan might still be in a fight. Lorelei and Emma were on the phone about it for two hours and fifteen minutes last night."

"Wow."

"And Dad is in the sewing room."

I frown. "What's he doing in there?"

The sewing room is a small room upstairs where Momma did all of her crafting projects. Lorelei and I started calling it the sewing room when we were little because we loved our mother's pale green Singer sewing machine. But the room was home to hundreds of varieties of crafting supplies, neatly stored in clear plastic bins with colorful labels. It still is; we get into the supplies from time to time, but the room looks just like Momma left it six years ago. I've only ever seen Dad go in there when he needs ribbons or wrapping paper.

"Not sure," Serafina says. "He's been hanging out there a lot this week. Maybe he's sewing you a princess dress for Family Weekend." She giggles.

I laugh. "Maybe he's sewing *you* a princess dress."

Dad has taken on so much since Momma died. He already handled the practical aspects of keeping our family running, but our mother was the imaginative one, the fun parent. Dad tries really hard. He tries to be everything. But the idea of him doing any sort of craft project in Momma's sewing room is pretty absurd.

More likely, he's missing her. He always gets quiet around the anniversary of her death, which is coming up soon. Better to let Serafina think Dad is on a crafting kick.

My little sister is lucky, in a way. She has stories about Momma, and pictures, but she doesn't really remember her.

If you look at it another way, she's the unluckiest of us all.

"Tell them I called," I say, but Serafina is already taking me into the kitchen, intent on showing me what's left of the cake Lorelei helped her bake after school.

28

I am skipping English for this.

I have never before skipped a class. I don't plan to make
it a habit. But I need the Den to myself, and the only time I
can be sure I won't be interrupted by any other ghosts is now,
while everyone is in morning classes.

When I get to the library, I find Ms. Bright and ask for
a pass to visit the stacks. She is a short, curvy woman with a
stylish, cropped haircut and glasses with cherry-red frames.
Her smile gives nothing away, but her eyes flash. Ghosts are
only permitted to use our back door keys after dorm check-
in. When students and faculty are around on campus, it's far
too risky.

While Ms. Bright consults her log book, I squint and try
to picture her at my age. A junior ghost. I know she graduated
from Tipton in 1992, which makes her three years older than
Momma. They would not have been in Haunt and Rail at the
same time, would have overlapped on campus only one year,
when my mother was a first-year and Ms. Bright was a senior.
She would not have known Aunt Mave at all.

I print my name: *Calliope Bolan, 10:36 a.m.*

Ms. Bright peers at me through her red-framed glasses and says, "Mr. Wheeler has an appointment to visit the stacks at noon. Please leave everything exactly as you found it by eleven forty-five."

I nod in understanding. I need to be out of the Den well before Ms. Bright sends someone else down to the basement.

"It won't be a problem," I tell her. What I'm planning shouldn't take more than a few minutes.

"Mind the time," she tells me, handing me a pass. Then she returns to her computer.

Inside the Den, I switch on a lamp, then take a moment to lean back against the door and breathe. When Momma was a ghost, they must have met somewhere else on campus. I know they didn't get the Den until Ms. Bright came back as a librarian, but even so, when I close my eyes, I can feel her all around me. Momma as I never knew her—young and not yet a Bolan. Momma as I always knew her—passionate, full of imagination, full of life. It is easy to imagine her as a ghost. Haunt and Rail is, in a way, straight out of a fairy tale: secrets, promises, the forces of good in an enchanted but sometimes corrupt kingdom, taking on real-life wolves and evil queens.

I open my eyes. The Den looks the same in the daytime, but also different. There are no windows in here; it could be the middle of the night. It would be easy to lose track of time. I set an alarm on my phone; I have no plans to get stuck down here, and it's time to get to work.

The room is strangely empty without nineteen other bodies

filling the space. The angry ghost glowers down at me from the exposed brick wall in the back, and as I make my way around to switch on a few more lamps, my footsteps sound loud and echoey in my ears.

Aside from skipping English, I'm not doing anything wrong, but I still feel guilty. My purpose for being here hasn't been expressly forbidden by Haunt and Rail, but I can't imagine they would condone it either. Hence, skipping class to ensure I'd have the place to myself. Hence, not asking for anyone's permission.

All my anxieties and justifications will be meaningless, though, if I can't find the book. I'm not sure why I expected to find it shelved in plain sight on one of the three bookcases. Of course it's better concealed than that; the book contains the names of every ghost, past and present. If someone found their way into the Den . . .

I think back to the two times I've seen it. That first night, Akari was holding the book when we entered the room, and it was displayed on the long table for our initiation ceremony. I don't remember anyone putting it away. I frown and start examining the rest of the room. It's possible that one of the seniors takes it back to the dorms with them, but that seems unlikely. Even our robes stay in the Den when they're not in use. It would be way too risky to store the book anywhere else on campus.

I lift couch cushions and slide open desk drawers. I peer behind tapestries, as if they might conceal a sliding door. I walk, listening for squeaky floorboards. I unlock the closet, shift robes aside to examine the wall behind them.

The book is nowhere.

When the closet door is closed behind me, I wander back to the center of the room, at a loss. I could just ask. The location of the book probably isn't even a secret; I just haven't been paying attention. Lee would tell me. But then Lee would want to know why I was asking.

Think, Calliope. I let my eyes skate over every inch of the room, one more time. They come to rest on the angry ghost, its railroad track teeth.

And then I see it.

The room's other three walls are plaster, but the back wall is brick. Except where it's been painted, the ghost in pale gray and black. My gaze focuses in on the mouth, on three bricks in the center that jut just slightly forward. Three loose teeth.

I climb up on the long table and wiggle the first brick with my fingers. It takes some patience, but eventually, it slides out. The other two bricks are easier. And behind them, on a narrow shelf carved into the insulation, is the book.

My phone vibrates in my pocket. Mr. Wheeler won't be here for a while yet, but I have no intention of skipping a second class today, which means I have five minutes to get to Creative Writing. Fortunately, the CW is right next door, but I need to hurry. I flip through the book's large pages until I find what I'm looking for—initiates from 1992, 1993, and 1994. I switch on my phone and snap photos of the names.

I can't be sure the man I saw in town was a ghost. But it's the best lead I've found, the most specific connection between Momma, me, and maybe, a stranger. My first yearbook search was too broad; I could have missed possible matches so easily, an awkward boy who grew up to be a very different man. But now I have access to a much more specific data set. Ten initiates who were tapped the year before my mother, ten from her class, and ten from the class behind her. The thirty ghosts Momma knew, roughly half of them boys. New names to examine. Possibly, new clues.

Over the weekend, I return to the library, but this time I am headed upstairs again, back to the yearbook archives. I open the 1995 yearbook first—Momma's class. Among the five male initiates in 1993, only one—Daniel Clark—bears a passing resemblance to the man I saw. His dark blond hair is curly, not straight, but that's something that might change with age or styling. I snap photos of Daniel and the four others, then flip to their names in the index to find their club and activities photos too.

I move on to the 1996 yearbook. There were only four male initiates in 1994, and none of them look remotely like the man I saw. I snap their pictures anyway.

I finish with the graduating class of 1994, matching the ghosts who were junior class initiates in the fall of 1992 to their senior pictures. There is one possible candidate, a ghost named Nathan Carey-York. He has shaggy, sandy blond hair that falls into his eyes. It's a lighter shade of blond, and his face looks too thin, but again, those are things that could have changed as he got older. And there's something about the way his shoulders are flung back, chest arced forward, that seems just a little bit familiar. So far, he is my most promising lead.

Two rows of photos down, something else catches my eye.

Someone has taken a Sharpie and blacked out the image of a senior named Adam Davenport. Adam wasn't a ghost, but I'm curious about this boy who someone clearly disliked, so I locate his name in the index too.

Page 24 is dedicated entirely to Adam Davenport, March 2, 1976 to November 10, 1993. It's a memorial tribute. In the black-and-white photo, Adam is grinning broadly and looks disheveled in the messy-on-purpose kind of way that certain wealthy, preppie Tiptonian boys cultivate to this day. It's hard to make out much of what was written about Adam because, like his senior photo, the tribute has been defaced. Across the page are scrawled the words *apologist*, *racist*, and *bigot*. And drawn in the lower right corner is the now-familiar symbol of the angry ghost.

29

Sunday dinner is just Aunt Mave and me this week; Teya is out with her teacher friends. I suffer politely through my aunt's regular roster of questions about my classes and activities, then as soon as I've satisfied her that I'm keeping up with everything and am not too homesick, I pull out my laptop, where everything I found in the yearbooks is now stored.

"Do you remember these students at all?" I start with the senior photo of Nathan Carey-York, class of 1994.

"Hmm, let me see," she says, peering at the screen. Under the kitchen table, Sebastian snores gently against my feet. Aunt Mave studies the picture. "Nathan, right. We didn't overlap; he graduated right before I came to Tipton. But I do actually know who he is because he did theater and sang a cappella with Alyson Effect, and your mom took me to one of their concerts when I was visiting her at school. He was gay and out—and this was long before I realized I was queer—but he made an impression on me."

"Oh wow. I didn't realize Alyson Effect had been around for so long."

Aunt Mave laughs. "Way to make me feel old."

"Sorry! Do you know where he is now?"

"No idea." Aunt Mave shakes her head gently back and forth. "I think he went to Princeton, but I never really knew him. Why are you asking?"

I ignore her question, for now, and open the next picture. "What about him, Daniel Clark? He was in Momma's class."

"Oh." Aunt Mave frowns down at the screen. "I really only got to know a few seniors that year, Kathy's closest friends, and then they all graduated."

That makes sense. Aside from Aymée, I've barely spent any time with the eighteen other ghosts outside our meetings. I'm sure even in the nineties, ghosts were careful about how much time they spent hanging out with each other on campus, so Aunt Mave probably didn't realize that he and Momma knew each other.

I pull open the notes I took from the yearbook index. "Daniel Clark was on the fencing team, in the hiking club, and he was the head of the Tipton Wilderness Society."

Aunt Mave's eyebrows knit together in thought. "That's right," she says finally. "Daniel Clark, he was Tipton's resident naturalist. After graduation, he grew a huge beard that swallowed his whole face. The last I heard about Daniel, he was headed to Oregon somewhere, to join an agricultural commune, I think."

"Oh." My face falls, and I slouch back in my chair.

"Now I get to ask why you are so curious about a couple of boys who graduated from Tipton a quarter century ago."

I consider my options. Lorelei doesn't believe me, and

Serafina is too young to remember anything. My family has always been my touchstone, but right now, I feel alone. I need an ally.

"This is going to sound strange, but hear me out, okay?"

"Promise," she says.

"During orientation, I saw someone in town. I mentioned him that first Sunday, remember, when you were dropping me off?"

"I think so," she says. "Yes, okay, I remember."

"He was a man about Dad's age who looked so familiar, maybe a bit like Nathan Carey-York or Daniel Clark, if they were in their forties. Dark blond hair, ruddy cheeks. But if Daniel's a beardy off-gridder in Oregon, and you haven't seen Nathan since he went to Princeton, it probably wasn't them."

Aunt Mave smiles. "Probably not."

I close my laptop and slip it back into my bag. "There's more, though. This man I saw—I recognized him. From that day. From the accident."

Aunt Mave sits up very straight. "What do you mean, Calliope?"

"Lorelei thinks I'm nuts, and please don't say anything to Dad. He's already anxious enough about me living away from home, and I don't need him showing up here for weekly visits or trying to convince me to come home. But when I saw this man, I remembered something. He was in the van with us that day."

Aunt Mave presses two fingers to her lips. She is looking at me very closely. I wait for her to tell me I am out of my mind, that my memory is playing tricks on me. Finally she pushes her chair back and begins collecting our plates from the table.

"I'm sorry, Calliope," she says finally, "but I'm not sure who that could be."

My heart sinks.

"Do you think it's possible, though? That someone was in the car with us that day?"

Sebastian emerges from under the table and follows my aunt to the counter, nose to the floor. He snarfs up a scrap of something from the tile.

Aunt Mave sighs and leans back against the countertop. "I don't think it sounds very likely, hon. But there are a lot of unanswered questions about what happened that day. For your father, it's easier to accept the unknown and move on. But your mind has never worked that way. Ever since you were little, you've been perceptive, filled with questions. I admire that about you, Calliope. But in this case, we may all have to learn to live without answers."

I get up and turn on the sink, start rinsing off dishes and loading them into the dishwasher.

"Just one more question." I know it's probably unrelated, but the angry ghost symbol on Adam Davenport's tribute page has been needling at me. I need to know more about how he died—why someone would have drawn the angry ghost in the yearbook. "Do you know what happened to Adam Davenport? You didn't overlap with him at Tipton, but—"

"I know who Adam was," Aunt Mave cuts in. "You're right, I never met him. He died the year before I started, but everyone was still talking about it a year later. The story was practically on the agenda at first-year orientation."

"When I was looking up the other pictures, I found a tribute to him in the 1994 yearbook," I tell her. "But it was all written over. Someone didn't like him very much."

"From what I've heard, lots of people didn't like Adam very much. I don't remember the specifics, but his dad was a prominent board member at Tipton. There was something about renaming a building; either his dad wanted something to be named after him, or he didn't want a building renamed. . . ." She shakes her head. "I'm sorry, the details are escaping me. But whatever happened, Adam was very vocal about it, and he made a lot of students angry over his dad's business. And then he died on campus, right in one of the dorms. Tripped down a flight of stairs in the middle of the night, and no one found him until the next morning."

"Oh my god."

"It must have been so shocking. I can't imagine finding the body."

"Did he . . . I mean, it was an accident, right?" I realize I've been holding the same plate for at least a minute, letting the water drain down the sink. I bend over and load it into the bottom rack.

"Yes, it was an accident. He was drunk, and the stairwell was dark. Adam had a lot of enemies on campus, and there were rumors, of course, but I don't think anyone ever seriously thought it was anything other than a tragic accident."

"Huh." I fit the last plate into the rack, and Aunt Mave

loads up the dishwasher with a detergent pod and closes the door.

Maybe it was an accident, but someone drew the angry ghost on his yearbook tribute. Someone wanted other people to think Haunt and Rail was involved.

30

When Aunt Mave drops me off at the front gate, I don't
know what to do with myself. My thoughts pinball between
Adam Davenport and the ghosts who were probably not the
man I saw and the knowledge that in a couple hours, my first
Haunt and Rail lark will be underway.

I stop by Chandler, but Nico isn't in his room. When
I text him, he says he'll probably be in the design lab until
dorm check-in, so I walk back to Anders. I fidget. I dig out
the watercolor Lorelei painted of our house and find the perfect place for it on my wall. Then I move it three inches to
the right. Slowly, the mysteries I'm no closer to solving give
way to pure nerves about the night ahead. I have found a new
reason to be thankful for my single. Clarice would know in an
instant that something was up.

After check-in, I return to my room and try to focus on
homework for an hour. Brit's face keeps floating in front of
my notebook pages, her pale eyebrows and smooth forehead,
blond hair scraped back from her face. The sly curve of her lips
as she ticked off my name on her clipboard tonight.

Two hours and sixteen minutes separate me from my very first Haunt and Rail lark. I wonder how the other juniors are keeping it together tonight. If we'll pull this off. If it will make an impact.

At twelve thirty, my phone buzzes. I throw back my blanket. I wasn't sleeping anyway.

Enter your password.
As we prepare for a new week at **Tipton**, I hope each of you will seek out moments of restoration and joy amid the hustle and bustle of Upriver.

The message reads:

Good evening, ghosts. Your
meeting location is Yardley
Pond, 1am. Don't get caught.
DELETE THIS MSG
—YFG

A cold fist closes around my guts. After Nico and Aymée told me that story about the seniors who sank frog floats in Yardley Pond two years ago, I meant to wander over there, check out the westernmost edges of campus. But I never did. Now, my first excursion to the outskirts of Tipton will have to be in the middle of the night, alone.

I grew up in a house nestled in a forest. I'm not scared of the woods. But it would be a lot easier to follow the ghosts' first instruction—*Don't get caught.*—if I knew where I was going in the dark. I delete the text and switch my phone to silent, then lace up my shoes and zip up my hoodie. It's only 12:35, but I decide to sneak out now, buy myself some extra time to find my way.

The first part of the walk is easy. I stay off the paths, out of the lamplight, and hurry through Quadrant West to Rhine. Past the dining hall, things get tricky. The moonlight is dim, and without any paths or buildings out here to cast a low glow across campus, I keep stumbling over rocks and tufts of long grass. Yardley Pond is out here somewhere, but how far? To my left? My right?

I crouch down beside a tree, realizing the flaw in my plan. Everyone else knows where they're going, is probably still in their dorms. Now that I'm out here, I need to hang tight, wait for someone I can meet up with or follow.

A few minutes stretch into an eternity, and just as I'm beginning to wonder if I'm entirely off the mark, I spot two shapes moving through the darkness. As they get closer, I recognize the twin flutter of blond hair in the moonlight: Kadence and Josh. I don't want to startle them, so I wait until the two junior ghosts are a few yards ahead of me, then fall in step behind them. Soon, I hear the soft brush of grass behind me, and I turn to find Spencer walking swiftly, closing the distance between us. Waving seems somehow inappropriate, so I give him a small nod, which he probably can't see in the dark, and let him catch up with me.

"Calliope," he acknowledges me in a whisper.

"Hi," I whisper back.

"Been out here before?"

"First time."

He nods. The moonlight casts a cool glow against his dark brown skin. "There's a dip in the ground coming up. Follow me."

I let Spencer walk a couple steps ahead, and I'm instantly grateful, because when the ground slopes down, I would have absolutely tripped without him leading the way.

Then Yardley Pond emerges in front of us, black and glassy in the moonlight. Kadence and Josh are there, and some ghosts must have approached from a different angle, because about half of us are already assembled in the tall grass by the water. I check my phone—12:57. Over the next three minutes, everyone else arrives, until I count twenty ghosts in the darkness.

At 1:00 exactly, Lee motions for everyone to gather around her. She has her hair twisted into a loose bun; I don't think I've ever seen it up before. She looks even tinier without all those red curls spilling down around her shoulders.

We're far out from any of the dorms, and there's zero chance anyone could hear us, but Lee still speaks in a stage whisper. "Juniors, line up behind me. Seniors, behind Lucas. Hands up to the sky."

A couple seniors grumble, but everyone falls in line as instructed. We all stretch our arms into the air.

"What's going on?" I whisper to Spencer, who stands across from me in the seniors' line.

"Phone check," he whispers back. "Hope you deleted your texts."

My fingers twitch against the night air. I did, didn't I?

I'm almost certain I deleted every one the second I read them. And all the photos I took of the yearbook pictures and the names of the initiates in the Haunt and Rail book are already off my phone, stored in a password-protected file on my laptop. Not that the ghosts should care who I've been looking up in old yearbooks, but keeping a photo record of initiate names probably wouldn't be looked upon kindly. I make a mental note to memorize the initiate lists and delete the pictures off my laptop as soon as I get back to my dorm.

Lee moves down our line, instructing the juniors to unlock their phones and hand them over, one by one. On the other line, Lucas does the same. When they're satisfied, phones are handed back and the ghosts return to milling around by the water. Lee gets to me, and I slip my phone from my pocket, hand it over. She checks my messages, gives me an approving nod, then hands it back. I exhale.

"What the hell, Wesley?" Lee's voice is bitter.

I step to the side, out of range, as if the infraction of the ghost behind me might somehow snare me in its net.

Wesley shoves his hands deep into his pockets. "I thought I deleted it," he mumbles. The moonlight catches the pale red in his hair, and I can't tell in the darkness, but I'd bet his cheeks are flaming. "I deleted all the others."

"Our meeting time and location are right here," Lee hisses, stabbing a finger at Wesley's screen. "What part of that seemed unimportant to you?"

My heart is beating hard in my chest. *Just apologize*, I want to say to him. *You screwed up. Just admit it and don't make this worse.*

Lucas finishes clearing the last senior ghost and steps over to check the two remaining juniors in Lee's line.

Instead of apologizing, Wesley says, "The text woke me up. I wasn't thinking clearly."

"Obviously not," Lee sneers. I've never seen her mad like this. It doesn't matter that she is petite or pretty or that I've seen her smile light up her face. In this moment, she is terrifying. She swipes left on Wesley's screen, deleting the offending text, then hands his phone back to him. "You're out for tonight," she says. "Go home."

"What?" Wesley balks.

"You heard her," Lucas says. "You'll sit out this lark. Show up to tomorrow's meeting ready to get your head back in the game. We don't need anyone out here tonight who isn't thinking clearly."

"Fine. Whatever." Wesley shoves his phone back into his pocket and stalks off, back toward the dorms.

No one else speaks. My heart is still pounding. I make a mental note to be even more careful than I've been. One little mistake, and that could have been me, slinking back to Anders, shamed in front of the whole group before we've even gotten started.

31

"Okay." Brit claps her hands, breaking the somber mood, and I realize my fellow ghosts have been speaking at a regular volume for a while now. I guess we've decided that whispering was an unnecessary precaution. My stomach churns. The instructions to delete our texts had been abundantly clear, but other rules seem slippery, impossible to grasp.

"We take our secrecy seriously," Brit is saying, "if that wasn't already plain. Let what happened to Wesley tonight be a reminder. Juniors, you must be vigilant. And seniors, don't get sloppy."

There are murmurs of assent all around me. I nod vigorously, roll my shoulders back, try to project that I am everything I am expected to be. On the inside, I feel a fresh wave of doubt. I was careful in the Den on Friday—careful with the photos, and careful not to get caught. But I should have just asked someone, explained why I needed to see the lists. Keeping secrets from the ghosts is probably a monumentally bad idea.

I don't have time to think about that now, because our lark is beginning. Lucas and Akari crouch down to unzip a large duffel bag I hadn't noticed before in the dark. Inside are several totes bulging with postcards and three family-sized boxes of plastic forks.

"Here's the game plan," Akari says, turning to two junior ghosts I haven't spent much time with yet: Mira, a Pakistani-American visual artist whose fan earrings catch the moonlight through thin stained glass, and Colin, a history and politics buff with a wide, braces-filled grin. "Colin, Mira, you'll go with Lucas to the athletic field." She tosses each of them a box of forks. Then she turns to the rest of us. "Seniors, find a junior to pair up with and grab a tote."

"You ready for this?" Spencer asks. He's nodding toward me.

"Yeah." I grin, relieved to have been swiftly picked. I reach into the duffel and sling a tote over my shoulder.

"Security rounds happen at the half hour," Brit says. "It takes Dante and Wallace ten to twelve minutes to do their checks and return to the security hut."

I swallow. If I'd been paying more attention to the patrol schedule, like the ghosts told me to that first night, I wouldn't have left Anders as early as I did. I'm lucky I didn't get caught.

Lucas pulls out his phone to check the time. "Which means we hang tight here for another six, and then everyone's got forty-eight minutes to complete the lark and get back to the dorms. But don't cut it that close."

"We'll divide and conquer, so this shouldn't take anyone longer than twenty-five, thirty tops," Akari says. She's going around to each pair, handing out key cards and assignments. "Lee and Josh, you've got the library and the CW. Quinn and

Kadence, take Tobin and Sloane. Brit and Aymée, you've got Wright, Anders, and Carrington." Then she turns to Spencer and me. "Spencer and Calliope, take the theater and Fortin Hall." She hands Spencer two key cards.

"On it," Spencer says, then he reaches for the tote. "Want me to grab that?"

It is heavy, and Spencer's biceps are at least twice the size of mine, but I'm not here to tag along. "I've got it," I say, and he shrugs.

Lucas gives us the all clear and a warning to keep our eyes open, just in case, and then we're off. When we're up the slope and headed back toward Rhine, I ask, "How'd Akari get access cards for every building?"

"That was all Quinn. They've got a student job on Campus Convoy."

"Is that the thing where you can text someone to walk with you if you're out after dark?"

"Yup. It's pretty popular in the winter, especially with first-years. Gets dark around here by five."

For the first time, I wonder if being out on campus at night might be dangerous. If Dante and Wallace ever find anything more serious than students breaking curfew on their rounds. Tipton seems a bit like a castle on a mountaintop, but I know it's not. The seniors didn't seem too worried about evading the night guards, and it hits me that past the security hut isn't the only way onto campus. There's a back entrance for delivery trucks, and if you're on foot, you could just walk up the hill.

My mind flashes to the man with dark blond hair. Does he know I'm a student here? It's been two weeks since our eyes met in town. Is he trying to find me? Or am I wrong about why he appeared in Alyson-on-Hudson right as I moved here? He hasn't tracked me down yet, and I'm not exactly hard to find. Possibly, I'm being paranoid.

"Quinn's family is loaded," Spencer is saying, drawing me back to the lark. "They mostly have that job for access to the spare key box and the key card machine. Security keeps the list of building codes taped to the back of the printer; it's not exactly high tech. Haunt and Rail always has someone on Campus Convoy."

"Wow." But I'm not really surprised. Prefects, student government, student housing, Campus Convoy. This is probably only the beginning of a long list. With twenty of us, it's not too hard for Haunt and Rail to secure positions wherever it benefits the society.

When we get to Rhine, back in earshot of a campus full of sleeping Tiptonians and resident faculty, we fall silent. We pass by Aymée and Brit opening the side door to Wright, the second boys' dorm on the path up from the dining hall. Aymée gives me a small wave before disappearing inside. I shift the tote bag to my other shoulder, and we walk past Anders, then Carrington, then Lynd, then take the path through Tobin and Sloane to Quadrant East. Between the buildings' hulking frames, it is so dark I have to run my hand along the wall as I walk. Above us, wings flap and something settles on the roof, out of sight. A bird, maybe a bat. Something drawn out by the darkness.

We reach the Ashbourne Theater first. Spencer beckons me up the steps where last weekend, Nico and Aymée and

I watched Alyson Effect perform. At night, the roof of the theater building glows bloodred where tinted floodlights sprout from the corners. It looks like a deserted disco or a landing pad for UFOs. Spencer presses the key card to the scanner, and a tiny light flashes green. We're in.

"Lobby last," he whispers. "It's visible from outside, so we want to hit everything else first."

"Got it," I whisper back.

We start in the theater itself, papering the stage and the theater seats with postcards. I switch on my phone and hover the screen above one of the cards to get a good look at what Lucas and Akari had printed. It's just what we'd discussed in last Monday's meeting: One side contains a series of historical facts and statistics about labor laws, wage parity, and the food service industry. In a bright, bold font right in the center is the hourly wage made by the food service workers at the Brecker School, Tipton's direct competitor in the mid-Atlantic region in all things admissions, athletics, Ivy League acceptance, and more. It's a startling four dollars an hour more than Tipton pays its employees at Fresh INC.

On the back of the postcard is our message:

We won't be out-Breckered. The students of Tipton Academy demand a $5 hourly wage increase for our food service workers. Sign a fair contract September 30—we'll be watching.

The food service workers have been asking for three dollars more per hour. Haunt and Rail decided to aim high in hopes of getting them what they've been asking for, at the very least. We'd spent nearly an hour discussing what tack to take for our lark, but the overwhelming sense was that appealing to Tiptonians' competitive spirit was the best way to mobilize the student body behind this issue.

"Sadly our less socially conscious classmates don't care about hourly rates or treating contract workers fairly," Lucas had said, "but they'll care about looking bad compared to Brecker. They'll care about winning."

Spencer and I finish up in the theater, and I take him backstage, to the green room and scene shop. We agree to do a few postcards here and in any classrooms that have been left unlocked, then hit the lobby before heading farther down the quad to Fortin.

Haunt and Rail's goal is to begin Monday morning with a giant jolt of awareness all across campus. "From there," Akari had said at our last meeting, "we can usually count on students to rally around an issue. It's our job to make our campaigns impossible to ignore. We get people talking— students, faculty, administrators. Outside this room and student gov, you could probably count on one hand the number of students who have even heard of Fresh INC. After Monday morning, there won't be a single person on campus who won't know all the facts. All we're doing is putting on a little display, applying a bit of pressure."

As we take the path from the back of the Ashbourne Theater over to Fortin, my gaze travels down the hill to the main entrance and the lights glowing inside the security hut.

"You sure they can't see us?" I whisper.

"Dante and Wallace never mix up their round times," Spencer whispers back. He presses the other key card to the scanner at the back door to Fortin, and the light glows green. We're in.

"And they're good about not messing with our stuff either," he continues at a regular volume now that we're inside. "Probably because Haunt and Rail always gives them a fat cash bonus at the holidays—anonymously, of course."

My eyebrows shoot up, not that I should be surprised.

"Last year during High Bluff, we set up this whole mannequin display in the courtyard behind Ashbourne, which they definitely saw on their rounds, but it was still there the next morning. They're used to us. They know a lark from an actual security threat—but we'd still be screwed if they caught us in the act, so don't get complacent."

I swallow. As we move through Fortin, first the assembly hall, then upstairs to the student lounge and the various club spaces, I wonder if tonight's lark will be enough or if next week, we'll be back out here again. With the end of the month approaching, we don't have a lot of time. I think back an hour, to how Lee shamed Wesley in front of us. It was awkward and kind of mean, but my gut says it worked. No one is going to forget to delete a text after that. In a way, what we're doing tonight is the same—calling the administration out on lowballing their contract workers, demanding that Tipton step up, do better.

We use up the last of our postcards, and I feel amazing.

I'm exhausted, but I can't imagine sleeping right now. I want to fast-forward to tomorrow morning, be everywhere at once, see the looks on my classmates' faces when they catch campus's overnight transformation.

"Get some sleep," Spencer says, as if reading my mind. He takes the tote bag and the key cards. "Your dorm should be unlocked. I'll drop these off at the Den."

"Thanks. This was . . . it felt important. I had fun."

And it was easy. I check the time on my phone. We have over twenty minutes to spare.

Spencer grins. "You juniors got a soft launch tonight. We are just getting started."

32

I sleep, heavy and dreamless. When my alarm goes off, I don't know where I am. I listen for footsteps below me, morning sounds of the radio and Lorelei switching on the hair dryer and Dad shuffling around in the kitchen. Then I remember.

Tipton. Monday. Lark.

I thought sleep wouldn't come at all, that I'd be up at the crack of dawn, but my body and brain are playing tug o' war, and as I stumble bleary eyed toward the shower, it's clear my body is winning. That I will be sneaking out again tonight for our weekly Monday meeting is almost unthinkable, but the hot water pelts my skin, and after five minutes in the shower, my brain fog has dissipated into the steam.

I skip my usual breakfast run to Manny's Joint and head in the direction of the athletic field instead, hoping it's not too late to see Lucas, Mira, and Colin's work on display. The Fleet Sports Center and athletic field are situated on the west side of campus, partway down the hill toward town. The incline makes for a great aerial view of the field from the path, and as I arrive at a prime viewing spot, I'm not the only Tiptonian with their phone out, snapping pictures of the field below, where our message is spelled out entirely in plastic forks stuck in the turf:

$5 FOR FRESH INC

I grin and snap a photo of my own before heading to physics.

In every class, students clutch postcards. Dr. Naylor has the field cleared by the end of first period, but there are photos all over social media. Everyone sees. Between classes, a chant springs up on the paths: *"We won't be out-Breckered! We won't be out-Breckered!"* Clearly, my fellow ghosts were right about what would motivate Tiptonians at large.

In assembly, Madison Blythe calls for a walk-out from Wednesday afternoon classes and a sit-in in front of Brisbane if Dr. Naylor and the administration have not committed to the wage increase in the next forty-eight hours. She speaks as if the demand was her idea, as if student government was going to step up and take action anyway, as if the assembly hall would be filled with students cheering and waving postcards in the air if we hadn't taken action last night.

Dr. Naylor stands coolly to Madison's right in a navy shirtdress and heels, allowing the student body president to say her piece, then calmly retrieves the mic to move on to morning announcements.

As our head of school steers the conversation toward the upcoming clubs and activities fair, it hits me that none of us will ever get to take credit for the work we do. If we succeed, even Akari and Lucas won't get any thanks. People will remember the forks and the postcards and Madison's speech at assembly, but they won't have any idea who made this happen.

"We don't do this for the glory," Brit had said at the end of last week's meeting, when we'd finalized our plans for the lark.

Now I understand what she meant. In a way, it's a letdown, but at the same time, I feel closer than ever to Momma. She carried the ghosts' secrets too. Now, across time, even across death, we share something special, something important. These secrets are ours.

I go to English, then Creative Writing. At the end of class, Mr. Ellis stays in his seat at the seminar table like he always does. He's almost too generous with his time. Sometimes people have real questions, but most of the students who stay behind are just angling for some face time with one of Tipton's most popular teachers. It can be hard to get a word in if you have something you actually want to ask. Today, though, everyone hurries out the door the second the period ends, eager to get to the dining hall and see what will unfold at lunch.

"Not in a rush?" Mr. Ellis asks. I'm still at my seat, packing up my backpack. Still thinking about Momma—what we share, and what sets us apart.

"I'll head down in a minute," I say. "But I actually wanted to ask something if you have a sec?"

"Of course." He smiles wide, dimples punching each cheek.

"I know we're doing flash fiction now, and short stories next, but I was wondering if we're going to be writing any poetry for class?"

He nods. "End of the trimester. I used to start with the poetry unit, but it scared off too many students. Now I do it last."

"Okay, that's great." I zip up my backpack and hoist it over my shoulders.

"Are you a poet, Calliope?"

I slip my thumbs through the straps. "When I was little, my mom was always reading us poetry. I didn't really like it at the time, but then the other day, a poem just kind of came to me. Something happened, something I didn't understand, but when I wrote the poem, I was able to think about it more clearly. Does that make sense?"

"It does." Mr. Ellis taps a finger against his lips. "Sometimes the creative brain outsmarts the rational one."

I nod enthusiastically. That's exactly what happened after I saw the man in town. Writing that poem had been a way to work through all my questions. "I want to write more poems, but I don't really know where to start."

"Well, what bothers you, Calliope? I always think that's a good jumping-off point."

"Fairy tales," I say after a minute. "We remember the princesses and happily ever afters, but most of the original stories were really dark. Maybe there's a poem in that."

Mr. Ellis slips his tablet into his bag and pushes his chair back. "That's always bothered me too. Those stories are riveting *because* of the violence and sex and cruelty at their core."

I nod slowly. Momma liked the good parts of fairy stories, but it's the dark stuff that makes them interesting, gives them something real mixed in with all the magic. Momma and I never agreed about that.

"I blame Disney," I say.

Mr. Ellis laughs. He starts walking to the door and beckons for me to follow. "Absolutely. Most of us have darkness in our lives, sometimes quite a bit of darkness. Our flaws make us human, don't you think?" He holds open the front door for me, and I thank him.

"There's a poem in there, Calliope. Maybe even a series."

I think about Momma and secrets and poetry and darkness as we step onto the lawn. Mr. Ellis says he is meeting a friend off campus, so I give him a wave and start down the path.

At lunch, I'm drawn back into the excitement of the lark. Nico and I eat flatbread pizza and join in when Rhine fills with spontaneous applause for Chef Andrea and her staff. Kitchen employees come out into the dining hall for a series of toasts, led by the prefects. People share memories of favorite meals and friendly interactions with the staff, who Quinn makes a point to identify by name in their toast. Juanita, Paul, Margie, Rahul. I look around, begin matching names to faces. I am embarrassed to realize that for over two weeks now, I haven't bothered to read the small brass name tags pinned to the collars of the people checking me in at the dining hall, serving me in the buffet line, refilling the hot water carafe at Manny's Joint. I wonder how many Tiptonians have been failing in the same way for months, for years.

The faculty dining with us join in, sharing their own stories. Several students have phones out, recording video, and I know the warm scene this afternoon in Rhine is going to make its way onto social media, onto administrators' screens. The ghosts were right—we ignited the kindling last night, and now it's a wildfire. This is no longer a Haunt and Rail campaign; it's a campus-wide initiative. And I get it—I get how a small secret society has motivated decades of positive change on campus. Momma made things happen here, and now we are forever bound by the ghosts. I raise my glass. I am glowing.

33

"Tomorrow's daily email," Lucas says at our late-night meeting in the Den. "I'm calling it." He is sprawled across the entire couch, forcing more ghosts onto the braided rug and beanbag cushions.

Akari shakes her head from her perch on the long table, feet on a chair. "Naylor will wait until Wednesday morning. She was playing it cool today, but she has teeth. We've seen it before. She'll announce something at assembly and threaten anyone who walks out of afternoon classes with Saturday service."

There is no consensus among the ghosts about when or how the Tipton administration will announce their decision to grant the Fresh INC employees a wage increase, but everyone is in a celebratory mood. Everyone agrees we have won.

It feels premature, but I am exhausted and giddy, and it feels good to be able to laugh and pass around snacks with the only people on campus who know what we did. It is a private kind of glory. I decide it is the best kind.

"We will hold off on hearing new campaign proposals until

the results are finalized," Brit announces. "We hope to resume regular society business in next Monday's meeting. But if last night's lark does not go in our favor, we may need to reconvene for an emergency meeting midweek. I want everyone to be brainstorming new larks in case we need to move swiftly. Got it?"

"Watch for a message," Lee says. Nineteen pairs of eyes land quickly on Wesley, then shift away. "If we need to meet off schedule, you'll be notified with a date and time. If there's no further business in the meantime, we're adjourned."

Brit and Quinn lead the way up the stairs, off to unlock the dorms. Everyone follows, except for Lee, Lucas, and Spencer, who are rounding up the leftover snacks and packing them away in a large plastic bin. I hesitate in the doorway. I'm so tired, but this might be my only chance to ask some of the ghosts about Adam Davenport until next Monday, and I think I can do it without bringing my clandestine trip to the Den into the conversation.

Lucas sees me hovering. "What's up, Calliope?"

I step back into the room, shut the door behind me. "I have a question about Tipton history. And the ghosts."

"Sure," Lee says. She hefts the plastic snack bin from the floor. "Grab the closet door for me?"

I make myself useful, then say, "This weekend, I looked up my mom's old yearbooks in the library."

"Kathleen Marie Callihan, class of 1995," Spencer says.

"That's her."

"And you want to know if you're here because you're a legacy?" Lucas says before I can go on. "Sorry, Calliope, no can do. Recruitment intel never gets shared with initiates. No one gets to know the specifics of why they were tapped."

"It's not that," I say. We've finished cleaning up, and Spencer takes a seat in an armchair, so the rest of us follow suit. "It's about something else I saw when I was looking through her junior yearbook."

"Okay," Lee says. "Shoot."

"So in the library copy, there was a senior's photo that was totally blacked out with Sharpie. I looked through the rest of the yearbook, and I found a memorial tribute to that student, Adam Davenport. He died on campus in November 1993."

"Oh god, yes," Lucas says. "Adam Douchecanoe Davenport."

"So you know who he was?" I can't keep the eagerness out of my voice.

"Adam's legend around Tipton," Lucas says. "And not in a good way."

"Your mom wasn't friends with him, was she?" Lee asks. She makes a face like she's bitten into something nasty.

"I don't think so. It's just, the tribute page was totally defaced. Whoever blacked out his senior photo wrote some pretty damning things about him on the tribute. And they drew our symbol."

"Oh," Spencer says. He draws the small word out into a long breath and leans forward. "So here's the deal with Adam Davenport. His dad, Richard Davenport, was a filthy rich old bastard on the board of trustees. He was a Tipton alum, an old guard southerner who moved to New York for school and stayed for business, but he was a racist shit, a Confederate sympathizer. He quit the board after Adam died. But at the time, he was the board's most vocal opponent of the motion to rename Calhoun, one of the boys' dorms."

"Named for former United States VP John C. Calhoun," Lucas adds, "a staunch defender of slavery."

"The 1993 motion to rename Calhoun failed," Spencer says, "largely thanks to Richard Davenport. Calhoun was eventually renamed Wright in 2015, after abolitionist Theodore Sedgwick Wright, a Black New Yorker. Which is great and all, but don't even get me started on the fact that it took Tipton *twenty-two years* from the original motion to finally change the name of the dorm."

"I actually remember that," I say. "I'd forgotten, but my mom followed the local stories in 2015, when the building was renamed."

That was the year before the accident. The year before she died. Aunt Mave's vague recollection about renaming a building hadn't sparked anything for me, but with this new context, it clicks. I remember Momma talking about it, but I don't remember her ever mentioning Adam Davenport.

"So what did all this have to do with Adam?" I ask. "Just dislike by association?"

Lee speaks up. "Story goes, Adam Davenport was a total daddy's boy. He was this uber-privileged asshole who no one really liked but lots of people sucked up to anyway. People just can't stay away from wealth and power. And Adam was super loud about supporting his father's bid to keep Calhoun Calhoun. The night the board's motion to rename the building failed, Adam was partying on campus, celebrating

Daddy's victory. After check-in, he kept the party going in his room, getting shitfaced by himself. He lived in Calhoun, how perfect is that? At some point, he must have wandered out into the hall. He tripped down the stairwell and broke his neck."

"Jesus. But he tripped, right? He was drinking alone, and he fell. Why would someone draw our symbol on his yearbook tribute?"

"There have always been rumors," Lucas says. "So many people hated Adam, and the way he was celebrating this racist victory must have pushed a lot of Tiptonians' buttons. It definitely would have pushed mine."

"His death was ruled an accident right away," Lee adds. "There was never a homicide investigation, but it didn't stop people from whispering." She wiggles her fingers in the air, as if casting a witchy spell. "Adam was pushed. Maybe by the ghosts."

"To be clear, Haunt and Rail doesn't claim responsibility for Adam Davenport's death," Spencer says. "Although I'm sure none of the ghosts shed any tears at his funeral."

"Do you think it's possible, though?" I ask. "That the ghosts were responsible."

"Probably not," Spencer says. "Can you imagine the meeting where they got a unanimous vote to murder a kid? Unlikely. But there was a Haunt and Rail campaign in support of renaming Calhoun. There's a definite record of that. And clearly that campaign failed with the board's vote. So who knows, maybe things got out of hand?"

"No way." Lee laughs. "We could barely get twenty people

to get behind releasing Ty Morrison's DMs last year after he spewed all that homophobic garbage to Jay and Leo. The society can be so *puritan* sometimes. Besides, if the ghosts were going to go after anyone, they should have gone for Davenport Senior. Adam was an ass, but his father held all the power."

"Maybe Haunt and Rail was more radical in the nineties," Lucas suggests. He grins and leans back on the couch. "I don't hate the rumors that we might have been involved."

My thoughts flash back to our conversation on the way to brunch after I'd been assured I'd be running for student government unopposed. Lucas is part of a long history of Tipton ghosts who have believed there are rules worth breaking, but that philosophy probably shouldn't extend to murder.

As we leave the library and walk back to our dorms, my mind won't stop whirring. It would be so extreme—for the ghosts to have killed someone, even someone horrible, in cold blood. But I can't escape the thought that there is something very suspicious about the way Adam Davenport died, drunkenly tripping down the stairs in the very dorm whose racist history he'd been celebrating.

In 1993, my mother was a ghost, Haunt and Rail's campaign to rename Calhoun failed, and Adam Davenport died. Two decades later, a year after the dorm was finally renamed, my mother was herself the victim of a terrible accident that everyone wants to think she caused.

I'm too tired to put all the pieces together, but the beginnings of a possible connection are starting to flicker. The question that has been turning over and over in my mind since the day I saw the man in town rises again to the surface: What if the car accident wasn't an accident at all?

Then new questions bubble up, and once they're there, I can't unthink them: Was someone trying to keep my mother silent? Or was it revenge?

34

On Wednesday, Nico and I sit on the lawn outside
Manny's Joint. I'm eating, and Nico is sketching on his
tablet, the beginnings of a new portrait. Campus has looked
highly seasonal since Hoards of Gourds, but today is the first
day that really feels like fall. This morning, the grass was
damp as I walked to class, and I swear it actually smells like
turning leaves. By midafternoon, the air is still crisp, but the
sun is hot overhead. I keep shrugging my sweater on and off,
on and off. Above us, the stallion's white body and teal-tipped
wings stretch above the entryway in an incongruous color pop
against Tipton's staid reds, whites, and grays.

"Why teal?" I tear off a corner of my sandwich. "It seems
so, I don't know, colorful?"

Nico looks up from his drawing and laughs. "Tipton
didn't have a mascot or school colors until the eighties,
I think. There used to be a very boring logo with a navy
shield and gold lettering. You'll still see it on old alumni
magazines and stuff in the library. Story goes, they let the
students vote for the mascot and colors. Someone's rich

parents paid for the rebrand, so there you have it."

"Eighties," I repeat. "Makes sense."

Nico places his tablet on the grass and crumbles two packages of crackers on top of his chili. "Food tastes even better today."

"It really does."

In the end, neither Akari's nor Lucas's predictions came true. Dr. Naylor's decision was not in yesterday's daily email, nor did the administration wait until the last second to make an announcement. On Tuesday evening, everyone received a Teal Alert notifying us that the school will be amending Fresh INC's new contract, which goes into effect October first, to include a four-dollar hourly wage increase. It's not the full five dollars Haunt and Rail campaigned for, but Madison Blythe sent an email to the student list-serv this morning calling off the afternoon walk-out and reminding Tiptonians that four dollars an hour is an improvement to our food service workers' initial ask, and while we're not besting Brecker, it's a match.

I remind myself that this is the kind of action the ghosts are known for—not shoving a student down the stairs, even if he was an overprivileged bigot. Maybe I let my exhaustion and vivid imagination get the best of me last night. But I can't entirely let the idea go. When it comes down to it, who *are* the ghosts? And what did they stand for nearly thirty years ago? If my mother's generation of Haunt and Rail really did have something to do with Adam Davenport's death, it's not like they would have kept a record of it for future classes.

As if reading my mind, Nico says, "After more than two

years at Tipton, I thought I'd know who's running Haunt and Rail by now. But I have zero idea."

I don't know what to say, so I stuff another bite of sandwich in my mouth.

Nico interprets my silence as confusion. He pulls out one of our postcards from his backpack and points to the angry ghost symbol below our message on the back. "Haunt and Rail is a secret society. That's their symbol, that ghost. You probably saw it on the whiteboards the first week."

"Right," I say, guilt gathering in my stomach. I don't want to lie to Nico, but what choice do I have? "I was wondering about that."

"They've been around forever. I think they go all the way back to the year the school was founded."

Close, I want to tell him. *To 1956.*

"No one knows how many students are involved, but it has to be a pretty small group." *Twenty.* "I think it's just seniors." *And juniors.* "They're activists, in a way, but they do a lot of pranks." *Larks.* "And they're smart. Usually they're pretty successful."

"Have they ever not been?" I struggle to keep my face blank. I am not good at this. "That you remember?"

Nico taps his spoon absently against the lip of his cardboard chili cup. "There was one prank my first year. Haunt and Rail called out this gross, misogynistic old board member, plastered the outside of Brisbane with printouts of the guy's emails. It was pretty amazing; when we left our dorms that morning, the building was entirely covered in paper. You couldn't even see the brick."

"Wow. What happened?"

"Not much. He got a slap on the wrist, I guess, but he's still on the board of trustees. I don't remember the details, but whatever he said in those emails wasn't enough to force his resignation. And Haunt and Rail must not have had anything else on him, because that was it. No other pranks."

"That sucks." I ball up my napkin and sandwich wrapper and drop them into the bag Nico is holding out for non-recyclables. When the campaign failed, it just . . . failed. And thirty years ago, when the ghosts couldn't get Calhoun renamed, they probably didn't lash out at that vile board member's obnoxious son. But the more I think about it, the less sure I feel. Am I thinking logically or trying to convince myself that my mother would never have been involved in something so horrible?

"Any others?" I ask.

"Probably. But it's hard to tell because sometimes there are copycats. Or at least I think they're copycats."

My eyebrows arch up.

"Like last May, someone moved all of the furniture out of the Lynd first-floor common area and set it up right over there." Nico points across Quadrant West to the grassy area outside the dorm. "They taped a big drawing of the ghost symbol to the coffee table. It was funny, but I don't think it was really Haunt and Rail."

"Why not?"

"It was just a joke. Haunt and Rail's pranks always have a purpose. Whoever moved the furniture outside was just messing around."

"Right. I guess Haunt and Rail is a good scapegoat." Which is how the Adam Davenport rumors got started too. Probably.

"Kind of. I think Dr. Naylor and the deans are smart enough to sort real Haunt and Rail pranks from the fake ones, but maybe it worked. No one got caught for the outdoor furniture display."

Nico walks over to the trash and recycling bins and deposits our bag. Then he sits back down on the grass and picks up his tablet.

"That's pretty amazing," I say, leaning close to peer at his drawing. "Even from the outline, it's so clearly Aymée. How do you do that?"

Nico shrugs. "I don't know how to explain it. I'd be an awful teacher, so I can probably scratch that career option off the list. Drawing faces has always come naturally to me. But other things are really hard, like capturing motion. I should really be working on my assignment for class, but this is more fun."

I wonder if Nico would ever want to try drawing me, but I don't know how to say it without sounding vain or like I was really asking, *do you like me?* Because honestly, I would be asking exactly that. I think I like Nico as more than a friend, but I am beginning to think it's one sided. That I misread those moments I thought he maybe wanted something more. I don't know how to read boys, how to read Nico. I am not sure there is anything more than friendship between us, but I want there to be. I bite my bottom lip between my teeth and wonder if I am brave enough to find out.

"Calliope," Nico says. His tone is soft, and for a second, I am sure my thoughts have been written plainly across my face. Horrified, I fuss with the buttons on my sweater.

"What's up?" I mumble.

"You haven't mentioned your family in a while. I just wanted to check if . . . well, if you'd remembered anything else about the man you saw. If you wanted to talk about that at all."

"Oh." I haven't said anything to Nico since my search for the man with dark blond hair got all tangled up in Haunt and Rail last weekend. I still want his help, but I don't know what to say. I scuff the grass below us with the toe of my shoe. "My family hasn't been particularly helpful," I say finally. "I haven't made much progress."

"But you still think he was there that day, right? You still want to remember?"

"Yes. Very much."

"Okay." Nico gives me a small smile. "Because I might have an idea."

35

"I get it," Lorelei is saying to me. "I just don't *get* it."

"You are infuriating." I return my sister's perplexed expression with an eyebrow furrow. It is just about the meanest thing I can make my face do, especially directed at my sister.

She laughs, and I toss my phone down on my bed.

"Hey, where'd you go?"

"Still here," I say. "I just can't look at you when you're laughing at me."

"I'm sorry, I'm sorry," she pleads, and I scoop my phone back up. "It's cool that the students helped get the staff a raise."

Not just "the students." *Me.* The ghosts. But I can't tell her that. Can't make her understand. I have never felt so far away from my sister.

"It's just that you've only been there three weeks," Lorelei is saying. She sits cross-legged on her bed. Behind her, I can see out the window to the woods beyond our house. "It's not like you really know any of these people."

I don't know how to explain this to Lorelei. How something can matter after such a short time. A place, the people in it. How life does not, in fact, begin and end in our small mountain village.

If you had tried to tell me the same thing, even a few weeks ago, I might have been unconvinced. I was desperate to get out of Plover Lake, but I didn't believe it could lose its hold on me so quickly. My first few days at Tipton, my mind roved constantly to whatever I imagined Alternate Universe Calliope would be doing back home in any given moment. What Beatrix and Erica were doing. What I was missing, for better or worse.

Now, I feel different. Has it only been three weeks since Dad, Lorelei, and Serafina dropped me off here? Tipton was so strange in those first days. But now, it has snaked its way inside me, put down roots. I am part of this school; I belong here now. Some days, I forget to think about home at all. With a guilty twinge, I realize I haven't opened the group chat with my friends in over two days.

"I don't know how to explain it," I tell her. But then I try. "Plover Lake is so small. It feels like the entire world is contained right in our village. We always say it's like a snow globe, right?"

She nods.

"In a way, Tipton is that way too. A campus on a hill, the universe captured in this glass bubble. It's easy to forget there's a world outside."

Lorelei looks sad. "Don't forget us, Calliope."

"I would never," I promise. Then, "How's Dad?"

Lorelei shrugs. "Same same."

My lips tug down at the corners. "Serafina said he was moping."

"When did she say that?"

"I don't know, last week sometime. She said he was hanging out in the sewing room."

"I don't think so," Lorelei says. "She likes to tell stories."

"The anniversary is coming up," I remind her, as if she needs to be reminded. "Next Friday."

"I know."

"Just keep an eye on Dad, okay? The twenty-third always gets him down."

"I *know*." Lorelei sighs. "I'm sorry. I just wish you were here."

"Me too," I say, but I'm not sure that's true. Do I wish I were home right now, in Plover Lake? I miss it and I do not miss it at the same time.

"I miss you," I add, because that is definitely not a lie.

36

"Here for a stacks pass, Calliope?" Ms. Bright adjusts her glasses with the cherry-red frames and checks her watch.

It is Friday, two hours before dorm check-in. The library is about as empty as it ever gets, but there are a handful of Tiptonians milling about, books or laptops open in front of them at long wooden tables identical to the one we have down in the Den.

"I actually wanted to ask you something." I drop my voice. "Privately?"

Ms. Bright glances to the other end of the check-out counter, where Rebecca, the library assistant, is loading returns onto a cart.

"Watch the desk for a few minutes?" she asks. "I need to open up a study carrel."

Rebecca nods, and Ms. Bright motions for me to follow her. We walk up to the second floor, and she unlocks an unoccupied group study room, then closes the door behind us.

"I noticed you've been visiting the yearbooks." She gives me a smile and pulls out a chair. We both sit.

"You've been paying attention."

She nods. "I always keep an eye on you ghosts. And every year, a few of you have questions."

"Right." Of course I am not the first to consult Ms. Bright for a history lesson. I fall back on the same broad explanation I gave Lee, Lucas, and Spencer the other night. "I was looking through my mom's old yearbooks, and I found something disturbing. The tribute to Adam Davenport?"

Ms. Bright nods. "Ah, Adam. He was two years behind me at Tipton. I was in college when he died, but he's certainly stayed in my memory. He was one of those people it was hard not to know."

"I don't know if you've seen it, but someone drew all over his tribute page. The Haunt and Rail symbol is there."

She nods. "I'm aware. I've had several copies of the 1994 yearbook over the years, and they've all been defaced. Eventually I gave up."

"Who's doing it?"

"We are." She smiles. "Several generations of ghosts, perpetuating the rumor that Haunt and Rail was responsible for Adam Davenport's death. You've stumbled upon one of the society's favorite myths."

"So you don't believe it?"

Ms. Bright shrugs. "Not really, but it's hard to say. Adam's peers were underclassmen when I was part of the society. They were an interesting bunch."

"What does that mean?" I probe.

"A mix of idealists, radicals, and wounded souls. Your mom, for instance. Kathy had such a good heart; she was always doing nice things for other students. My friend Iris went through a bad breakup our senior year, and Kathy organized an impromptu spa day for her. Iris was so surprised; she and Kathy barely knew each other, but that's the kind of person your mom was. Always trying to make a difference in other students' lives."

"That's really nice," I say. "Thanks for telling me about that."

Ms. Bright nods. "So there were the dreamers like your mom. But there were a few ghosts that year who hadn't been treated kindly by Tipton—or by Adam Davenport in particular."

"Like who?" I have deleted the photos I took of the initiate lists, but not before committing their names to heart.

"Well, Monica Zisk was teased mercilessly for a speech impediment, and Adam was one of the ringleaders. Nathan Carey-York was one of the only out gay students at Tipton in the early nineties, and the lacrosse team made his life miserable. Adam was the captain. And then there was Ron Graff, another recipient of campus ire, from Adam and nearly everyone, I'm embarrassed to say. Ron was quiet, a loner, the type of kid people whispered would grow up to be the Unabomber."

"The who?"

Ms. Bright shakes her head. "Ted Kaczynski? One of the most notorious domestic terrorists in the US from the late seventies through the midnineties."

"Oh. Right." I give her a sheepish smile. "Before my time."

"Well, in my *many years* of experience"—Ms. Bright's lips quirk into a half-smile—"nearly everyone tapped to join Haunt and Rail has had an underlying love for Tipton. This school has a lot of flaws, but the ghosts have always worked to make it a better place, not tear it down. But I've often wondered about the dynamic that year. There was more than one ghost who would have been happy to see Adam's reign of terror come to an end."

Monica Zisk. Ron Graff. Nathan Carey-York.

"Bad enough to shove him down a flight of stairs?"

Ms. Bright stands and collects her key ring. "Probably not. But I really don't know. The only thing I'm sure of is this: If the ghosts were responsible for what happened to Adam Davenport, it definitely wouldn't have been a unanimous decision. That's not what the society is about."

"So you think a few of the ghosts might have, what, gone rogue?"

"Maybe." She starts toward the door. "Or more likely they only wished they had, and they spread rumors after the fact. Either way, it must have been a turbulent time to be in Haunt and Rail."

Ms. Bright excuses herself, saying she needs to get back to the desk, but I can stay in the study room until close if I want. When I'm alone, I pull my laptop out of my bag and start writing down everything I know:

- Several ghosts had a reason to want Adam Davenport dead, including Nathan Carey-York, one possible yearbook match for the man with dark blond hair.
- My mother would have been against doing anything

to hurt a classmate—even if he was a contemptible person. Presumably she is not the only ghost who would have been against cold-blooded murder.

- Whatever happened, at least one ghost, probably a few, took credit for Adam's death behind the shield of Haunt and Rail. But his death was ruled an accident.

- In 2015, the year before Momma died, Calhoun was renamed Wright. The news coverage my mother was following so closely would have definitely mentioned Adam Davenport, the student who died there in 1993, the son of the former board member so against renaming the dorm.

- Also in the year before the car crash, Momma was away from home more than usual. She took a lot of trips to Alyson-on-Hudson to visit Aunt Mave—and conduct her own investigation?

A possible theory: One or more students in Haunt and Rail killed Adam Davenport, and Momma knew something, but she didn't have proof. For years, it bothered her. Then in 2015, Adam Davenport's name was back in the news, stirring things up again. In the year before the accident, all those times Momma was visiting her sister, she was also going back to Tipton, asking questions, maybe gathering evidence. On the day of the accident, we were on our way to Alyson-on-Hudson because Momma was planning to meet someone or go to the police.

Maybe Momma trusted the wrong person, a fellow ghost. Maybe that person made sure my mother would stay silent forever.

I shiver, save my notes in my password-protected file, shut my laptop down. If my mother was driving to Alyson-on-Hudson to meet with someone about Adam Davenport, or to talk to the police, I don't know why she would have pulled us out of school that day, taken us with her. Maybe she thought she'd be safer that way, that no one would try to harm her daughters. Maybe she miscalculated. Or maybe I'm on the wrong track altogether, but my gut says I'm closer to the truth than I have ever been.

37

Nico insists on paying for our taxi from the train station to the Sunrise Memory Center in New Paltz. The driver hands him the receipt, and we step out of the car.

"This might be a complete waste of time," he says for the third, or possibly fourth, time since we left campus this morning. "And money. I didn't realize how expensive—"

"Nico," I cut him off. The taxi backs out of the tiny gravel lot, and we're left standing in front of a small, freestanding office building on a pretty side street with a used bookstore and a coffee shop on one side and a bunch of small brick and stone houses with sloped, grassy yards on the other. Above the door to the center is a navy blue awning with ALEXA STONE, MS ED., CHT. printed across the front in white block letters. Master's in education. Certified hypnotherapist.

"It's fine, I want to do this. And I get that it's probably a crock."

After Nico suggested the memory center, I'd done a deep dive into memory recovery therapy and hypnosis. Basically everything I read online suggested that medical hypnosis can have real value, but probably not when it comes to recovering memories. There are a bunch of cases from the eighties and nineties of people who thought they were recovering memories of childhood abuse that turned out to be entirely false. There was even a whole FBI investigation into alleged satanic ritual abuse, and false memories "uncovered" during hypnosis contributed in a big way to the spread of the rumors. The memory recovery industry was largely discredited after that, but there is still a school of hypnotherapists that practice memory recall.

So basically, I have every reason to be wary of this place. But I am not trying to recover memories of abuse or messed-up cult stuff. If there's even a small chance that Alexa Stone, MS Ed., CHt, can help me remember more about the man with dark blond hair, it's worth it. And I have several years of babysitting money saved up; I can swing one session.

"That satanic panic stuff was wild," Nico says. "I can't believe I'd never heard of that. I should have done more research before I suggested this." He scratches at the back of his neck, a nervous gesture. "I just saw the ad and instantly thought of you." He peers at the awning. "And she has all those letters after her name. . . ."

I laugh. "It's going to be fine. Worst case, I don't remember anything, and I'm out some cash. And either way, it'll be a good story."

Best case, I'll remember everything. But I can't bring myself to say that last part out loud. I want it too badly.

"Can we go in now?"

"Yeah." Nico grins and extends his arm toward the door. "After you."

The woman seated behind the reception desk is in her early twenties. Her light brown hair is cropped close to her head, revealing a string of small diamond studs running up the curve of one ear. The name plate positioned in front of her computer reads ANGELINA.

"Welcome to Sunrise," she says. "Do you have an appointment?"

"Um, yes. I'm Calliope Bolan. I'm supposed to see Alexa Stone?"

Angelina smiles. "Eleven o'clock. While you wait, will you please fill these out for me?" She hands me a clipboard and a pen attached with a string.

"Sure." Nico and I take a seat in the small waiting room. No one else is in here. He grabs a copy of *Sports Illustrated* while I fill out the New Client Intake forms. Name. Date of birth. Check boxes for a litany of medical conditions that don't apply to me. Family health history and emergency contact information.

When I'd called to make the appointment, Angelina, or whoever I'd spoken to, had been clear that the Sunrise Memory Center is not a medical practice, and they do not accept insurance. The paperwork is nonetheless pretty similar to the forms you're handed at a doctor's office. On the last page is a request for credit card information.

"Do you take cash or check?" I ask, back at the desk.

Angelina takes the clipboard. "Check is fine," she says. "You're a student?"

I nod. "Tipton Academy."

"We offer a discount to students and teachers. I'll note that on your file."

"Do I pay now?" I ask.

"We'll do billing after your session."

I adjust the strap of my bag against my shoulder. "Can I ask you something?"

"Sure."

"Have you . . . I mean, it's my first time doing anything like this. Have you done hypnosis?"

She leans toward me, across the desk, and lowers her voice like we are sharing a secret. "I was super skeptical the first time I came in here. I get it. And hypnosis doesn't work for everyone, but it can be a really effective tool. Alexa helped me recover all these things about my birth parents, before I was adopted."

I think about that. This is obviously very personal, but I can't help asking, "Did you live with them for a while?"

"Only four days. But the mind is *amazing*. You never really forget anything. You just lose access to many of your memories over time. Alexa can help you unlock things that will *blow your mind*. Like my birth mom, she named me Angelina. Isn't that wild? I had my name legally changed after I remembered that."

"Oh, wow." So this is definitely a racket. Maybe I should quit while I'm ahead, walk away now. I look back at Nico, but he's not paying attention to what Angelina's saying. He's on his phone, texting intently.

Angelina glances at her screen. "Alexa is ready for you

now, Calliope." She gestures down the hallway to my right, where a door is swinging open. A woman in her thirties steps out into the hall. She is wearing khaki dress pants and a pale blue top. She doesn't look like a scam artist or some woo-woo hippie type. In fact, she looks pretty boring. Straight, shoulder-length hair, pale pink lipstick, stylish tortoiseshell glasses.

"Right this way, Calliope," she says.

I glance at Nico again. He looks up and gives me an encouraging smile.

38

I sit across from Alexa Stone in a small, dimly lit room. It smells good in here, like vanilla and something vaguely spicy. Rainforest sounds pipe softly from a little speaker mounted on the wall. Alexa instructs me to make myself comfortable, so I kick off my shoes and draw my feet up under me in the soft leather chair.

Angelina was right—this is nothing like a medical practice. It's not much like a therapist's office either. I've never been to a spa, but I can imagine getting a massage here. The bird calls and oil diffusers are nice, but can't sounds and smells trigger memories? I wonder if she's going to somehow cleanse this room before she hypnotizes me.

"I'm glad you've found your way to Sunrise, Calliope," Alexa Stone is saying. A tan folder is spread open in her lap, displaying my New Client Intake forms, but she doesn't look at them. "When we experience a trauma, the unconscious mind can block some of our memories. I like to use the metaphor of a sealed box. Those memories are still inside us, but the lid is closed. Do you follow me?"

Not very original, but I nod.

"When the unconscious mind seals off those memories, the conscious mind loses access to them. It's a survival mechanism, but an imperfect one, because the damage"—she places the palm of her hand on her chest—"is still there, sealed inside the box."

I keep nodding slowly, but I'm starting to feel a little weird. What she's saying doesn't sound crazy, exactly, but it doesn't sound rooted in science either. I don't know what I was expecting. Maybe I was too focused on those degrees after her name. My mind travels to the bright, sparsely decorated room where Dad, Lorelei, Serafina, and I spent hours and hours in family therapy in the years after the crash. Dr. Nguyen had been warm but always professional. I was probably expecting something like that.

"When we say we don't remember something, it's not because the memory is gone," Alexa says. "It's just out of our grasp, stored in that sealed box." She leans forward, drops her voice to a dramatic stage whisper. "But we can unlock it."

I swallow.

Then she sits back in her chair, peeks down at my folder for the first time. "Can you tell me a little about why you're here, Calliope?"

"Um, okay." I kind of want to leave, but would that be disrespectful? My body feels glued to this soft chair, and I find myself telling her about the accident, what I remember of it. I stop before I say anything about the man with dark blond hair. It's why I'm here, but part of me doesn't want to share that with her. "I've been trying to remember more about that day," I wrap up vaguely. "What really happened."

"I see," Alexa says. She is looking at me intently. "You can absolutely access those locked memories through hypnotherapy. We are going to increase your awareness to a heightened state of vivid recall." She leans forward again, locks her eyes with me. Something about her confidence makes me flinch. "Did you know that we unconsciously remember almost everything that has ever happened to us, Calliope?"

My quick dip into Google revealed heaps of research indicating this is almost certainly not true. I break her stare, drop my eyes to my hands. I felt more comfortable in this room before Alexa Stone started speaking.

"Hypnotherapy will allow you to tap into your stored memories. You can pry the lid off that sealed box, permit them to come rushing to the surface, reclaim them." Alexa flips her hands over so her palms are open, facing the ceiling. Her face is alive with passion. She looks like a spiritual healer in pink lipstick and khakis. "Are you ready to remember, Calliope?"

My throat feels like sandpaper. The room was pleasantly warm a minute ago, but now I'm suffocating. I am not ready to remember. Not like this.

A loud, booming voice at the back of my head says going through with this would be a very bad idea. I wanted this to be the real thing, but I should have listened to my gut. What if she suggests stuff that isn't true, like those hypnotherapists I read about? Doing this could mess up my memory even more, lead me further away from the truth.

Screw politeness.

"I'm sorry." I shove my feet back into my shoes and stand up. "I don't want to do this. I've changed my mind."

Alexa Stone stands too, passion draining from her face, replaced by concern. Before she can try to convince me to stay, I'm back out in the hallway, beckoning to Nico.

Angelina is staring at me, openmouthed. "Not my cup of tea," I hear myself saying to her, a strange adult phrase I'm absolutely sure I've never uttered before. Thank god I didn't pay before going in there.

Nico is already at the door, holding it open for me. Then we are outside, and I am wrapping my arms tightly around his shoulders and pressing my face into his shirt.

"I am so sorry," he says, over and over. "This is all my fault." His arms close around my back, and he pulls me in.

We are almost the same height. I straighten up and extract my cheek from the soft fabric of his T-shirt, try to get myself together. "It's not your fault. You were trying to help me. And I wanted this to be real." Tears gather at the corners of my eyes, and I blink them back. I'm not sad, not really. Or rather, I am sad and happy and furious and giddy all at once. And most of all, I am brave.

I walked out of that office. I can do anything. I can tell Nico exactly how I feel.

I find his eyes with mine. "I would very much like to kiss you right now. Would that be all right?"

Nico's lips part into a slow smile, and my gaze travels down to the tiny chip in his left front tooth. I am on a roller coaster, traveling up up up. He pulls me even closer, and I am teetering at the top, waiting for the drop, waiting for my brain to shut off and the ride to take over.

Then he leans forward and tilts his chin just slightly to the left. Our lips brush lightly once, then come together, and I am falling, falling, the cart plunging into sweet nothingness, and I don't have to think anymore. It is like breathing, but better. I never want to stop.

39

When Nico and I have drawn apart again, the goofy grin on my face is reflected on his. Which of course makes me grin even harder. My eyes stray to the center's door, half expecting Angelina to come chasing after me, or Alexa Stone, but it stays firmly shut, and the moment remains mercifully intact.

"I've never done that before," I tell him, bravery bubbling over into a level of honesty I should probably reel in, but can't. I have no chill, as Lorelei often tells me. "Except once at a party. I'd known the guy since we were toddlers, and I wanted to like him, but I didn't feel anything. I just kept picturing him in kindergarten, burying ants in the sandbox and stealing cookies out of my lunch." I bite at my lower lip, force the word vomit to stop. "Sorry, too much?"

"Not too much," Nico says. "Did you feel something, this time? Because I felt something."

I grin even harder, if that is possible. "I definitely did." *The climb. The sheer, perfect plunge.*

I used to love roller coasters. But after the crash, after my dream of riding The Comet while the minivan swerved off the road, the thrill kind of lost its shine. Until right now.

Nico slips his hand into my hand, and our fingers lace together. He glances up the street, toward the shops. "We have time until the next train. Since you're not being hypnotized and all."

I laugh and step out from underneath the awning, gently tugging Nico with me. "Yeah, let's get away from this place."

"Herbal tea?" he asks, nodding toward the coffee shop.

My smile reaches all the way to the top of my head and down to my toes. He has been paying attention.

Inside the Village Brew, I order a peach tea while Nico scours the menu hanging above the barista's head. She has fair skin like me, but no freckles, and her hair, which is so dark brown it's almost black, stops just below her shoulders. She is a couple of years older than we are, probably a college student. Nico finally lands on something complicated involving chocolate and the espresso machine and places his order. The barista hands me a mug and a tea bag and tells Nico she'll give him a shout when his fancy coffee drink is ready.

It's midday on Saturday, and the coffee shop's mismatched array of lounge furniture and wobbly wooden tables is packed with a mix of students in SUNY New Paltz gear and young couples with stroller-aged kids. I set off to find the hot water and honey while Nico pounces on a table tucked to one side of the café counter, which is in the process of being vacated by two people packing up their laptops.

"Do you want to talk about it at all?" Nico asks when I'm back.

I blow across the top of my mug, an enormous maroon

thing decorated with owl faces. To our left, the barista is working on Nico's drink while her goateed co-worker takes orders at the counter.

"I should have turned right around when the receptionist said Alexa Stone had helped her recover memories from her first week of life."

Nico's eyebrows shoot up. "Whoa."

"Yeah." I draw the word out into two syllables, then sip at my tea. "But I really wanted to remember. I thought maybe there was still a chance it could work."

"What happened after you went back there? Did she start to hypnotize you?"

"We didn't get that far. Alexa Stone started talking—"

"Nico?" The barista is standing at the side of the counter, a steaming coffee cup beside her. "Caffe mocha, extra whip."

Nico stands to retrieve his drink, but the barista doesn't move. She is looking at me intently.

"I wasn't trying to eavesdrop," she says, "but were you talking about the Sunrise Memory Center?" Her forehead is creased in concern.

"Oh. Yeah. I just bailed on a session there."

Her shoulders relax. "Good call. That place should be shut down."

"Have you been?"

She looks behind her. There's no one in line at the moment, and her co-worker is busy cleaning an espresso machine. She places her forearms on the counter and leans toward me, almost-black hair spilling over the fronts of her shoulders.

"Two years ago, someone important to me died, and my memories of that night got all tangled up with another tragedy. By the time I started at New Paltz, I'd already done a lot of work to untangle things, but there are still gaps. Things people have told me, but I don't actually *remember*."

"Oh wow." I lean toward her, fascinated. Across from me, Nico dips a spoon into his whipped cream, lets us talk.

"I was curious about hypnotherapy," she says, "so I looked into it. The thing is, if you black out from drugs or alcohol like I did that night, your brain actually stops recording memories. There's nothing there to recover. Alexa Stone makes a lot of claims about what hypnosis can do, and she's probably well-intentioned, but it's bad science."

"Yeah, I pretty much figured that out," I say. "Thanks for affirming."

"Sure." She smiles and sticks out her hand. "I'm Anna."

"Calliope. Hey." I take her hand and give it a small shake. "Can I ask you something, Anna?"

She glances behind her shoulder, but there are no new customers. "Sure."

"You said you'd done some stuff to untangle your memories. What did you do that actually worked?"

Anna nods. "Not everything I'd forgotten happened while I was blacked out. Some of it was from early childhood. Going back to the place where the memories were formed started to trigger things for me. But you have to be open to the unexpected. There were things I was absolutely convinced of, but I'd mixed up when events happened or who was there. My mom helped a lot with that. Looking at photo albums, listening to her stories. I was able to sort out most of the stuff I'd jumbled."

"Yo, Anna." A line has formed again, and the other barista is waving to her. "I need you on counter, okay?"

She tells him she'll be right over. To me, she says, "I have to go. Good luck getting your memories back, Calliope."

"Thanks." I smile up at her. "You've already helped."

Anna returns to the front of the counter, and I turn to Nico. "What she said made a lot of sense, about mixing up details. When I saw the man in town, I remembered his face, and I thought he was with us in the car that day. But what if I knew him some other way?"

"That's what your family thinks, right?" Nico asks.

I nod. "And I haven't wanted to listen to them. But maybe I should. Maybe he was someone my mother knew, and I'd met him at some other point, and my memories are tangled."

Maybe he was Nathan Carey-York or Daniel Clark. Maybe he was the ghost my mother trusted. Maybe he was in the van with us that day, or maybe we stopped along the way and Momma met up with him at a gas station or rest stop. Maybe he did something to the minivan, something the investigation didn't turn up. . . .

Nico is nodding. He reaches for my hand across the table, slips it gently into his. Hypnotherapy wasn't the answer for Anna either, but she found other ways to remember. I need to do the same thing.

I've already been brave twice today, but I can't stop there. This trip to New Paltz wasn't a magical solution, but coming here still opened my eyes. The answers are out there, and the man I saw has them. I am going to stop sitting around, wondering if he's looking for me, waiting for him to make a move. I am going to find him.

IV
The Campaign

40

After my trip off campus yesterday, I have more home-work than I could possibly cram into one day, but I spend most of Sunday composing a note, then deleting it, then composing something new. There is so much I want to know, starting with the man's name, but also how he was involved in Adam Davenport's death—and if he caused my moth-er's. I can see all the dots, and he is my key to the connec-tions between them. Accusing him of something will scare him away, but he saw me inside the coffee shop that day. He knows I'm in Alyson-on-Hudson, must know that sooner or later, I'll have questions. He needs to know I mean business.

Finally, I settle on this:

> *I think you know something about the*
> *day my mother died. I want to talk, but first,*
> *you need to prove yourself to me. Tell me*
> *your name. Tell me who I am. Tell me what*
> *happened on November 10, 1993.*
> *Leave your response here. I'll find it.*

That evening, Nico walks into town with me, and I tack my note in a sealed envelope to the bulletin board across from Frances Bean, where I saw the man reading flyers that day. *To the man in his 40s with dark blond hair and sunburned cheeks.*

"He's never going to see this," I say. "Or even if he does, it's too vague."

"This town is small. If he doesn't see it, maybe someone will get it to him. It could work." Nico gives my elbow a reassuring squeeze, but he sounds doubtful too.

Since I don't have any better ideas, all I can do is hope. We turn and trudge back toward the arch, where Aunt Mave is picking me up for Sunday dinner.

I've made my move. Now, I wait.

On Monday night, the center of the Den floor has been cleared for Akari and Lucas, who are performing their "victory dance," a ballroom number with lots of dips and twirls that they have clearly spent time choreographing. His black hair swishes against the tops of his shoulders as he moves, and the low lamplight catches the highlights in Akari's newly blue bangs. Dramatic classical music swirls from a small set of speakers, and my fingers keep wanting to flinch toward Spencer's phone on the side table to my right, turn the volume down. But it's the middle of the night, and none of the seniors seem worried about the noise, so I shove my hand instead into the bag of fancy, pink-salted chips that Aymée and I are sharing and try to enjoy myself.

Then Brit is hovering over our beanbag poof, hands extended with an offering of two sparkly plastic cups. "Chillax, Calliope," she says, taking in my stiff back and twitchy fingers. "We're celebrating."

The cups are filled to the brim with golden, fizzy stuff.

"Is this real champagne?" I register the note of naiveté in my voice, but the words are out there now. I can't swallow them back.

Brit laughs, and heat fills my cheeks. "It's Veuve, my dear."

I don't know what "Veuve" is, but I raise the cup to my lips and take a sip. It is definitely actual alcohol.

"Where do you think she got this?" I ask Aymée when Brit has returned to her pouring station on one end of the long table, where a tea towel and six green bottles with orangey-yellow labels are laid out. I squint. The labels read *Veuve Clicquot Brut* in an elegant font.

Aymée shrugs. "Brit's family isn't exactly 'traditional.' She grew up in this rambling old mansion in the Finger Lakes, and her parents run a winery. They probably shipped it to her."

My eyes pop. My dad has been a bartender since before I was born, but that didn't mean he was supplying us with booze growing up. The opposite, in fact—Dad's seen just about everything at his job, and he can sniff out even the faintest whiff of alcohol. The Bolan girls do not participate in underage drinking.

I raise the cup to my lips and take another sip. Dad isn't here now. And this isn't "hard alcohol"; it's the stuff people drink at weddings. No one here is going anywhere near a car tonight, so what's the harm in some victory champagne?

Akari and Lucas finish their dance and collapse onto the

couch to a round of applause and hoots. Her body drapes across his, and he presses his lips to hers, and it hits me for the first time that they are a couple. I bury my surprise in my drink. I barely see them together on campus, and I've definitely never seen them kiss or hold hands. I wonder if this is a new development or if they are very private outside Haunt and Rail.

My thoughts wander to Nico, to our first kiss in front of Sunrise, then our second kiss on the train platform. How an elbow squeeze was the extent of our physical contact yesterday in town. How today on campus, I reached for Nico's hand at the same time he shoved his hands into his pockets, and it was maybe a coincidence but maybe not a coincidence. I wonder if we will also be very private, if Saturday's trip to New Paltz counts as our first date, if he has changed his mind, if it is possible to analyze a relationship to death before it even becomes a relationship at all.

Before I can spiral out completely, Lee clambers up onto the long table and lifts her cup. Her red curls spill down her shoulders.

"First, a toast to Haunt and Rail. Without the sparks we ignite, I swear this school would die of apathy. You all know I don't do sappy, but seriously. We make things happen. We keep this place on its toes. And this week, we inspired Tipton to level up again."

"Here's to Lucas and Akari," Aymée says.

Lee flashes her a smile. "To Akari, to Lucas, and to all of us. Cheers!"

There is a chorus of cheers all around, and when I raise my

cup to my lips again, I am surprised to find it nearly empty. I feel warm and suddenly giddy. Aymée leans against me, and I lean my head against her shoulder.

"Okay, okay." Lee is clapping her hands, angling for our attention again. Her empty cup rests on the table at her feet. "Sorry to cut this celebration short, but we have business to get down to. I am up here to present a proposal for Haunt and Rail's next campaign on behalf of myself and another member of our society who wishes to remain anonymous, at least for now."

"Is that allowed?" Mira asks. She leans forward in her chair.

"There is precedent." I'm surprised to see the speaker is a junior, Colin. He has sandy brown hair, long eyelashes, and a mouth full of braces. Colin has kept a low profile in meetings so far, but he did really nice work with Lucas and Mira on the athletic field for our first lark.

"The financial aid act of 2002," Colin says. "The year before it passed, my uncle thought he'd have to drop out of Tipton. His mom lost her job, and his parents were struggling to come up with tuition for his senior year. He worked with another ghost, Trina Sullivan, on the campaign proposal. They both put in the work, but Trina presented it to Haunt and Rail and kept my uncle's name out of it. He wanted to get the ghosts' support before they knew it was personal for him. He didn't want pity votes."

So Colin's uncle was also a ghost. I wonder how many of us in this room have a legacy connection to the society.

"Thank you, Colin," Lee says. "There are various reasons

a ghost might not want to present a campaign proposal, and that's fine as long as another member is willing to present in their stead. And in this case, I am very willing and very much behind this proposed campaign. This is sensitive, so I need you all to listen up."

She pauses, and the rustling of a chip bag fills the room. "Sorry," Josh mumbles.

Lee takes a seat on the table, and her legs swing over the edge. "Several times in Haunt and Rail history, we have taken action against a problematic member of the faculty or administration. These are our most difficult campaigns, and they have not always been a success. Tipton guards its own, even when it means protecting very bad people."

My thoughts dart to the story Nico told me the other day, about the sexist board member whose emails Haunt and Rail exposed, to no avail. Then to Richard and Adam Davenport.

"What I'm about to share will come as no surprise to some of you. But this teacher has managed to stay in tip-top standing in the eyes of the Tipton administration for six years now, so I imagine his actions aren't widely known, even among the students."

"And we're all going to give Lee our uninterrupted attention while she presents," Quinn cuts in. "Questions after."

There are murmurs of agreement all around.

"Thanks, Quinn. Okay, here goes. Stephan Ellis started teaching English at Tipton in 2016. At twenty-nine, Mr. Ellis is still one of the youngest full-time teachers on Tipton's faculty. He has won teaching awards five out of his six years here, and he recently announced a deal for his first novel with Random House. He's a Tipton darling, a rising star. But Mr. Ellis is also a predator."

A chill zips down my spine, and the energy in the room shifts instantly. I hear "no way," but also "finally," and "I've never liked that guy." Next to me, Aymée stiffens.

"Let her finish." Quinn's words rise above the chatter, and we all fall silent again. I place my empty cup on the floor beside me, suddenly wishing I was sober. Mr. Ellis—*a predator?* I squeeze my eyes shut and try to focus.

"What we have on Mr. Ellis goes beyond rumors," Lee says. "Without going into too much detail, to protect my anonymous co-chair's privacy, I can assure you they have experienced Ellis's harassment firsthand. Inappropriate touching, sexually explicit speech, private invitations to visit his faculty apartment without other students or teachers present. And we are almost certain there are other students, past and present."

"Why has no one reported this?" Wesley asks. He sounds genuinely shocked. After getting kicked off our first lark, Wesley has been super attentive during meetings—first to arrive, first to volunteer to help with anything that needs doing. I think Quinn is going to jump on him for interrupting, but Lee smiles.

"A very good question, which brings me to my next point: Mr. Ellis has been getting away with this behavior for two key reasons. First, he's smart enough to not get caught. And without proof, these students have nothing against one of the brightest stars at Tipton. Second, coming forward is a big risk. As I'm sure you know, survivors are systemically silenced and disbelieved by people in positions of authority. Dr. Naylor calls herself progressive, but she's in the board's pocket. Mr. Ellis is young, handsome, and well-liked by basically everyone. He would absolutely spin this so it looked like a couple of students with crushes on him lashing out after he turned them down.

"This is where Haunt and Rail comes in," Lee continues. "We need to stop Mr. Ellis before he ruins any more lives. We propose that Haunt and Rail take up exposing Mr. Ellis's behavior as our next fall campaign. This will absolutely be harder than our first campaign, and may take more than one lark, but I believe we have a moral obligation to take this on. I hereby propose a vote."

"Seconded," Akari says. Her eyes gleam, and I wonder if she is Lee's co-chair.

Lucas rises from the couch and moves to stand next to Lee at the long table. "All in favor of adopting Lee's proposal for action to expose Mr. Ellis, vote in the affirmative by raising your hand."

I love his Creative Writing class, and Mr. Ellis has never done anything remotely creepy or inappropriate around me. But Lee warned me to steer clear of him before classes even started—and now I know why. I don't want to believe Mr. Ellis is anything other than a young, enthusiastic English and writing teacher, but I trust Lee. And whoever her co-chair is, I believe them. I raise my hand.

"The motion does not pass," Lucas says, and I whip my head around. Josh's hands rest in his lap—as do Amyée's.

"Fuck," Lee says. She smashes her open palm against the long table with a loud smack.

"Lee, you know the rules. You may present again next Monday. If you are able to turn eighteen votes into twenty, Haunt and Rail will take on this campaign."

"Fine, I know," Lee says. Her voice is bitter, and I feel Amyée's body shrinking into the beanbag cushion beside me.

41

On the way to Manny's Joint Tuesday morning, a text from Nico:

> I might lose the nerve to say
> this in person, or when I'm fully
> awake, so here goes: can I ask
> you on a proper date, Calliope
> Bolan? You, me, somewhere off
> campus this evening?

A "proper" date. I beam.

Now it is evening, and we are walking into Alyson-on-Hudson. The moment we step through the entry arch and into town, Nico slips his hand into mine. Our feet keep time against the pavement, left and then right. Together, together, together.

We turn onto Chicory Lane, and I know I need to be brave again.

"Can I ask you something a little uncomfortable?"

"Sure, go for it." Nico's voice is light, but his hand twitches against mine. Or maybe it is my imagination.

I draw in a deep breath. "So on Saturday, we kissed. Twice. But since then, on campus, it's been like before. Before the kiss," I clarify unnecessarily. I hope Nico can't see how red my cheeks are in the semidark. "Is there a protocol I don't know, or are you embarrassed of me, or . . . ?"

"Oh my god, no!" Nico looks horrified. He scrapes his free hand through his hair. "I thought I was following your lead, but now I don't know why I thought that exactly. I may have kissed a couple more people than you, but the truth is, I don't know what I'm doing either." The streetlamp light catches his smile, shy and perfect.

"Oh!" I laugh, the tension inside my chest breaking into a thousand tiny bubbles. "We can be bad at this together."

Nico laughs too. "Deal. I like you so much, Calliope. I was trying to not be too pushy, I think? I've never had a girlfriend at school before, so this is pretty new to me too."

He likes me so much. I grin, big and goofy and uncontrollable. "Then we will figure this out."

Nico tells me he has had two girlfriends, ever. Emily was his "camp girlfriend" for three weeks the summer between seventh and eighth grade, which sounds legitimate enough to me, but he insists hardly counts. A girl called Simone was his first real girlfriend. They started dating after his first year at Tipton, when he was home for the summer in New Hampshire. They stayed together long distance for all of sophomore fall, then broke up over winter break.

"So I don't want you to think I have all this experience or

anything," Nico says. "I might do more stuff like forget to ask you what you actually want and assume I have things figured out when I clearly don't. I might need you to tell me when I'm being dense, but please do tell me and don't just let me keep being dense. Can I ask that? Is that okay?"

"That is more than okay."

Nico wants to show me his favorite spot in Alyson-on-Hudson, but before we do that, I insist we check the bulletin board. I've been back three times since leaving the envelope— twice yesterday and once today at lunch. Yesterday, my note was still there, tacked to the spot where I left it. But this afternoon, it was gone.

"Oh my god." I tug Nico over. There's a new envelope where mine used to be. *To the girl with freckles and long auburn hair* is typed across the front.

I snatch it from the board and tear it open. Inside is a regular white sheet of paper with a short note printed out in plain Times New Roman.

> *I can't tell you my name. Not yet. Not until*
> *I'm sure I can trust you.*
> *But I know who you are, Calliope.*
> *And I know what happened on November 10,*
> *1993. That's the day Adam was pushed.*

"Holy shit," I breathe.

Nico plucks the paper gently from my fingers to examine it. "Who is Adam?"

"Adam Davenport?" I'm not sure how to explain this without getting into Haunt and Rail territory, but it turns out, my worry is unnecessary.

"I know who Adam Davenport is," Nico says. "The kid who died on campus. I thought he tripped down the stairs."

"He did. Officially."

Nico frowns and hands the note back to me. "This is kind of dark. And it's shady that he knows your name and what you look like, but he won't tell you his name."

"Yeah," I agree. "But he wrote me back. That's the important thing."

And now I need to figure out how to earn his trust.

Twenty minutes later, Nico and I are perched on top of a tall, triangular platform in the middle of the town commons. It is either a public art project people use as a hang-out spot or a public space that looks kind of like an art project. The staircase built into one side is so narrow it almost seems decorative, but we managed to scramble up without spilling our drinks.

"You can see a lot from up here," Nico says. "During the daytime, it's great for people watching."

"I will remember that." I sip at my herbal tea—raspberry this time—from Frances Bean while Nico drinks something tall and frothy that he swears won't keep him awake at night. We have about forty more minutes together until we need to start walking back to campus for dorm check-in.

I am trying to focus on Nico, the debate we are engaged in about the merits of hardcore camping versus car camping versus glamping. We're in agreement that glamping should barely be considered a wilderness activity, but Nico is hung up on the idea of having a vehicle nearby. I am trying hard to listen to his case, I really am, but my thoughts keep wandering back to the envelope tucked inside my bag.

"So you concede?" Nico says when I've been quiet too long. He takes a long sip from his to-go cup.

"Never." I fidget with the clasp holding my bag shut. "First off, most of the best camping spots in the Adirondacks can't even be accessed by car. Hiking in is the only option."

"But day trips!" he protests. "Don't you get bored just hanging out at the campsite? Calliope?"

"Sorry." Without really thinking about what I was doing, I must have opened my bag. The envelope is now pinched between my fingers.

"I should have come up with a better plan for tonight. Sitting on a platform isn't much of a date."

"This is a great date," I insist. "I'm just distracted. It's my bad."

"I get it," Nico says. "Do you want to walk around until we have to go back?"

"Yeah. I'd like that." I drain my tea, and we climb carefully down off the platform, moving backward like we're climbing down a ladder.

Back on Chicory Lane, I steer us away from the bulletin board. Up the street, Jeremiah holds open the door to the Thai restaurant, and Brit steps out and onto the sidewalk, a takeout bag in her hand. He wraps his arm around her shoulders, and they start up the sidewalk toward school. Unlike Akari and Lucas, there is no mistaking that Brit and Jeremiah are a couple. According to Aymée, they have been together since the end of their first year here, which is basically a lifetime. Aymée says they broke up for a while last year, but now, it's hard to believe they were ever apart.

Has she really never told him about Haunt and Rail? I slide my arm hesitantly around Nico's waist, and he returns the gesture. I have already told Nico so much about my family, about my life before I came here. It doesn't seem right that I can't tell him about one of the most important parts of my life right here at Tipton—especially now that it is becoming more and more tangled up with my past. I watch Brit and Jeremiah turn toward campus, then vanish into the darkness, and I wonder how she has kept this secret for so long. If I am as strong as she is. If I want to be.

42

Aymée is distracted during morning assembly. We are supposed to be seated by dorm, but a month into the trimester, those boundaries have begun to fray. She is sitting next to me in the plush seats in Fortin Hall, but her gaze is locked on her phone. When Dr. Naylor announces that afternoon activity period will be canceled, as staff are needed for setup for a donor's reception this evening, Aymée doesn't react.

I nudge her gently with my elbow. "Free afternoon, Ayms. Want to do something?"

Normally I'd welcome the open stretch of time. We are so scheduled at Tipton, so much more that I used to be at home, but today I need to keep busy. Today is Friday, September 23. The sixth anniversary of the accident. The anniversary of Momma's death.

"What?" she asks, eyes flying up from her screen.

"We could go into town," I whisper. "Stop by my aunt's shop." And check the bulletin board—again. It's been almost forty-eight hours since I left my response, but as of yesterday, it was still tacked to the board, untouched.

Aymée twists her lips to the side. She has been asking to meet Aunt Mave, and I know she'd give us tons of samples if we stopped in. But Aymée says, "I don't think so." She doesn't even make an excuse.

At lunch, Aymée is nowhere to be found. Nico is eating with the soccer team today, so I sit with Clarice for a change. It is nice to catch up, to hear about her weekend plans, a trip home to the city to see her parents and her boyfriend, but now I am the distracted one. Where is Aymée? Is she avoiding me?

After history with Mr. Wheeler, I make a beeline for Lynd, the large girl's dorm where Aymée lives. I stop to say hi to Prisha, who is sitting on the lawn out front with a fat science text. She gives me a polite hello, then resumes reading. At home, I saw every person in my school every single day. There were only forty-six of us across all four grades. Here, it is so much bigger. There are people I met during orientation who have now faded into the background of my world. I feel like I've done something wrong, but maybe that's just the way things are at boarding school.

I take the stairs to the third floor, then knock on Aymée's door. No answer. I sit down on the carpet, back pressed against her closed door, and wait. In the room next to Aymée's, someone is having a party. Music blares, and I can hear people jumping around and dancing. When Aymée has still not appeared ten minutes later, I start to get antsy. Someone pokes their head out of the door to the party room and asks if I've seen Elsbeth. I don't know an Elsbeth. I say sorry.

Another five minutes pass; then my patience is rewarded.

Aymée emerges from the stairwell, and I shove myself to my feet.

"Are you mad at me?" I ask. I am not capable of letting things go. I do not know if this is my best quality or my worst.

"What? No." Aymée looks up and down the hall, as if someone might be there, watching us. She unlocks her door in a hurry, then pulls me inside.

In a minute, her door is firmly closed again and we are both sitting on her bed.

"This is a hard day for me," I tell her. "With the anniversary and everything. I'm sorry if I'm being oversensitive."

"No, I'm sorry." Aymée looks miserable. "You told me last week, and I forgot. I've had my own things going on, but it's no excuse. I'm a bad friend."

"You're not," I say, and I mean it. "But you are being weird. What's up?"

Aymée lets out a long, rasping sigh that wants to turn into tears. She swipes at her eyes. "It's Haunt and Rail," she whispers, although no one could possibly hear us above her neighbor's thumping bass. "The new campaign."

I have had so much on my mind—New Paltz, Nico, Adam Davenport, the envelopes, the anniversary—that I had almost forgotten that Aymée was one of the two dissenting votes against Lee's proposal. I am not sure if we are supposed to talk about society business outside our meetings, but no one has said it's forbidden. Besides, who would know?

"You didn't raise your hand," I say. "Do you want to talk about it?"

Aymée sniffs. "It's just . . . I've never liked English before; it's always been my hardest subject. I'm math and computer science. Numbers make sense. Books do not. But Mr. Ellis takes the time to go over stuff with me outside class. I'm actually doing well this year, and it's because of him. He's a really good teacher."

"I know," I say quietly. "I think he's a good teacher too." There's a reason Mr. Ellis has won all those teaching awards Lee mentioned, why he's so well-liked at Tipton.

"But you voted for the campaign," Aymée says.

"Do you think it's possible to be a good teacher, but a bad person?" I ask.

Aymée presses her lips together. "I don't know. I know we're supposed to believe survivors, but I don't want what Lee said to be true. And I don't want to do anything to hurt Mr. Ellis."

"Ayms, we're not going to hurt him! Just expose the truth about him. He's the one hurting people, and if we don't do something, he's not going to stop."

"*If* he's guilty." Aymée's eyes flash. "We don't even know who Lee's co-chair is—the person Mr. Ellis is supposed to have harassed. We're going based on what a mystery person in Haunt and Rail told Lee. It's secondhand gossip, and we're supposed to just accept it as gospel?"

"Okay." She has a point. I squeeze my eyes shut and try to make sense of everything. "You're not wrong. I hadn't looked at it that way. But here's what I'm thinking: I trust Lee. And Lee must trust whoever told her, who must have a good reason for staying anonymous. I don't know why Lee, or anyone in Haunt and Rail, would lie to us about this."

Aymée pulls her knees into her chest. She looks very small. "I still don't want to vote yes."

"It's a democracy, right? You don't have to."

"It's not." Aymée reaches for her phone, then holds it out to me. "Not really."

A vote against the new proposal
is a vote against the sisterhood.
Do you hate women, Aymée?
Don't let us down. DELETE THIS
MSG
—YFG

"This is just the latest one," she says. "I already deleted the others."

"So I guess Lee's co-chair is female," I say. "I think I assumed that, but I wasn't sure."

"So what?" she mumbles.

"Sorry, not the point." I hand Aymée's phone back to her. "Do you know who's sending these?"

She shrugs. "Who sends any of the messages? The seniors, but I don't know who."

"This isn't right. I'm going to find—"

"Don't." Aymée cuts me off, voice trembling. "You can't tell anyone I told you about this." She grasps at my wrist, eyes wide.

"I could just ask who usually sends the texts, something vague."

Aymée shakes her head violently back and forth. Her black curls whip against her cheeks. "They know we're friends. It'll be obvious why you're asking."

I slip my free thumb between my teeth, bite down.

"You have to promise me, Calliope. I shouldn't have said anything." She squeezes my wrist, hard.

"I promise." I extract my wrist gently from Aymée's grasp. "I won't say a word."

"Okay." She wraps her arms around her knees again and rests her back against the wall.

"What are you going to do on Monday?"

She shakes her head again, softly this time. "I don't know."

43

They are sitting on the back porch this time, Serafina and Lorelei on the swing Dad built; Dad in the Adirondack chair. The tripod must be set up at the base of the porch steps, because Dad's phone is tilted at an angle. They are bottom heavy; bowling pin people.

"This is strange. Not being there with you."

"Maybe I should have asked you to come home for the weekend," Dad says. His face is a cloud, heavy with gathered rain. "I thought it might be too soon."

"A month is a really long time," Serafina says.

I frown. "I didn't think of it until this morning. I'm not used to this yet—being here, when you're all in your world."

"This *is* your world," Lorelei says. "Don't say that." She gathers her hair, which is the same rusty auburn as my hair, over one shoulder.

"Don't be sour. That's not how I meant it."

Lorelei makes a face at me. I make my face into a mirror.

"No fighting," Dad says. "Not today."

He is right. Of course he is right. We call a silent truce.

"Dad made a collage," Serafina says. "For the living room."

Dad reaches off screen, toward the picnic table, and returns with a large frame filled with family pictures—our mother with each of us as babies; Dad and Momma together, before we were born; Momma and Aunt Mave; all of us at Six Flags, the summer before the accident.

"I meant to do it last year," he says. "For the fifth anniversary. Better late than never."

"Now is perfect," Lorelei says. She reaches out to rest her hand on Dad's shoulder.

My throat is thick with tears. Photo collages were Momma's terrain, not Dad's. She would have drawn us all into it, made it a family project. Dr. Nguyen reminded us over and over that it wasn't any of our responsibilities to replace Momma, who she was to the family. But it's never stopped Dad from trying. It clicks that this is why he has been in the sewing room. He's been going through Momma's photos, building a collage, never asking for our help. Not that I've been around to help anyway. My heart shudders inside my chest, and hot, salty tears streak down my cheeks.

"It's beautiful," I choke out.

"Oh, pumpkin." Dad's face is a raincloud again. He thinks I am crying because I miss her. Because the pictures remind me of the before times, when our family was still whole. And he is not wrong, but it is the other thing too. The truth about what happened that day. The puzzle that seems to worry no one but me, the solution still maddeningly far from my reach.

"Dad made you one too," Lorelei is saying. "We'll bring it on Family Weekend. To hang on your wall."

"Thanks." I swipe at my cheeks, force the tears to stop. "I miss you so much."

And I do. I miss them so much it hurts, a hollow ache in the cavity beneath my ribs. This is true, but it is also true that it is a relief when the call ends, when I am alone in Anders 1D again.

I sit cross-legged on my bed, all the puzzle pieces I can't make fit on my own hovering in the air around me. It's not too late to walk into town, but I've already checked the bulletin board twice today. My second note is still tacked there, unread.

After many discarded drafts, I'd written:

> You want proof? I know you went to Tipton.
> I know you were a ghost. And I know you knew
> my mother. But I haven't told a soul.
>
> I can keep a secret. That's how you know you
> can trust me.
>
> Now tell me your name. Tell me what really
> happened to Adam. And tell me where you were
> at 4:00 p.m. on Friday, September 23, 2016.

I was so sure he would acknowledge the anniversary, respond to my note, but either he's a coward, or I've come on too strong, or he just doesn't care about what he did, if I'm right about all this. The last possibility lands on my chest, presses until all the air rushes out of my lungs, and I'm sobbing again, faced pressed into my pillow.

44

We are hushed hellos and twitchy glances tonight. No one is chatty. No one is hungry. Everyone files into the Den and finds a seat.

Lee leans against the back wall, arms crossed, one foot propped against the brick. The angry ghost glowers behind her. She is beautiful, electric—hard angles and a chiseled glare in the lamplight. Her curls flicker and flare against the gray paint. If I had Lee's skills as a photographer, I'd ask to take her picture.

Lucas joins her, and they bend their heads so they are almost touching. Their whispered conversation is urgent, private.

At ten after one, Lucas pushes away from the wall. "We need to get started."

"Where's Brit?" Akari asks. Nineteen sets of eyes turn toward the closed Den door.

Quinn scowls and rubs at their glasses with their hoodie sleeve. "We can't hold a vote without everyone present."

I am seated in a hard chair at the long table. My eyes stray toward Aymée, who occupies one corner of the couch. She looks relieved.

"Chill," Spencer says. "She'll be here."

We wait in silence. Thirty seconds, sixty. I don't know what to do with my hands, so I shove them beneath my thighs. Ninety. When I left Anders, Brit's door had been closed, dark at the threshold. But she is always out of the dorm before me on Monday nights; I never see her leave. Could perfect Brit have forgotten to set an alarm?

Fifteen more seconds, then the soft click of a door shutting above us, then the quick patter of feet on the stairs. The Den door swings open, and Brit does not look disheveled or out of breath. Her shoulders are perfectly square. Every hair is scraped neatly back from her face. She does not apologize for her lateness.

She nods at Lee. "Let's get started. Together."

Lee's eyes widen, but she smiles. "Okay then."

Tonight, Lee does not hop up on the long table. She stays where she is, back to the wall, while Brit joins her. Side by side, their differences are stark. Brit is almost a full foot taller than Lee. Against the backdrop of the angry ghost, Lee's energy seems to radiate outward, while Brit's is contained, cool, her spine arrowed toward the ceiling. She does not smile.

"As Lee has already shared with all of you," Brit begins, "Mr. Ellis targets students at Tipton. I declined to present last week because I didn't wish to make this about me, and I still don't. But because it has come to my attention that there are some questions circulating about the accuracy of Lee's presentation, I've changed my mind about staying anonymous."

She draws in a deep breath, and her eyes flutter up toward the ceiling. It is the only indication I've ever seen that emotions course beneath Brit's skin, that she is not entirely unflappable.

"This isn't easy to talk about, okay? It's embarrassing. Some of you remember I was a mess for a while last year. I almost dropped out of Tipton, but a few of you convinced me to stay, and I'm grateful for that." She locks eyes with Lee, then Lucas. "Mr. Ellis is a predator. He's sick. He reels you in, then spits you out when he's done with you. I know I'm not the only one, but I don't have proof. If I take this to the administration, it's just my word against his. And you know how that would go." Her eyes shine, but she bats the tears away. I have never seen Brit like this. So vulnerable. So real.

"I can't do this alone," she says. "I need you."

I look across the room to Aymée, who is staring at her hands, folded in her lap.

"Brit didn't want to make this about her," Lee says, "but if that's what it takes to get your vote, then so be it. Everything Brit's talking about went down last year, and we're sure there have been other girls, before that. Now we're a whole month into Upriver. If Mr. Ellis hasn't zeroed in on a new girl yet, he will soon. We need to act now. We need to expose him for the dangerous person he is, keep this from happening again."

"Let's vote." Lucas's voice is flinty, a dare. His eyes flicker across the room, landing on Josh, then Aymée. "All in favor, vote in the affirmative by raising your hand."

My heart bangs in my chest. Twenty hands rise up, and

the room lets out a collective exhale. I smile at Aymée, but she won't meet my eyes.

"Fantastic," Lucas says. His voice is flat, satisfied. "We have ourselves a lark to plan."

"Listen up." Lee claps her hands together and shoves off the wall. "This campaign will probably take more than one lark, so we need you to keep your schedules clear for the next few weeks. Be on campus, be available. Like I said last week, this is going to be a challenge, but I know Haunt and Rail is up to the task. If we had hard evidence, this would be a whole other matter."

"Not that hard evidence is any golden ticket," Spencer says. His voice is bitter, calling up the ghosts of campaign failures past.

"A high school teacher preying on his students is a scandal," Lee says. "Or it should be, but no one's talking. We need to get people talking."

"But I thought . . ." I start to say, then trail off. I don't want to say the wrong thing, cause Brit any more pain. "I thought the problem was, we don't know who the other girls are. And with just Brit . . ."

"Not Brit," Lee says. "Not the victims. *Everyone.*"

A smile spreads across Brit's face. "I believe what Lee is suggesting," she says, "is some good old-fashioned gossip."

45

Tuesday morning descends like a thick, viscous wall I
am supposed to walk through. My head is jammed with
static, and my legs feel like I went swimming with my jeans
on—heavy, dragging. After assembly, navigating the path
from Fortin Hall across Quadrant East to my English class in
Sloane, I trip over my own feet and careen toward the pavement. A hand shoots out and grabs me just above the elbow,
keeps me upright, just in time. Lee.

"You okay there?"

"Just clumsy," I mumble. This is true. Bolan girls have
always been clumsy; narrow ankles and big feet. But truer is
that I have never been so tired.

Lee's lips curve down at the edges. We determine we are
headed in the same direction. She walks with me, rises to her
tiptoes so her mouth is close to my ear. "Power naps. The noc-
turnal schedule takes some getting used to."

"When do you have time?" I whisper back.

"Lunch is an hour fifteen. You don't need that long to eat.
And there's time between afternoon activities and dinner."

"Right." I nod. "Okay."

We are getting close to Tobin and Sloane now. "How are your grades?" Lee asks, voice resuming a regular volume.

"Oh." I wasn't expecting that. "Fine I think?"

She purses her lips together, skeptical. "Find a study buddy. The first trimester is a big adjustment for everyone." Her eyes find mine; lock. By *everyone*, she means all the new ghosts. "You especially, being a transfer. They don't call it Upriver for nothing."

"Yeah. It's a lot," I admit.

She lowers her voice again. "There's mandatory tutoring next trimester if your grades aren't up to par. And don't think we won't ban you from larks until you bring them back up."

How *are* my grades? I got a B on my first unit exam in physics, and Mrs. Stiver seems to like what I've handed in for English. We're midway through the trimester, and most of the major exams are still ahead. I haven't missed any assignments, but I know my classroom participation has left a lot to be desired. I'm just so tired all the time.

"Thanks for the heads-up."

Lee's hand falls squarely on my shoulder. "Just looking out for you, Calliope. I'm serious about the study buddy. Or get a tutor."

I swallow. She is so much smaller than I am, but the weight of her hand is unmistakable. Every part of me believes her threat about being banned from larks.

She tips her head up until her mouth hovers beside my ear again. "Don't fall back on bad habits. Cheating will get you kicked out of Tipton so fast your head will spin. No Tipton, no ghosts."

I flinch. I want to explain that it was *one time*, that I panicked, that Haunt and Rail has nothing to worry about, but Lee is already giving my shoulder a squeeze, reaching for the large glass door at the front of Sloane.

"After you," she says, holding it open. "Your academic future awaits."

After dinner, Nico and I walk up the path through Quadrant West toward Chandler. I left lunch early to take a quick nap back in my room, but I'd barely fallen asleep when my alarm went off and I had to leave for history. Several hours later, I am still dragging.

"Meet me on the theater steps ten minutes before?" he asks.

"Oh." I hook my thumbs through my backpack straps. I lugged it with me so I'd be sure to go straight to the library. "I'm not sure. I have a lot of homework."

Nico places one hand on his chest and takes a step back, his face a picture of mock horror. "You are seriously considering homework over Alyson Effect's fall concert?"

He is playing, but my heart dips anyway. "They don't call it Upriver for nothing," I mumble.

Nico laughs. "I think it's a Henry Hudson reference."

"I mean—"

"No, no, I get it. Do you want company? I have homework I could do."

I whip my head back and forth. "Go to the concert. I'm

going to get a tea—maybe even a coffee—and hit the library. If I finish in time, I'll text you."

Nico smiles. "I'll go with you to Manny's Joint. I could use a coffee myself."

We shift direction, cut across the lawn.

"Subject change," Nico says. "Any response yet?"

He means to my second note. Tomorrow will be a week since I left my reply on the bulletin board, and the silence is killing me. Someone finally picked up my envelope on Saturday, the day after the anniversary of Momma's death, but I've been back to check every day since then and so far, nothing.

"Maybe my version of proof wasn't what he was looking for. His note wasn't very specific. And honestly, he *shouldn't* trust me. Not if he hurt my mother. But I tried."

"What did you write?" Nico asks.

"I think I scared him off. I basically implicated him in my mom's death and said I'd been keeping his secret. What better proof that he can trust me, right? But it came off like a threat. I went too hard."

I leave out the part about saying I know he was a ghost. I can't get into that with Nico, and there's also the possibility that I'm wrong. Maybe he hasn't written back because I'm on the wrong trail, and now he knows it.

I want to tell Nico all of it, but how can I? As far as he's concerned, I barely know about Haunt and Rail. My theory doesn't make any sense without the context that my mother was a ghost. That I am. On the one hand, I am sworn to secrecy, but on the other, a lie by omission is still a lie. The unspoken words sit like a rock on my tongue.

I fiddle with my backpack straps, sure that *I am hiding something from you* is written all across my face, but if Nico notices my discomfort, he doesn't act like it. He is nodding, face serious.

"Maybe he's just taking his time," he says. "I think you'll still hear back. And when you do, if I can help at all, I'm here for you."

"Thank you." I stop fiddling, angle my body toward his. He tilts his head down, and his lips meet mine, a soft brush stroke. A warm rush floods my chest.

"There's something else I've been wanting to ask you," he says as we walk up the steps to Manny's Joint. We push through the door, the winged stallion disappearing overhead, and the typical evening mix of fryer smells and slightly burned coffee hits my nostrils. We weave through the bottleneck of Tiptonians clogging the entrance and head back toward the row of steel urns.

"I'm listening." I grab a large cup and survey my options. Coffee smells so much better than it tastes, and caffeine is not typically my friend, but tonight I really need the jolt. I go for a mix of French vanilla and hazelnut.

"This might be too soon. It's totally too soon. But my mom can't come for Family Weekend, it's the same weekend as her annual conference for work, so she's been on me to pick a time to come home instead." He turns to me, and I nod, waiting to see where this is going.

"I thought . . . well, she'd really like to meet you."

I grin and dump three packets of sugar into my coffee. "You told your mom about me?"

"We're really tight," Nico says. He squirts chocolate sauce into the bottom of his cup, then tops it off with regular brew and four creamers. "And I know it's fast, but I promise she's very cool. She won't make it awkward or anything."

Nico is rambling now—something about fall foliage and train routes and optimal weekends—but my mind is reeling. I've never been to New Hampshire. I want to go with Nico, too soon or not. But Lee's words from last night batter my eardrums, drowning Nico out: *We need you to keep your schedules clear for the next few weeks. Be on campus, be available.* I can't go away right now, not when Haunt and Rail needs me.

"Can I think about it?" I blurt out. I fit a lid on my cup and grab a napkin. "I want to go, I really, really do, but I just need some time—"

"Totally. I get it." Nico stirs his coffee, then blows across the top of the cup.

"It's not too soon," I add. "I'm just barely keeping my head above water right now, with homework and everything."

"Sure, sure." We get in the line to pay, and I dig my Teal Cash card out of my backpack. "I can put her off for a few more days."

"Thanks." I give him a small smile. "I'll try to sort out my schedule."

But part of me knows I am just postponing the inevitable. I can't exactly force Brit and Lee to nail down dates for our larks several weeks in advance. There will be other weekends with Nico, other chances. When I voted for this campaign, I made a promise to Haunt and Rail; more—a promise to every girl at Tipton. It is a promise I fully intend to keep.

46

"You're hiding something." Lorelei's lips quirk into a half smile. She leaves the general store with a jangle of bells, steps out onto the sidewalk. Then she turns, raising a soda to her lips, and behind her, the mountains of Plover Lake are a blur of greens fading to brown in some spots, flaming to red in others.

"I'm not," I insist, but that is a lie. There is Haunt and Rail of course, but the secrets have only sprawled out beneath me like an iceberg beneath its unassuming tip. When I was home, my sister knew every moment of my day, and vice versa. But now, even though we talk often, I find myself carefully choosing the parts of myself to share, the parts to keep hidden. I am being selfish, or maybe I am protecting her from things that might be darker and more unsettling than she can handle, at least until I have proof. Maybe it is both.

Never have I ever kept so many secrets from my sister.

"You are," she says. She presses her soda bottle to her forehead as if it is a receptacle for communiqués from above. "And I'm thinking . . . it's about a boy."

I laugh, relief spilling over. "Busted."

She has not found out about Haunt and Rail. My flailing investigation into Momma's death, my failed attempt to get the man with dark blond hair to trust me. I tilt my head back against the sugar maple and adjust my phone in my grasp. I will not have to lie to my sister's face. But still, I am nervous. I cannot pinpoint why I have been keeping Nico to myself, why I have not told my family when he has told his mom about me. But Lorelei is staring at me expectantly; on this one thing, it is time to come out of hiding.

"It's not a secret exactly, it's just new."

"It's the boy from orientation, isn't it?" Lorelei asks. She sips at her soda again. "The one who butchered your name."

"Good guess. How do you even remember that?"

She taps her temple with the base of the bottle. "Like a steel trap."

"His name is Nico Hale," I tell her. "He's a junior too."

"You owe me pictures," Lorelei says. "I can't believe you've been keeping him from me."

"It's just very new. I didn't want to jinx it." This is not a lie, but it is not wholly the truth. Lorelei is onto me, squints skeptically into the phone.

"You know I've never dated anyone before," I plead. "It feels precarious. Like if I talk about it too much, it might all go away."

"You will be forgiven when I see pictures."

I promise to text her as soon as we are off the phone.

"Can I tell you something?" she asks.

"Always."

"I kissed AJ Kimmler."

"When?" The Kimmlers moved to Plover Lake when AJ was twelve. Three years later, he is still the new kid. I've always thought he was cute, but he is younger than me, Lorelei's year.

My sister twists her lips toward the sky. "Last weekend."

"Now you're the one keeping secrets."

"Maybe I was waiting for you to tell me about Nico."

I ignore her jab. "So is this a thing now?" I ask. "You and AJ?"

She shrugs, a casual gesture that does not seem casual at all. "Maybe. We're going to Reagan's birthday party on Friday."

"Have fun. Don't do anything I wouldn't do." I think about drinking champagne with the ghosts, another small secret buried along with all the bigger ones.

Lorelei frowns, all serious. "How would I know, Calliope? You never tell me anything anymore."

47

Enter your password.

As the fall trimester progresses and you **immerse** yourself in your studies, I want to take this opportunity to remind you of the many campus resources available to meet your academic, social, and spiritual needs.

The message reads:

Ready to give them something to talk about, ghosts? Your meeting location is Brown Rock, 1am. Wear clothes you can get dirty, and don't get caught. DELETE THIS MSG
—YFG

I slip out of bed, slip into my battered jeans and a plain black T-shirt. Outside Anders, I fall into my now-familiar routine: stay off the paths, avoid the lamplight, walk fast. Brit is a few yards ahead of me, blond ponytail catching the moon-light, swishing across her back. I wonder if Jeremiah knows what happened between her and Mr. Ellis last year, if he is the reason they split up for a while. I wonder if Brit is okay, if she will be okay.

If I get up the nerve, I will ask her that last thing. The rest is none of my business.

I keep walking, through the space between the hulking frames of Tobin and Sloane, fingers grazing the brick, over to Quadrant East, then through the trees to the north side of campus. I emerge behind the library. To my right, some-thing skitters through the grass, and I stop short, heart in my throat. *Pulse, pulse.* The thing moves again, then darts up a tree trunk. A fat gray squirrel.

When I arrive at Brown Rock, no one is speaking. To the left, all the lights inside Perry Cottage are dark. Our plan is brilliant, but also dangerous. If Mr. Ellis gets up to grab a glass of water, raises the shades to look out those two northeast-facing windows in his second-floor apartment, we'll be caught.

We all know our jobs; this lark will be conducted in silence. On the grass in front of the boulder, Mira and Kadence, who are both enrolled in visual arts electives, pry lids off paint cans. Kadence's feathery blond hair is pinned up at the nape of her neck, but her bangs still fall across her eyes; Mira's hair spills in light brown waves around her shoulders as she sets her last can aside and reaches toward a tote filled with paintbrushes, probably lifted from Hunt, the studio arts building.

She nods at me and holds out the bag. I grasp it, note her long nails, which are slicked in black polish. Mira has a slightly edgy, perfectly put together look that projects *artist* but also *affluence*. I believe she is the only Pakistani-American student at Tipton, which can't be easy. I tear my eyes away and start digging in the tote—hand rollers for Quinn, Josh, and Wesley, who are going to do the base coat in two layers of gray; brushes with medium bristles for Kadence, who is going to wrap our message around the rock; and smaller brushes for everyone else.

Lee holds up her phone, and for a moment I think we're in for another random check, right here in the middle of campus, but she is telling us to make sure our ringers are on silent. *No vibrate*, she pantomimes, shaking like a leaf. I bite back a grin.

When everyone has double-checked their settings, she nods to Lucas, and he begins sending texts. My eyes find Aymée's in the darkness. *Lucas has access to the message app.*

Quinn, Josh, and Wesley get to work on the first layer of gray, covering up the autumnal motif. Akari grabs a sponge and touches up spots their rollers miss. When my text arrives, I enter the password, then stare down at the list of names, all pulled from Mr. Ellis's class rosters over his six years at Tipton. He has taught a lot of students in that time, primarily for eleventh and twelfth grade English and creative writing electives.

Saadiqa

Summer

Lauren

Tara

Megan

Shayne

Chantal

Charity

Wynn

Lisa

Jasmine

Jillana

Tipton girls, past and present. Now that I am staring at my list, all those names illuminated on my phone screen, my stomach tightens. We will be painting first names only—not just victims, all the girls. Most aren't even at Tipton anymore. And as Lee and Brit contended when planning this lark, including everyone's names means not singling anyone out. It is simply a record of every girl he has taught, accessible to anyone with the right permissions on Tipton Teal. Which should be limited to administrators, but that is where Wesley's student job in the dean's office came in. Every ghost has a role.

It made perfect sense at the time, back in the Den Monday night, but now, looking down at all those letters dancing across my screen, I'm not so sure. Painting someone else's name, deciding for them, is starting to feel a little like an invasion of privacy. A little like taking a choice away from these girls instead of giving them a voice.

My eyes rove across the faces around me. Everyone looks excited, amped up. Fingers tap against brushes, against phone screens. At 1:25, Lee signals for us to bring everything with us and follow her down into the Den. We'll wait out the security rounds inside while the base layer of paint dries, then come back out to do the more detailed work.

As we shuffle down the stairs, file into the Den, no one looks like they are having second thoughts. I tell myself it's nerves, the straight shot from Mr. Ellis's kitchen to our handiwork, and squeeze my eyes shut. I remind myself why I am doing this, why we came out here tonight: To expose the truth about Mr. Ellis. To keep him from preying on any more girls. That is the main thing.

When the coast is clear, we file back outside. The rock is deemed dry enough for Kadence to get to work, then the rest of us. With so many ghosts painting, the last stretch of our lark goes quickly. When we are finished, Akari squats down, paints the angry ghost on the side of the rock directly facing Mr. Ellis's kitchen windows. We stand back, admire our work. A sea of names fills every inch of the seven-foot boulder, impossible to ignore. Then we gather paint cans and brushes in silence, and when there is no evidence left behind, we scatter back to our dorms.

48

Gossip flares with the sunrise. Friday morning brings a flurry of pilgrimages to Brown Rock, photos, texts. Our warning passed from Tiptonian to Tiptonian in a highly functional game of telephone, the message unchanged: *Don't stand so close to me, Mr. Ellis*, surrounded by hundreds of names and one angry ghost. Snatches of that Police song hummed between classes, in Rhine, on the theater steps, the speaker flipped in our demonstration—the demand on the girls' lips this time.

"Don't stand so close to me, Mr. Ellis."

Not everyone is thrilled about the lark. Our paint job includes the names of current students as well as alum, and I hear more than one grumble—*this has nothing to do with me; what right do they have to drag me into this*—on the path between classes. Lee snags my arm on the way to lunch, says ignore them, people will simmer down soon. I say sure, but I get how they feel. Aymée's name is up there. My name is too.

Friday afternoon, at Dean Sadler's instruction, I troop over to Brown Rock with the rest of student government. By the end of afternoon activity period, it is an autumnal mural again, not quite as detailed as before. My eyes stray to Akari's again and again. We paint in silence.

The weekend comes. Whispers fade into football, homework, apple picking.

Now, we are gathered in the Den, debriefing. Aymée and I share a beanbag chair again. She picks at her nails.

"They're nervous," Lee says. She is sitting on the long table, fingers tapping against the wood. "Dean Hiland called an all-faculty meeting for Thursday afternoon. We need to get in there."

"I wish," Wesley says. "They lock those meetings down, even under normal circumstances."

Lee frowns. "Quinn?"

Quinn shifts around in their beanbag. "Not much I can do. We don't need a key to access the conference room, we're just not allowed to be there."

"There's an A/V closet," Wesley offers. "I could hide in there?"

Lee's face lights up, but Brit stands, and the room falls silent. She folds her arms across her chest.

"No need." Her voice is crisp and even. "They'll chastise him at best, give him the benefit of the doubt at worst. There's no way that meeting leads to Mr. Ellis's dismissal, so who cares what exactly is said."

"This is what we do," Lee cuts in. "*Haunt* and rail."

"We already know everything we need to know about Ellis," Brit counters. "Our smartest move is to assume we haven't succeeded yet and start planning the next lark."

Lee looks ready to protest again, but Kadence speaks up.

"She's right. We'd all love to be a fly on the wall, but unless anyone knows how to bug a room, it's not worth the risk."

"Spencer?" Lee asks. "Aymée?"

"Yeah, we don't have access to spy equipment in engineering," Spencer says, palms turned up toward the ceiling. "Sorry, Lee."

Aymée looks up from her nails. Her jeans are a mess of flaked pink polish. "In theory, I can remotely turn on someone's laptop camera. Record the meeting. But I'd need access—"

"Thank you," Brit cuts her off, "but fuck this faculty meeting. We have nothing to gain from eavesdropping aside from satisfying our own curiosity." She tilts her head to the side, thinking. "How good are your hacking skills, Aymée?"

"It's why I'm here, right?" she says.

"We can neither confirm nor deny," Lucas deadpans from the couch, where he is lying on his back, feet kicked up on the back cushions.

"We got people talking, but now we need a new plan," Brit says. "Something that goes beyond gossip this time."

"What we need is action from the faculty," Lee says.

"Let's take a beat." Lucas swings his legs down and sits up. He leans forward, fingertips steepled together. "Brit's right; Ellis isn't going to get fired, not yet. But let's wait a couple days, see what goes down after that meeting. Take some time to plan our next move."

"What exactly does it take to get someone fired?" I ask.

For a moment, the Den is silent.

"We've laid the groundwork," Lucas says finally. "He's

on everyone's radar now—students, faculty, admin. Whether they believe it or not. But now we need proof."

"And for that," Brit says, "we're going to need Aymée."

Her head jerks up, and my stomach twists. They wouldn't use the fact that Aymée is friendly with Mr. Ellis. . . .

"We need to talk hacking," Brit continues, and I breathe again. Of course that's why they need Aymée.

Lee claps her hands together. "Meeting dismissed. Aymée, meet with Brit and me in my room after dinner tomorrow? We need to know what you can do."

49

After dinner on Thursday, Nico says he will walk with me to the student government meeting. I slide my hand into his as the shadows of Tobin and Sloane swallow us and we emerge onto Quadrant East. It's getting dark so early now. At not quite seven thirty, the walk to Fortin Hall is 80 percent lamplight and 20 percent deep blue daylight fading to black.

"What happens after all-faculty meetings?" I ask. "Do we get to hear what they talked about?"

The faculty convened in Brisbane a few hours ago, following afternoon classes. Since then, I've been on alert, but there's been no word from the ghosts, no announcements flashed across Tipton Teal.

"Not really. Sometimes, if they voted on a new hire or if there's a new policy that will impact students, there'll be something in the daily email about it. But it's not like they circulate the meeting minutes to students."

"Right." Of course not. I don't know what I'd been expecting, but now that the meeting is over, I feel deflated. This is why Lee was so set on getting someone in the room.

Haunt and Rail got this conversation going; it feels like we have a right to know what was said, even if Mr. Ellis just got a warning. Even if his colleagues came to his defense, allowed him to laugh it off. But of course we don't have a right. That's not how it works.

That's why Haunt and Rail exists. To even out the imbalance of power. To set wrongs right. A surge of something I can't quite name zips through me. Pride spiked with a kind of righteous outrage. I am a part of this.

"You have him for writing," Nico says. "What do you think about Mr. Ellis?"

We are walking past the theater now. A group of Tiptonians on rehearsal break sits on the steps, hunched into sweaters and scarves. Two boys break into an impromptu interpretive dance, and everyone cheers them on.

"I love his class, and he's always so friendly. Not in a creepy way, just kind and encouraging. But Creative Writing has been weird this week—he's been standing up at the teaching station instead of sitting around the seminar table with us, and he's jumpy. On edge. I feel bad for him, kind of? But then I feel bad for feeling bad. Ultimately, it doesn't matter what I think. We should believe survivors."

"Sure, agreed. One hundred percent. But what survivors? All we have to go on is dozens of names on a rock. Your name was up there, and you just said he's never been creepy to you."

"Right. I mean, if he was doing whatever he's doing with most of his students, I'm sure he would have been reported a long time ago."

"If Mr. Ellis did something to any of his students, Tipton should fire his ass. No question. But what did he do?" Nico gently releases my hand and shoves both of his into his pockets. "The song lyrics, the girls names on the rock. I buy that he did something sketchy, but what exactly is he being accused of?"

I open my mouth, about to protest, then close it again. He's right. Not only do we have no evidence, we don't have a specific accusation. Our lark alluded to something inappropriate going down between Mr. Ellis and his female students, but that's where it stopped. The ghosts got to hear an account from Brit, but no one else did. If anything is going to come of Haunt and Rail's campaign, we're going to need to get a lot more specific next time. But how can we without putting Brit in the spotlight?

"Subject change," Nico says when I've been silent too long. We stop in front of Fortin; I am a few minutes early for student gov. "I don't mean to pressure you or anything, but I was wondering if you'd been able to look at your schedule at all? Mom is really feeling the Family Weekend FOMO, and I want to give her some dates. Maybe the weekend after?"

"Oh." Shit. Mentally, I decided I couldn't go to New Hampshire with Nico almost as soon as he asked. Not with the next lark still up in the air, not when the ghosts need me here. But I never said anything to Nico. I've kept him hanging for over a week. "I'm really sorry. I'm still struggling to keep up with my classes, and with my family coming to visit, I already feel like I'm losing time."

"I totally get it." His voice is bright, but his face flickers with disappointment. I feel terrible. I don't know what to do with all the disconnected parts of me, how to find a balance.

"You should pick a weekend that works for you," I say. "But maybe next trimester, ask me again?"

"For sure. You need to keep your grades up. There will be other opportunities for Mom to smother you with affection and apple crumble."

"Thanks for understanding." Even that is a lie; how can Nico understand what I haven't been able to tell him? I dig the toe of my boot into the dirt.

"There's actually something I wanted to tell you," I offer. I drop my voice, make sure no one else is within earshot. "I went into town before dinner. And there was an envelope, finally. On the bulletin board."

Nico's eyes pop. "How are you just mentioning this now?"

"I know, I'm sorry. I wanted to say something the second we were alone, but we started talking about Mr. Ellis."

"So what did he write?" Nico asks, impatient.

"Basically, he said to stop digging."

The actual message had been a little more detailed than that, but after two weeks of waiting for a response to all my questions, what I got was a giant letdown.

> *I'm sorry for your loss, Calliope. But grave digging does more harm than good. You should really let it lie.*
>
> *You've got me thinking about Adam though. A fitting death for one of Tipton's worst specimens. Your mother was a good person. But*

whatever happened to Adam, don't you think
Tipton is a better place without him?

I want to show the note to Nico, but I've already kept part of this exchange from him. I'm not sure how to explain why this conversation is still circling around Adam Davenport. And I'm mad at myself too—I asked too many questions, opened the door for the man with dark blond hair to sidestep the most important thing. My mother.

Nico scowls. "So he wants you to stop writing to him?"

"He wants me to stop searching for answers about my mother's death. Which means he has something to hide."

Akari brushes by me, then Clarice, who promises to save me a seat. It's almost time to go inside.

"Talk more later?" I ask.

Nico nods. Then he pulls out his phone, taps open an app. "Before you go. When I first saw the picture, I thought for a second this was you."

I peer at his screen. *New friend request from Lorelei Bolan.* "Ah. My sister."

"Figured that out as soon as I read the name. I just wanted to check with you before I accept? I mean, we're not even friends on here."

I laugh. "I'm barely online. But yeah, of course you should accept, if you want to. She just wants to get to know you." And check up on me, no doubt.

If I was dating someone from home, Lorelei would know him already. She would know every little thing about him from whatever gross thing he did in kindergarten right on up to the present. I'm the one who has been secretive. Lorelei feels left out.

I resolve to be a better sister. I am glad Family Weekend is coming up, that in a week, they will all be here. I will make it up to her then.

50

"I need a sounding board. Before the meeting tonight."

Aymée and I are sitting on the far bank of Yardley Pond, splashing pebbles into the water and nibbling sandwiches from Manny's Joint. The tops of the buildings on the west side of campus are just visible from here—Rhine, the Preston Music Building, and Hadley, Quinn's dorm. There's no one else around.

Afternoon classes will be starting soon, and Aymée has spent the last half hour dancing around the point of this clandestine lunch. I give her an encouraging nod.

She draws in a deep breath. "So on Friday, I finally got a few minutes alone with Mr. Ellis's tablet. I've seen him using it around campus, but he always keeps it in his bag during class. But on Friday, I knew he had a PowerPoint planned, so I snuck into the room early and scrambled all the wires on the teaching station. When he couldn't get the classroom computer to work, he hooked his tablet up to the projector."

"Smart."

"Thanks. After class, I stayed for help like usual, and when it was just Mr. Ellis and me in the classroom, Spencer called him with a credit card fraud alert. We were able to make it look like the call was coming from a one-eight-hundred number and everything."

"This is some *Mission Impossible* shit."

"Hardly, but thanks." Aymée grins. "Anyway, when Mr. Ellis stepped out of the classroom to deal with it, I took a peek at his tablet."

Her face darkens again. She hurls a rock the size of her fist into the pond, and the surface shatters into a million ripples.

"I'm guessing you found something."

"I wish I hadn't. But I found two things. First, Mr. Ellis watches teen porn on his tablet."

"Gross."

"Very. I captured some links. And I looked at his messages. I don't know who his contacts are—he has them saved under fake names—but he's been chatting with someone called Rainy Day as frequently as this week. Sexy messages."

"You took screen shots."

"Of their whole message history. I texted them to myself from his tablet, then deleted the evidence."

"Is she for sure one of his students?"

"That's the thing. It's definitely someone at Tipton. There were references to places on campus. But what if he's dating a teacher? Or someone on staff? The texts looked like they were written by someone our age, but that's not exactly ironclad proof."

"Can you look up Rainy Day's number?"

Aymée scowls. "I don't have it. If I'd had more time, I

could have drilled into his contact info, but I only had a few seconds to take screen shots and get out of there. Here's the other thing, though. The screen shots I sent myself? They came in from a number I didn't recognize. It's not the same as Mr. Ellis's cell phone. He's using a second number."

"Right. Because clearly don't use your regular phone to send sexy texts to your students." Aymée and I both scrunch up our faces. "Can you prove the tablet number is registered to him?"

"I think so. I have to do some investigating."

"Then what?" I ask.

"Brit and Lee think what I got is enough to take him down. They want us to use it, but I don't know. If we had messages Brit could confirm were between her and Mr. Ellis, I'd feel more comfortable about using them to put him on blast, but Brit says she never texted with him. So Rainy Day is all we've got."

"And the porn. That's a giant red flag."

"True. I mean, I believe Brit, okay? I like Mr. Ellis, and I didn't want to do this at first, but I believe he's a predator. I'm not trying to protect him, I just don't feel great about using something we can't totally verify to expose him. It's not smart." Aymée's voice drops, even though there's no one around. "This is personal for Brit. She's not thinking clearly, and Lee's stoking the flames."

"So worst case scenario," I propose. "What could happen?"

"Easy. Let's say the Rainy Day texts *are* with a teacher, or any adult. She comes forward to identify herself, and our whole campaign is destroyed. Not only that, but everyone's on Mr. Ellis's side after that. He basically gets a free pass."

I crumple up my sandwich wrapper and stuff it in our trash bag. "I don't know, Ayms. If he was messaging someone age-appropriate, why save her contact under an alias? Why use a second number?"

"You're right. But I still have a bad feeling about all of this."

Aymée needs time. Another chance with Mr. Ellis's tablet. Airtight evidence. And I am going to help her stall.

Before tonight's meeting can really get started, before we dive into planning the second Mr. Ellis lark, I shift around in my seat and clear my throat. Josh tosses Colin a tube of Pringles. Mira compliments Akari's new cherry-red bangs. No one is paying attention.

I eye the long table. If I'm doing this, I'm doing this.

"Um, hey, everyone?" I clamber up onto the table and turn around. Nineteen sets of eyes lock on me. For better or worse, I have their attention now. "I wanted to propose something. A new campaign?"

Lucas leans forward on the couch, fingertips steepled like he does when he's deep in thought. "Good initiative, Calliope, but I think we have our hands full."

"I know. But hear me out. You wanted me on student gov for a reason, right? And I have something."

Lucas settles back on the couch again, hands falling to his knees. "Point taken. Proceed."

"I know we have a lot going on," I start. "But while we're planning the next Mr. Ellis lark, there's something else that deserves our focus. And I don't want it to fall by the wayside."

This speech isn't quite impromptu, I've had a few hours to plan, but nonetheless my stomach is a jumble of knots. Public speaking isn't exactly my thing. But if I don't do something, Haunt and Rail is going to move forward with this half-baked lark. And Aymée has already put her commitment in question by voting no the first time around. If she tries to divert the group's focus, it'll look way too suspicious. So it's on me to buy her the time she needs.

"At yesterday's student government meeting," I begin, "we heard guest speakers representing Tipton's student athletes. In brief, the budget for girls' sports is only two thirds the budget for the boys' teams. Part of that money comes from the Student Activities fund, and that's divided equally, but most of the funding comes from a budget line voted on each year by the board of trustees. A decade ago, there were several more boys' teams at Tipton. That hasn't been the case in years, but the budget has stayed the same. This is just blatant sexism."

"She's right." My heart lifts—Kadence plays field hockey, and she's not the only student athlete among the ghosts. I picked this proposal because it *is* really unfair. But also because maybe, my plan will actually work.

"The girls' program is stretched way too thin," Kadence says. "A few of the captains actually presented at a board meeting last spring, and it seemed like such a cut and dried argument, but the budget didn't change."

"Last night," I continue, "the student athletes came together to ask student government to shift our funding one hundred percent to the girls' program. It wouldn't even things out, but it would make some difference. There will be a vote at the next meeting—but I don't think this is the solution. If anything, it incentivizes the board to maintain the status quo. And like Kadence said, there was already a presentation to the board last spring. The official channels have stalled out. I move that Haunt and Rail get involved."

"Question," Spencer says. "What's the timing on this? I mean, the budget for this year is already set. When does the board vote on next year's budget?"

I swipe my palms against my jeans. "Not until spring. But student government votes in less than two weeks. If student gov adopts the athletes' proposal, the board can use that as an excuse to not make any changes when they meet in a few months."

Akari taps two fingers against her lips. "It's a catch-22, isn't it? If we vote yes in student gov, the board will say the problem is already solved. But if we vote no, it sends the signal that even the students don't support equal funding. Damned if we do, damned if we don't."

I beam. "Exactly. Haunt and Rail needs to get ahead of the student government vote, expose the dilemma, and demand the board take this seriously in the spring."

"No shade to student athletes," Lee says, "but we've tried to run two simultaneous campaigns before, and it sucks, to put it lightly. Everyone remember High Bluff last year? It's not like the campaign we've already committed to is a cake walk. Do we really think we can juggle this too?"

There are murmurs of agreement, and my heart starts

to pick up speed. I can't lose them. "We can walk and chew gum, right?" My voice is pitched high, brimming with nerves I'm fighting to hide. "We focus on this for a week or so while we gather more evidence against Mr. Ellis, then we're back to the first campaign, full stop. We're ghosts, right? We can handle it."

The Den is an explosion of noise, and that's not good. I can only make out scraps of what people are saying, but this sounds like bickering, not unanimous agreement.

"Let's vote," Lucas says, and the room falls silent. "Anyone want to second Calliope's proposal that we run a campaign in support of equal funding for the student athletics programs simultaneous to the Ellis campaign?"

"Seconded," Kadence says, and I flash her a smile.

"All in favor?" Lucas asks.

My eyes skate around the room. Eight hands lift into the air, nine including my own. All juniors.

Just like that, it's over. My proposal is dead.

51

They arrive on Friday afternoon, just as classes are ending—Dad, Lorelei, and Serafina. Activity and club periods are canceled for Family Weekend, so at three o'clock, I walk over to the visitor's lot to meet them.

It is the middle of the month, campus a blaze of fall color. We join the other families snapping photos under the sugar maple, its brilliant coppers and rusts. Dad thinks that Momma lived in Carrington when she was at Tipton. In the nineties, long before it was an all-gender dorm, Carrington was one of the smaller girls' dorms. Dad says he doesn't know what specific rooms were hers, so we sit in the common area for a while, the three of us imagining her here.

"I bet she had one of those canopy beds," Lorelei says.

"And pink sheets," Serafina adds.

"That's not far off," Dad says. "Your grandparents replaced all the school-issued furniture with a bedroom set from Bergdorf's."

"No way." I laugh. *"Bergdorf's?"*

Dad laughs too. "Your grandparents are something else.

Only the best for their daughters. According to your mom, when she graduated, the furniture was passed to your aunt. It's probably still in her house."

Serafina wants a backstage tour of the theater, so we leave Carrington behind and troop over to Quadrant East. I take them into the scene shop where I have been building sets and painting backdrops. When we're through, Lorelei wants to explore the library; her interests have moved underwater, from bees to octopuses.

"Octopus can be pluralized in three ways," she tells me as we step through the Henry Hudson Library's main doors. "*Octopi* is from the Latin because octopus is a Latinate word; *octopuses* is the English way; and the rarer *octopodes* comes from the Greek." She likes that no one can seem to agree.

We search the catalogue online, and Lorelei is disappointed by the lack of octopus texts in Tipton's collection. "The common octopus only lives for about a year," she says. "Their minds become senile near the end, which might be a kindness of nature. When their time is up, their tentacled bodies sprawl in a final repose across the ocean floor." She sweeps her arms out dramatically, and Serafina giggles.

My mind travels instantly to the accident. Water everywhere. *Momma.* Lorelei has already moved on to describing the rocky crevices where octopuses like to make their dens, and I am jealous of my sister. She can talk about an octopus dying and think only of an octopus dying. I listen until Lorelei runs out of steam and Dad suggests there is more to Tipton than books.

Everyone wants to see my new room.

"Why did you move again?" Lorelei asks. "I thought you liked your roommate."

"I did. I do."

"Are you lonely?" Serafina asks.

"Maybe Calliope doesn't want to make friends," Lorelei says.

"Girls." Dad cuts them off with one word.

The truth is, the secret society I joined had me upgraded to a single so I can break curfew and sneak out.

"Some rooms were open at the start of the trimester," I offer. "Students on exchange programs and stuff. A few of us got moved around." I leave it there, vague and unsatisfactory, tell myself there is nothing I have said that isn't true. Nothing that could be called a lie.

Serafina makes a game of finding herself in the photos from home I have hung around my room, exclaiming that she was such a baby in all of them, even pictures taken only last year. Dad says my copy of the collage he made is in the trunk with the rest of their stuff, and Lorelei points to an empty spot on the wall, next to her painting of our house. "It can go right there. Perfect."

I pack an overnight bag so I can stay with them in the hotel tonight, then we drive into town to check in.

"We're going to have a real sleepover," Serafina says, slipping her hand into my hand as we hoist our bags across the hotel parking lot. "Like we used to at home."

Our house in Plover Lake is a drafty, rambling thing. Lorelei and I shared a bedroom when we were little, but the Bolan girls have all had our own rooms for years. Mine is the largest, a third-floor space with its own bathroom and lots of privacy that Lorelei has threatened to take over while I am at Tipton, but hasn't. On the first Saturday of every month, we'd drag Lorelei's mattress up the stairs, and Serafina would set up her sleeping bag on my floor, and we'd have a sleepover. For years, it has been a Bolan tradition.

"That's right." I give her hand a squeeze. "Two nights in a row, to make up for the sleepover I missed."

We walk into town together. We are going to dinner at Scarpettini's, a family Italian place on a side street off Chicory Lane. Dad insists I bring Nico. He is being kind since neither of Nico's parents are here, but mostly, he wants to meet "this boy" I've been spending time with at Tipton. I shoot Lorelei a glare when he says it. She has been talking to Dad, spilling my secrets.

When we're close to the restaurant, I tell them I need two seconds, that I'll meet them inside. I squeeze Nico's hand, silently apologizing for abandoning him to my family. But I just need to check the bulletin board. I'll be right back.

His last note told me to stop digging, but of course, I won't. I wrote back anyway, and last time I checked, my envelope was still pinned to the bulletin board. But this time, it's gone. Good.

I spin on my heel, head back to Scarpettini's. My focus is clear now, my demand in his hands.

Forget Adam. I'm sorry I asked. I got us off track.

But we have to talk about my mother,
Kathleen Marie Bolan. Or Kathy Callihan, as
you knew her.
    She deserves better than secrets and games.
Her family deserves better. Meet me at 3:00
p.m. on Sunday 10/16 at the platform in the
town commons. Let's talk.

In two days, my family will be gone. In two days, fingers crossed, I will meet the man with dark blond hair face to face.

I arrive at the restaurant along with Aunt Mave and Teya, who hold the door open for me. Dad, Nico, and my sisters are already inside, holding court at the largest booth, a round giant in the corner with a high, sweeping leather back. We join them.

The meal progresses without Dad's usual sullenness or my aunt's glances toward the door, commonplace occurrences when they are together. Tonight, the unnamed tension between them is in hibernation. Dad even engages her in a friendly conversation about the shop, and Aunt Mave recommends a new bleu they've gotten in that she thinks he will like. Maybe my presence in Alyson-on-Hudson has tipped the invisible scales that are never quite even between them. Maybe by leaving, I have restored some kind of balance.

Lorelei spends the majority of the meal craned around me, peppering Nico with questions. She starts off easy. How does he like Tipton? What's his favorite class? Does he miss New Hampshire? But as dinner progresses, my sister's line of inquiry gets increasingly personal. How old was he when his parents split up? How often does he see his dad? Are either of his parents remarried? Has Nico had other girlfriends? How many?

"Lorelei, enough." I prop my elbows on the table, creating a barrier between them. "You're so intense."

"It's fine," Nico insists. He is being too nice. It is not fine.

"Calliope's right." I didn't realize Dad was paying attention. "This isn't twenty questions. Let Nico eat his pizza, okay?"

Dad flashes him a grin. I think he approves. My sister glowers into her water glass.

When thick slabs of tiramisu and plates of crisp cannoli have been placed on the table, my phone pings. I excuse myself and stand in the hallway outside the bathrooms.

Enter your password.

What an absolute pleasure to welcome so **many** of your families to Tipton today for our seventy-fifth annual Family Weekend!

The message reads:

We have a plan, ghosts.
Tomorrow night, 1am. Meet
outside the back entrance to the
library. Take full precautions—
conceal your hair, cover your
face, wear black. And don't get
caught. DELETE THIS MSG
—YFG

52

"Dorm question?" Brit asks. I hover in her doorway on Saturday afternoon while my family takes a campus tour. It's a beat before I absorb the subtext. Brit wants to know if I am coming to her as a prefect or as a ghost.

"Not exactly," I say.

She motions me inside with her chin. "Close the door."

Brit's room is pale yellow and robin's egg blue. Everything is perfectly coordinated, from her laptop case to the curtains to the pencil cup on her desk. She swivels around in her desk chair, but does not invite me to sit on her bed. I hook my thumbs through the tops of my jeans pockets.

"It's about tonight. My family is here. I'm supposed to be staying with them at the hotel."

She tilts her head slightly to the side, perhaps waiting for me to go on. When I don't say anything else, she shrugs. "Get out of it."

My heart begins to beat double time. "I don't think I can. I made a promise to my sisters."

Brit narrows her eyebrows. "You made a promise to the ghosts."

"I know." Sweat begins to collect under my armpits, across the backs of my knees. "And I'm available, literally every night. I'm not going anywhere, I kept my schedule clear. But it's Family Weekend."

"Precisely." She crosses one leg over the other, leans forward. "Four hundred families are here this weekend, Calliope. Nearly half of all the parents at Tipton. Why do you think we've waited all week to make a move?"

"Oh. I thought . . ." I thought maybe they'd listened to Aymée's concerns. That even without my failed proposal stalling the campaign, Haunt and Rail was taking things slow, ensuring we'd get this right.

"The timing is perfect. Tonight's lark will have an enormous reach. The administration won't be able to bury the issue with hundreds of concerned parents tuned in."

"I get it. I hadn't thought about it like that."

Brit stares at me like she's not sure why I'm still in her room. "Well, go," she says. "Hang out with your sisters. But tonight, you're ours."

After their tour, Dad suggests apple picking, and we pile into the car, Lorelei in the passenger's seat, Serafina and me in the back. My sisters are debating the particulars of tonight's hotel sleepover—the movies, the snacks—and my stomach twists. I squeeze my nails into my palms and tell them I have to stay in the dorm.

"If I catch up on reading tonight, I can spend the whole day with you tomorrow," I offer. Even to me, the excuse sounds thin. Clichéd.

"Noooo," Serafina wails.

"We're only here until noon tomorrow," Lorelei protests. "That's hardly the whole day. Can't you do your homework after we leave?"

"Tipton is different." Different from our school at home. Different from what you're used to. "I can't do all my homework in a few hours."

This is not a lie. I am drowning in work, as always. And I will probably spend a couple hours catching up on my reading for English before the lark. But still.

"You can read at the hotel," Serafina says at the same time Lorelei says, "Oh, I'm sorry. I didn't realize a few weeks away from Plover Lake had turned my sister into little miss prep school."

"Lorelei." For the second time in two days, Dad puts my sister in check. "If Calliope has to study tonight, it's fine." He finds my eyes in the rearview. "You can still have dinner with us, right? We'll drop you off on campus after."

"That works." I avoid Serafina's and Lorelei's eyes. I can be a bad sister or I can be a bad ghost. I guess I've made my choice.

53

Breaking into Perry Cottage is easier the second time.
Quinn holds a key card to the scanner, and five of us file
through the main entrance. My hair is pinned up, and I'm
dressed in all black, as instructed. The bandana tied around
my face makes me feel like a bank robber, but it's effective.
Beneath all this, I could be anyone.

Once we're inside, we become real ghosts. Unseen,
unheard. There's an energy coursing through us, a heightening
of the senses. Above us, Mr. Ellis is sleeping. One stumble,
one banged door, and we'll give ourselves away. The best
disguise in the world won't be of any use if he catches us in
the act.

Quinn beckons us toward Mr. Ellis's office and slips a key
from a small kraft paper envelope—a spare borrowed from
their job. Slowly, slowly, they turn the latch. Beneath the
door, a hazy blue light pulses at the threshold, and it hits me
that Mr. Ellis might not be upstairs at all. What if he's a night
owl, working late? I picture him sitting at his desk, hunched
over his computer, revising his novel. His face lit by the blue

computer screen light. If he catches us now, we'll fail, and worse. Would we get suspended? Expelled? I extend a hand toward Quinn's shoulder, but it's too late, they're already pushing the door open.

Silence. I dig my nails into my palms, try to control my breathing. Mr. Ellis's office is lit by a dusty lava lamp, glowing on top of a bookcase. Probably something confiscated from a student's dorm room. I unclench my fists, and my hands twitch against my sides. It's a fire hazard to leave on at night, but that's about to be the least of Mr. Ellis's problems.

We file inside, and Quinn pulls the door shut behind us. Akari reaches into a tote and begins distributing supplies to Josh, Kadence, Quinn, and me. Rolls of tape and printouts of stomach-turning home pages ripped from the browser history on Mr. Ellis's tablet. We get to work papering his office walls.

Our part of the lark is largely performative. As Lee put it, we're decorating Ellis's office to shame and intimidate—we're not slapping up content from just any gross site. Our printouts are from the specific sites he's visited. He'll know we're watching.

Aymée is doing the real work from the safety of the Den, Spencer is keeping watch, and everyone else is scattered around campus, turning on public computers, testing it out. Tomorrow, the login screen on every school machine will display a new background: proof that the second number is registered to Mr. Ellis and screen shots from his message history, all superimposed over the angry ghost.

I work quickly, taping my stack of printouts to the office walls, and make a silent wish that the evidence we have will hold up. The fact that Mr. Ellis registered his second number under his real name was a real coup. Without that puzzle piece, the screen shots Aymée took would be next to meaningless.

But there's still the sticky matter of the identity of Mr. Ellis's contacts. We have no way to prove that Rainy Day is one of his students, just the hope that the combination of a second phone number, the disguised name, and the youthful tone of Rainy Day's replies will all point toward wrongdoing. The evidence doesn't have to be ironclad, it just has to be enough for the school to open an investigation. Maybe other students he has harassed will decide to come forward. Maybe our speculation will transform into hard evidence.

Six phones vibrate in our pockets, but Quinn has theirs out first.

"Shit." Their eyes travel from their phone screen to the window. "Everyone get down."

We drop to the floor, out of sight.

"What's going on?" I whisper.

"Text from Spencer," Quinn says. "Dante's out sick. Security shouldn't be doing rounds yet, but one of the day guards is on the paths now."

We wait, stomachs and cheeks pressed to the scratchy carpet in Mr. Ellis's office, for what feels like an eternity. Finally, another text.

They caught Wesley.

54

"Who is Stephan Ellis?" Dad greets me in front of Anders
Sunday morning with a frown. "He's one of your teachers,
right?"

"Creative Writing." I start walking toward Rhine and
motion for them to follow me. At home, Dad knows every
single teacher at school, but here, he's only put a couple names
to faces around campus this weekend.

"We heard his name at least five times between the visitor's lot and your dorm," Lorelei says. "What'd he do?"

My eyes are lined with sandpaper, and my tongue is
sluggish in my mouth. I want to crawl back in bed, burrow
beneath the covers. But I have to run damage control. Wesley
got caught by security outside Brisbane, where he'd been
testing the lobby computers, but the rest of us still pulled off
the lark. A selection of Mr. Ellis's messages with Rainy Day
are the background to every campus computer this morning.

"There have been some rumors," I say carefully. For the
first time, it hits me that staging our lark on Family Weekend
could have an even more drastic effect than Brit imagined.

Maybe the "enormous reach" she'd mentioned will go beyond visibility. Parents will demand their daughters are removed from Mr. Ellis's classes, start threatening to pull their students—and their students' tuition money—from Tipton.

Is that what they—we—wanted to happen?

"Such as?" Dad prompts, pulling me back to my family, to the path beneath my feet.

"Relationships with students," I say. No point in sugar-coating it. They're going to find out. "There's a group on campus who has been trying to expose him. They want the school to open an investigation."

"Jesus." Dad runs his hand through his hair. "He hasn't tried anything with you, has he? You know you can tell me, if anything happened—"

"No," I assure him. "Seriously, nothing like that. But I believe what the other students are saying."

"I want you out of his class, Calliope. I'm finding one of your deans before we leave."

"Okay," I agree. Maybe I want out of Mr. Ellis's class too, after this. I'm just relieved Dad hasn't said anything about me coming home with them.

Rhine is pure chaos. There's the usual brunch din, times four because of all the families present, but it's more than that. Students are pulling out school-issued laptops, passing them around their tables. And rising above all the other conversations is a refrain, hushed, then biting, electrically charged— *"Mr. Ellis, Mr. Ellis, Mr. Ellis."*

We find four seats at a table in the middle of the room.

Even with the extended brunch hours today, Rhine is at capacity. Dad instantly joins a conversation with the mother of a first-year, whose family is occupying the other half of the table. She talks a mile a minute: Her son graduated from Tipton last year; he had Mr. Ellis two years in a row. Her daughter had been planning to take his creative writing elective next year. She's been trying to get her son on the phone this morning, but he's in college now. On weekends, he's never up before noon.

My head spins. I leave them to their conversation and tug Lorelei and Serafina toward the waffle stations, even though I'm so amped up, I can't imagine eating right now. This doesn't feel like the morning after the Fresh INC lark. Everyone's talking, like before. A response from the school feels inevitable, like before. The taste of almost-victory coats my tongue. But my stomach is in knots. Wesley lied to the guard about why he was out in the middle of the night, of course— something about insomnia and searching for a stronger phone signal. He got sent back to his dorm with a warning, but that was before the school woke up to the lark on full display. Wesley will definitely be questioned, and then what?

"This sounds like Melissa." The girl in front of me is holding her phone out to her friend. It's the login screen; she's zooming in on one of Mr. Ellis's texts with Rainy Day. "Doesn't it? She signs everything xx0, with a zero instead of an oh. Who else does that?"

In unison, their necks crane toward a girl sitting in a back booth with a few Tipton students I don't know well. All seniors, I think, no parents. Which makes sense—Family

Weekend is less of a thing for upperclassmen, whose families have been to campus a bunch of times already. The girl who must be Melissa is laughing at something one of her friends is saying, but I can see her pushing scrambled eggs around her plate. It's hard to tell from across the room, but her smile looks forced.

Of course. Someone was going to be affected by this, personally. I've spent so much time wondering if Rainy Day was really a student here that I forgot what would happen if she was. Sure, the messages are anonymous, but that doesn't mean they're impossible to identify. Someone's very private business just became gossip fodder for every member of the Tipton community. In our attempt to expose Mr. Ellis, we just put one of his victims on blast.

Before I can wonder too hard if the girl in the booth is the real Rainy Day, what she must be going through because of us, two things happen at once: A waffle maker opens up, and a hush falls over Rhine, gradual at first, and then no one is talking. I reach to help Serafina with the jug of batter, and a roomful of heads swivel toward the front of the room, where Dean Sadler is standing beside the check-in station.

He clears his throat, even though he already has our rapt attention.

"Good morning, families. I wasn't planning on interrupting your breakfast, but given the events of the morning, I wanted to put in a few moments with you before our closing reception." Dean Sadler is a short, stocky man in his late forties or early fifties, I'd guess. Older than Dad. He's wearing light-wash jeans with a belt, a button-down shirt, and a jacket, in a stiff attempt at weekend casual.

"At the moment, we don't know any more than you do about the vague, but troubling accusations against our English and Creative Writing teacher, Mr. Stephan Ellis. We do not yet know if there is any truth behind the rumors of misconduct, but I want to assure you that Tipton takes such accusations very seriously, and I have opened an investigation into the matter. We will be looking carefully into Mr. Ellis's behavior, and we will be looking just as carefully into the campus pranks that have suggested possible wrongdoing."

"What's going on?" Serafina whispers, and I lean over to check her waffle's progress.

"A teacher might be in trouble," I whisper back. And I might be too.

"Tipton does not condone these kinds of pranks," Dean Sadler is saying, "but the screen shots shared through our campus computer network this morning suggest that a member or members of our community have more information that could be valuable to us. It is our desire to get to the bottom of this situation as swiftly as possible. Mr. Ellis will be taking two weeks of leave, effective immediately, and in the meantime, we are asking for the person or people who changed the campus network login screen to come forward. If you don't come to us, we will come to you."

I flip Serafina's waffle onto a plate and force my eyes to stay focused on the toppings. They want to rove around the room, land on every ghost eating brunch at Rhine this morning. Haunt and Rail has been drawing attention to itself for years, and the society hasn't been caught yet. But as seasoned as the seniors act, they've only been doing this for a year. And this time, one of us got caught. I squirt a huge dollop of whipped cream on top of Serafina's waffle and wonder if this lark might mean exposure for Mr. Ellis—but also the ghosts.

My family stays for the closing reception in the courtyard behind the theater. We walk into town, and Aunt Mave loads them up with cheese from her shop. We say goodbye. We say we will see each other at the end of the trimester, in four weeks' time. That we will talk much sooner.

When they are gone, I draw in a giant breath. I am relieved to be alone, then I feel horrible for feeling that way. But I am a complete jumble of nerves, and on top of my anxiety about Haunt and Rail, I have somewhere to be. At three o'clock, I am meeting the man with dark blond hair. If he shows.

Nico offers to walk into Alyson-on-Hudson with me, and I am grateful. I picked a public space in broad daylight, but a small voice at the back of my head says maybe asking the man to meet me wasn't such a great idea. If I'm right, if he had something to do with my mother's death, with Adam Davenport's . . . I might be putting myself in danger. But a louder voice says I need to know the truth. I'm going.

When we get to town, I ask Nico to wait for me across the commons. He finds a seat on a bench, keeps his phone out and ready, while I climb up to the top of the platform. Nico was right the other week; this is a prime spot for people watching. I can see the entire commons from here, and I spin in a slow circle, scanning faces. The man with dark blond hair is nowhere.

At 3:05, Aymée walks by with her friend Keana. They don't see me.

At 3:15, two elementary-school boys climb up on the platform and inform me I am now a captive on their space ship. I say fine. I'm not leaving, not giving up.

At 3:25, they get bored. They tell me I am released, and I say okay, I'm staying. They climb down the narrow steps, and I am alone again.

At 3:30, Nico texts me.

I think you've been stood up.

At 3:45, I text him back.

I'm coming down.

"Let's check the bulletin board," Nico suggests when we are together again. He wraps an arm around my shoulders. I lean my head into the curve of his neck.

"Good idea." It's hard to keep the disappointment out of my voice.

I don't expect to find anything, but in the center of the board is a new envelope with my name typed across the front. I tear it down, tear it open.

> *You're not going to find what you're looking for here, Calliope. I have no answers for you. Don't bother responding; I won't write again.*

> *But I would like to thank you. This exchange*
> *has reminded me of something very important.*
> *ACTIONES SECUNDUM FIDEI.*

"What does that mean?" Nico asks. "Is that Latin?"

"I think so," I lie. "I'll have to look it up."

My heart sinks to my shoes. That coward probably saw me waiting for him on the platform. And instead of climbing up to meet me, he left me this spineless send-off. *I won't write again.*

But the note does one useful thing. *Actiones secundum fidei.* Confirmation, once and for all, that the man with dark blond hair was a ghost. If Adam Davenport was murdered, whoever killed him must have believed they were acting according to their convictions. Action follows belief. And if Momma figured it out, threatened to expose what he'd done?

In my mind's eye, the man with dark blond hair reaches across the van from his spot in the passenger's seat, grabs the wheel, and sends us careening into the lake.

55

Enter your password.

I had planned to write this morning **about** the joy of
meeting so many of your families this past weekend, but
I woke yesterday to an unexpected turn of events that I
feel compelled to address first.

The message reads:

Location change for tonight: the
woods beyond Yardley Pond.
Find the tree with the yellow
marker, then follow the path.
Bundle up, ghosts. And don't get
caught. DELETE THIS MSG
—YFG

On my walk past Rhine, past Yardley Pond, out to the
woods, I tell myself everything is going to be fine: Mr. Ellis
is taking a two-week voluntary leave, has moved temporarily

off campus. Tipton Academy is investigating. Our campaign is over; the school will take it from here. All those concerned parents won't let Tipton drop the ball. And if something had gone down with Wesley, I would have heard about it. Maybe the guard believed him.

I tug my coat sleeves over my hands and tuck my chin into my scarf. I am cold because it is cold out. Simple as that.

The tree with the yellow streak of paint is the start of a hiking trail I didn't know existed. Quinn and Mira arrive at the same time, and we shine our phones' flashlight beams on the path until we hear voices. The ghosts are gathered in a small clearing, sitting on the forest floor. The ground is cold; as soon as I sit, I wish I'd brought a blanket.

People are talking, but not about Mr. Ellis. Not about why we're out here instead of tucked into the warm comfort of the Den. I shift my legs under me and try not to freeze. It's pitch black under the canopy of leaves, but a few ghosts have brought flashlights, which they set up in the center of the circle. This feels like the worst version of camping—no fire pit, no tent, no marshmallows.

When everyone has found our spot, Brit and Lee exchange glances.

"Are you going to tell us why we're out here?" Josh asks. He is hunched into a puffy vest, blond hair spilling out around the neck.

"We're here because Wesley was questioned by Dean Sadler this afternoon." She casts a look at Wesley.

"Don't worry," he says. "I stuck to my story. But Sadler's suspicious as hell, and the Den is compromised."

There's an eruption of questions until Brit tells us to shut up. She turns to Aymée. "Walk us through the tech from Saturday night."

"Okay?" Aymée says it like a question. "Wesley gave me the ID and password to use. Only a few admins have access to change the login screen background. Wesley's supervisor in Brisbane is one of them."

"Right," he says. "Staff aren't supposed to hand out their login info to student workers, but Ms. Vance hates updating student records on Tipton Teal. She always asks us to do it."

"'Us' being?" Lee asks.

"Me, Prisha, and Kurt. The Brisbane student workers."

"So you used Ms. Vance's login info?" Brit asks.

"Right," Aymée confirms. "That's how I was able to access the network and change the background."

"Which you did from the Den," Brit says.

Aymée nods.

"A couple of problems." Lee's voice is sharp. "One, the school knows whoever changed the background was logged in under Ms. Vance's account. And they don't suspect Ms. Vance or any of the full-time staff, so they're looking at the student workers. On Saturday night, Prisha was traveling with the volleyball team and Kurt was off campus in his parents' hotel room. But Wesley was caught by security right outside Brisbane."

"That's just bad luck—" Aymée starts to protest.

"Is it?" Brit asks. "Maybe you should have done your research."

"How was I supposed to know Dante would call out sick?"

Aymée snaps. "The new guard changed the round times. You can't pin that on me."

"Maybe not," Brit agrees, "but even if Wesley hadn't been seen, Dean Sadler would have traced Ms. Vance's login to him eventually. We'd still be in this mess because you didn't think this through."

"This never would have happened if Bodie was here," Lucas grumbles.

Aymée whips her head toward him. "Bodie graduated. And you tapped me."

"Which was clearly a mistake," Brit says.

"Maybe so," Aymée quips back.

"*Maybe*," Lee cuts in, shushing everyone else, "you shouldn't have done the lark from the Den. That's problem number two. They've already traced the IP to the library router."

"You told me to use the Den!" Aymée explodes.

"I'm not the techie!" Lee yells back. "It was your job to speak up if that was a bad idea."

"Real question," Spencer cuts in. "Why does it matter that Aymée's login happened in or around the library? The basement doesn't have a separate router as far as I know. Nothing should point to the Den specifically."

Brit scowls. "It matters because they put a padlock on the back door this morning. Our library entrance is out of commission until we get a key." She turns to Quinn.

They look skeptical. "Might take some time. But I'll try."

"And twenty of us entering through the front after hours isn't an option," Brit continues. "Way too visible."

"I'm sorry," Aymée mumbles. "I didn't think—"

"You sure didn't," Lee snarls. "Your lack of thinking cost us our clubhouse, and Wesley's in the hot seat. Because of you, we are very much in danger of being exposed."

"This isn't fair!" The words are out of my mouth before I've thought them through. They sound childish, hanging in the air. Everyone stares at me. "Okay, so Aymée messed up. But she's not the only one who could have looked into Prisha's and Kurt's weekend plans. They're Wesley's co-workers." I cast him a glance, and he drops his gaze to the forest floor. "And if no one thought to confirm it was Dante and Wallace on the night shift like usual, that's on all of us."

A few ghosts start to speak up, either pushing back or agreeing with me, but I'm not done. I talk over them.

"And the IP address thing isn't rocket science. Any one of us should have thought about that too. You can't pin this all on Aymée."

A flood of voices again. Next to me, Mira squeezes my hand, starts to speak up in my defense. Josh nods his head in agreement, but Lee cuts them all off.

"Aymée has been against this campaign from the beginning. This was sabotage."

"What?" Aymée's voice pitches up in surprise. She stumbles to her feet. "That's bullshit."

Brit is on her feet next. She steps close, towers over Aymée. "Sure, there were some other missteps. But you voted no on Lee's proposal. Without a little encouragement, you would have voted no the second time too. And since then, you've questioned the campaign every step of the way."

"Because it was rushed," Aymée spits. Her head is tilted back; she glares up at Brit. "Because I knew something like this could happen, but I went along with it like a good little ghost. *You* fucked this up, Brit. You're too close to this, and you let that get in the way."

"You bitch." Brit's words are like ice.

For a moment, nothing happens. Then Aymée lunges at Brit, shoving her to the ground, and they are a tangle of limbs and snarls. All around me, people gasp, stumble to their feet. Lee clambers on top of Aymée and pulls her off Brit.

"Cool the fuck off," she says. "Both of you."

Aymée scrambles back in the dirt, then shoves herself to her feet. Her hair is a mess of twigs and leaves, but she's fine. Brit stands slowly, then swipes the back of her hand across her mouth. It comes away red, and she grimaces.

"You're out." Lee is glaring at Aymée.

"What?" Aymée gasps.

"You sabotaged the lark, and you just fucking assaulted Brit. You. Are. Out."

"You're twisting everything," Aymée begins to protest, but Spencer steps beside Lee, puts his arm around her shoulders.

"She's right," he says. "Maybe you have a point, maybe we should have slowed our roll with this campaign, thought the lark through more. But you were running tech, Aymée. That's your bad. And attacking another ghost?" He shakes his head back and forth. "You crossed a line."

"Wait." My heart is beating so fast I can hear the blood banging against my eardrums. "Don't we take a vote? Decisions have to be unanimous, right?"

"Consider this an exception." Brit spits onto the leaves at her feet, saliva mixed with blood. "You make the society unsafe for the rest of us, you're out. You have a problem with that, Calliope?"

I do. We all screwed up. Aymée didn't sabotage anything; they're just looking for a scapegoat. But the words are stuck in my throat.

"Save yourself," Aymée sneers when I still haven't said anything. Her face is filled with disappointment. I deserve that.

"I—" I start to say, but I can't finish.

"Key," Lee says. She holds out her hand.

Aymée scowls, but she digs in her pocket and presses her Den key into Lee's open palm. Without a word, she spins around on her heel, grabs a flashlight, and starts walking down the path, toward Yardley Pond. It is only a matter of seconds before the darkness swallows her.

I drag my eyes back to the ragged circle of ghosts. Brit is still staring at me, waiting for my response.

"There's no problem," I say to my feet.

"Good," Brit says, voice smug. She looks around, and eighteen faces stare back, some stunned, some satisfied. She folds her arms across her chest. "In case you've forgotten, being part of Haunt and Rail is a privilege. Want to keep your membership in the society? Don't cross your fellow ghosts."

V
COLLATERAL

56

The temperature spikes back into the low seventies on Wednesday afternoon. All over campus, sunlight glints off treetops, and Tipton glows like a bonfire. Nico is determined to take advantage of one of the last warm days of the season, so we grab lunch at Manny's Joint and camp out on the lawn. Aymée sits across the quad, picking at a salad and scrolling on her phone.

Nico looks back and forth between us, then sighs.

"What's going on with you two this week?"

"Huh?" I whip my head around, pretend I wasn't just staring.

"You and Aymée. You have a fight or something?"

"No." She's pissed because I was a coward. Because I backed down the second Brit tested my limits, and if the situation had been reversed, I know Aymée would have stood up for me. "Nothing like that."

"What then?"

Nico looks genuinely concerned, and I want to tell him everything so badly my chest aches. How Aymée got thrown under the bus for something that was everyone's fault, how we all just stood back and let it happen. How Haunt and Rail is one of the best things that's happened to me at Tipton and also one of the worst. How it's supposed to be democratic, but it isn't. How there isn't supposed to be a leadership structure, but it's clear who's in charge. How any question can be twisted into a breach of loyalty, any mistake into treason.

I want to tell Nico all that and more. How I know the man with dark blond hair was in Haunt and Rail with Momma, how her death might be tied to Adam Davenport's, but I haven't been able to prove it. How now that he's stopped writing to me, I don't know what to do. Everything I was building here at Tipton is crumbling, and I'm crashing with it. I can't stop it from happening—I'm just reaching out on the way down, clawing at air.

But I have no words for any of that.

"Let's talk about something else." I crumple up my napkin and stare at the grass.

"Okay," Nico agrees. "But if you change your mind . . ."

I give him a small smile. "I know where you live."

"So," he says after a minute. "Subject change. Possibly awkward."

I can't imagine anything more awkward than this, all the secrets I am keeping. "Go for it."

"I really loved meeting your family last weekend. They're very cool."

I swallow hard. Nico is going to ask me to come with him to New Hampshire again. And after Monday night, I am on thin ice with the ghosts. I can't leave, not now. I already feel bad for saying no; the thought of having to do it again makes my breath catch in my throat.

"But Lorelei, she's been messaging me. Kind of a lot."

"Oh." My head snaps up. That wasn't at all what I expected.

"And, I mean, it's fine; I think she just wants to get to know me. But I thought you should know."

"Thanks, I had no idea." I start gathering the rest of our trash. "What is she writing you about?"

"All kinds of stuff. She's really into octopi."

"God. Yes, she's always into something."

"But mostly it's questions about the other girls I've dated. Why we broke up. Where I see this relationship going."

My cheeks are flaming now. They match the trees. "I am so embarrassed. You don't have to write her back."

"She's just being a good sister," Nico says. "I think, anyway. She cares about you a lot."

"She could have come to Tipton this year too," I tell him. "She didn't want to. I think a part of her regrets it."

"It's probably FOMO. She misses you."

"I'm sorry. I'll tell her to cool it."

Night, fifteen minutes before lights out. I am hunched over my physics text and about ready to crawl into bed when my phone beeps.

Enter your password.
In the wise words of our guidance **counselor**, Ms.

Nassar, the middle of the week is an excellent time for balance and self-reflection.

The message reads:

Our work isn't done, ghosts. Ellis
was on campus for questioning
this morning, but he'll be back
in the classroom in a week and a
half unless the school nails him
on something. We're laying low
this week and monitoring the
situation. Stand by for further
instructions. DELETE THIS MSG
—YFG

57

Lorelei bombards me with facts: The larger Pacific striped octopus was first documented in the 1970s. A baby in the world of animal classification, the LPSO has no official scientific name, but is known for its intelligence and unusual sociability. Most female octopuses are known to be cannibalistic during mating, the males keeping their distance. Not so among the LPSO, who engage in close, personal mating rituals, coming together beak to beak, embracing in an intimate tangle of sixteen arms.

"We need to talk about Nico," I say, cutting my sister off.

"Any mating practices you'd like to tell me about?" She is sitting on the wall outside the high school, auburn hair tangled in the breeze.

"No." I twist my face into a scowl. "No 'mating.' Not that it's any of your business."

Lorelei presses one palm flat to her chest, feigning horror. "None of my business? I am your sister."

"We need to talk about *boundaries*." I am sitting on the theater steps in the free minutes before afternoon activity period. Soon, I will need to go inside, paint the new backdrop for *Guys and Dolls*. "Nico says you've been messaging him. A lot."

"I have a right to get to know my sister's boyfriend."

"You're interrogating him," I clarify. "Just like at dinner."

Lorelei's face falls. "Did he say that?"

"Not in so many words. He's too polite."

My sister grins. "I think he's a keeper, Calliope."

"Then maybe you could try not to scare him off?"

"I would never."

"Maybe I'll find AJ Kimmler online," I tease. "Start peppering him with questions."

"Don't." Lorelei narrows her eyes at me, all the fun drained from her face.

"You're not still making out?" I ask.

"I didn't say that. We're just not all official like you and Nico."

"Maybe I'll tell him he should make it official." I grin.

"Seriously, Calliope. Just don't."

"Jesus, fine." I hold up my free hand in mock surrender. "I wasn't really going to message him."

"Good."

"You do get the irony?" I ask.

"Not really. This is entirely different."

I sigh. Mr. Cruz walks up the steps, beckons me to follow him into Ashbourne.

"I have to go," I say to Lorelei. "Theater tech."

"Call me later. I miss you."

At dinner, Aymée is sitting with her other friends. Her friends who are not ghosts, are not me. I am reminded that she had an entire life at Tipton before Haunt and Rail, before Calliope Bolan, and it hits me that she is going to be okay.

Shame washes over me. Maybe the world doesn't have to be as small as I have made it. Maybe Aymée is lucky. Maybe now that she is out, she doesn't miss it. Maybe all Aymée feels is relief.

She has been avoiding me all week, or have I been avoiding her? I adjust my grip on my tray and walk over to her table.

"Hey."

She looks up at me like I am a stranger. Blood batters my eardrums, but I am here now. I am not turning back.

"Can I sit?"

"We're almost done," Aymée says. "Maybe some other time."

Even mean Aymée isn't cruel. But her words slice straight through me all the same.

"I'm hanging around for a while." The speaker is Keana, one of Aymée's friends. We're in history together, and once, the three of us walked into town for bubble tea.

"I'm not." Aymée picks up her tray and pushes her chair back. "*Queer Eye* later?" The question is not directed at me. I spot Clarice walking in with a couple student government reps and mumble something to Keana. I can't walk away fast enough.

My cheeks are hot, and tears sting the corners of my eyes.

When I had a choice to make, I chose the ghosts. I should have seen it before, but now it's clear. I can't have both.

Halfway to the front of Rhine, Aymée grabs my arm. The silverware on my tray rattles.

"I get why you did what you did," she whispers, pulling me close. Her voice is hot in my ear. "And I don't blame you. But we can't be friends. Believe me, it's better that way."

Just as quickly, she releases my arm. A hot ring remains where her fingers just were. I watch until she's pushing through the door, until she's gone.

58

Enter your password.

I hope you will join me this **evening** at seven for a screening of our own Jeremiah Whelan's short film, *Deceit and Insurrection*, in the Fortin auditorium.

The message reads:

Your presence is required in
the Den this afternoon at the
start of lunch. Enter through the
front, get a stacks pass from Ms.
Bright. DELETE THIS MSG
—YFG

At twelve thirty, Lee, Wesley, and I slip silently through the door. I am more than a little surprised to see Aymée already seated at the long table with Lucas. Brit is nowhere— nor is anyone else in Haunt and Rail.

"What's going on?" I gravitate toward the chair beside

Aymée, then stop myself and pick a spot on the other side. Her warning from dinner last night is still loud in my ears.

"Everyone find a seat," Lucas says, voice giving nothing away.

"This all of us?" Wesley asks.

"We're keeping this intimate," Lee replies.

When the five of us are seated, Lucas turns to Wesley. "Want to update the room on this morning's events?"

Wesley shifts uncomfortably in his chair. "Yeah, so, they called me back in to meet with Dean Sadler and this guy Rich from IT this morning. Someone sent screen shots of Rainy Day's complete message history with Ellis to Dean Sadler last night. They asked me a bunch of questions about this encrypted email service, and they searched my laptop and phone."

"Shit," Lee says. "Can they do that?"

"They can definitely search our laptops," Lucas says. "School issued."

"My phone was clean," Wesley says. "Believe me, I learned my lesson. They weren't going to find anything on either device, so I let them look. Thought it would look suspicious if I put up a fight."

"Good," Lee says. "You did the right thing."

"Anyway, they seemed satisfied that I didn't send the screen shots to Sadler last night. But they're still suspicious about Saturday. Their working hypothesis seems to be that I provided Ms. Vance's account info to someone else, who used it to change the login screen background. Which isn't off base, but I keep swearing I don't know anything."

"Are they buying it?" I ask.

"Kind of? Getting caught by security is actually working in my favor because I keep reminding them that as her student worker, I already knew Ms. Vance's login info. If I wanted to do something with it, I could have done it from anywhere. Same as Prisha and Kurt. Their evidence—which is basically that I happened to be in the proximity of Brisbane after curfew on Saturday—doesn't actually tie me to anything, and they know it."

My gaze travels between Lee and Lucas. "So why are the screen shots such a big deal? It sounds like Wesley is managing things."

"Agreed." It's the first time Aymée has spoken. "I played nice, I came down to meet you guys. But it seems like you have this little techno thriller under control." She pushes her chair back from the table and starts to stand.

"Hold up." Lee's hand shoots out, clasps Aymée around the wrist. "Please. Have a seat."

Aymée scowls but sits back down.

"They're a big deal," Lucas says, "because they think Wesley's 'accomplice' from Saturday is the same person who contacted Sadler with the screen shots." He glares at Aymée. "And I think they're right."

"That's bull—" Aymée starts to say, but Lee cuts her off.

"Only two people had the screen shots of Rainy Day's complete message history," she says, eyes fixed on Aymée. "You and Brit."

"Then maybe you should talk to Brit," Aymée says through gritted teeth. "Because I sure as hell didn't send anything to Dean Sadler."

"Show me your laptop," Lucas says.

"Seriously?"

Lucas glares until she digs it out of her bag and places it on the table. "Come on, Aymée. Unlock it."

She enters her password, then slides it across to him. "Go wild."

"What's the program?" he asks.

"The IT guy was asking about Hushguard," Wesley says. "It's one of those encrypted email services. Servers in Switzerland, no personal info required on sign-up, basically untraceable."

After a minute, Lucas slides the laptop over to Lee. "It's clean. Nothing on here."

"Of course not," Aymée growls. "I deleted those screen shots. And I don't have a Hushguard account."

"Phone," Lucas says.

"Oh my god." Aymée pulls it out and holds the screen up to her face, unlocking it. "Go ahead. But you're looking at this all wrong. Why would I go rogue now? I'm not putting my ass on the line like that."

"Because maybe you want us to get caught," Lee snarls. "I can think of a couple reasons you might be pissed at the ghosts right now."

"If I wanted you to get caught, I would have made it look like the email came from one of you," Aymée bites back. "Not used some untraceable account. Brit's the one who wasn't satisfied with the last lark. It's been almost a week, and no one's fired Ellis yet. No one's pressing charges. I'm telling you, you're interrogating the wrong girl."

"Also clean." Lucas tosses Aymée's phone back to her.

"Of course it is." Aymée shoves everything back in her bag and stands.

"Because you'd never leave a trail," Lee says.

"Because I didn't *do* anything."

"Well, neither did Brit," Lee says. "She would never endanger the society."

I scan Lee's face, try to get a read. Maybe she is simply set on throwing Aymée under the bus again, but I think she genuinely believes what she's saying.

"You're all fucking brainwashed." Aymée's voice is hollow. She starts toward the door.

Lee ignores Aymée's comment and turns instead to me. "Calliope?"

I swallow. I was entirely fine with never finding out why I was invited to this meeting of the minds.

"You and Aymée are friends."

It's not a question. I look back and forth between them. "We were," I say slowly, because it's true. Because I think it's what Aymée wants me to say. She stops walking and turns back to face me.

"Would you vouch for her?" Lee asks.

"What do you mean?"

"Would you vouch for Aymée? That she's telling the truth?"

My eyes lock with Aymée's. I don't think she is a vindictive person. But Haunt and Rail burned her pretty bad. If I'd gotten kicked out for something that wasn't really my fault, maybe I would want to take everyone else down with me. Maybe I would want to lead the administration straight to the society. Burn it all down. Is that why she told me we couldn't be friends? If she was planning to send those messages to Sadler, maybe she was just trying to keep me in the dark.

"I think," Lucas says dryly, "that Calliope's silence speaks volumes."

"No, wait." I tear my eyes away from Aymée's, turn to face him. I've already let Aymée down once. I won't do it again, let my doubts get the better of me. "She isn't lying. She didn't do this. And you know what happened on Saturday wasn't entirely her fault."

"Don't waste your breath," Aymée says. "They'll believe what they want to believe."

She turns, heel grinding into the Den floor, and lets the door slam behind her.

"You're cruel," I say to all of them. "Anyone can set up an email account. How are you so sure it wasn't Brit?"

"Because I asked her," Lee says. "And unlike Aymée, I trust Brit. She wouldn't lie to me."

"How do we know Aymée didn't share the screen shots with you?" Lucas asks me. "You could have sent them."

I shove back from the table. "Before Saturday, Aymée had more than one friend in Haunt and Rail. Maybe you should ask everyone. And if you want to search my stuff, be my guest. Anders 1D; stop by any time."

I throw open the door and walk out into the stacks. I feel angry and vindicated and very, very alone. I look for Aymée, but she's already gone.

1:45 pm:

Enter your password.

join me this **evening** at seven for

The message reads:

This is your first warning,
Calliope. There won't be a
second. DELETE THIS MSG
—YFG

3:12 pm:

Enter your password.

join me this **evening** at seven for

The message reads:

Aymée Rivas is not the only
person who can set up a
Hushguard account. Check your
school email. DELETE THIS MSG
—YFG

59

Forbidden Love Is in the Air!
Anonymous Cat <kittyanon@hushguard.com>
to tipton-student-listserv

October 21, 3:10 p.m.

Happy Friday, my dears. Turns out "Rainy Day" isn't
the only Tiptonian with a lust for forbidden love. Our
own Aymée Rivas had herself a little tryst with an older
gentleman before joining our elite campus community.
Guess we know why Mommy and Daddy sent her all the
way from Miami to Alyson-on-Hudson.

Coincidence much?

Or perhaps it's no coincidence at all. Maybe Aymée and
Mr. Ellis were keeping their rainy days a secret.

Guess the cat's out of the bag!

Below the note are four photos of a younger Aymée, thirteen or fourteen, with an older teen. He's in high school, probably a senior. He's definitely too old to be dating a middle schooler, but there are at most four years between them. Not nearly fifteen, like Mr. Ellis and his students. In three of the shots, Aymée and the guy are kissing. They clearly have no idea anyone is watching them, taking their picture. In the fourth, Aymée's head is resting on the older guy's shoulder, and the side of his face nestles into her curls.

"Oh my god." I am standing outside Sloane, eyes locked on my phone screen. All around me, students are checking their phones, reading the email. Looking at those pictures.

Aymée's collateral.

I shove my phone into my bag and break out running across the quad, toward Lynd. I run all the way up to the third floor and bang on Aymée's closed door.

"It's Calliope!"

No answer. I press my ear to the wood, listen.

"Aymée, if you're in there, please open up."

I sink down to the carpet, not caring that I'm missing the start of theater tech.

Where are you? I'm outside your room.

I know you're mad at me, but I'm here for you. 🩶

No one's going to think you're
Rainy Day.

You're not Rainy Day, right??

Aymée?

60

On Saturday morning, Aymée is not at brunch. Over potatoes and omelets that I'm barely eating, Nico tries to reassure me.

"She's just laying low this morning. Who wouldn't be?"

I pick at a piece of toast. I tell him I'm sure he's right. "She hasn't answered any of my texts, though. I'm worried."

"It's hasn't even been twenty-four hours since Kittygate."

"Kittygate?"

"That's what people are calling it. It's stupid."

"And cruel. Didn't we all make mistakes before we came to Tipton?"

Nico nods. "Sure. Hell, most of us screwed up this week. But Haunt and Rail has the whole school on high alert with the Mr. Ellis accusations. Any other time, something like this might blow over fast. But not right now."

"She doesn't deserve this. They shouldn't have . . ." I don't know how to finish what I want to say. "Forget it."

Nico stares at me hard.

"What?" I ask.

"The whole school is coming up with theories about who sent that email. Who might have a vendetta against Aymée. Do you know who 'they' are?"

"What?" I splutter. I tear my toast in half. The pieces fall to the plate. "No. I just meant the general 'they.' Whoever did it."

Nico frowns down into his coffee mug. "Okay."

"I don't care who sent it," I insist. "I'm just worried about Aymée."

Aymée who never wanted this campaign to begin with. Aymée who went along with it because she had no choice. The same question that's been on my mind since yesterday rises again to the surface. *Is* she Rainy Day? Maybe Aymée didn't know there were other girls until Brit and Lee laid it all out. But she could have told me. She could have trusted me, but she didn't. My stomach sinks. After everything that's happened, Aymée probably made the right call. I didn't deserve her trust.

I draw in a deep breath. This isn't about me. Whatever the truth is, Aymée did everything the ghosts asked her to do. And they exposed her collateral anyway.

Nico drops his voice. "Listen, Calliope. I don't know if this is Haunt and Rail, but it's on theme, don't you think? If they did this to her, if you're involved with them, you have to tell someone."

"I'm not," I hiss.

"But if you were, you could talk to me."

"I said I'm not." My voice is too icy. I try to make it soft. "Really."

I stare at my still-full plate. My cheeks burn hot.

"Okay," Nico says again. "I believe you."

Tears gather in the corners of my eyes. I don't know if I should feel relieved that he believes me or horrified at what a good liar I've become.

"I can't eat this." I push my tray toward the center of the table. "I'm going to go check on her."

Nico places his hand on top of my hand. "I'll come with you."

I pound my fist against Aymée's door. There's no answer.

"It's Calliope and Nico," I shout, louder than necessary. "I know you're in there." I pound again. My fist stings, and I pound harder.

The door next to Aymée's swings open. Her neighbor is a squinty-eyed senior in Tweety Bird pajamas who was clearly still sleeping.

"Chill," she tells us. She scrapes a hand across her face. "She's not in there."

"Do you know where she is?" Nico asks.

Tweety Bird shrugs. "She was up all night, banging around. She left really early this morning, like five o'clock. I think she went home."

"Home home?" I say. "To Miami?"

"Yeah. She was on the phone a lot. Sounded like she was talking to her parents." Tweety steps back into her room and narrows her door until only a crack of light remains.

"Sorry," she says through the crack. "I don't know anything else." Then the door clicks shut.

61

When I was a kid, I used to love running. Then I joined track in middle school, and I wasn't fast enough or strong enough or coordinated enough. Competing killed everything I loved about running—how for a while, you don't have to think about anything at all. How sometimes, if you're lucky, it feels like flying.

I tell Nico I need some time alone, then I pound down the Lynd stairs and head back to Anders. In five minutes, I've exchanged my boots for sneakers and my jacket for a hoodie, and I'm back outside. I take off down the hill, toward town.

It has been a long time since I've really run. At first, I can't switch off the ache in my lungs, my jumble of thoughts. How Aymée didn't deserve this. How I could so easily be next.

I run until the voices stop, until the ache subsides, until the world shrinks to just my body and the sidewalk in front of me. It's not like flying this time, but it's quiet. It's working.

I run farther down Chicory Lane than I've ever gone before, past the Thai restaurant and the smoothie place and the bulletin board and Frances Bean. I run until the buildings on either side of me are mostly houses with big lawns.

Eventually, the road curves to the right, and I follow it. The buildings change again. Now, the houses are interspersed with blocky gray office buildings and auto shops. To the right is a grocery store with a big orange sign. An SUV is blocking the sidewalk, waiting to pull out into the street, so I jog behind it, into the lot. And that's when I see him, standing beside a gray sedan, chatting with a woman who gives him a wave, then gets into her car. Dark blond hair, square shoulders, ruddy cheeks. The man from the van. He turns and walks toward the entrance.

"Hey!" I shout. He doesn't turn around. I take off across the lot, toward the store. I don't know what to call him. He never told me his name. "Hey," I shout again. He disappears through the sliding glass doors.

Inside, I whip through the lobby, past the carts and baskets, and into the front of the store. It's a sprawling, suburban market with the haphazard kind of layout that Momma used to love but Dad hates—sections eventually dissolving into aisles that are supposed to be charming but in reality make it impossible to find anything without combing the entire store. There's produce to my right, then artisanal candy and a popcorn machine. Beyond that, a sushi bar and home goods. To my left are the registers, and beyond them, a deli and seafood counter, then aisles. I stand in the mouth of the store, heart pounding, turning in a slow circle.

I only saw him for a second—but his face was clear. It was him, I'm almost sure. I start to my right and work my way through the store. I scan every specialty counter, every register, every aisle. But he is nowhere. He is gone, if he was ever here at all.

After I've been through the store twice, I admit to myself that it's useless. My stomach is a hard knot, and it hits me that I barely ate anything at brunch before setting off on this run. I'm starving. I buy a chicken wrap and sit down at a table in the little café in the back.

There is a world in which the truth about what happened six years ago is revealed, poof, a giant cloud lifting, and there is a world in which I never get to understand. In both worlds, Momma is dead, but my sisters and I got to live. Maybe that is the only thing that matters.

I finish my sandwich and stare out into the store, all those people who hold no answers for me. Finally, I pull out my phone and pull up a familiar number.

62

It takes Aunt Mave under ten minutes to collect me from the grocery store. When I tell her I want to spend the rest of the weekend at her place, she doesn't ask questions. We drive back to Tipton so I can pack a bag and she can check me out with the guard, and then we're gone.

I tell Aunt Mave about Aymée, the highly abridged version. I tell her the end-of-trimester stress is catching up to me. She frowns and fixes us mugs of tea.

That night, Aymée sends me a single text.

Taking a leave of absence for the
rest of the trimester. Be careful,
Calliope.

I text her back, then three more times. Eventually, I accept that she's not going to text me again.

On Sunday morning, Teya makes us cinnamon apple pancakes and chicken sausages from the farmer's market. All through breakfast, my phone pings, but it's not Aymée.

Enter your password.

Enter your password.

Enter your password.

I stare at the screen. What if I just . . . don't? After the third prompt, I turn my ringer off.

For most of the morning, I actually work on my English paper. Aunt Mave has to go into the shop, but Teya sets me up at her desk in the living room, and with my phone out of sight in the guest room, it's not that hard to concentrate. By two, when Teya is pulling bowls of tarragon chicken salad and roasted beets and a block of sharp cheddar out of the fridge, I realize I haven't thought about Haunt and Rail or the man with dark blond hair in hours. Maybe I should do this more often.

After lunch, I'm sleepy. The words on my laptop screen begin to blur.

"You look like you could use a break," Teya says when my head visibly jerks. She is sitting on the couch, grading papers.

"I'd love to look through Aunt Mave's old photo albums," I tell her. "Pictures of Momma and Aunt Mave when they were at Tipton. Do you know where they are?"

"Of course." She slides open their living room closet and points to several leathery albums on a shelf. "These are Mave's from before we got together. Have a look."

I find one album from Aunt Mave's first year of high school and a fatter one that goes from sophomore through senior year. Unlike Momma's, my aunt's photos are neatly organized. Momma loved the magic of discovering a forgotten memory. Her sister is more like I am—thoughtful, thorough.

"May I?" Teya asks. She clears her papers off the couch and sits down next to me. "I could use a break too. I haven't looked at these in years."

"Sure." I spread open the first album between us.

In many ways, Tipton looked exactly the same in the nineties as it does today. Same two quadrants surrounded by the same redbrick buildings, same clusters of trees and bright blue sky. The students are a little less diverse, their clothes and hairstyles dated. Where the sports center is now is a much smaller gymnasium. I flip through Mave's first trimester. There are a few photos of Momma, but mostly it's fourteen-year-old Mave with her friends. Mave as a Pink Lady in a production of *Grease*. Mave brandishing the remote like a sword in a dorm common area.

Then I flip the page, and my jaw hinges open. On it is a series of photos of Mave getting ready for a school dance with her friends. It's the last photo that catches my eyes, a group shot taken on the lawn in front of Carrington: Mave, Momma, and four other students in dresses and suits, mugging for the camera. Standing next to Momma, arm wrapped around her waist, is a Tiptonian with short blond curls, sun-bleached. In the posed shot in the yearbook, I wasn't sure, but in this candid photo, the resemblance is unmistakable: Square shoulders. Thick eyebrows. Ruddy cheeks.

His hair is lighter, but it's him. Daniel Clark is the man I've been looking for.

I jab my finger at the page. "Do you know him?"

Teya peers at the photo. "I don't think so. Did your mom have a high school boyfriend?"

I slip the photo out of its sleeve, turn it over to read my aunt's neat handwriting on the back: *High Bluff Dinner Dance with Joey, Kathy & Danny, Marissa & Kent. February 1995.*

But Aunt Mave said she barely remembered Daniel Clark. She definitely didn't say he was Momma's boyfriend. Or that she knew him well enough to call him by a nickname—Danny.

"I don't know," I say to Teya. "Momma never talked about old boyfriends. I wish I'd asked her, but I was ten when she died, you know? I didn't care about boys." Tears well in my eyes, and I blink to fight them back.

"I'm sorry." Teya places her hand on top of mine, gives it a squeeze. "It's not fair."

"It's definitely not." I swipe at my cheeks, which are flushed and wet despite my best efforts.

"You should ask Mave," Teya suggests. "Maybe they just went to that one dance together. But she might remember him."

I did ask Aunt Mave. And she lied to me.

"I will," I say.

We flip through the rest of the album together, but there are no more photos of Danny Clark. When we're finished, I return to my laptop, but I can't focus on my English paper. Instead, I open up my password-protected folder and find the list I made the day I spoke to Ms. Bright. My eyes skim over the last two bullets.

- In 2015, the year before Momma died, Calhoun was renamed Wright. The news coverage would have definitely mentioned Adam Davenport.

- Also in the year before the car crash, Momma was away from home a lot. She took a lot of trips to Alyson-on-Hudson to visit Aunt Mave—and gather evidence?

Then I add to the list:
- The man with dark blond hair is Danny Clark, who Momma knew from Haunt and Rail. Also possibly her high school boyfriend?
- Did Danny Clark kill Adam Davenport?
- In the days before the accident, did Momma confront Danny? Confide in him?
- Did Danny kill Momma to shut her up?

When Aunt Mave comes home, I am all over her. I hold out the picture.

"You said you barely knew him. But you all went to this dance together. Was Danny Clark my mother's boyfriend?"

Teya says she is meeting a friend for happy hour. She offers to bring home takeout, says she will be back in an hour or so. She is giving us space.

When Teya is gone, my aunt sighs and sinks into a chair at the kitchen table. She pats the chair next to her. "Have a seat, Calliope."

"I saw him again," I blurt out before she can answer my first question. "Yesterday. At the grocery store. I doubted myself, but now I'm sure it was him. Danny Clark isn't living on some commune in Oregon. He knew Momma at Tipton. And now he's back here, in Alyson-on-Hudson. She trusted him, and he caused the accident. We have to—"

"Hold up, Calliope." Aunt Mave throws up her hands. "I wasn't entirely honest with you earlier, and I'm sorry. But Danny Clark had nothing to do with your mom's accident—I am one hundred percent certain."

"Then why did you lie?"

"Because I was embarrassed. Because the truth won't shed any light on what happened in the car that day."

"Embarrassed of what?" I press.

Aunt Mave removes her glasses and sets them down on the table. "Danny Clark was your mom's boyfriend. I knew him very well. They got together sometime in their junior year at Tipton, and they stayed together long distance through most of college, while Kathy was at Yale and Danny was at Cornell. But then their senior year, they split up because of me."

My eyebrows arch toward the ceiling. "What happened?"

"It was my first year out of high school. I was living in an apartment in town, working retail at this little boutique. Over her winter break, Kathy flew to Fort Lauderdale to stay with our parents. They'd retired there a couple years before, and I should have been in Florida for the holidays with the rest of the family, but we were fighting. They were all horrified I was working retail instead of going to college, even Kathy, and I was angry with them for being snobs. So I refused to go to Florida for Christmas, and I stayed in Alyson-on-Hudson by myself."

She pinches her bottom lip between her thumb and forefinger, and I squirm impatiently in my chair.

"Danny was an Aly; he grew up here. When he came

home over winter break, he was missing Kathy, and I was furious at her for taking your grandparents' side. We wound up spending a lot of time together that Christmas, and we made a mistake. We slept together."

"What?" Of all the possibilities racing through my head, that had not been one of them.

Aunt Mave grimaces. "I was spiteful, and Danny was lonely. It's the worst thing I've ever done, and I paid for it, believe me. I regretted it instantly, begged Danny to pretend it had never happened. That was the second worst decision I made that winter. Danny told Kathy the truth, and she broke up with him. And for nearly two years, she didn't speak to me."

"Oh my god."

"I deserved it." Mave picks up her glasses, slips them back on. "I'd destroyed her relationship, and I hadn't even been honest about it. I let Danny break the news to her. You may have noticed the lack of photos of Kathy and me in the couple years after I graduated."

I shake my head. "I didn't get that far in the albums. I was just looking at pictures from Tipton."

"It's why your dad and I have always had some coldness between us. When Kathy met your father, she was only twenty-two. We still weren't speaking."

Momma met Dad on a summer vacation to the Adirondacks. I've heard the story a thousand times, from both of my parents. They fell in love at first sight, which Granddaddy called nonsense and Grandmommy called undignified. They most certainly did not approve—their oldest daughter falling head over heels for a small-town bartender of all people—but she followed her heart and moved to Plover Lake that fall. Momma got her fairy tale ending.

"Kathy did not paint the kindest picture of me to your dad," Aunt Mave continues, "and I don't blame her, but that first impression has been hard for him to shake. He's never fully warmed up to me, knowing how badly I hurt your mom all those years ago."

My mind is racing. Maybe I've been wrong about Adam Davenport—but right about Danny Clark. I try to construct a new picture of how Momma's ex-boyfriend was tied to the accident, but my mind stalls out. "This is a lot."

"I know. And yes, Danny lives here, in Alyson-on-Hudson. He did move out to Oregon in his twenties, to work on an agricultural commune. And he used to have a thick beard. That was all true, but after he and his wife divorced, he moved home to New York. It is probably Danny that you've seen around town. I only lied because I knew if I told you the truth about who he was to your mother, I'd have to tell you why they broke up. And honestly, I'm still ashamed. Kathy forgave me eventually, but I've never entirely forgiven myself."

I reach over and slip my hand into my aunt's. "Fortunately for you, I am not known to hold a multidecade grudge like my father."

Aunt Mave laughs, then she wraps her arms around me and pulls me close. "I sure hope not," she says into my hair. "You have a lot of time at Tipton left, and I'd miss our Sunday dinners too much."

I let her hold me for a minute, then gently pull away. "I

get why you lied, but this doesn't explain how I recognized him. What he had to do with the accident."

Aunt Mave shakes her head. "There is more to the story, but I promise you Danny wasn't in the car with you that day. I don't have any idea why seeing him this fall could have made you think that. But . . ." She trails off, pinches her lower lip between her fingers again. "I need to make a few phone calls, Calliope. Give me a couple of days, okay?"

"Fine," I agree. "A couple days." But if Aunt Mave doesn't come through, I'm tracking down Daniel Clark myself, whether he wants to talk to me or not. I am too close to the truth to give up now.

63

Back at Tipton, I tell myself after weeks of waiting, I can
do a couple more days. The temperature plunges overnight,
and I wake Monday morning to sunless skies. Hard, chilly
rain washes the leaves from the trees until skeleton limbs
remain. When the rain stops, crows scream overhead. Below
our feet, campus is coated in a slick carpet of oranges and
browns that the grounds crew will struggle to clear before a
new layer of dead leaves coats the paths.

Quinn's boss has the only padlock key, and it's too cold
to go back to the woods, so on Monday night, we meet at
Gray Space, the student-run performance venue at the far end
of Quadrant East, beyond the Ashbourne Theater and Fortin
Hall.

"This is where Haunt and Rail used to meet," Spencer
tells me as we claim spots on a sagging pea-green couch.
"Years ago, before we got the Den. The Gray Space student
managers all have keys, which isn't ideal, but the chance of
anyone aside from us breaking curfew to come here in the
middle of the night is pretty slim. It'll do for now."

I've been to Gray Space a couple times, but it's not my favorite spot on campus. The furniture is worn and speckled with mystery stains, and the floor and inside walls are painted black, like a box theater. Some Tiptonians come here to study, but the dark walls and tiny windows up near the ceiling put me to sleep.

Tonight, though, I can see the benefit of the remote location and squinty windows. It's much better than shivering in the woods again.

"Listen up," Akari says. She is sitting on top of a wobbly wooden table near the small stage. "The past couple weeks have been rough on all of us. And I have some feelings about what went down with Aymée last week." She flashes Brit a glare.

Turns out, I am far from the only ghost upset about what happened to Aymée. This morning, when I finally opened all the Haunt and Rail texts I'd let accumulate over the weekend, I learned a few things. First, Brit and Akari both have access to the message app, because the texts were a series of barbs between them. Lucas used it during our lark at Brown Rock, and Spencer sent the security alert during the last lark. At this point, I'm fairly sure all the seniors have access and none of the juniors. Yet another testament to the myth of equality within the society.

Second, the decision to expose Aymée's collateral was all Brit. She should be the last person tearing another girl down over a relationship with an older guy, but Brit's vengeful streak won out over any sense of sisterhood or sympathy.

Akari folds her arms across her chest. "Things happened

fast, and decisions were made without the input of the group. That's not how Haunt and Rail is supposed to operate." She casts a glance across the room at Lucas, who is leaning against the wall by the small refreshments counter, and I realize this is the first time I've ever seen them not sitting together at a society meeting. It looks like he took Brit's side on this.

Brit starts to say something, but Akari holds up her hand. "Let me finish. Exposing Aymée's collateral was petty, and worse, it opened us up to retribution. We're lucky she hasn't ratted us out to the administration yet."

"She won't," Brit snaps. "Aymée pulled information off a teacher's personal tablet without permission. She hacked into the campus network and changed the login screen background. If she reveals our identities to Sadler or Naylor, she knows we can pin it all on her. She'll get suspended, maybe expelled. I knew what I was doing, whether you trust me or not."

"Enough." Mira pushes herself to her feet from the spot where she's been sitting cross-legged on the stage. "I don't like what Brit did either. When Aymée comes back from leave, we owe her a huge apology, not that I expect she'll accept it. But what happened happened. I love this group. I love what we stand for. Over the past couple months, Haunt and Rail has become my home at Tipton. And we can't let ourselves fall apart over this."

There are murmurs all around me. People want to forget what we've done. What we stood by and let happen. They want Mira's words to patch us up.

Akari sighs. "Mira's right. We can let this divide us, or we can put it behind us and focus on the work we have ahead."

"I'm with Mira," Quinn says from a rickety metal folding chair near the door.

"Yeah, me too," says Colin. Then Kadence. Then Spencer. Everyone agrees. Everyone wants to move on, look forward. Or after what happened to Aymée, they are too afraid to say otherwise.

I nod my head, still feeling like a traitor.

"Good," Lee says. "Because we have work to do."

Brit squares her shoulders. "Ellis returns from leave on Sunday, and he'll be back in the classroom on Monday unless something changes." As always, there's not a hair out of place on her head, but she looks tired. I wonder if beneath all her bravado, she feels any doubts about what she did.

"But what about the investigation?" Kadence asks. "How could the school not find anything?"

"Easy," Brit scowls. "Ellis lies and covers his tracks. I don't know if they'd even look at his personal tablet, but if they do, he'd be smart enough to erase his search history."

"Or explain it away as 'research for his novel,'" Lee sneers.

"Tipton Academy doesn't want a scandal," Brit continues. "They don't want to find anything. If Ellis can convince them it was all a bunch of rumors, they'll be thrilled."

"Someone needs to come forward," Lucas says. He looks at Brit. "We're out of leads. It's the only way."

"I can't." Brit wraps her arms tightly around her waist. "It would still be just my word against Ellis's. And besides, me coming forward puts a target on the back of the ghosts."

I press my lips together and silently fume. If Brit isn't

ready to speak up, I respect that. One girl's voice against Mr. Ellis isn't likely to succeed. I understand Brit not wanting to put everything on the line unless she thought she could win. Unless there was a chorus of voices to drown Mr. Ellis out. But that is a personal decision. She's using Haunt and Rail as a shield, presenting her choice as if it's for the good of the group. It's just slant. Brit speaking up only puts a target on our backs if she feeds them our names.

But everyone else seems to have forgotten how angry they were with Brit a moment ago. No one wants her to do anything that would put her in an unsafe position. Lee says we can't give up. She calls for ideas for the next lark. There are halfhearted suggestions for tapping Mr. Ellis's phone (beyond our skill set, especially without Aymée) and planting a nanny cam in his bedroom (too gross, and also probably illegal).

"Awareness is what we do best," Quinn says. "Our larks work because we get other Tiptonians to care about the things we care about. We get them to take up the cause, make things happen."

"Okay," Brit says. "Got any ideas?"

"We've gotten people talking. And we've already presented our evidence. Now we need to remind Tipton why this all matters. We do an info-driven lark focused on the harmful impact of sexual harassment and abuse. Or maybe on successful cases—remind people it is possible to bring perpetrators down. We need to refocus students' attention on the core issues, not the scandal."

Listening to Quinn talk, I feel the first bit of calm I've felt all night. They're right—we got off track, and I hate what

Brit did to Aymée, but maybe it's not too late to salvage this campaign. This is what Haunt and Rail is all about. It's the reason I joined, the reason I'm still in this room tonight.

"The Fresh INC lark worked because we appealed to Tiptonians' competitive spirit," I say. "The comparison to the Brecker School on the postcards. We need something like that this time."

"Calliope's right," Spencer says. "And so is Quinn. We do something info-driven with a personal touch."

"Good work," Lee says. "Keep the ideas coming. We make our move on Sunday night."

64

Dad calls a family meeting. On Tuesday, he tells me that he has spoken to Aunt Mave, that he has already informed the school that I will be missing class for the rest of the week. I press, but he won't say anything else over the phone. He says it's better if we discuss this in person, as a family.

My heart lifts, just a bit. Dad knows something about Daniel Clark. This is progress.

I text Lee, let her know I will be gone for a few days. I promise I will be back by Sunday night.

When classes end, Aunt Mave and Teya collect me from campus. They will stay over in the guest room tonight, like they used to when Momma was alive. On the drive home, Sebastian sprawls across the back seat with me. No one will answer my questions. They say we have to wait until we are all together. Just a couple more hours. I grit my teeth and burrow into Sebastian's warm doggy fur.

All along the twisty mountain roads, the trees snatch at us with their skeleton shadows. By the time we get to our house, twilight has faded to a deep winter dark that our headlight beams barely slice. Dad has the porch lights on, and a warm glow lights up the windows. When I left Plover Lake two months ago, I thought I was making my escape. I fantasized then about never returning to my small village with its many eyes.

It doesn't hit me how badly I have missed my home until I see it, waiting at the end of the driveway like a giant hug.

Sebastian leaps out of the car as soon as I open the door and runs up to the porch. I grab my bags and get ready to follow. There is an unfamiliar car parked in the driveway, and I ask Aunt Mave if she knows who it belongs to.

She rests a hand on my elbow and shifts uncomfortably on the gravel, right foot, left. "Let's just go inside."

Sebastian fusses at the front door, and my dad swings it wide. "Right on time." He is smiling, but he looks nervous. He does not step out of the doorway to let us through until we have all bunched together on the porch.

Everyone is being weird. "Where are Lorelei and Serafina?" I ask. "Whose car is that?"

"Serafina is at a friend's," Dad says. "She'll be home in the morning. And Lorelei is in the dining room. With Danny."

My eyebrows shoot up. Dad motions for us to set our bags down and follow him.

Sitting at the long dining room table are my sister and the man with dark blond hair. Danny Clark. Up close, his features come into focus. Thick eyebrows, skin ruddy from too much time spent in the sun. He is older, but he's unmistakably the boy from the photos, grown up. The man I have seen in Alyson-on-Hudson. My tight-lipped correspondent.

He stands abruptly when I walk into the room. "You must be Calliope."

His voice is smooth and warm. I stand there, staring. He is acting like we are two complete strangers, meeting for the first time, like he hasn't been stringing me along for weeks.

"Let's all sit," Dad says, and we pull out chairs. I take the seat next to Lorelei, and she slips her hand into my hand beneath the table. Sebastian flops at our feet.

Danny clears his throat. "May I?" he asks, and Dad nods.

"My name is Danny Clark," he says. "As I gather you've figured out." He glances at Aunt Mave, and I realize the adults have spoken about this beforehand. Only Lorelei and I have been kept in the dark.

"As Mave has told you, Kathy and I were together during the end of high school and most of college. Then we broke up, and we went our separate ways." He looks down at his hands. Under the table, Lorelei swings her legs back and forth, back and forth. She holds my hand tighter.

"Years later, my wife and I divorced, and I moved home to Alyson-on-Hudson. Kathy was in town visiting Mave; we ran into each other on the street. It had been such a long time." Danny's eyes stray to Dad. "Kathy and your dad were going through a rough patch. Your mom and I started talking on the phone a lot. Visiting each other."

"You had an affair," Lorelei says, voice flat. Her eyes bore holes into his.

"That's right," Danny says, eyes flickering down to the table. All the air rushes out of my lungs.

"Dad?" I squeak. Tears are pooling in my eyes. I cough, hard. This isn't the story that Danny is supposed to be telling. This doesn't sound like the same man who wrote those cryptic notes. Everything I thought I knew starts to waver.

Dad gets up and stands behind my sister and me, wraps his arms around our shoulders. "I know this is a lot for you girls to take in. But I don't want you to worry about me. I've known about what happened between your mother and Danny for a while now."

"And you?" I look to Aunt Mave and Teya.

"I knew," my aunt says softly. "Not the whole time. But the year before she died, your mother told me." She glances at her wife. "I made the decision not to burden Teya with this."

"You kept her secret," Lorelei says. It is a question or an accusation.

"I thought my sister was making a terrible mistake, but what moral ground did I have?" Aunt Mave says. "Kathy wouldn't listen to me. She was convinced she'd been reunited with her true love."

Danny clears his throat. "And I'm afraid there's more."

Together, they tell it—Dad, Aunt Mave, and Danny.

It starts like a fairy tale.

Prince—young, handsome, idealistic—meets princess—beautiful, rich, going places. For two years of high school, they are together. Then the prince goes to study agriculture at Cornell and the princess ascends her ivy tower at Yale. For three more years, they defy the odds. They stay together. Love wins.

In year four, everything collapses. The wicked little sister interferes, rends love asunder, tests everything the princess has come to believe. The king and queen have been rich and miserable for years—money never made them happy. The princess believes in love, not money, or at least she thought she did.

For a dark year, it seems as if all is lost. The next summer, the heartbroken princess's friends whisk her away to the Adirondacks for a week, and the princess meets a pauper—a handsome bartender named Peter. The princess moves to his small Adirondack village to give love a second chance, but she is hasty. They marry when she is twenty-four, have their first daughter when she is twenty-eight, then their second the year after. Their life together is good, but it is imperfect. It is real. And as the years go by, the princess comes to realize that it will never be a fairy tale.

For a time, the princess puts on a happy face. She plans fantastical adventures for her daughters, spending the king and queen's money on parties and trips and riches that make the bartender frown. But he surrenders. He wants the princess to be happy.

When the princess is thirty-five, she meets her prince again. Fourteen years have passed. The heartache is old, easy to forget. In fact, what happened then seems forgivable now, the possibility of a fairy tale love once again at the princess's fingertips. They know it is wrong, but the wrongness does not stop them. They keep their love a secret. The princess thinks that this way, it is even more like a fairy tale.

Two years later, a baby girl is born. The pauper keeps his

suspicions to himself. He knows the princess is unhappy, but he loves their third daughter, who they name Serafina. He never asks the questions he wants to ask, and as the months pass, it becomes easier to keep them buried deep inside.

Then the fateful day arrives—Friday, September 23. The princess has pulled the girls out of school, another adventure, is going to introduce them to her prince. It is a terrible idea, and the girls' aunt knows it. She has been keeping her sister's secret for a year now, since the birth of her youngest niece. That morning, she tries to talk her sister out of it. They fight. She tells the princess she wants no part of this plan, that the pauper deserves to know the truth, that she will not come to dinner with them that night. She closes her shop early and drives to Scarsdale to visit some childhood friends, clear her head.

Then horribly, tragically, the princess dies.

The girls' aunt panics. When she speaks to the police, she tells them she did not know where her sister was taking the girls that afternoon. Not to visit her—she wasn't in town. Not to Scarsdale—she would have to ask her friends to lie. And for the girls' father to find out about the affair like this, through the investigation into his wife's death, seemed cruel. Unnecessary, really, when telling the police about the prince wouldn't bring her sister back.

So the affair remained a secret for a little while, but the princess had left bread crumbs scattered all around, and when he resigned himself to truly look, the pauper pieced the truth together. It didn't change how he felt about his youngest daughter, not even a little bit. But he knew the truth would change everything for all three of his girls, would cast a shadow across their mother's memory, so he kept the princess's secret safe.

Until the oldest daughter began asking questions. Until the pauper and the aunt spoke—really spoke—about it all for the first time. Until they agreed it was time to tell the girls the truth.

65

"Were you with us in the car that day?" I ask when they have finished speaking and it is silent at the dining room table again.

Danny shakes his head, no. "I was at home, waiting for you. When you didn't arrive, I thought Kathy had changed her mind. She wasn't responding to any of my messages. I didn't find out what had happened until late that night when Mave called me."

"This is fucked up." Lorelei glares at him.

My mind is spinning. Maybe my theory was way off the mark, but what happened that day wasn't a psychotic break or a murder-suicide attempt. The police investigation was just as far off. If my mother was in love with Danny Clark when she died, if she was dreaming about taking us to start a new life with him, there is no way she drove off the road on purpose. Momma was making a horrible mistake, but she wasn't trying to kill herself.

I turn to Aunt Mave, heat rising in my throat. "You told me the truth wouldn't shed any light on what happened in the car that day. But that's a lie. If you or Danny had told the police the truth about where Momma was taking us, it would have ruled out their murder-suicide theory. Don't you understand how much that would have meant to the rest of us?"

Before Aunt Mave can respond, Lorelei shoots back in her chair. Her hand rips from mine. "She was texting. Before the van swerved off the road, I saw Momma texting."

"What?" We all turn to Lorelei in unison.

"You were sleeping," Lorelei says to me. "You sleep like the dead. But I saw what happened, and I'm the one who should have told the truth. But I was a kid, okay? And I didn't want everyone to blame Momma. So I said I was sleeping too."

"Pumpkin." Dad gets up and folds Lorelei into him. "She couldn't have been texting. The investigators thought distracted driving was a possibility at first, but her phone records didn't show any activity at the time of the accident. They ruled that theory out."

"Then maybe she was doing something else on her phone," Lorelei insists. "Checking Google Maps or the weather."

I glare in turn into each of their faces—Danny, Aunt Mave, Lorelei, Dad. Anger churns hot and sticky in my gut. "What is wrong with you?" My voice pitches up, and Sebastian whimpers at my feet. "If you'd all told the truth six years ago, the accident wouldn't have been this huge mystery. You're all selfish."

Dad pinches his forehead between his index finger and thumb. "I'll call Dr. Nguyen in the morning. This family has a lot of work to do."

I spin to face Danny, who is cradling his forehead in his hands. "I have a few more questions for you," I say. "In private."

I start toward the back porch, motion for Danny to follow me. I wait for someone to stop me, to tell me I'm not allowed to speak to Danny alone. But they let me go. Danny follows.

When the porch door has swung shut behind us, I say, "The notes on the bulletin board. Did you write them?"

Danny frowns. "Notes? No, I don't know what you mean."

My stomach twists. "You saw me in town that day. August twenty-sixth. Through the window at Frances Bean."

He scrubs one hand across his face. "I'm sorry, Calliope. I don't remember that. I might have taken a walk on Chicory Lane that day, but if I saw you, I didn't recognize you."

I shake my head back and forth. My chest is tight, and I force myself to keep breathing. Maybe he is lying, or maybe I'm the one who got everything wrong. My eyes rove across his face, and there's only confusion there. That day in town, I thought we'd locked eyes, but he was looking at something else through the glass. The realization that he never saw me at all knifes through me, and I dig my nails into my palms to keep from screaming.

Which means someone else watched me tack that first envelope to the bulletin board. All this time, someone has been messing with me. The double blow is too much to process right now, so I force myself to tuck that thought away.

After all this time, I am face to face with Daniel Clark. I need to get it together, need to focus.

"Okay," I say. "Fine. But when I saw you in town, *I* recognized *you*. How is that possible if Momma was taking us to meet you for the first time?"

Danny sighs. "I came to Kathy's funeral. Maybe you remembered me."

"Maybe." I feel like I know everything and nothing all at once. My theory may have been nothing more than wild speculation, but while Danny is here in front of me, I'm determined to find out. I drop my voice low. "I know you were in Haunt and Rail together."

Danny's eyebrows arch up. "You're a ghost?"

I nod.

Danny sighs again. "Haunt and Rail had a deep hold on Kathy and me. Being a part of the society was foundational in a way I didn't fully realize until years later. Your mom and I were young and idealistic then. When we found each other again, what we had felt unstoppable. It was like we'd never been apart. We were the romantics we'd been at Tipton all over again, sneaking around for the glory of love."

I feel like I've been punched in the gut. Danny folds his arms across his chest. "Now of course," he continues, "I can see how shortsighted we were."

I fix my eyes on his. "I know about Adam Davenport."

He looks a bit surprised, but he doesn't flinch. "What made you think about Adam?"

"Did you kill him?" I ask point-blank. "Did the ghosts?"

Danny's mouth curves into a deep frown. "No, of course not. As far as I know, that rumor was started by Ron Graff and Nathan Carey-York, two victims of Adam's bullying.

Adam Davenport falling to his death in Calhoun was a tragedy, but some thought it was poetic justice. Some of the ghosts couldn't resist stoking the flames. But his death was an accident, pure and simple. I had no idea that rumor was still going around."

My mind travels back to my conversation with Ms. Bright. All of Danny's claims line up with what she'd told me. My heart sinks, but I can't pinpoint why. It should be good news that Adam wasn't murdered in cold blood, that my mother's death had nothing to do with his. But for some reason I can't entirely explain to myself, I wanted that version of the truth. Maybe I just wanted to be right, for her death to have been the tragic consequence of her crusade for justice. Instead, if Lorelei is telling the truth, our mother died as the result of distracted driving. The least mysterious possibility of all.

I should feel relief—but I don't. If anything, I feel more unsettled than I did before coming home.

"And the year before my mother's accident," I say, intent on tying up the final loose end, putting the last scrap of my theory to bed, "she was traveling a lot. Visiting Aunt Mave, taking a lot of 'me' time. But she was with you."

Danny nods. "We were involved for two and a half years. But things really accelerated between us after Serafina was born."

My stomach churns. "She doesn't know yet, does she?"

He shakes his head. "Not yet. I'd like to have a relationship with her, Calliope. But I've agreed to follow your father's lead on when and how to tell her."

I feel ill. Danny Clark was not in the car with us that day, but he still destroyed our family. I was right about that. "This is all your fault," I hiss. "You broke us apart."

I don't wait for him to respond. I run back inside, and the porch door slams behind me.

66

We retreat to my room on the third floor, just Lorelei and me. The scarf I knit her last summer is looped in two loose rings around her neck.

"Did you really see Momma texting?" I ask. "Or whatever she was doing on her phone."

"Yes." Her voice is small. She plays with the end of the scarf.

"How many times did we see Dr. Nguyen?" I ask. "Why didn't you ever say anything?"

"Because you'd know it was her fault. Because I didn't want her to get in trouble."

She is staring out my window into the darkness. She is not looking at me.

"How could she get in trouble?" I ask. "She was dead, Lorelei."

My eyes drill holes in her head. I will not let this go. For weeks now, I've been chasing what I wanted to be true, shuttering myself to the other possibilities. It would be easy to take Lorelei's word at face value, accept that this is the truth, move on. Maybe I would find some peace. But Dad's words ring loud in my ears. *Her phone records didn't show any activity at the time of the accident. They ruled that theory out.*

My sister is still not looking at me. We are sitting on my bed, cross-legged. She drops the scarf and picks at the bedspread. She will not meet my eyes.

"Tell me the truth," I insist. "I know you're lying."

"Fuck." A dark shadow crosses over Lorelei's face. Finally, she turns to look at me. "If I tell you, you have to promise you'll never say a word."

I promise. I am too close to the truth to have it snatched away from me now.

"The day before the accident, I saw them together. You were over at Erica's, Dad was working, and I was supposed to be having dinner at Jodi's, but Jodi's sister got sick, and her mom brought me home early. When I walked into the house, Serafina was napping in her crib, but Momma wasn't inside. I went around back, looking for her, and she was in the woods behind the house with some stranger. They were half naked, rolling around in the pine needles."

"Oh my god."

"It was so stupid. If Dad had come home early from the bar, he would have caught them. They had Serafina's baby monitor with them, and they were just going at it."

"What did you do?"

"I screamed." She laughs, a short, hollow sound. "Momma said Danny was her 'special friend' and tried to sell me some bullshit story about what they'd been doing. I didn't fully get what was happening, but I knew it was bad. I knew what kissing was, obviously. I wanted to tell Dad, but he came home late that night, like usual, and Momma took us to school in the morning before he got up. I never got a chance."

Lorelei twists a coil of auburn hair between her fingers. "When she pulled us out of school early on Friday, I threw a fit. Do you remember? Before we even got on the road."

I shake my head. "I'd forgotten about that."

"Momma took me aside and tried to calm me down. She said we were going to see her special friend, and everything was going to be wonderful. She was trying to spin what I'd seen into this secret adventure."

"You knew we were going to meet Danny."

Lorelei nods. "She let me ride shotgun. We were too young to ride in the front, but Momma let me sit up front with her that day, like a bribe. When we pulled over at the gas station, I dug around in her bag, and I found pictures she'd put in there, of Momma and Danny together. I showed them to you. I told you that Momma wanted us to go live with this bad man, which wasn't even what she'd told me, but clearly I wasn't so far off the mark."

The realization hits like a fist to my chest. "That's why I recognized him. That's why I thought he was in the car with us."

She nods. "Guess so."

Then the second realization hits. "You weren't in the middle row with me. You were in the passenger's seat."

Lorelei stares at me. She doesn't say anything.

Suddenly, the room is very cold. My arms break out in gooseflesh.

"What did you do, Lorelei?" It is half question, half whisper.

Even before she tells me, I know it is bad. Like Momma, Lorelei has always believed in true love. But she has never trusted a fairy tale. My mind travels to Nico, how my sister has been raking him over the coals. Testing his worth. How she wouldn't let me close to the guy she has been seeing here, AJ Kimmler. Maybe she knows he is not good enough. Maybe she made the whole thing up.

Lorelei's eyes well with tears. "I never planned for it to happen. I didn't plan anything at all. You were sleeping in the back. Momma was listening to music loud, singing along. She was so happy, like this was the best adventure ever. I didn't want anyone to die. I just needed the car to stop, and I kept asking Momma, and she told me to be quiet. She said we'd be there soon, and I knew I had to do something. I screamed at her to turn the car around, take us home, but she wouldn't listen."

"What happened then?" I ask, dread snaking through me, cold and terrible.

"Then Serafina woke up; she was screaming too. Momma still wouldn't pull over, so I grabbed the wheel. I just wanted us to turn around, go home, but the van spun out, off the road. Then we were in the lake, and Momma wouldn't wake up. You wouldn't wake up either. I climbed out of the front seat, and the water kept rushing in. I was shaking you."

I close my eyes, try to shut the memory out, but it won't stop coming. "I was dreaming we were at Six Flags. We were riding The Comet, and everyone was screaming. I remember your foot was tangled in the seat belt. You'd lost your shoe."

337

Lorelei nods. "Climbing into the back. When you said you'd seen someone in the passenger's seat, I thought for sure you'd remember. For weeks, I've been waiting for you to remember that it was me. Me who showed you his picture in the car that day, me up front with Momma. Me steering the car off the road—but I never meant it to happen. You believe me, don't you, Calliope?"

She clutches at my hands, and I don't remember, not really. But I can picture us at the gas station, Momma filling up the tank, Lorelei showing me photos of the bad man we were going to meet. Lorelei losing it when Momma wouldn't listen to her, Lorelei grabbing the steering wheel, trying to make the car stop. Everyone screaming.

My sister's hands feel like hundred-pound weights in mine.

"Do you forgive me?" she asks.

For my entire life, I have forgiven my sister everything. She is my person, the other half of my heart. When she threw an epic tantrum on my fifth birthday and half of my friends went home, I forgave her. In second grade, when she wouldn't tell Dad the truth about the fight at the pool and we both lost TV privileges, I didn't tell on her. Last summer, right before I left for Tipton, when she borrowed my favorite dress without asking and brought it home from a party torn up the side, I forgave her.

But now, my heart is shattering into a million bits of blood and salt and grit. Where my chest used to be is a giant crater, air rushing through.

"You killed Momma," I choke out. "She's dead because

you were reckless. Because you didn't think."

"I know," Lorelei sobs. She snatches her hands from mine, wraps them tightly around her knees. "Don't you think I don't know that, Calliope? That this hasn't been eating away at me for six years?"

I thought we told each other everything. I thought Lorelei's anger this fall was justified, when I'd been keeping secrets from her. A boyfriend. A secret society. But all that pales in comparison to the one big secret Lorelei has been keeping from me.

My sister's friends, her parties, her collections of useless facts. I thought she had bounced back fast after the accident. I envied how easy it was for her, living in Plover Lake, letting all the attention roll off her shoulders. If the truth about Momma's death has been eating away at her, she has never once shown me. There is something very dark about that.

I know I should fold my sister into my arms, comfort her, say *we were so young*, and *it wasn't your fault*. But I don't do any of that. I can't. Every molecule inside me is vibrating with hurt. The pain is so bad I think I might scream.

I push myself to my feet, hug my arms to my waist. My insides want to spill out; I am barely holding on. "Get out of my room," I say through clenched teeth.

Lorelei scrambles up, clutches at me. "You have to forgive me, Calliope."

I stumble back, leave her snatching at the air.

"Get out," I repeat, louder this time. "Leave me the fuck alone!"

My sister doubles over at the waist like I have kicked her in the stomach. Good. I want her to hurt the way I am hurting. She staggers to the door, struggles for a moment with the handle. And then she is gone.

VI
CRIMINAL

67

A Siren in the Water

A memory, revised—
There was a man that day, six years ago.
Dark blond hair, thick eyebrows, sunburned
  skin.
In his castle, waiting for us to arrive.

A prince, a wolf, a thief.

Inside the chariot, three sisters—
One was too young to remember.
One was sleeping.
One made a terrible mistake.

A beautiful maiden . . .

Lorelei, her name plucked from the old
  German tale.

It starts dark and grows darker. A forlorn lass
throws herself into the Rhine
to spite a faithless lover.

. . . turned deadly siren.

Legend has it, she lured guileless fishermen
to their watery graves. So much drowning.
So much rage. In our story, Momma
is the faithless one. Everyone pays.

Here be dragons.

This is the wrong kind of ending. Lorelei,
I don't know how to cast you as the villain.
How to hate you. I don't know how
to forgive you either.

68

I am so angry at Lorelei, I can barely breathe. For what she did to Momma. For asking me to keep her secret. But most of all, I am angry at myself. For making her tell me the truth.

I spend Wednesday hanging around Plover Lake, alone. The movie theater is damp and cold. At the general store, they're out of peach tea. Everything feels hollow. I think about calling Erica and Beatrix, asking them to ditch school, but I don't want to see my friends. I don't want to lie to them, and I don't want to explain anything either.

I wind up at the library, dozing in a beanbag chair at the back of the children's room. Anything to avoid my family, the secrets I pried from their throats. Anything to avoid Lorelei.

The texts from Nico pile up.

8:10 p.m.

You get in OK?

10:26 a.m.

Hey didn't hear from you last
night. Everything good?

Just got out of assembly. Tipton
without you is like Manny
without his wings.

10:29 a.m.

Sorry that was weak. Just miss
you. Hope you're having a good
time with your fam! 😊

12:32 p.m.

Are you punishing me for that
Manny simile? Allow me to try
again:

Tipton without you is like coffee
without the whip. It's like Alyson
without the Effect. Haunt with no
Rail. I'm improving, right? 🤣

I switch my phone to silent. The sweeter Nico's texts, the
more my stomach hurts. I could write back and say what?
Everything is decidedly not okay. I am having the polar

opposite of a good time with my family. I have some updates about the man with dark blond hair, but the thing that's killing me, the thing that hurts the most? I can't tell you about that. So on top of everything I've already been hiding, I'm coming back with more secrets. Buckle up.

I settle for the coward's play, the path of least resistance. It is astonishingly easy to say nothing at all.

Eventually, I drag myself home to suffer through a short family dinner. Dad asks if I will stay another day, go to see Dr. Nguyen, but I say I am not ready. If I go there, I will slip up, say too much. I have never felt anger like this before, raw and cavernous. It storms through my insides, leaving its wreckage behind: a stone in my gut, copper on my tongue, knives behind my eyes. There would be something satisfying about spilling my sister's secret, ratting her out, but watching her squirm is better. Maybe I want her to keep suffering. Maybe I just need some time. Or maybe I am crueler than I knew I could be.

After dinner, I lock myself in my room. Nico calls, and I turn off my phone. When Lorelei knocks, I pretend I am sleeping.

Thursday morning, Aunt Mave and Teya drive me back to Tipton. They put on music to drown out the silence. Who did I think I was, playing detective, forcing the truth into the light? Murders linked across decades, a villain I could hate with every fiber of my being . . . Momma wanted to live in a fairy tale, and I loved her for it, but I judged her too. It's so clear now, so painfully obvious I don't know how I missed it before—I am exactly the same. I've spent these past two months trying to twist reality into a story with good guys and bad guys, a terrible injustice, and a hero swooping in to ferret out the truth, set old wrongs right. But reality is so much messier than that. The good guys aren't all good. The bad guys aren't all bad. And sometimes the hero just screws it all up.

As the mountains shrink in the rearview, I remind myself why I left Plover Lake in the first place. I went to Tipton to leave the accident behind—and I failed epically. But I did some things right. I found a connection to Momma that I never expected. And I found my place, my passion.

Haunt and Rail isn't what I thought it would be. The ghosts keep secrets. They lie. They screw up. They hurt people. They are messy and imperfect, just like my family is messy and imperfect. Just like me.

When we pull up to the main entrance, I draw in a long, deep breath, and I feel like I haven't really breathed since I left. I am back, eyes wide open. I am ready for the imperfection and the mess. Ready to do whatever it takes to make sure Mr. Ellis pays. Brit can be cruel and selfish, but she is also a survivor. The ghosts can be rash and quick to cast blame, but they are passionate, and they are brave.

I got swept up in a fairy tale, but that's over now. When the wounds have scabbed over, I will deal with my family. When I am ready. But right now, I am going to take all that anger, all that hurt, and put it to work.

I pull out my phone and send Quinn a text asking if they

can meet up after dinner. A million ideas about Sunday's lark are buzzing through my head. We have a campaign to finish.

I find Nico sitting on the wall outside Chandler. It is after five, and the light is already fading. He looks up from his tablet.

"You're back!"

I give him a small smile, no teeth. His grin fades to hurt or worry. Probably a little of both.

"You okay? You didn't write me back."

"I know." I scuff the toe of my boot into the ground, digging until the grass tears, exposing dirt. I am feeling mean, destructive. And Nico doesn't deserve any of that. Unless . . . there's something that has been needling at me. Something I need to get off my chest.

"My dad called a family meeting. That's why I went home. I met the man with dark blond hair—Daniel Clark."

"What?" Nico's spine straightens. "No way."

I shake my head back and forth. "I was way off the mark. He knew my mom, but he wasn't there the day she died. It's a long story. But also, he wasn't the person leaving me notes."

"Oh." Nico frowns. "I'm sorry."

"Yeah. There's a lot going on at home. I don't really want to talk about it. But, Nico, someone was writing to me. Someone put those notes on the bulletin board." I draw in a deep breath. "And you're the only one who knew what I was doing."

"Wait a sec." Nico's face goes dark. "Calliope, I would never do that."

I cross my arms over my chest. He looks horrified. But who else knew as much as Nico, who else would know exactly what to write? That last letter convinced me that the man was a ghost, but maybe the society's motto isn't a well-kept secret. And I put the date of Adam Davenport's death in the first letter; all Nico would have needed to do was look it up.

"Shit, I swear to god, Calliope, it wasn't me. I would never hurt you like that. Look." He holsters his stylus on the side of his tablet and turns it to face me. "You've been gone for two days, ignoring my texts, and all I've been doing is missing you."

The drawing takes my breath away. On the screen is my face, vivid and full of life. The girl in the picture is me, but so much more beautiful, drawn with love. She knows how to forgive, how to accept hard truths, how to see beauty in the world. Her eyes are a wide, piercing green. She is not a girl who just accused her boyfriend of lying to her. She is not a girl made of secrets.

"It's . . ." Tears teeter along the bottom of my eyelids, then spill over, run down my cheeks.

"You hate it." Nico flips the tablet back, switches it off. "It's not finished. I shouldn't have shown you yet."

"Nico." I step back, swatting at my cheeks. "The picture is perfect. More than perfect. And I'm sorry I accused you of writing the letters. But I need some time, okay? I'm not thinking straight."

Nico hops off the wall and takes a step toward me. He reaches out his hand, and I leave it hanging in the air between us for much too long. Finally, I take it.

"I leave for New Hampshire tomorrow after school. Mom visit, remember?"

"Right." But the truth? I'd forgotten all about Nico's trip.

"So take the weekend, okay? Take as much time as you need to deal with your family stuff. But I'll be back on Monday. And if you need me, call me, okay?"

I drop his hand so I can swipe at my face again. The tears are streaming down harder. "Why are you being so nice to me?" I ask. "I blew you off for two days, and then I came back flinging accusations around."

Nico shoves his hands into his pockets. "When my parents divorced, I was a nightmare for months. I get bad family stuff. And in my case, no one died. So you get a pass, okay? This time. But I need you to talk to me, Calliope. Sooner or later."

I nod. And that is precisely the problem. First Haunt and Rail, now Lorelei. Keeping those promises means never telling Nico the truth.

69

We meet at Yardley Pond at midnight, nineteen pink-cheeked ghosts bundled in coats and hats. I blow hot breath into my mittens—warm, woolen things from last winter's craft fair in my village. They remind me of home, before home became so complicated; a plump little plover is knitted on the back of each one.

It is Sunday, the night before Halloween—Devil's Night—and Mr. Ellis's leave is up. This morning's daily email included a note welcoming him back to campus, as if he'd been on sick leave or away on a trip. A separate email went out to parents, assuring everyone that a thorough internal investigation had turned up absolutely no evidence of teacher misconduct. The school promised continued vigilance, but it's clear the whole administration is breathing a giant sigh of relief.

We're here to shake things up again. And I am in—wholly, completely in. This campaign is what I need to get my mind off my family, off Lorelei. I can't go back and undo what happened six years ago. But I can make a real, tangible difference here at Tipton, for Brit, for Rainy Day, and any girl who Mr. Ellis has hurt. For the girls we can stop him from hurting in the future. No mystery, no fairy tale, just action. Justice. I catch my fellow ghosts' eyes and smile.

The grass is brittle beneath our feet; the first frost of the season is coming. Lee and Lucas run another phone check, and this time, everyone passes. When we've all been cleared, Akari and Spencer pass out tote bags stuffed with the bright teal T-shirts I helped design. The angry ghost graphic is printed in white on the back of each shirt. The front reads *#GenZ: We Are Survivors*. Below the header are the names of young people who have won cases against perpetrators of sexual harassment and assault. At the bottom of each shirt is my contribution to the design, a blank line: _____, inviting Tiptonians to fill in their own name or the name of a survivor in their life.

The message has broad generational appeal, and the school colors make the shirts feel personal. I hold a tee out in front of me, reading all the names, and I feel powerful, inspired in a way I haven't felt since the start of the Fresh INC lark. Haunt and Rail did good work with this, combining Quinn's ideas with mine. This is going to make a real impact; we can still win this fight. I slip a bag over my shoulder, energized and ready to give Haunt and Rail my whole heart again.

Brit pairs us off, sending teams to each dorm to make tote drops. "And we've got a bunch set aside for Alys, so we'll hit student spaces too," she wraps up. "Lucas and Calliope, you've got the mail room; Lee and I will take Gray Space."

"And that's it?" Kadence asks. "Just make our drops, then we're done?"

Brit laughs. "Not every lark is a whole production."

"Trust me," Lucas says, "there's power in simplicity. Drop off your totes, then go home. Get some sleep."

Lucas opens up the mail room, and we leave our totes on the benches in the center of the floor. Thirty seconds later, we're out on the path again, headed back toward our dorms. My head is still fizzy with caffeine pops of energy, but my feet are dragging and my fingers are stiff with cold. Being out here tonight felt amazing, but it's been a long week, and I am crashing. Thankfully in five minutes, I'll be back in my room, burrowing under the covers. Like Brit said, not every lark is a whole production. When Tipton wakes up to find the shirts tomorrow morning, the real fun begins.

We part ways in the middle of Quadrant West, me toward Anders and Lucas toward Stratton, the boys' dorm beside Brisbane.

"Good work, Bolan." He gives me a little salute, and then I'm slipping through the entrance, which Brit or Quinn has left unlocked and ajar, into the warmth of my dorm.

I'm halfway down the hall toward my room when I realize my mittens are missing. They're not on my hands, and they're not in my pockets. I remember wearing them at Yardley Pond; I must have slipped them off when we got to the mail room. Which means they could be inside, right by our totes.

The lure of crawling into bed is strong, but my mittens aren't exactly run of the mill. If I dropped them with the T-shirts, I'm basically advertising my involvement in the lark. With the Wesley incident still fresh, I can't risk exposing the ghosts to more scrutiny. I have to get my mittens back.

Lucas has the mail room key card, so I turn on my heel, hurry back outside. I'm pulling out my phone to send him an SOS text when I see him—walking away from Stratton, back in the direction we came from. His back disappears between Tobin and Sloane. I slip my phone back into my pocket and break into a jog. Catching up to him will be faster.

When I emerge onto Quadrant East, Lucas is veering left, toward the break in the tree line, the one that leads to the back entrance to the Den. I follow. On the other side of the trees, the library is washed in dark. The back door is still padlocked. Where'd you go, Lucas?

I'm digging for my phone again when a twig snaps to my left—by the CW. I circle around to the front and find the door cracked open. My gaze floats up to the apartment windows above. Everything is dark, but then a tall shadow passes behind the glass. Mr. Ellis is home, and whatever Lucas is doing, he's going to get caught.

Before I can think better of it, I swing the door all the way open and step inside. Lucas is standing at the base of the stairs leading up to Mr. Ellis's apartment. Footsteps echo above us. *Thud, thud, thud.* He has to hear them. Wildly, I motion for him to turn around, get out of here, but of course he doesn't see me. He starts up the stairs.

I freeze. I could turn around now, leave Lucas to his fate. But something is keeping my feet nailed to the floor. *Thud, thud, thud.* Footsteps again, louder this time. I should be running out the door, but I'm moving toward the stairwell instead, toward Lucas. He'll hear them this time. He'll turn around.

But he keeps going up.

"Hey," I whisper, frantic, following him up two steps, three. I can't say his name, Mr. Ellis will hear, Mr. Ellis will—

Lucas whirls around, but it's too late. The door at the top of the stairs swings open, and the stairwell is flooded with thin white moonlight. It washes over Lucas, spills down to me, bares our faces.

"Calliope?" he hisses.

"What the fuck is this?" Lee says. She steps out onto the landing, peers down at me.

Lucas slams his open palm against the wall. "She must have followed me."

"Jesus," Lee says. "Well, she's here now."

Lucas mutters something I can't make out, then steps around her, through the doorway, and disappears into the apartment.

I slump against the side of the stairwell. My heart is a sparrow, trapped in my chest. "I lost my mittens . . ." I start to say, words trailing off.

Lee lets out a sharp, silvery laugh. With the light behind her, her face is a dark mask. "Well, come on, Calliope. Party's up here."

"Holy Christ," I hear Lucas say from inside the apartment.

"The Devil is more like it." Brit's voice this time.

I get myself together. I take the stairs two at a time. Lee grabs my hand, pulls me through the front door, into a narrow hallway. I let her lead me around to the right, into Mr. Ellis's kitchen.

Brit and Lucas are standing in the middle of the floor. They're not alone. In front of them, Mr. Ellis is slumped over in a wooden chair, head, chest, and arms draped across the top of his kitchen table. His eyes are open, empty bowls. A dark pool halos his head and drips down onto the tile. I squint in the semidark, eyes failing to register what I'm seeing. Blood—no, vomit. The acrid stench pierces my nostrils, and I smash my coat sleeve to my face.

Mr. Ellis isn't moving.

70

"Is he dead?" I ask through my sleeve.

No one answers me. Lee digs into a cardboard box on the counter and pulls out a pair of vinyl gloves. She thrusts them toward me. "Put these on."

I do as I am told. They are all wearing them. No one is answering my question.

I try again. "What happened? Should we call nine-one-one?"

They respond in a jumble of snarls and snaps.

Lee: "Don't touch your phone."

Lucas: "You weren't supposed to be here."

Brit, to Lucas: "This is your fault."

"The mail room key card," I splutter. The need to explain myself burns hot in my throat. "I dropped my mittens. Maybe by the shirts."

"Forget your mittens." Lucas whirls toward me. "If they're in the mail room, who's to say you dropped them tonight? They don't prove anything."

An iron fist squeezes the air out of my lungs. All I wanted

was to throw myself into Haunt and Rail. Instead, I have found a worse way to disappoint them.

I struggle to gulp in air. I wish I'd never noticed my mittens were gone. That I hadn't tried to go back. I could be in my room now, swaddled in a dark cocoon of blankets and sheets. I could be far from this, whatever this is.

"We need to focus," Brit says. "I'll get the blinds. Ellis always puts them down at night. Then we can turn on some lights."

Lucas goes to help her. Lee grips my shoulder, gives me a small shake. "I need you to listen to me," she says.

I can't meet her eyes. My breath comes in ragged gulps. My gaze is snagged in her hair; all that red. I let out a small whimper.

"Calliope." She jostles my shoulder again. "They were never going to make him pay. He was never going to stop. You understand why we had to do it, right? For Brit. For all the girls he hurt."

She is telling me that they killed him. I think I knew it already, but now the truth of it slices through me in a dark, cold rush.

"I think so," I whisper. But I don't understand, not really. Lee is shaking me again, but her hands are by her sides. I am the one who is shaking. I wrap my arms around my waist, try to stop.

"Give me your phone," Lee says. She sounds exasperated.

My fingers fumble against it in my coat pocket. I hesitate.

"You'll get it back," she says.

I hand it over. Lee checks to make sure it's on silent. I

never turned the ringer back on after the lark. Then she slips it into her pocket. "You'll get it back *later*," she clarifies.

There is a strangled sound then, a half choke and half moan, and I realize it is coming from my throat.

"Calliope, look at me." I do as instructed. Lee places one hand on each of my shoulders, gently this time. She tilts her head to the side. "It's fitting that you're here. You inspired us, after all."

Before I can ask what she is talking about, light floods the kitchen, yellow and much too bright. My arm flies up to shield my eyes.

"Shit," Lucas mutters. Just as quickly, the light flickers back off.

"Here." Brit is in the apartment's small living room, just off the kitchen. She switches on a floor lamp.

"Better," Lee says. We blink for a moment, our eyes adjusting. "Now let's get to work."

Lee dictates assignments as if this was any other lark. Her voice doesn't waver. Lee will clean and disinfect. My gaze falls on a cardboard box of cleaning supplies on the kitchen counter, beside the box of gloves. Brit and Lucas will wrap up the body. Brit pulls a crisp set of bedsheets from a plastic shopping bag and rips into the packaging. They have brought everything with them. Nothing in Mr. Ellis's apartment will be unnecessarily touched. Everything will be bagged up and carried out with us.

In the lamplight, my eyes land for the first time on the large wicker gift basket sitting in front of Mr. Ellis on the kitchen table. It is filled with gourmet cookies, tea, fruit. A card reads: *Welcome back, Stephan! —Your faculty colleagues.* The basket's silky blue ribbon is unspooled beside it, and the yellow cellophane wrapper is unpeeled from the top. A corner disappears in the pool of vomit. My stomach roils.

"It was poisoned?" I choke out.

"Everything in it," Lucas says.

"But how——?"

"Do you really want to know?" Brit asks.

I do and I do not.

"He could have invited someone over," I splutter. "He could have offered——"

"But he didn't." Brit cuts me off.

"Give us some credit," Lucas says. "Obviously, we were careful."

Nothing feels obvious. This is how it feels: like everything around me is in free fall, but I am rooted to the floor, unable to wake up from this nightmare.

"Breathe, Calliope," Lee says.

I breathe.

"I need you to look at me."

I tear my eyes away from the basket. Lee is the smallest person in the room, but she grabs all my focus. She is determined, calm, unhurried.

"I need you to get it together," she says. "Can you do that?"

"I think so."

"Good. Now go into Ellis's bedroom and find his suitcase. It's probably still packed. If he has family photos around the apartment, put those in. It will look like Ellis came back this afternoon, packed up a few more things, and left."

"The guilt was eating at him from the inside," Brit says. "When it came down to it, Ellis couldn't face his colleagues. He couldn't face his students. He knew that sooner or later, he'd get caught, so he ran. Simple as that."

"And where did he go?" I ask.

Lucas grins and flings his gloved hands into the air. "It's a mystery!"

Brit grins, baring all her teeth. They glint in the lamplight.

Lee grabs a fat roll of paper towels. "Let's get to work."

In half an hour, the kitchen table and surrounding areas are clean. All evidence of the gift basket has vanished inside a garbage bag. Mr. Ellis's suitcase is filled with a few additional clothes and personal items. In a separate bag, Lee has packed all his electronics—laptop, tablet, phone, chargers. We never removed our gloves, but everything we touched is wiped down, just in case.

Mr. Ellis's body is tightly wrapped in bedsheets and fastened with duct tape. I stop thinking of him as Mr. Ellis. I stop thinking of it as a body. It is easier to think of the thing wrapped in sheets.

Finally, Lucas goes over to the fridge and pulls the door open several inches.

"What are you doing?" Brit asks.

"Smells like chemicals in here," Lucas says. "Now it will smell like old food instead."

"Waste of energy," Lee says, "but smart. Now let's go."

"Where are we——" I start to ask.

"No time for questions," Brit says. "Just take the suitcase and follow our lead."

It's a struggle, even with four of us, but we get everything down to the first floor. Lee turns off the lamp and locks the apartment door behind us.

Mr. Ellis's midsized gray sedan is parked outside, the spot bathed in shadow from the empty apartment.

"Stand watch," Lee instructs me, and I do. I don't have my phone anymore, but it must be close to two o'clock by now. Security won't be making rounds again for another half hour. Campus is very silent and still.

Brit pulls Ellis's keys out of her coat pocket and pops the trunk. At first, I think the thing wrapped in sheets is too long to fit, but Lucas bends it one way, then heaves, then another, and then the thing is inside. They jam the trunk with the roller suitcase, the laptop bag, the garbage, the cleaning supplies—everything.

"I have it from here," Brit says. She tucks her long ponytail into a swimming cap and pulls on a fresh pair of vinyl gloves. Then she pulls out a disposable mask and fits it across her face.

"What is she doing?" I whisper.

"No one is ever going to find this car," Lee says. "But if they do, they'll search for DNA. We can't let them find a trace."

Brit drapes a plastic trash bag over the back of the driver's seat, then a second across the seat cushion, and a third on the passenger's seat. Then she pulls her wallet, her phone, and something that looks like a motel key with a green plastic tag out of her coat pocket and places them on the seat beside her, on top of the trash bag. It strikes me that they have been planning this for more than a few days. They have thought of every detail, have taken every precaution. I am the only wrinkle in this meticulous plan.

Brit turns on the car and immediately cuts the lights.

"Delivery entrance," Lee says, and Brit gives her a tight nod through the window. Then she pulls away, and the car disappears into the dark.

"Where is she going?" I ask.

"We don't know," Lucas says. "And it's best that we keep it that way."

71

I don't sleep. All night, I toss and turn, on the edge of slipping into a sweet, empty nothing, until I am pulled back by any little sound—the heat cycling on, then off; a toilet flushing down the hall; a phone turned up too loud. Way too early, someone is pounding on my door. I pull the blankets up over my head. I decide I will stay in bed forever, until sleep comes.

"You're not sick, Calliope." Brit's voice.

I don't respond.

"I'm coming in there."

My door is locked, but Brit slides a key into the latch. A minute later, the door is shut behind her, and she is standing over my bed, flinging the covers back.

"Don't," I groan, grappling for the blanket.

"Get up," she hisses. "Act normal."

I force my eyes open. Brit is standing over me, clean hair scraped back, burgundy lips, neatly dressed in flared jeans and one of our teal T-shirts. Over it is a fitted black blazer with the sleeves cuffed below her elbows. She thrusts a tee out to me. "Take a shower. Put this on."

"I'm going back to sleep," I tell her.

"No, you're not." She grabs my upper arm, yanks hard.

"Ow." I sit up, rub at the pink skin where her fingers dug into me.

"You will go to all your classes. You will eat your meals in Rhine. You will go to the Halloween party in Fortin tonight, and then you will come to the Haunt and Rail meeting like absolutely nothing has changed. Understood?"

I shove myself up and grab my towel from the back of my closet door. "Fine. Understood."

I skip breakfast, but I drag myself to my first class. Campus is an unnerving patchwork of teal tees and Halloween costumes, both looks vying for control. My vision crosses and uncrosses—teal zombies, teal pop stars, teal ghosts. A few students have filled in the blanks on their shirts, and my heart lifts for one single second until I remember. What they did. What I helped them do. The bright teal T-shirts seem garish now. Is it grave dancing if no one knows he is dead?

On the way to assembly, something catches my eye in the center of Quadrant East. Someone has picked up my mittens and placed them on a bench. They were never in the mail room. They were out here, on the path, and I missed them. My eyes well with tears. I clutch them as if they are a time machine, as if they could transport me back to last night, to the moment before I realized they were missing.

"Fancy meeting you here."

I jump.

"Didn't mean to sneak up on you." Nico grins at me, sheepish. "I'm glad I caught you, though. I missed you this weekend."

I shove the mittens into my pocket. Nico. Weekend. New Hampshire trip. My mind is reeling; the world has turned inside out since the afternoon he showed me the drawing, since we agreed to take some time off over the weekend. But not for Nico; for him, the world is the same. Guilt gathers in my stomach; all this time, I didn't think about him once.

Brit's voice fills my ears: *Act normal.* How can I act normal when things are as far from normal as they've ever been?

I compose my face into a smile. "Just jumpy this morning," I tell him. I do my best imitation of a normal girl. "It's all the costumes. A witch scared the crap out of me on my way to physics."

Nico laughs. He goes to slip his hand into mine, then hesitates, shoves them into his coat pockets instead. "I was going to put on my werewolf suit, but then I found this T-shirt." He spreads his arms into wings, and his coat parts down the center. "Pretty cool."

We start walking toward Fortin. "You don't really have a werewolf suit."

"No." He laughs again. "You caught me."

"How was New Hampshire? Did your mom bake apple crumble?"

"She did. There might be a Tupperware for you in the Chandler fridge."

My stomach twists. "Oh wow. That was so nice of her."

Nico tells me about the college kids behind him on the

train last night, and for a few moments, I don't have to do anything but listen.

Inside Fortin, Dean Sadler brings us all to attention. Dr. Naylor stands at the podium. She is dressed in a burnt-orange wrap dress, and tiny jack-o'-lantern earrings dangle from her ears. My eyes latch onto them as she speaks.

"As some of you have already heard, Mr. Ellis was unexpectedly absent from his morning class. We apologize for the disruption to your studies, but we assure you it will be temporary. Ms. Soto, who covered Mr. Ellis's classes these last two weeks, has agreed to return to Tipton until this has been sorted out. She is on her way now and will take over Mr. Ellis's classes starting next period."

Fortin Hall ripples with hushed conversations.

"You hear about this?" Nico whispers in my ear. He is seated in the row behind me with the rest of Chandler. I spin around to face him, shake my head, no. I don't trust myself to speak. Madison Blythe steps up to Dr. Naylor and says something to her privately while Dean Sadler attempts to restore our attention.

When the room is quiet again, Dr. Naylor returns to the mic. "I know there are a lot of questions about Mr. Ellis's whereabouts. This is an unusual situation, and I'm afraid I don't yet have the answers. I want to be perfectly upfront with you, and the truth is we have not been able to reach Mr. Ellis yet today. He did return to campus for a short while yesterday, but he appears to have departed again overnight or sometime this morning. We are currently trying to establish contact."

"He saw the shirts," someone shouts. "He's a coward."

I whip my head around, searching for the speaker, but it's useless. Dr. Naylor's and Dean Sadler's attempts to regain control of the room are drowned out in an explosion of voices. I hear *misconduct* and *guilty* and *on the run* and *criminal.* I hear *Haunt and Rail.* They think our lark has succeeded, that we have driven Mr. Ellis away.

I expect to feel something then, something ugly and raw, but all I feel is blank. Scraped out. The feeling is a memory, sticky and cold. *This is what shock feels like.* After the accident, I felt this way for days. Is it still an accident if Lorelei made it happen? Mr. Ellis; Momma and Lorelei; Lee, Lucas, and Brit . . . all the secrets I want to unhear, unsee, are swirling together, inky and dark, and I am back there again, cold water dragging me down, down, a deep, swallowing pool, then the caustic stench of vomit, no light, no air. Nothing.

"Calliope?" Nico's hands are on my shoulders, his breath hot on my neck.

I turn around in my chair, try to focus. All around me, a thunder clash of voices. "What?" I ask.

His face is creased with worry. "You were screaming."

72

With trimester finals approaching, a reminder that the
library will be operating with extended hours beginning
next week, and additional appointment times have been
added to the schedule in the advising and peer tutoring
centers.

The message reads:

A key advancement has occurred
in the padlock situation.
Tonight—usual time, usual spot,
don't get caught. DELETE THIS
MSG
—YFG

We are back in the Den and things feel normal, but
tipped on its side. Nineteen ghosts. Fifteen are passing
around mini Snickers and Twix and Swedish Fish, grinning,

engaging in smug speculation about the role of our lark in Mr. Ellis's disappearing act.

Four ghosts know the truth.

I try to follow Lee's, Lucas's, and Brit's lead. They blend effortlessly with the others, crunching candy, praising Quinn for their success with the key, tossing around a foam football that someone found on a bookshelf. How are they so calm, so unrattled?

I did everything Brit told me to do today, right up until the Halloween party in Fortin. All day, Nico has seesawed between hovering and trying to give me space. After dinner, I retreated to Anders 1D, choosing three hours of sleep that never came over the "Monster Mash" and a sugar rush that might jolt my body out of shock and into territory I can't handle.

Now, I am jumpy and adrift all at once. I decide I am post-tired. My thoughts are like a thousand little sparks that flicker, then burn out before I can grasp onto them. I wish the Aymée-less beanbag would swallow me whole. I close my eyes, testing. When I open them and I'm still here, I try again.

This time, I press the heels of my hands into my lids. Last night unfurls against the blackness like a massive bolt of fabric. Two fists grasp the cloth and pull and pull until a tear splits down the center. The gash grows wider and wider until it is all I can see, a dark, ugly wound. Something wet is seeping from its edges, blood or bile. I try to duck, but I can't get away from it, and it's coating my skin, slithering down my hair, into my nose, my mouth—

"Okay, okay." My eyes fly open. Akari has clambered onto the long table. She claps her hands.

No one sees that I am covered in gore, that I am choking. I cough into my elbow, and Spencer leans over, thumps me on the back.

His hand comes away clean.

"You okay?"

I swipe at my face. Tears leak from the corners of my eyes, but otherwise, my skin is dry.

"Fine," I mumble. "Thanks."

"Listen up, ghosts," Akari says. "Mr. Ellis turning tail is definitely a win, and praise is due to Quinn and Calliope for developing this lark." There's a round of applause. People are staring at me. I force myself to move my hands together, *clap clap clap*. "But," she continues, "our success means there are a lot of eyes on Haunt and Rail right now. More than usual. We need to tread very carefully."

Spencer gets up, joins her on the long table. "Akari's right. I'm sure Mr. Ellis is perfectly fine, crying it out in some motel room or crawling back home to Mommy and Daddy. But the school will spin what happened as bullying, and they will be looking for students to blame."

"Which is why Haunt and Rail needs to lie low until the end of the trimester," Akari says. "No new campaigns, no meeting next Monday, nothing. We have two weeks until break, and when we get back, we'll see where things stand with Ellis. At that point, we'll reassess."

"Agreed," Spencer says. "Everyone with us?"

I say yes. I am with them.

It feels like a lie.

I have never felt so alone.

73

Tipton Daily Update
Head of School <a.naylor@tipton.edu>
to tipton-student-listserv
cc tipton-faculty-listserv, tipton-admin-listserv

November 2, 8:00 a.m.

Dear Students,

I write this morning with a frank, transparent update
about the ongoing situation concerning our teacher
Mr. Ellis. While it is often the instinct of school officials
to shield our students from uncertain news, our entire
campus community has been shaken by the rumors of
misconduct circulating over the past several weeks, and it
is my belief that you are owed as thorough a report as it
is possible to provide at this time.

While there remains no cause for alarm, two days have

now elapsed since Mr. Ellis did not report for his Monday morning classes, and it has been well over forty-eight hours since his car was last observed parked at Perry Cottage. It is the school's working assumption that sometime late Sunday or early Monday, Mr. Ellis chose to leave campus. We believe that the T-shirts distributed around school late Sunday night may have contributed to Mr. Ellis's decision to not resume his teaching responsibilities at Tipton Academy.

I must emphasize that for now, this remains an assumption. We are concerned about the safety of Mr. Ellis, and we likewise remain concerned about the rumors of misconduct. Our attempts to reach Mr. Ellis have not been successful, although the school has been in contact with his parents and two sisters. Last night, we were informed that Mr. Ellis's family has reported him missing. This afternoon, you will see law enforcement officers on the Tipton campus. Police will be conducting a search of Perry Cottage. Please give them space to work and do not interfere. If you are asked to speak with an officer, a school official must be present for that conversation. I know I can count on all Tiptonians to be helpful and cooperative.

In happier news, I am delighted to report Ms. Shannon's promotion to senior director of student activities! Please join me in congratulating . . .

On Wednesday evening, we huddle in Brit's perfectly coordinated room, pale yellow and robin's egg blue. Lee, Lucas, and Brit are keeping an eye on me.

They use words like *justice* and *warranted* and *vigilante*. Loud music is playing on Brit's laptop. It swallows their words whole. Lucas says we are on the wrong side of the law but the right side of history, and his eyes flash. My thoughts roam back to our first real conversation, the day I self-nominated for student government. We'd talked about moral authority and political authority, about pushing back against corrupt systems. About breaking the rules. It had all checked out in light of the Fresh INC campaign, even locking in that transfer student representative spot. But *murder?*

The shock that's been keeping me numb is starting to give way to questions. Lots of questions. I want to ask point-blank what, specifically, Mr. Ellis did to *warrant* this *vigilante justice*. Before, Brit's trauma was none of my business. I understand how it feels to have too many eyes on you, everyone staring, licking their lips at your tragedy. I didn't need to know the particulars; that he had harmed her was enough. Now nothing feels like enough. But what could she say that would make me feel like what happened on Sunday night was justice and not a crime?

I decide there is nothing. I stay silent while their words crackle in my ears. They reassure each other that if the police had found anything at Perry Cottage this afternoon, there would be crime scene tape, a campus-wide lockdown.

"They didn't find anything," Lucas says. "We're in the clear. No crime scene, no crime."

"Take a deep breath, Calliope." Lee rubs her hand in wide circles across my back. Her words are at once comforting and snide. "We made something happen. Something *big*."

"*You* did this," I bite back, surprising myself. "I just stumbled into your mess."

Brit *tsks* her tongue against the backs of her teeth.

"Take some credit, Calliope," Lucas says. "You gave us the idea. Action follows belief, am I right?"

I stare at him, jaw hinging slowly open. *This exchange has reminded me of something very important. Actiones secundum fidei.*

"You wrote them," I say slowly. "The letters."

He shrugs. "Lee and I saw you leave that envelope on the bulletin board. We were just messing at first, but yeah, all your questions about Adam Davenport gave us the idea. A lack of support from the whole society didn't stop the vigilantes in 1993, if that's what happened. We *had* to act, with or without Haunt and Rail behind us."

Lee's voice clangs in my ears, the puzzling thing she'd said to me in Mr. Ellis's apartment finally landing: *It's fitting that you're here. You inspired us, after all.* My stomach heaves, and I draw my knees into my chest.

"You've got it all wrong," I choke out. "Adam Davenport's death was an accident. The ghosts didn't kill him."

"Who cares." Lee flaps a hand in the air, dismisses my words as if the way a person died is no more than a matter of semantics. "Ellis deserved what he got, just like Adam deserved his fate thirty years ago. What's done is done, and we need to stick together. Got it?"

What I get is this: Not only did I help them cover up a murder, but this all started with my attempt to connect some dots that were never actually linked. Now, in a sick, horrible twist, three ghosts *are* actually responsible for cold-blooded murder. They did this on their own, but I can't escape the horrible thought that if I hadn't asked all those questions in the Den that night, if I hadn't written those letters, Mr. Ellis might still be alive.

"And you're going to stick with us, aren't you, Calliope?" Brit asks, her voice a flat sneer. "Because if you tell, you know no one would believe you. Where is your evidence? Where is the body?"

I squeeze my knees harder. I wish I could make my body disappear. "You don't have to worry about me," I mumble.

"Good girl," Brit says. "Because if we go down, you go down."

"Concealing a body," Lee says. "Accessory after the fact. They're both felonies."

"You've done your research," I say, unable to keep the bitterness out of my voice. When Lee and Lucas saw me pin that envelope to the bulletin board, they could have left well enough alone, but instead, they chose to screw with me. And now, they're blackmailing me into silence. My eyes skate across their faces, and there's no compassion there. No regret. These people were never my friends.

My thoughts drift, hilariously, to my collateral. Proof I cheated on a test. Holding that sheet of paper, I had been terrified. Two little months ago, getting kicked out of Tip-ton had seemed like the worst possible thing Haunt and Rail could do to me. And still, in that moment, it had all seemed worth it.

"We're not going to get caught," Lucas says. "Chill, every-one."

"Which reminds me." Brit reaches into a sparkly gift bag on her windowsill and withdraws a bottle of champagne. "Air chilled."

She pops the cork, and foam spills down the side of the bottle.

"To justice," Lee says.

"To taking the fucker down." Brit tilts her head back and raises the bottle to her lips.

In that moment, it's crystal clear: Brit's refusal to come forward about Mr. Ellis wasn't driven by fear. She wouldn't come forward because she was planning this from the start. For Brit, this was always about taking revenge. And to pull it off, she needed Haunt and Rail to launch a campaign, to cre-ate an atmosphere on campus that could have plausibly driven him away. Aymée threatened that plan, even if that threat was mostly in Brit's head. So Brit took her out. She used us all.

I wonder if Lee and Lucas were with her from the begin-ning or if she convinced them somewhere along the way. Maybe it doesn't matter.

Brit lowers the bottle, and a few stray drops trickle down her chin. She laughs and swipes them away. "I feel fucking fantastic," she says, but her eyes are flat. She passes the bottle to Lucas.

I scour Brit's face for another flicker of evidence that this isn't a celebration, that she is drinking to forget everything that happened to her, everything she's done. She flashes me a cold, toothless smile, and I look away.

When the bottle comes to me, I pretend to drink.

74

"I'd like to ask you a few questions, Calliope. Would that be okay?"

I nod. I am sitting in a small conference room in Brisbane with Dean Sadler and Detective Merrill from the local police department. Dean Sadler sits next to me at the round oak table, like we are a team. We have only spoken once before, a few polite words about the cookies after a student government meeting. He wears a suit and tie, and I feel scrubby in my leggings and long knit sweater. I tug at the sleeves. He is here on my behalf, but it doesn't feel that way.

Detective Merrill sits across from us. She is a tall woman with a square jaw and blunt, shoulder-length hair. A tablet is open on the table in front of her; she taps the screen with a pen.

"As you have been notified by your school," she says, looking up at me, "Stephan Ellis was reported missing two days ago by his family. The Alyson-on-Hudson Police Department has opened a missing persons investigation, and over the course of the next few days, we will be speaking individually with members of the Tipton student body, faculty, and administration."

"You're talking to everyone?" I ask.

"We will be," she confirms. "Our interviews began earlier this afternoon. We're in the early stages yet."

I clasp my hands together under the table and try not to let my relief show. They're probably working alphabetically. Bolan—of course I'd be called in on the first day. It's not a bad omen. They don't know anything.

"Do you know Stephan Ellis?" Detective Merrill asks.

Lee's voice echoes around the back of my skull. *Concealing a body. Accessory after the fact. They're both felonies.* I straighten up in my chair like I have nothing to hide.

"A little. He's my Creative Writing teacher."

"Did you have any contact with Stephan Ellis outside class? Extracurriculars? Casual conversations?"

"Not really. We'd say hi if we passed on the path. But I just transferred to Tipton at the start of this year. I've only known him since September."

"You're doing great, Calliope," Dean Sadler says. He can sense how nervous I am. I lean back in my chair and try to relax.

"Are you aware of the rumors that have been circulating on campus about alleged misconduct between Stephan Ellis and an unnamed female student or students?"

I nod. "Not until a couple weeks ago. But there have been some pranks." I speak slowly. I am careful not to say larks. "I think it's safe to say that every student on campus is aware of the rumors now."

"And do you have any idea who has been behind these pranks?"

I shrug. "I'm a transfer student. I've only been here a couple months."

"Have you heard of a secret student group on campus called the Haunt and Rail Society?"

"I've seen their logo," I say, noncommittal. "Like a ghost with teeth."

"Okay. And do you know anyone who is a part of this secret society?"

I want to shift in my chair, to stare down at my feet. I resist. "Like I said, I've only been at Tipton since the start of the trimester. I'm not really in the loop on a lot of things yet."

Detective Merrill smiles at me. "I understand. But sometimes fresh eyes are exactly what we need in a situation like this. If you think of anything, please reach out to me anytime."

She slides a business card across the table, and I reach out to accept it. I smile back at her. This was easier than I thought it would be. I didn't even have to lie.

75

That night, I am on my way back to Anders when my phone beeps.

Enter your password.

During this ongoing period of uncertainty and **unknowns**, I am reminded once again of the extraordinary respect, compassion, and drive demonstrated by this community every day.

The message reads:

You heard it here first, ghosts:
we have it on good authority that
Rainy Day has come forward.
The student who sent the screen
shots to Dean Sadler was Rainy
Day herself, Melissa Vaughn.
This is major—when Ellis crawls
out from under the rock where
he's been hiding, there will be

hell to pay. Keep this to yourself
and DELETE THIS MSG
—YFG

I stop in the middle of the path, reading the text again and again. Then I hit delete.

Never mind that Mr. Ellis will never return to campus, will never face a hearing or arrest or any form of legal justice.

Never mind that Aymée did not send those screen shots. That Brit made the whole school—even me—think Aymée was Rainy Day for no good reason. There's no admission that the ghosts were wrong, no apology. It's like it doesn't even matter that they kicked her out of Haunt and Rail, then humiliated her and ran her off campus. She was nothing to them, expendable. Guess it's easier to pretend she never existed at all.

I open my messages, pull up my conversation with Aymée, which went silent two weeks ago. I don't care if it's insider information; Aymée deserves to know.

FWIW, Melissa Vaughn sent the
screen shots to Sadler. Everyone
knows you didn't do it.

I know it's too little too late,
but I hate what went down and
I'm really sorry for my part in
it. I was a bad friend. And I
miss you.

Three dots spring up on my screen, and I suck in my breath.

Are you still with them tho?

Them. The ghosts.

> **Yes. It's complicated. When**
> **you come back after break,**
> **let's talk okay?**

Aymée doesn't write back.

My thoughts swirl and churn, dark water. If Mr. Ellis hadn't vanished, would Melissa Vaughn have come forward? Maybe his disappearance, her likely assumption that she'd been discarded, the dawning realization that he wasn't coming back, was the only thing that made her feel like she could tell her story, say her name, make herself vulnerable like that.

There is a world in which Mr. Ellis is not held accountable for his actions, and there is a world in which he is dead. What if there is no world in between?

For the first time, I really try to understand. Brit, Lee, and Lucas saw two worlds, and they made a choice. A tiny voice inside my head says maybe they are not good people, but maybe they were right.

A louder voice says I might be losing my mind.

Bang bang bang.

It is ten thirty; half an hour after check-in, half an hour until lights out. I am curled up on top of my comforter, listening to music, something mellow and folksy Lorelei sent me, an olive branch I haven't yet acknowledged. I am thinking about my sister, whose secret I am keeping, who I still haven't spoken to. It has been over a week. She wants to know how long I am planning to punish her, when I will forgive her. I don't have any answers. I may never be ready.

Bang bang.

"What?" I don't want to get out of bed, don't want to face whoever is pounding on my door.

"Open up, Calliope." Lee's voice, thick and mean. "Now."

I drag myself out of bed and over to the door. I intend to open it a few inches, keep her in the hall, but the second I undo the latch, she is shoving herself inside, slamming the door behind her.

"I didn't see you at check-in." It sounds like an accusation.

I shrug. "I was there. Left fast."

"Brit saw you going into Brisbane today." Her face is flushed red, and her eyes rove around my room, taking in my photos, my posters, the laptop open on my desk. "What did you say to the detective?"

I glare at her. She is half a foot shorter than me, but I have no doubt she could hurt me. I take a step back. "None of your business."

"It absolutely is." Her breath smells like booze, and her gaze is unfocused. In the half hour since check-in, Lee has been getting plastered in her room.

"I didn't say anything, okay? Swear."

"Really?" Lee glowers up at me.

"Yes, really." I snatch my phone from my bed and send

the music to my speakers, turn up the volume.

In that moment, Lee seems to wilt. All the fury drains from her face, and she sinks down onto my crumpled comforter. When she tilts her head up at me, tears well in her eyes.

"You really didn't tell the detective anything?" She slips a flask from her hoodie pocket and takes a drink. She doesn't offer it to me.

I pull out my desk chair and sit across from her. "Swear to god. You think I want to go to jail for what you did?"

Lee swipes at her eyes. "I wish you hadn't followed Lucas. I wish you'd never gotten tangled up in this."

"On that, we agree completely."

She draws her knees up to her chin. I have never seen Lee look so scared. "We haven't been very fair to you," she says finally. She takes another drink. "You probably think we're terrible people."

"You killed a man," I hiss. "What am I supposed to think?"

Lee's chin quivers. She swipes at her eyes again, and I grab the box of tissues from my desk, toss it over.

"Thanks." She grabs one and presses it to her eyes. "Look, you deserve to know the truth. The stuff I said to Haunt and Rail about unwanted touching and inviting girls over to his apartment, that wasn't the half of it. Ellis wasn't just some run of the mill creep. He drew girls in, made them think they were goddesses. For a while last year, Brit broke up with Jeremiah over him. She almost didn't come back to Tipton after Ellis stopped returning her texts over spring break."

"Why didn't she tell anyone?"

"She told me," Lee says, voice hard. "But if you mean her

parents, the school, the 'authorities,' Ellis has pictures. When they were together, Ellis got her to do a lot of stuff she'd never want anyone to see. He said he would send them to college admissions offices if she told. And to her parents. Brit's family may be permissive in some ways, but they're devout Catholics. They would have pulled her out of Tipton, sent her to some reform school. So that's why she was hesitant to speak up. I'd venture to guess same goes for Melissa Vaughn."

"I get it," I say slowly. Maybe Brit had more than one reason for not speaking up. Maybe my truth and Lee's truth are both right. "He was a horrible person, but . . ."

"But you don't think he deserved what he got."

"To be murdered? No, I don't. There's a criminal justice system in this country. Why should you get to decide?"

Lee stares up at the ceiling. "Three years ago, when Brit and I were first-years, Ellis went after my older sister, Lacy." My mind's eye travels to the girl from the photos on Lee's wall. Older, sharper features, same explosion of red hair. So much has happened between orientation and today, I'd almost forgotten Lee had a sister.

"Lacy was a senior," Lee continues. "He did to her the same thing he did to Brit. She was so wrapped up in their relationship, she nearly failed out of Tipton. He makes you feel like what you have, it's the only thing that matters. But she graduated, abandoned her USC plans to go to a community college here in the Hudson Valley. Partway into her first year, he dropped her cold. He'd moved on to another girl."

"That's terrible." It feels inadequate, but I'm not sure what else to say.

"For Lacy, it was devastating. Two months into the school year, she killed herself."

"Oh my god." My hand flies to my mouth.

"I knew the truth. Lacy told me everything, warned me to stay far, far away from Ellis. But our parents didn't want to believe it. Lacy had never mentioned Ellis to them, for obvious reasons, and before she died, she deleted every trace of him from her phone. It was like nothing had ever happened between them."

Lee takes another swig from her flask. This time, she offers it to me. I shake my head, no thanks.

"My sister's death destroyed our family. My parents divorced. My mom's basically an opioid zombie. If our campaign had succeeded, Ellis would have lost his job. But what about Lacy? The criminal justice system isn't perfect, Calliope. My sister's blood is on his hands, and he was never going to pay for that."

"I'm so sorry." Lee is too far away for me to touch her. I think about getting up and walking over to the bed, sitting beside her, but I don't think she'd want that. I tuck my hands between my knees.

"I've been living with that for two years now. Before our junior year, Brit and I barely knew each other. Different circles, you know. But after we became ghosts, after it happened to her too, we became close. We made a promise to each other that one way or another, Ellis would pay for what he did to her. What he did to Lacy."

My mind is spinning. "You didn't say any of this to Haunt and Rail. They don't know the truth about Lacy, do they?"

"The less the others know, the better," Lee says. She screws the cap back on her flask and tucks it into her pocket. "We couldn't tell the whole society how much was at stake. Some ghosts would never have gone for a revenge campaign, and even if they did, when Ellis disappeared, they would have seen straight through me if they knew the truth about Lacy. Four can barely keep a secret; we weren't going to test it with nineteen."

"And what about Lucas?"

Lee smiles. "Lucas and I were together for a long time. He may be with Akari now, but he was with me when Lacy died, all through that horrible year. We'll always be part of each other. You know how it is."

She makes the same flapping motion with her hand that she made the other night, as if I would know anything about that, as if having a hold over another person, to the point that they would kill for you, is entirely normal.

"The campaign was never endgame," Lee continues. "We wanted him to suffer a little, but mostly, it was the perfect cover-up. Once everyone knew Ellis was a creep, once rumors were swirling, it made perfect sense he'd cut and run."

"Yeah, I'd pretty much figured that out."

"But now, the detectives are starting to think something bad happened to poor Mr. Ellis. Which is why we need you, Calliope. You understand, don't you? We need you to stay strong. Keep going to class, theater tech, student gov. Keep your grades up."

"Yeah," I say, voice flat. "I'm working on it."

"Work harder. Remember there's mandatory tutoring if

you don't pass your exams. The ghosts will put you on probation."

"Fantastic," I snap. "Because I'm done with the ghosts. I'm keeping your secret because what choice do I have? But I am not at your beck and call anymore."

Emotionally, I've been over Haunt and Rail since the second I saw Mr. Ellis's body. I didn't expect to blurt it out, but now that it's done, something unlocks inside my chest. Through all this wreckage, one tiny bit of peace.

Lee sighs. I expect her to press back, to tell me I can't just quit like that, but instead she asks, "You have a sister, don't you, Calliope?"

My head jerks up. I wasn't expecting that. "I have two."

She nods. "Stephan Ellis was a monster. Lacy took her life because of what he did to her, and I owed it to Lacy to get the justice she never got. Wouldn't you do anything for your sisters?"

I can't move. I feel naked, exposed. In that moment, Lee's face and Lorelei's blur in front of my eyes. My sister made a terrible mistake, but what happened was an accident, a childish impulse gone horribly wrong. A week ago, I thought my anger was so righteous. But now, I am complicit in something much darker than a tragic accident. I helped cover up *a murder*. What Lee did was wrong—I still believe that. But unlike Mr. Ellis, she is not a monster, and neither is Lorelei.

I don't know if I can forgive the three of them for drawing me into their crime. But I need to forgive my sister.

Lee's eyes are still locked on me, demanding an answer.

"Yes," I whisper. "Maybe I would."

76

Nico catches up to me on the path, halfway to Manny's Joint.

"Can we talk?"

He looks concerned, and I can't blame him. I owe him an explanation for why I have been shutting him out, why I am not the girl I was at the start of Upriver. I still don't have any words for what I am tangled up in, all the secrets I am keeping. But I have been avoiding him for a whole week now, and my time is up.

"Sure." I hook my thumbs through my backpack straps. This is going to suck, but then it will be done. Nico will be better off without me and all my secrets, and I won't have to feel bad about hiding things from him anymore.

I am still snared in Lee, Lucas, and Brit's sticky net, still locked in indecision—bury our secret or come clean, destroying all our lives in the process. If there is a third choice, I haven't found it. But this is simple. This I can fix.

It is too cold to eat outside, so we take our lunches to an empty table in the middle of the grill's small seating area. A few seniors crowd around a Ping-Pong table jammed into the corner, and a couple seats are occupied by students with laptops and headphones. Otherwise, it's pretty empty in here; everyone is at Rhine or cramming in an extra study hour in the library.

Nico frowns into his soup. "It's like you're not really here anymore," he says. "I've barely seen you in days."

"Yeah," I say, noncommittal. Why is this so hard? "School stress." I pick at the paper holding my turkey wrap together.

"You said you needed space, and I've been trying to give it to you, but . . ."

I wish he'd finish the thought, put me out of my misery. *But space has become an abyss. But I'm tired of waiting.*

"I know."

Nico leans across the table. His face is so close to mine. "I'm worried about you. Did I do something?"

"No." I flinch back, take a big bite of my wrap so I don't have to say anything else. But I can't stall forever. I need to do this, need to rip the Band-Aid off. I don't have any real explanations to offer, but I can blame it on my grades, make the situation sound more dire than it actually is.

I swallow, make my voice cold. "I'm failing physics. And I might not pass English either. I'm sorry, but I don't have time for this right now. For us."

"Okay." Nico's head bobs up and down as my words settle in. "Okay, that sucks, but I get it. I can still be your friend, though, Calliope. Something's going on with you, and I want to help."

My stomach clenches into a hard fist. I've been the worst

girlfriend ever, and I just told him I was choosing homework over our relationship. He should be furious with me, or at least pissed off, but instead, he's being *nice*.

Nico is a good person. The best. Which is why he deserves to be far, far away from me. I have been incredibly unfair, and I can't take any of that back. But I can do one kind thing in return—push him away. "Just back off," I spit. "I don't need any help."

Hurt blooms across Nico's face. I did that. "Come on, Calliope. You don't mean that."

"I do." I shove myself away from the table. My chair scrapes the floor, and I push myself to my feet. "Leave me alone."

Nico leaps up, reaches for my arm. "Wait. Let's go to the health center, okay? You don't have to talk to me, but you should see someone. A counselor."

I shake my head back and forth. My hair flies into my eyes. He is making this as hard as humanly possible. "Just stop, okay, Nico? Seriously, back off."

"Fine." He drops my arm, holds his hands defensively in front of his chest. "I hear you. I won't bother you anymore."

This is exactly what I wanted, but it doesn't hurt any less. Tears spring to the corners of my eyes. "That's probably for the best."

Nico tugs on his coat, shoves his hands into his pockets, stung. After all that, he still expected me to change my mind. "I don't understand you, Calliope."

He takes a step away from me, then another, until he is

gone and I'm left at our table, alone, hand clutching the back of my chair so I won't crumple onto the floor.

Tears stream down my face, but no one notices. No one asks if I'm okay.

I deserve that.

77

Take a break from the end of **trimester** rush: All Tiptonians are invited to stop by the first floor of Brisbane between afternoon classes for tea, cookies, and conversation.

The message reads:

Over a week and still no sign of
Ellis. It appears Tipton's Icarus
has truly fallen from grace. This
campaign may be in the books,
but stay vigilant, ghosts. We'll be
accepting new proposals when
we return from break. DELETE
THIS MSG
—YFG

I have been staring at my phone, then the collage on my wall, then my phone again for two minutes that feel like twenty. It's the hour between check-in and lights out, the time shapeless, unassigned. I told Lee I was done with Haunt and Rail, but apparently I'm still on their distro list. Maybe she didn't tell anyone I quit. Maybe they are afraid to let me go. For the first time, I let myself wonder if I have some power after all. I am afraid of them, but maybe, they are more afraid of me.

Finally, I delete the text and turn to my laptop instead. I should be revising my English paper or working on the history take-home essay I haven't even started. Only a few days remain until Upriver ends and I go back to Plover Lake again. Back to my family, to face everything we haven't really faced yet. I'm not failing like I told Nico, but I'm not exactly sailing through my fall classes. In front of me, the screen is a jumble of blue folders. I need to focus, but my brain is an endless cycle of the hurt on Nico's face; Mr. Ellis, his eyes cold and dead; Lorelei grabbing the wheel, steering us into the lake; Momma, not breathing; Lee, Lucas, and Brit passing around a bottle of champagne like what we did was cause for celebration.

Concealing a body. Accessory after the fact. I open an incognito window and run a search. The charges are serious; I could be tried as an adult in New York State. I search some more. In a murder trial, a person convicted of being an accessory after the fact can face as much time as the person who committed the crime. That's life in prison. I shudder and tear my eyes away from the screen.

I need to make a choice, break out of this horrible, endless limbo. Take their secret and lock it away forever. Or tell the truth—and lock us all away for life.

Anger burns hot and bright in my throat every time I think of Lacy, the life Mr. Ellis destroyed. I ask myself the question I keep coming back to, the question with no easy answer: Does that make it okay? Wrong, but justified. A necessary evil. Or maybe that is just spin, using persuasive words to talk about terrible things. What they did was still cold-blooded murder. And every day I keep their secret is another day I'm complicit.

Unless . . . maybe there *is* a third option. Maybe I can break away from the three of them, save myself. If I confess to my part in what we did, maybe I could get a plea deal. That's how it works on TV; a shorter sentence in exchange for information. Maybe I'd even go free—if anyone believed me.

But why would they? We did a thorough job cleaning up the crime scene; the police found nothing in Perry Cottage. Brit left through the delivery entrance, undetected, and she did something with Mr. Ellis's electronics, destroyed them or disabled the trackers. And most of all, there's no Mr. Ellis. No crime scene, no missing car, no body—just one girl's outrageous story with a big blank space where the ending should be.

My third option starts to crumble. Only Brit knows what happened next. I press my thumbs into my eyelids and picture her that night, lining the car interior with plastic, tossing her things onto the passenger's seat, pressing Ellis's key into the ignition.

The key.

My eyes fly open. There was another key on the passenger's seat, beside Brit's wallet and phone. It looked like an old motel key with a green plastic tag in the shape of a diamond. Did she rent a room somewhere? Leave Mr. Ellis inside and ditch the car in the lot? Surely by now, someone would have noticed the abandoned vehicle, the locked room, the smell . . .

I shiver. Not a motel room then. I open another incognito window and start a new search. Brit wasn't just concealing a body; she was concealing a car. *Best places to hide a car.* The search takes me to Reddit. Someone is soliciting ideas for hiding their car from the repo man. I'm not even sure what that is, something about being in serious debt, but I click on the thread. Someone suggests the woods. Another user suggests renting a space in a parking garage. A third user recommends renting a large storage locker. My breath catches in my throat. Not a motel key. The key to a storage locker.

Brit drove off in Mr. Ellis's car around two o'clock. By seven thirty, she was banging on my door, showered and dressed. She couldn't have been off campus for longer than five hours, tops. Factoring in the time it would take to access the locker, leave the car, and wait for a Lyft back to campus, or a bus, or a train, the locker she rented couldn't be farther than two hours from Alyson-on-Hudson.

It's not an answer, but it's a solid lead. Something I could give Detective Merrill. Maybe, it would be enough to get my life back. I dig around in the bottom of my backpack until I find her card. *Detective Tara Merrill, Alyson-on-Hudson PD, t.merrill001@a-hpd.org.*

Then I navigate to Hushguard and open an account, silently thanking Melissa Vaughn and the ghosts for introducing me to the world of encrypted email. By lights out, I've composed a note.

> *You're looking for storage lockers within a two-hour drive from Tipton Academy, large enough to park a car inside. The facility uses keys with green diamond tags.*

My finger stalls on the trackpad, hovering over the send button. No matter how many precautions they—we—took, if the police find the car and Mr. Ellis's body, it's going to lead back to us eventually. I could admit I sent in the tip, but even if I did get a plea deal, when it came down to it, could I stomach throwing the others to the wolves? Is that who I am?

Head spinning, I turn away from the computer and pick up my phone instead, open my conversation with Lorelei. I reread all the notes I haven't returned from the past week, then I type out the message I should have sent days ago.

> I'm sorry. I love you. I forgive you.

I send the text.

It's not enough, but it is a start.

The clock ticks to eleven. I get up and turn off the lights, then I push the curtain aside and stare out my bedroom window, across the silent quadrant toward Brisbane. In the darkness, Lee's face and Lorelei's swirl together again until I can't tell them apart anymore. *Wouldn't you do anything for your sisters?*

I came back to Tipton ready to open my eyes to the real story, messy and imperfect, and that's exactly what I got. The curtain falls shut until the only light left in the room is the pale glow of my laptop screen, the unsent email hovering there. My fingertips reach for the keyboard.

I know what I need to do. I draw in a deep breath, and finally, the churning inside my head comes to a stop.

ACKNOWLEDGMENTS

Two years ago, I was struggling through the draft of an entirely different book and envisioning the swift demise of my writing career. When I finally told my editor it just wasn't going to happen, and she conveyed the doomsday message to the rest of the publishing team, I likewise envisioned the worst. Instead, I got the gift of time to write a new story, a story I was dying to tell. Thanks go, first and foremost, to my wonderful, insightful, and supportive editor, Nicole Fiorica at Margaret K. McElderry Books, who gave me the time and space I needed to make my fourth novel happen. Not to overstate it, but I am absolutely euphoric that we landed on *Very Bad People*.

Also at McElderry and throughout S&S, much gratitude to Justin Chanda, Jenny Lu, Lauren Carr, Alissa Nigro, Bridget Madsen, Ellen Winkler, Brian Luster, Elizabeth Blake-Linn, Irene Metaxatos, Anne Zafian, Karen Wojtyla, Lauren Hoffman, Caitlin Sweeny, Nicole Russo, Anna Jarzab, Emily Ritter, and the whole Riveted team. I am so thankful for your support now, and through the years. (Wow, that feels strange to write, but as we launch book four, it is wildly true!) To Mackenzie Croft and everyone at S&S Canada for your ongoing support up north. To Gee Hale for bringing Calliope so vividly to life on the cover and to Debra Sfetsios-Conover for the stunning design. To Mike Hall for mapping out the Tipton Academy world in such incredible detail, and for designing the perfect angry ghost! And finally, to the amazing team at S&S Audio for your work on the audio book. You are all so appreciated; my biggest thanks for getting behind my dark academia world and my righteous, morally gray teens.

Thank you to my incredible agent, Erin Harris, who encouraged this book from its earliest stages and continues to fervently support every facet of my career. You are simply the best. Also at Folio, my thanks to Madeline Shellhouse, Mike Harriot, and Kat Odom-Tomchin. At WME, I am so grateful to have Hilary Zaitz Michael in my corner.

To the early readers whose invaluable feedback at various stages helped me develop *Very Bad People* from an interesting spark of an idea into a fully-realized story with "a beginning and rising action and well-rounded characters": Karen M. McManus, Carlyn Greenwald, and Lindsay Champion. Also key was the insight of Osvaldo Oyola, Dora Fisher, Jo Watson Hackl, and Don Zolidis, who took the time to answer my questions and allowed me to pick their brains about boarding school life. I took some liberties anyway; any dark detours or questionable details are by my own design.

To the writers whose friendships I value every day, with special shout-outs to: Rachel Lynn Solomon, Anica Mrose

Rissi, Maxine Kaplan, Kara Thomas, Carlyn Greenwald, Derek Milman, Karen M. McManus, Sarah Nicole Smetana, Katie Henry, Amelia Brunksill, and all the Electrics. To Sara Shepard and Jennifer Moffett, thank you for your kind words. To Osvaldo, again and always, for your unending support. To the Ladies Social Wine Club for continuing to show up for my books, but mostly just for being you. And to my family— Mom, Dad, Aunt Sally, Sonia, Lissette, and Angel—for your boundless enthusiasm and love.

To the booksellers, educators, librarians, and bloggers across platforms who have supported and shouted about my books. Your creativity, enthusiasm, and support mean the world. To the readers who have followed me from *See All the Stars*, *All Eyes on Us*, and *I Killed Zoe Spanos*, thank you for continuing this journey with me. And to the readers who are joining me for the first time with the twisty world of Tipton Academy, welcome to the gray. I couldn't do this without you.